Advance Comments on *The*

The Centaur Legacy is a work of towering in courage, knowledge, skill, nor the understanding shattering work!
Jeremy James, FRGS, Author of The Tippling Philosopher, Saddletramp, Vagabond a*nd* Debt of Honour - The Story of the International League for the Protection of Horses

Hugely entertaining, thought-provoking and informative, this impressive book takes a fresh and sometimes irreverent look at the closely linked history of horse and man.
Caroline Burt, Editor for J. A. Allen Publishing, London, England

I believe we have something absolutely new on riding here. With a scientific approach, the fact-finding characteristics of a journalist, and a pinch of humor, Rink has had the audacity to interweave physiology and biomechanics with equitation's long history.
Dr. Renan Sampedro, Professor, Federal University of Santa Maria, Brazil.

You'll find no greater insight into the complexities of horsemanship than when you look into old questions with the new eyes of life sciences presented in *The Centaur Legacy*. Enjoy your journey.
Roberta Jo Lieberman, Editor, Equus Magazine.

Rink has done a terrific job of reviewing a subject long neglected in literature. *The Centaur Legacy* is comprehensive, accurate, and holds one's interest throughout.
Dr. Holm Neumann MD, American Board of Orthopaedic Surgery,

The Centaur Legacy is interesting and provocative, with novel and challenging ideas.
Dr. Matthew Mackay-Smith, DVM; Author of The Fit Racehorse, *Inductee into the International Equine Veterinary Hall of Fame and Medical Editor of Equus Magazine.*

Revolutionary! The most important equestrian book of the 21st century. Rink's concepts cannot be confined to a single language or country. Read it and be amazed.
CuChullaine O'Reilly, FRGS, Founder of The Long Riders' Guild, author of Khyber Knights.

THE CENTAUR LEGACY

**HOW EQUINE SPEED AND HUMAN INTELLIGENCE
SHAPED THE COURSE OF HISTORY**

Bjarke Rink

Copyright © Bjarke Rink, 2004

All rights reserved. Copyright under Berne Copyright Convention, Universal Copyright Convention, and Pan-American Copyright Convention. Without limiting the rights under copyright reserved above, no part of this publication may be reproduced, stored in or introduced into a retrieval system, or transmitted, in any form or by any means (electronic, mechanical, photocopying, recording or otherwise) without the prior written permission of the author and The Long Riders' Guild Press.

ISBN 1-59048-156-9

www.horsetravelbooks.com

FOREWORD
By Jeremy James

When a book comes along and bangs you round the head, seizes you by the lapels, leaves you staring into space, head filling with questions, head ringing with answers – what do you do? *What do you do?* I know what you do: you go and yell at somebody about it: talk to them: lend it to them - dash round to their place and shout: "Hoi! look! Drop whatever you are doing and READ THIS!" Push it into their hands. Then go home. Twiddle your thumbs. Wait. Wait for them to call. When they call – and they will – there will be a minute's hesitation before they speak: a minute's pause before the torrent comes. Then you will know that they too have encountered what you did. And that's a terrific moment.

When first handed this book by The Long Riders' Guild, I approached it hesitantly. It seemed perhaps somehow abstract, not that I dislike the abstract, far from it, but abstract in a way which didn't have much relevance for me. Moreover the fact that the author Bjarke Rink himself called it an anthology of essays made it sound remote and perhaps overly academic for my palate. I wasn't quite sure what I was getting into because the publishers said nothing. On reflection, thinking about it, I realise now what the enigmatic smiles were all about.

Anyway, I took the book, grunted something, closed my door, sighed, sat back, opened the book and began reading.

The words moved: the pages turned. All distractions faded. Noises from the outside world silenced. Everything around my peripheral vision vanished. Just those words stayed. Moving on the page.

Sitting bolt upright at my desk, holding this book in both hands, eyes wide open and hearing myself saying: "good grief!" again and again, I glanced at my watch. Four hours had passed.

That is the first time a book had seized me like that since I read Dudinsev in the 1970's.

The Centaur Legacy is a staggering work. It is profound. It is erudite. It is elegant. It is absolutely surprising. It takes your breath away. It is pithy; it is witty, it is full of fun. It is rude. It's great! It takes you down alleys no-one has ever trod, makes connections that no-one has spotted. This book brings out the richness of the entire philosophy of equitation which no-one has ever assembled, and in so doing, is the first complete Philosophy of Equitation ever composed. And that on its own is a stunning achievement.

But it is so much more.

When I was young, there were a number of wonderful television series screened in England. One was Lord Clarke's *Civilisation*, the other Jakob

Bronowski's *The Ascent of Man* and the last, Carl Sagan's *Cosmos*. Each of these programmes had a remarkable effect: you could actually feel your mind being expanded, being taken in head-bending directions, have things revealed to you that had profound impact upon your thinking. I remember sitting cross-legged on our sitting room floor as a teenager, mouth open and moved to tears as Jakob Bronowski explained to me, in my family sitting room, how the Theory of Relativity worked. I, who had failed every exam in mathematics: I, who was condemned never to be allowed to take Physics as a subject because I was too stupid. I understood the Theory of Relativity at a stroke, in my family sitting room, because of Jakob Bronowski's ability to present it in a cogent form. Not only was I able to understand but actually repeat it. These three series were fabulously enriching. And they were watched by millions. From all walks of life. They topped the soaps, they topped the every day programmes: they were unmissable.

This book, *The Centaur Legacy*, falls into precisely the same category. Like the three distinguished men from these three distinguished productions, Bjarke never talks down to you. He never assumes superiority, never takes the high ground. Instead, like them, he takes you by the hand and shows you. Reveals it you. Look, he says, see for yourself. I'm just laying it out in front of you. It's all there. Always been there. Like the master of his craft, like Bronowski, Sagan and Clarke, he has no time for artificial props: gone is obscurity: gone is myth; gone is the hocus-pocus. He offers room to neither mystery nor mystique, so-called horse lore, the mumbo jumbo of secrecy, horse whispering, special knowledge, all the tosh and nonsense that goes with those who can neither explain nor properly understand their subject. Any claim for the need to be some kind of special adept to understand or to control horses is rightly dismissed for the rot it is. He articulates what you have sensed intuitively but never put into words. He gives you the facts, the truth, laid out, bare, lucidly, comprehensible and absolutely emulateable. All you have to do is sit back and take it in.

How many people can actually manage that? How many people can present complex ideas in the simplest terms, as though you have known these things all your life, as though all Bjarke has done, is turn on the light.

Isn't it wonderful when intellect speaks to you like this? It's so comfortable. It's so reassuring. It's so dazzlingly enlightening. It's like seeing something for the first time, seeing something when the veils are ripped off.

I am not going to attempt to explain what lies in these pages but leave you the reader, to find out for yourself. Let Bjarke take you there. It's a memorable journey. A journey that might leave you with one final insight, with which I was left. I felt that had I not read this work, I would have missed out on a whole new world of horsemanship that had not only improved my understanding of it, but made me grasp a human-horse relationship I had not previously appreciated was even there. Bjarke had shown me, better than anyone I have ever read, or known, how to be with a horse and left me knowing for certain, that if I had not read this book, I should not be keeping horses at all.

Jeremy James, FRGS
Powys, Wales
February 2005

Jeremy James is the author of *Saddletramp, Vagabond, The Tippling Philosopher* and *Debt of Honour - The Story of the International League for the Protection of Horses*. A Founding Member of The Long Riders' Guild, Jeremy was made a Fellow of the Royal Geographical Society in recognition of his equestrian explorations.

www.horsetravelbooks.com

www.horsetravelbooks.com

CONTENTS

Page

I – THE CATALYST OF HISTORY
1. Homo Who? 13
2. Homo Sapiens, the Learning Machine 16
3. Equus Caballus, the Running Machine 19
4. The 'Big Bang' of the Biological Revolution 22
5. Horsemanship, the Catalyst of History 25
6. Horsemen Break the Human Time Barrier 29
7. On Attila and Einstein 33
8. The Rule of the Centaurs 37
9. 'Equestrian Dynamics' Powers the World 42
10. The Masters of Speed and the Masters of Space 46
11. Horsemanship Throughout Fifty Centuries of Adventures ... 51
12. To Implode History Subtract Horsemanship 54
13. A Slow World Devoid of Horses 58
14. Horsemanship in Sedentary Civilizations 63
15. The Rise of the Horsemanship in Europe 66
16. The Working Rider 72
17. The Sporting Rider 75
18. The Saddle Artist 78
19. Xenophon, Academic Equitation is Born 81
20. Federico Grisone, the Painful Renascence 84
21. Antoine de Pluvinel, Equitation as the Seventh Art ... 87
22. La Guérinière, the Heir to "Scientific" Equitation 92
23. François Baucher, Civil War in Horsemanship 95
24. Gustav Steinbrecht – The German System 98
25. Federico Caprilli, the Unfinished Revolution 102
26. The "Golden Years", Where and When 106
27. The Last Myth 110
28. Horse Power Supreme 113

II – IN SEARCH OF THE CENTAUR
1. An Auspicious Beginning 117
2. The Centaurs Last Stand 122
3. A World Without Horses? 125
4. The Centaur Spirit Lives! 128
5. On Horses and Automobiles 131
6. Scientific Equitation in the 20th Century 135
7. Horsemanship on the Rise 138

www.horsetravelbooks.com

8. In Search of the Centaur 141
9. The Miracle of the Physiology of Equitation 145
10. Neuroscience Reveals the Principles of Equitation 150
11. Organizing Equitation into Conditioned Responses....................154
12. The Code of Riding Cues 157
13. The Merging of Homo and Caballus 160
14. Doctor Pavlov and General L'Hotte...163
15. On Horsemanship and Leadership..166
16. On Horsemanship and Draftsmanship 170
17. The Power of Pleasure 174
18. Equus Ludens 177
19. The Bit, a Connection to the Mind 181
20. The Saddle, a Double-Lane of the Senses 186
21. Other Thoughts on Whips and Spurs..191
22. Cracking the Centaur Enigma 194

III – ODYSSEY IN SCIENCE

1. Are the Echoes of the Past the Music of the Future?....................201
2. A Revolution in the Making..206
3. Equitation: Symbiosis and Slavery?..209
4. Dancing with Horses? 216
5. Emotional Intelligence in Equitation 221
6. The Natural Language of Movements...225
7. Communicating With Horses 229
8. Life Cycles and Strategies in the Training of Horses....................236
9. Building a Centaur from a Horse 241
10. A Rider Named Homo-Caballus 246
11. Bioequitation – Turning "I Wish" into "I Can".............................250
12. Caprilli and Beyond...255
13. The 'Cybernetic Zone' of the Centaur...260
14. Riding in the 'Comfort Zone' 265
15. Why Ride?...271
16. Nomad Wisdom in an Urban Civilization 276
17. On Culture and Horsemanship 282
18. On Modern Riding Ethics...287
19. Odyssey in Science 290
20. Sport is War By Other Means 294
21. A Modern Structure for Equestrian Sports 300
23. The Centaur Legacy 305
Acknowledgements 310

www.horsetravelbooks.com

THE ROAD MAP TO THE TOP OF THE WORLD

This anthology of essays was written to reach the horse world and beyond, I hope. The theme is the never really understood impact that horsemanship had on humankind in the past and why horses make people more influential even today. I have tried to answer some anthropological questions, which scholars mysteriously seem to have overlooked in the past. For example:

Q: Of all human machinations to dominate the natural world, was there any single development that can be said to have boosted Homo sapiens from antiquity towards the technological revolution of the 20th century?

A: Yes. Equitation. With this incredible complex biological technique, mastered some six thousand years ago, horsemen were able to break out of the human genetic space/time limit and conquer the Planet at a dizzying rate. Undoubtedly, had the horse gone the way of the mammoth, today we would have no cars, computers, genetic engineering and global strategies.

Q: From the scientific point of view what is equitation really about?

A: Equitation can be said to be the symbiotic blending of the human and equine key features—brains and speed—that historically resulted in the most feared predator that ever stalked the planet. A combination of survival skills that the Greeks called 'Centaur.'

Q: After accelerating World History and providing the steep upswing of the Western World, has equitation any further role to play in humanity's future?

A: Certainly. This complex biological technique is probably still the best strategy for humans to perform physically and mentally beyond their original capacity. Equitation is without doubt humanity's most important cultural heritage, and its physical benefits will be perpetuated by equestrian sports.

I do realize that this book should have been written by an anthropologist whose profession it is to chart human evolution; or by a biologist whose life has been dedicated to the study of symbiotic connections; or yet, by a historian whose business it is to remember what other people forget (thanks Hobsbawm); or, better still, by three capable hands.

But, for one simple reason this book was written by a horse person: we are the only human beings who work on the frontier of the senses where Homo sapiens merges with Equus Caballus – an area of human enterprise, which is still virtually a 'no man's land' from the scientific point of view. As I sincerely doubt that any non-equestrian scholar could guide you safely through this uncharted land, a hazardous trip that will eventually lead us to unravel the Centaur enigma, you'll have to come with me. I have a reliable road map and a good horse, so saddle up and let's be on our way!

Bjarke Rink

www.horsetravelbooks.com

I – THE CATALYST OF HISTORY

1. Homo Who?

Hundreds of millions of years ago there lived an anonymous little creature that spent most of its time avoiding a closer acquaintance with Tyrannosauruses, Apatossauruses, Brontosauruses, Stegosauruses and other sauruses of lesser importance. Eons later, tired of running away from its own insignificance, the little nameless beast took a break up in the trees with its boisterous cousins the monkeys. But after a couple of million years the insignificant being, eternally unsatisfied with its own wretchedness, jumped back to the ground and reoccupied a position between the earth-bound species. As it had never developed any special strategy for survival – claws, jaws, horns, a good kick, or great speed – the creature found itself standing at the end of the mammalian evolutionary line, and there it remained until a few million years ago when it began to reveal to the world its scary biological difference!

Some four million years ago, in the Laetoli savanna of Kenya, appeared a biped mammal. This strange but seemingly inoffensive creature didn't impress the magnificent horses, zebras, elephants, giraffes, lions, hippopotamus, rhinoceros and gazelles that lived there. The new neighbor was about forty inches tall and lived in small family groups on the shores of lakes such as Turkana. To its animal neighbors, the strangest thing about this negligible creature was that it had a monkey face, a monkey body and monkey manners – but it had no monkey hair and like the birds it had only two legs – but couldn't fly! The new animal moved around with a pair of big floppy feet outfitted with two big toes very handy for tree climbing. As this bipedal form of locomotion was slower than the quadruped, and required more energy per kilometer, the new mammal was not a good hunter, thank heavens. And, although it had multichromatic and stereoscopic vision, improved hearing, a fine sense of smell, a good touch and a loud screechy voice, the apparently inoffensive species had no big teeth or mighty claws to hunt animals and rip open their skin to feed itself. The creature spent most of its time peacefully rummaging for insects, leaves, fruits, nuts, seeds, roots and, despite occasional outbursts of high pitched chatter, troubled nobody. The anthropologist Raymond Dart, a descendant of this strange creature, denominated it *Australopithecus*.

Nevertheless, after some million years of this joyless way of living, concerned mainly with foraging for eatables, raising children and with the daily routine only broken by sporadic gibbering and much ado about nothing – the other animals on

www.horsetravelbooks.com

the savanna were horrified to note that the 'naked ape'[1] was slowly changing its habits… for the worse!

The weird creature had begun to form bands of hunters to chase the other animals to kill them! Afterwards, in camp, it could be seen ripping open the hide and cutting out chunks of raw meat with chipped stones that had been sharpened like knives! The little biped monster had also learned to use sharp-edged stones to scrape the skin off the dead animals and fabricate rough garments to wrap around its ridiculous nudity. The anthropologist Louis Leakey, a descendant of the strange species, denominated this evolutionary stage *Homo habilis*.

One million and a half years later its increasingly concerned neighbors began to note another alarming change in the 'naked ape's' habits. It had learned how to manipulate fire and was now seen cooking its gory food to soften its texture – a really nauseating sight! (Although this type of hominid was already erect since the Australopithecus stage, some later bureaucrat called it Homo erectus). But, even then the 'naked ape' was not a great menace to the other animals, all of them endowed with efficient strategies for survival – claws, jaws, horns to fight or great speed to get out of its way. Fitted with only two chubby legs that any healthy quadruped could outrun,[2] red meat was fortunately a small part of its daily diet. But undoubtedly, the eerie creature enjoyed meat a great deal. Sometimes the horrified neighbors would see the 'naked ape' struggling with hyenas, wild dogs and birds of prey for the leftovers of the mighty ruler of the savanna, King Lion.

A mere 480,000 years after learning to handle fire, the 'naked ape' came out with a new idea – this time a really dangerous invention: the bow and arrow. One of its descendants Carolus Linnaeus, in an inexplicable impetus of enthusiasm, denominated this evolutionary stage Homo sapiens ("sapiens" Carolus? whatever for?). Now, to compensate its slow footwork, the 'naked ape' shot arrows after its targets. All members of the fauna acknowledged that as it was developing technologically the 'new ape' was becoming a real inconvenient neighbor – a nuisance and a true menace for the other animals in the savanna (and they hadn't yet seen a fraction of the ruin that this creature would cause the environment in the 19th and 20th century).

Thirty thousand years ago, Homo Faber (the denomination for the creature that we'll use in most of this work) was already dominant over most of the other species. He was the number two in the evolutionary line and was now harassing

---

[1] *Naked ape:* Prof. Desmond Morris' splendid definition of mankind, a great contribution to the deeper meaning of anthropology and the human zoological condition.
[2] Michael Johnson, the fleet-footed American sprinter, who shattered the 400-m world record in 1999 with a 'dazzling' 43.18 seconds, could be out-sprinted by a common sewer rat.

www.horsetravelbooks.com

even His Majesty, the Saber Toothed Tiger. Fourteen thousand years ago, and only eight thousand years after inventing the bow and arrow, the 'naked ape' came out with one more of his eye popping schemes: he began to domesticate animals – dogs, goats, pigs and cattle. Now he didn't need to do much hunting anymore – when his belly rumbled he'd just amble over to the pen and grab his squealing lunch. His creativity seemed boundless. Some ten thousand years ago, and only four thousand years after the domestication of animals, he made his biggest discovery yet: he found out how to sow and harvest plants in the soft and nutritious soil by the riversides. This caused a real revolution in his way of life, and modern biologists, his descendants, would call it the Biological Revolution. Soon afterwards, a mere thousand years, he invented ceramics, and within another thousand years he was fabricating ropes, rafts, bricks and scythes. Note that time was diminishing between one invention and another; at first there had been hundreds of thousands years between one scheme and the next, but now he was having new inspiration with only a few thousand years interval. *The mind of the 'naked ape' seemed to be able to accumulate experiences that led to new inventions with the progression of a brakeless downhill mammoth!*

Six thousand years ago, Homo Faber took an important step by discovering the technology of smelting bronze. That would substitute the sticks, stones and bones that he then used to fabricate his weapons and tools. In the following centuries, Homo Faber unfolded his creativity in full – he invented writing, navigation and ox-drawn carts with wheels. As a matter of fact, by accumulating all this technology: fire-making, the domestication of animals, agriculture, ceramics, rafts, boats, scythes, irrigation, wheels, copper, bronze, candles, writing and the calendar, he established one of the first cultural organization that could be called a nation – a riverside country where all his united inventions would form what historians would later call a "civilization". At last the 'nobody' of the treetops had become somebody on the planet. His animal neighbors were flabbergasted by this unworthy creature's amazing success.

Showing the technological ability of building a glittering nation like Egypt, Homo Faber reached what seemed like the climax of his creativity. But, in that very moment this surprising creature took a parallel technological leap, which started his greatest adventure of all! But before we resume the history of this adventurous 'monkey-hero' let us take a look on how and why this weird creature had changed so much in his appearance and behavior, while the others animals of the fauna had changed so little.

www.horsetravelbooks.com

2. Homo Sapiens, the Learning Machine
With the involuntary help of Richard Leakey

The latest progress in neurological science is helping to rewrite, among other subjects – anthropology. With the understanding of the functioning of the brain, neuroscientists are setting the evolution of mankind in a whole new perspective. Today it is understood that Homo sapiens bet his evolutionary chips on developing his brain. The discussion that involved several generations of philosophers – whether education or nature determines human behavior – is now turning in another direction. Scientists are now concerned about how genetics interact with the environment *in the constitution of cerebral patterns and how this establishes man's behavior. According to contemporary science, social organization was the main catalyst of the size, the structure and the functioning of the human brain. The material conquests – the making of tools, the control of fire, the bow, iron, agriculture, wheels and writing, are thought to be mere consequences of his cerebral development. Which also means that the history of mankind's social formation is more important than the history of his material evolution.*

What the other animals that lived alongside Homo habilis didn't know was that to compensate for his poor locomotion system, the 'naked ape' was gifted with a cerebral structure of great capacity for learning. The activity of his neurons actually modified the physical structure of his brain! This means that the more experiences humanoids underwent, the more connections linked their neural cells – which in turn permitted new experiences in one infinite *chain process* of brain wiring and learning. (Nature didn't endow the 'naked ape' with claws, jaws or horns – but what his brain would be able to conjure even God, the creator, may now feel hard to believe.)

But what had stimulated the 'naked ape' to develop his brain? What was the motor of his intellectual evolution? In the past, anthropologists thought that environmental pressure, the struggle for survival, had compelled Homo to accomplish new inventions and that this had developed his mind. After all, the finding of many stone, bronze and iron tools tell them, with *material evidence,* the history of his economic progress. Karl Marx, the philosopher of materialism, thought that the fundamental difference between men and animals lies in the fact that to fulfill their needs men invent tools, and with them he transform his surroundings.

Richard Leakey, in his book *People of the Lake,* offers us a more up to date explanation about the development of the human intellect. He says that the group is a *dynamic entity,* an ever-changing kaleidoscope of practical matters and social

www.horsetravelbooks.com

moods. The material world itself is relatively predictable. Although considerable cognitive skills are required for exploiting diverse and widely scattered food resources, they become relatively simple when compared with the intellectual demand of making and maintaining social alliances, of political maneuvering for gaining subtle advances in social status, and of simply interacting with another essentially unpredictable individual. The behavior of plants and prey is more or less certain; the behavior of humans in a complex social organization is not. You need a keener wit for dealing with relative uncertainties than you do for coping with relative certainties. Leakey's argument is based on the premise that the pressure of social life was the main force to promote the evolution of primitive man's intelligence. Technology and other subsistence demands must have played some part too – says he – simply because a basic technology needs be only very basic to endow economical advantages. So the locomotive of Homo's brain growth was obviously his social interaction.

Between three and one million years ago the Old Stone Age technology developed from some few tools to cut and scrape, into the Mesolithic, where a 'kit' containing about twelve tools with specific functions to cut, scrape, splinter, mill, drill, polish, and so on, appeared. But in spite of being a big advance, it can't be said to have been the 'apex' of human technology. And, even so, the brain of Homo in this period, increased two times in weight and size! And though between 1 million and 250 thousand years the invention of utensils had advanced rather slowly, man's brain increased one-third in size. "The crucial part of operating the mixed economy of gathering and hunting, apart from the mechanics of knowing where or when to find food, was the intensely enhanced social interaction" – argues Leakey. "And being a part of a group co-operating in different ways to achieve the same goal can be a very frustrating business, as everyone who has ever served on a committee certainly knows! Restraint, persuasion, tact, submission, aggression, perception and a good sense of humor (a lot of that) all play their part in successful cooperation".

When a reporter once asked Einstein why man was able to discover the atoms but not how to control them, he answered with his celebrated wit – "that, my son, is because physics is a much easier subject than politics". Today scientists agree that, despite giving no preponderance to any force as a catalyst of the enormous development of the human intellect – evolution never works in such a simplistic way – social relationship was the biggest responsible fact for current technological and social development. *Therefore the social web should be considered mankind's masterpiece.*

But what's all that got to do with horses and riding? asks the impatient reader. Just you wait and see, fellow traveler. In the Laetoli savanna, the insignificant hominid did much more than invent and manufacture new instruments – he started to organize raids in search of food and materials for his basic technology. "Without a commitment to the social order, without loyalty to the group, and without a place in the chain of tasks, an individual in the hunting and collecting economy would simply perish," is how Leakey put it. If, at first, the scientists saw the invention of utensils – the use of stones, fire, bows and arrows – as the motor of human intellectual development, now they know that the key factor that definitely modified the behavior of the 'naked ape' was his psychological and emotional development stimulated by social relationship. Some 35,000 years ago, Homo's brain had already the *same potential for* thought that is has today. Let's remember that.

After more than two million years collecting cultural experiences, man had seemingly reached the peak of his intellectual development. From the Paleolithic, the Old Stone Age, to the Neolithic, the New Stone Age, humanity had given a series of large steps to conquer the environment. And this accumulation of knowledge and technology allowed the ever-building Homo Faber to found, on the banks of the river Nile, one of the first big land development projects in history. But the building of Egypt is really no big deal, if humanity's later exploits are considered. About 6000 years ago a more important fact in relation to the cerebral development of Homo sapiens took place – an invention that provoked an explosion of his neural connections and impelled man as a rocket towards the twentieth century.

Endowing Homo Faber with a brain capable of making infinite associations between the natural phenomena God, on the other hand, equipped him with the poorest locomotive apparatus of the mammals – the bipedal system. (It was certainly for the same reason that He didn't outfit snakes with wings; this could have become another ecological disaster). However, during the millions of years in which Homo was wiring and expanding his incredible neuron web, another mammal in the evolutionary chain had bet all its biological resources in perfecting its locomotive mechanism.

www.horsetravelbooks.com

3. Equus Caballus, the Running Machine
With the involuntary help of Bruce J. MacFadden

In the chase of life and death, if a predator makes a mistake and its prey escapes, it will live to hunt another day. But if a horse is attacked by a predator and makes a mistake, it may be its last. "To survive, everything in the horse has been sacrificed in favor of speed, making the animal a 'cursorial machine,'" defined E. Scott. This means that the horse's physiology evolved around the ability to run; it is the animal best perfected for agility, speed and resistance. The horse's circa 58 million years of successful survival on the Planet is due to its continually developing motor system and the rest – the alimentary system and the social behavior – was adapted to this key strategy. Many specialists affirm that extant Equus Caballus is at the pinnacle of its evolutionary progression.

Since pre-historic times, the beauty of the horse's motion has fascinated humanity. Paleolithic cave paintings show the horse almost always in action. All studies in equine movement indicate that the horse, in all the animal kingdom, was blessed with a unique combination of locomotion assets – speed, agility and resistance. A modern horse can sprint up to 70 kilometers an hour and a racing-horse take more than two strides per second.

As some animal species developed horns, and others claws and teeth as key strategies for coping with the hardships of the environment, the horse bet his biological chips on speed. The forms of Equus body were designed for swiftness and his whole diaphragm is aerodynamic – muscles and bones, and his two, three and four beat gaits were designed for rapid and sustained propulsion. The horse's long and slender legs produce maximum leverage, with fewer movements, and the animal touches the ground with the tips of his toes with the lightness of a dancer.

"To move on tip-toes is difficult for man, and can only be attained by long practice – but for the horse it is the natural position," comments Harold Barclay in his work *The Role of the Horse in Man's Culture*. The *locomotive system* is the key character of Equus evolutionary strategy. Now, with the help of Bruce Mac-Fadden, author of *Fossil Horses: Systematics, Paleobiology and Evolution of the Family Equidae*, let's examine how this running machine has changed from the dog-size, pre-historic creature known as *Hyracotherium* to the glorious animal we know today.

Modern *Equus Caballus* is a much-changed version of its ancestors. In the thousands of physiological mutations occurring over 58 million years, all the modifications have to do with the performance of the horse's locomotor system. The alimentary tract was perfected so it could eat and digest on the move. Horses, in their natural life, cannot gorge themselves with food like humans. Endowed with a very small stomach, it must eat almost constantly to maintain a continuous digestive flux, which avoids having to carry a big bellyful of edibles – yet another strategy that contributes to endurance and speed. The newborn colt is able, after a few hours practice, to follow the mother and the herd with astonishing velocity.

S.J. McNaughton, an American paleontologist, published a very interesting study in 1985 in which he demonstrated that the capacity for moving at speed for extended periods was a favorable adaptation for equines to roam over big distances to take advantage of food resources found in far and different places. This study strengthened the theory that many changes in the horse's motor-system developed to give it the resilience to undertake long journeys (as Alexander, Motun,[3] Attila, Genghis Khan, Pope Urban, Tamerlane and Napoleon can attest to). Other physiological modifications enabled the horse to explode into instant action and reach top speed in a few seconds. These adjustments permitted *Equus* to wander over great distances in a relatively short time.

One of the most important changes of Equus was the evolution from his three-toed (tridactyl) foot to the single-toed (monodactyl) hoof, as we know it today. This change in design afforded the horse greater torque and speed. For short distances and long, hard wear and tear the single hoof is a better solution than the two-toed design used in the majority of hoofed animals. Cloven hooves are more prone to diseases and to accidents under pressure. For this reason, most cloven-hoofed animals developed horns to help "stand their ground" in case predators overtake them. But though the cheetah is the fastest land animal on Earth, it is not a horse predator because of its diminutive size. Tigers, lions, bears and wolves, whose average speed falls in the same range, are prime predators of horses. Even so, to have any chance of success, the attack must be sprung at 50 yards or less. In a longer run a healthy horse can outrun any of these large predators with relative ease.

Equus motor system reveals another unique feature inherited from his ancestors: a "stay apparatus" that locks the horse's kneecaps in position so he can sleep in an upright position. Standing up saves energy and keeps muscles, joints, and tendons warm for instant action, allowing the horse, if attacked, to attain top speed in a split second. This mechanism became an important part of *Equus Caballus'* long-running survival strategy on the planet. Considering both speed and endurance, the horse is thought to have the best locomotive system in nature.

In his work, MacFadden also cites paleontologist Dr. E. Renders' study of ancient hoof-prints preserved in the soft volcanic mud in Laetoli, Tanzania,

---

[3] *Motun* was the mounted nomad war leader who in the third century BC began to turn the Eastern Huns, horse and animal herders living north of modern China, into a great imperial power.

Africa. This 3.5 million year-old paleoanthropological site is of great interest because it also contains hominid footprints. In a detailed study, Renders concluded that the imprints of the Hipparion indicate the animal was performing a running walk. This way of moving permitted a speed slightly more than nine miles per hour (15 kilometers) using the same safe four-beat motor coordination as the walk. Unlike the trot and the gallop, there is never a moment in this steady gait when all four legs are off the ground at once.

Equus, the specialist in speed, has the option of multiple gaits for fast and steady moving, including the running walk. At the running walk, Hipparion could sustain greater speed for a longer time with less energy and with a reduced risk of falling. Stumbling, in a hunter's world, is tantamount to death. And Equus' biped neighbor, Homo sapiens—a frequent target of predators himself—may well have looked on the horse's speed and surety with envy.

Perhaps the human ancestor whose footprints share the same paleoanthropological site tried to grab a Hipparion on the run but with very little chance of success. Or possibly these footmarks were made by hominids, endowed with only two legs and two floppy feet, who were shuffling down to the horses' stamping grounds on what passed as a weekend to gawk at their agile, capering, beautiful movements and speed. These early hominids may well have spent a lot of time watching the horses in the savanna, but in the meantime, they were spending most of their lives in and among the trees developing their own survival tools: a finely tuned sense of balance, agile and dexterous hands, and a relatively large, very clever brain.

Equus Caballus' motor system and the human cerebral structure are unique in the animal kingdom. If these two creatures could ever join forces they would form a superior physiological being – greater than Homo Faber and Equus Caballus individually. In the improbable case that such a splendid creature could be formed, the resulting animal would posses all the makings to become the master of Mother Earth. But, naturally -- it would be easier for man to go jump on the moon than for such a miracle to happen. Don't go away!

www.horsetravelbooks.com

4. The 'Big Bang' of the Biological Revolution

Three million years separate Australopithecus *of the Laetoli savanna from* Homo Faber, *the builder of Egypt. To us this seems an enormous space of time; to our forebears this was the time necessary to connect their neurons to organize the first grand civilization on the planet. In a mere 5,500 years following this great achievement, another advanced nation disembarked one of their men on the moon while a good part of humanity followed the adventure sitting in their living rooms! What are the main factors, which led to such a gigantic technological leap in such a relatively short time? Is there any historical evidence of what might have sparked this astonishing feat? There is. Some 6000 years ago, Homo sapiens accomplished his most improbable achievements ever: he overcame the time constraints imposed by those two floppy feet.*

About 30,000 years ago, Homo Faber's brain had achieved its present size and potential for thought, meaning that it had definitely outgrown its corresponding footwork. In other words, the human brain had achieved the capacity to enter the Digital Age while the human foot remained mired in the distant past as one of the slowest locomotive structures among the mammalian species. The locomotive system was definitely the weak link of the human body structure.

The great intellectual development that followed the domestication of plants and animals started the greatest technological advance then known to Homo sapiens. To live by foraging nature's resources, you only have to know certain peculiarities of plant and animal life cycles. But to raise crops, you have to understand a lot more about nature's laws – knowledge constituting the basic principles of biology. The Biological Revolution was brought on by different peoples on different parts of the planet, and the technology involved in planting and reaping flourished in those parts of the world where this enterprise had the best chances to succeed—on the rich earth of the shores and deltas of the big rivers of Asia, Europe and Africa. The people who settled to work the soil also built the world's first cities and nations. Anthropologists call these human gatherings urban-agrarian sedentary communities—urban settlements surrounded by farmland.

And so, as we were taught in school, the most important adaptation of man to his environment—the single fact that would transform the face of the earth—was the adoption of agriculture as a way of life. They knocked into our tender skulls that the Biological Revolution was achieved by the incessant capacity of the imagination of Homo sapiens, alias Homo Faber. What nobody ever explained to us was that the Biological Revolution had a "big bang"—a crucial happening which forever changed the physical capacity and potential of human beings.

www.horsetravelbooks.com

The most dramatic chapter of the entire revolution was the symbiotic union of Homo sapiens and Equus Caballus which produced a third entity in every way superior to them both. The Greek called the combination 'Centaur' and we shall sometimes call the synergetic beast Homo-Caballus.[4] Let's see how this new creature came to be and what impact the biological unity of horse and man had on the social and economic career of the human species.

Anthropologists tell us that with each new invention, Homo Faber changes his behavior and enlarges his capacities. The ball, the bike, the corkscrew, the can opener, the funnel, the fax, the hatchet, the hammer, the knot, the knife, the needle, the nail, the pan, the pin, the rope, the reeve, the saw, the screw, the tap, the toaster, the zipper, the zapper, and the silicone chip are all small (though significant) technological improvements that have given Homo Faber greater control over his environment.

But the invention of equitation was more than just another new tool or commodity; it was a species-changing technological milestone that was just as important as the control of fire and the invention of stone tools, the wheel, agriculture and other machinations of Homo Faber's inventive mind. The merger of Homo and Equus into one galloping being was like the smelting process that amalgamates iron and carbon into steel. To connect two different nerve systems into a third, more powerful organism is infinitely harder to do, as any novice rider can attest. Therefore, if all the small discoveries and inventions made by Homo Faber changed his behavior, you can well imagine the creative leap that Homo went through when he started a cooperative relationship with another creature that was five times his size and instinctively driven to keep intruders at a mile's distance. Imagine the doses of persuasion, induction, intuition, auto-repression, tact, emotional balance and analytical skill needed to attain cooperation from such a highly developed and complex creature as Equus Caballus.

J. Bronowski, in his book, *The Ascent of Man*, tells us, in a romantic tone, that with the Biological Revolution "suddenly man and plant unite their lives as in a genetic fairy tale." Well, if the betrothal of man to the beetroot, or to any other plant for the matter, is like a fairy tale, the sensory-motor connection of Homo sapiens and Equus Caballus is the greatest epic in human history (which in fact it became).

The cooperative union of Homo and Caballus represents a qualitative leap in human psychology and physiology that permitted man to act beyond his original biological means and made possible the careers of a series of supermen, the likes

---

[4] We will henceforth use the word Homo-Caballus to identify the creature resulting from the symbiotic merger of Homo sapiens and Equus Caballus. Homo-Caballus will thus represent the scientific version of the mythological Centaur.

www.horsetravelbooks.com

of which our world will probably never see again. Alexander, Julius Caesar, Charlemagne, and especially Attila, Genghis Khan, Motun and Tamerlane—the greatest of the nomadic war leaders who all made their fame and fortune in partnership with their horses, leaving a cultural imprint on the planet that will probably never be deleted.

It is true that with the domestication of wheat, spinach and all those other eatable plants, man increased his intake of carbohydrates and vitamins. With the taming of plants, man increased his food supply, and later with the taming of the ox, he increased his muscle power. But carbohydrates and vitamins are found in other foodstuffs, and the strength of five or six men corresponds to that of an ox. With the invention of agriculture, humanity simply increased the 'quantity' of what people already possessed. This part of the Biological Revolution represented a significant but simple quantitative conquest in the process of human development.

In contrast, the 'big bang' of the Biological Revolution was the physiological merging of Homo and Caballus that changed human nature. Not five, ten or even 100 men will ever attain the speed of one horseman, making the incorporation of the horse's physiology by mankind a qualitative leap and, thus, the pinnacle of the entire Biological Revolution. The development of equitation was the pivotal moment of history, allowing man to break his biological time barrier and become the first and only animal ever to have done so.

If the latest research coming from neurology and physiology is seriously considered, advanced horsemanship is probably the most complex biological technology ever invented by man and has given him his greatest influence and power to date.

To turn wild horses into the core of a strong economy was a process of trial and error that probably took thousands of years to perfect. The archaeological remains of this part of recorded history are relatively few. As testimony to the steppe nomad's dazzling success, we have evidence of his devastating impact on urban-agrarian civilizations. In the clash between agriculturists and pastoralists, a star was born that would shine in the sky of every advanced civilization for the next 50 centuries. His name: Homo-Caballus, the catalyst of history.

5. Horsemanship, the Catalyst of History

The cultural and economic underpinning of nomad societies sprang from a profound knowledge of horse husbandry on the open range, one that relied upon the absolute confidence in man by the horse. To control the herd in open country, with no corrals or containment facilities, man must possess a deep knowledge of the mind, habits and social organization of the horse. To understand and transform wild horse herds into a way of making a living demanded a greater burst of creativity from Homo Faber than stone chipping, food gathering, hunting with bow and arrow or even farming. Even before the invention of equitation, through pastoralism the steppe people had achieved a successful social and economic organization. But in the beginning of this new way of life, the horse herder was faced with one very difficult question. Contrary to wheat, barley and rye, the horse had a mind of its own, and when it started running, nobody knew how to stop it.

Thousands of years ago, in Central Asia, somewhere between the Black and Caspian Seas, the first nomadic tribes began to specialize in horses, which were ubiquitous on the steppe. Think about it: there they were, running after the horses with their bows and arrows, just like you see the scenes painted on the ancient cave walls. But over time they stop chasing the horses and learn to mingle with the herd, following the horse's year round pasturing circuit. This new manner of living demanded special behavior techniques that were arguably more difficult to accomplish than hunting but ultimately brought greater economic advantages. By following horses and behaving as part of the herd, these people avoided all those wild goose chases of the hunting parties, which more often than not saw them return home with empty bellies.

While the farmers down south were learning to foresee the seasons for planting and reaping, the nomads up north were learning to adapt their lives to the nature and pasture circuit of the horses. And the first rule of this technique was to live with the animals in harmony. "Nature has to be dominated, but yet, the goal has to be harmony. It is like training a dog or gentling a horse. Real mastery is impossible without the understanding that springs from profound sympathy," wrote Virgil more than 2,000 years ago.

And so to establish the relationship of mutual trust needed to dwell together on the open range, it was first important that the horses accept the human presence. For this reason, the herders developed an approaching technique,[5]

---

[5] Although Monty Roberts' *join-up* technique was not the first time an ethnic European put into practice a language for mutual cooperation between man and horse – Oscar Gleason at the turn of the last century and Horace Hayes in the nineteenth were early "horse whisperers" – Monty undoubtedly was the first to treat the matter as a technique

www.horsetravelbooks.com

which would, throughout time, turn into the cornerstone of a relationship of interdependence and trust. From this new way of approaching horses, a code of social relationship was born between the human and equine species. Man cared for the horse, would defend the herd against predators, dress a wound and offer other small services, which only human hands could do. In biology this sort of relationship based on mutual cooperation is called a symbiosis.

To maintain this symbiotic relationship, the nomad herder would never slay a horse in sight of the herd. With great psychological insight, he also learned that horses are organized in a social hierarchy much like his own, and by understanding the rules he learned how to control the herd—mainly the lead mares. With such subtle ways of horse handling, the nomads slowly took control of the herd. The domestication of mares for milking was an important step in establishing this leadership. As all matters concerning horses require fast thinking, detailed organization and much sensitivity, the nomad herder greatly developed his intelligence.

For example, if a mare were tied up overnight, in the morning when she was freed she would lead the owner to the herd! To control the herd it was also necessary to castrate the excess stallions. To determine ownership of individual horses it was essential to mark them. This was done with a cut in the ear or a brand on the skin. To cure diarrhea in the youngsters, to recognize and remedy diseases and stop pain with herbs—all were part of the everyday duties of the nomad herder. To follow the horses' feeding circuit all year round, the nomad pastoralists moved their camp whenever the grass started to grow scarce on the surrounding plains. This kept the community on the move for most of the year. The result was that these Asiatic tribes slowly undertook full leadership of the horse herd and built a new way of life around the horse.

The nomad's existence amid his horses turned him into an expert in the delicate art of horse husbandry. Please note that all these equine experiences are highly sophisticated, from the point of view of the human learning process. (Neuroscience has already taught us that the interrelation between living beings requires a greater understanding of cause and effect than the use of tools, planting or tinkering with cars and other inanimate objects.) So while the Outer Eurasian farmers down south were developing agriculture, the Inner Eurasian horse herders up north were learning to handle horses successfully.

While the planters invented hoes and scythes to help to plant and reap, the horse herders invented the hobble and a host of knots and loops to help restrain and treat their horses. One day a clash between these two cultures would upset

---

that anybody could learn, rather than some sort of metaphysical boogy only practiced by the "initiated."

www.horsetravelbooks.com

THE CENTAUR LEGACY

the world and show which social system—nomadic or agrarian—was best equipped to develop the harmony between human body and mind and bring economic and social success. (See *The Masters of Space and the Masters of Speed* coming up soon).

The herd was the *'leit motif'* to the nomad, as the crop was the *'raison d'etre'* of the farmer. The horse transported the pastoralist's belongings from camp to camp and supplied him with meat; the mares produced milk with which he made cheese and curdled milk; horsehide covered his tent and was useful for myriad other tasks: from horsehair he made felt, rough cloth and braided ropes. The horse was a form of currency and the nomad herders became great animal merchants. In horse husbandry nothing is lost, everything is transformed, as Antoine Lavoisier would have said before he himself was "transformed" by the French Revolution.

But there remained a serious, seemingly insoluble problem for the herder. When the horses spooked, nobody could stop them. These occurrences became a source of deep worry to the herder, a slow biped equipped with the worst motor system in nature. If a tiger, wolf or lightning startled the herd, in a wink it would be over the hill and out of sight. Afterwards, it could take many days and lots of luck for people on foot to find the animals without loss. Naturally the steppe herder suffered greatly before finding an answer to this problem. The solution turned out to be as simple as Columbus' standing egg[6]. Even though nobody really can prove how riding techniques developed, Harold Barclay[7] mentions several authors, but shows special sympathy for one of the theories, which seems to be the most likely.

Riding was probably developed as a means to control the herd. By riding one of the horses, man was up to the task of following the stampede wherever the horses would go and eventually bringing the animals back. Simple. Now, to ride a horse may sound easy to you who have seen and known about riding all your life. But it must not have been easy to invent. To dominate the movements of the horse from a position on the animal's back would have seemed more like commanding a tornado sitting on a barrel picked up by a storm. The back of a horse is theoretically the worst place to be if you want to overpower a horse.

---

[6] It is said that Christopher Columbus in his endeavor to convince a congregation of royal seafarers, astronomers, geographers and scientists of his apparently harebrained scheme of reaching the east by sailing west asked the noble audience if they knew how to make an egg stand alone. As nobody did, he took an egg and knocked the roundest side gently on the table, thus making it stand!

[7] Harold Barclay: professor of Anthropology at the University of Alberta and author of the book *The Role of the Horse in Man's Culture*.

www.horsetravelbooks.com

Well then, how did someone think about climbing aboard a horse so as to ride it and keep track of the herd?

Here is probably how: *children got the idea.* Brats in play may have started it. Probably nomad children herding the milk mares to and from the pasture started to climb onto the horse's backs, for a free ride. You know kids and what they are capable of. Let's focus on them. There they are, those naughty brats. One boy is trying to climb onto one of the young colts and is nimbly bucked off. A spirited girl tries the same prank and is handily bounced over. The other kids hoot. It turns into a game. Another child tries to mount an older mare that just runs a little, but feeling it's just for fun, stops and starts cropping the grass. The child slaps her croup and she runs a little bit more and stops again to graze.

Now the mare is getting the hang of the game and doesn't mind being ridden any more. It's clearly all for fun. After that, going from the camp to the pasture and back, the little herders learn to ride the tame mares. Now just look at that: an unusually bratty kid is riding the older mare all over the place, guiding her with a rope around the muzzle! The grown-ups puttering around the camp chores stop their work to look at the brat – kids will be kids – and shake their heads in merriment and go back to work.

But naturally, one day, it dawns on a brighter somebody that the impossible has happened in that camp: it was possible to guide a horse sitting on its back! This new understanding of the horse solved the nomad herder's greatest problem and started the rise of a star — *Homo-Caballus* — that was to govern humanity for the next 60 centuries.

By riding a horse, man can reach a much greater speed than the one programmed by his biological constitution. Homo-Caballus started having a different relationship with space and time than the rest of humanity. For him the distances diminished and the future drew closer. All of a sudden, tomorrow can be today and next week tomorrow! The world shrinks and everything comes within the reach of his ambition. With the invention of equitation, Homo-Caballus broke the human speed barrier and 'equestrian dynamics'[8] shaped history.

---

[8] *Equestrian dynamics*: the force and speed derived from equitation that gave human affairs an exponential velocity beyond the human genetic capacity.

www.horsetravelbooks.com

6. Horsemen Break the Human Time Barrier

By incorporating the horse's speeds the Central Asian mounted nomads gained the same autonomy of the wild horses that roamed the endless steppe that stretches from central Europe to northwestern China. Ethnologists generally name these people, which include the Cimmerians, Scythians, Sarmatians, Huns, Turks, Avars, Magyars and Mongols, as steppe nomads. Archaeologists usually don't care much for them. They prefer the sedentary Sumerians, Egyptians, Indians, Greeks, Romans and Chinese, who reward their diggings with splendid archaeological treasures — artifacts, monuments, and even whole cities can be unearthed. From Homo-Caballus relatively few traces are found – mainly bones, pieces of art and riding gear from their trash-midden and burial places. But ultimately the pastoralist nomads of Central Asia would offer the greatest contribution to human progress: the breaking of humanity's biological time barrier. After that exploit, man's strategic thought pattern and most important time saving inventions would be related to this new technology.

It is most probable that riding was developed by the nomad herders to control the horses on the Inner Eurasian steppe in the manner that the gauchos, vaqueros and cowboys manage the cattle herds in the Americas. A horseman will have the speed to follow the stampeding herd, and besides that, the animals will be more willing to accept the leadership of a horseman than of a man on foot – just ask any cowhand.

Now, the technology of riding, invented by the nomads, must have consisted of an important *neurophysiological adaptation* between horse and rider. To achieve total mobility, the nomad must have merged his *sensory-motor system* with his horse. That is, when riding, he connected all his senses and coordinated his reflexes to those of the horse to produce precise cooperative movements. He was not worried about *striking a pose* and showing *who is in command here,* as you often see in the Western world. As a predator, the only objective of the nomadic horseman would be to achieve a high standard of mobility to handle his herd, down his prey, or vanquish his enemy. This meant that when riding, the sensory-motor system of horse and rider should merge into one fine-tuned machine.

This neurophysiological merging of horse and man also resulted in a *super-predator* equipped with the ambition of man and the speed of the horse. A totally new predator of great velocity and maneuverability who would become specialized in preying on humans – mainly the city-building, food-storing sedentary farmers dwelling by the rich river deltas in southern Eurasia.

As we shall see, there is no evidence in the past of an invention which had a greater impact on modern civilization than equitation – the perfect symbiosis of man and horse carried out on the Central Asian steppes. And, as we have recently learned with neuroscience, the relationship with the *incertitude of* animals is more stimulating to the human brain than the *certainties* of dealing with plants, these people must have developed a mind prepared for fast action performed beyond the human speed limit.

With the absolute control of the horse herd gained through riding techniques, the steppe people must have *wired their brains* with trillions of new neuronal connections to cope with the infinite complex situations of horse husbandry and horseback riding in a society always on the move. The nomad herder must have developed a tactic-strategic reasoning unheard of in any other society that would have a profound impact on history. And by dominating the technology of breeding, selecting, feeding, gentling, training, handling, hunting, and specially wielding arms on horseback, the Central Asian horseman must have reached the highest level of *brain wiring* of any human group.

Everything in his way of life concurs to brain development: the agility of the society, always on the move; the forming of warrior leaders schooled for the fast-armed confrontation, characteristic of the steppes; the invention of all the riding equipment needed for horseback warfare: bridles, reins, bits, stirrups, saddles, surcingles, saddle blankets, straps, and látigos, the accessories which help connect and fine-tune the sensory-motor systems of horse and rider; the expert handling of the composite short bows – the most dreaded weapon of light cavalry; the technique of horse repositioning during warfare without the cumbersome 'remuda' system. The military strategy of advancing, falling back, dispersion and reorganization at the speed of nerve synapses. As their brains were exposed to an ever-changing environment, where new neurons structures had to be connected to cope with fast changing situations, everything in this way of life conformed to quick thinking and swift action.

The sum of all these experiences formed a vivacious and intelligent fast moving people with their eyes always set towards the horizon and the opportunities that the future might bring. The Romans named them Sagittarius – the dart throwers – and depicted them as a human figure with a horse's body. A nomadic attack had the precision of a flight of eagles and thousands of riders could maneuver on the battlefield as one body. But, they obviously never received a good press. They were too fast, too dangerous, too successful, too foreign and always on the wrong side of our history's cheerleaders.

The Huns, say ancient Chinese witnesses, are always on horseback. Sometimes they sit sideways if that position is more convenient – to take a leak, for example. Everybody in that nation, man, woman or child, is able to ride nights and days if necessary. Astride a horse they buy, sell, eat, drink, gossip and when tired lean forward and sleep.[9]

Their favorite sport, called Buz Khazi, is still played in Afghanistan. It is a fast game and sometimes as many as 300 riders join the contest. Instead of a ball, they play with the body of a calf. It is not a team game – it's every man for himself. The calf is disputed by the mass of riders and the victor is the horseman who is able to catch and hold onto the calf, turn a post in a corner of the field and carry the prize back to a circle in the center. No mean feat, and it's unnecessary to describe the expertise needed of horse and rider in this game, which is the forerunner of polo.

"These people make their war councils while mounted, and their country is the back of their horses," wrote a Chinese emissary. Which of course made the ground where their horses were standing their fatherland. According to Chinese chronicles, Hun children learned to ride when other children learned to walk. The Hun's diet was horse milk and horsemeat. The meat was eaten fresh, smoked or dried. The milk was drunk fresh or curdled. When necessary the Hun would open a vein and drink the blood of his horse, which of course gave their military forays extra autonomy.

Every penalty in their strict legal code was paid in horses. The killing of a free man was punished with the payment of one hundred horses; the killing of a woman, girl or slave, 50 horses; the killing of a sultan 700 horses; the loss of a tooth, a broken leg or a wound in the head was redressed with the payment of one horse. To cause the abortion of a woman was punished with one horse for every month of pregnancy. But to steal or kill a favorite horse carries a death penalty! They became the greatest horse societies in the world, with the greatest equestrian achievements in the history of humanity.

When the Central Asian nomads invented equitation and broke their *biological time barrier,* they also broke out of their frontiers, invaded the agrarian civilizations and gave the world a show of military strategy which was never to be surpassed by any other power. The sum of the speed of their thinking,

---

[9] As normally happens with city-bred people, the ancient Chinese were not aware of the neurophysiological merger of horse and man during top performance equitation. Exactly like us, they would describe only what they could see with their own eyes: people sitting on horses, sleeping on horses, gossiping on horses, working on horses and fighting on horses. The horse was simply seen as the vehicle of the rider. The deep feelings of 'self' that arise when man and horse have achieved complete understanding of each other's intentions and are capable of blending into one biological unity was beyond their understanding. Probably the Chinese, like us, had good individual riders but the 'Homo-Caballus symbiosis' never spread out to become a cultural feature, as appears to have happened with the nomadic horse-people of Central Asia.

www.horsetravelbooks.com

the speed of their horses, and the speed of their arrows, turned their military campaigns into lethal military operations. The cavalry actions of the Scythians and Huns initiated the military cycle of the warriors of the steppes – and started the first weapon scramble in history, as sedentary societies struggled to dominate the equestran techniques and form their own cavalries to save themselves from the waves of lightning fast horsemen of the steppe.

The equestrian societies of Central Asia started an entirely new philosophy in the use of time, which later would be emulated by Western societies with many new time saving inventions such as trains, automobiles and electronic communication. But for six thousand years – all the way up to the 20th century – *the people who made the best use of the speed of the horse were the heirs of the earth and of all the wealth that it contained.*

The incorporation of Equus Caballus' splendid motor-system liberated Homo sapiens from his biological speed limit and unbridled his ambition. Attaining the mobility of Equus, the Huns of Attila achieved one of humanity's greatest exploits. They captured parts of China, the Middle East, and Central Europe and built their capital in Hungary – occupying in successive generations 8000 kilometers of the Old World. The principle of this phenomenon – the diminishing of time with the increase of speed – a real Homo sapiens named Einstein defined many years later with the Theory of Relativity.

7. On Attila and Einstein
With the contribution of J. Bronowski

Some 6000 years ago, in Central Asia, the steppe nomads formed the symbiosis that evolved into equitation, and with this extraordinary biological technology they broke humanity's time barrier, which had kept man chained to the speed of his genetic motor program. Attila can be considered the first great leader of a nomadic horse society to dominate parts of Western Europe. Einstein, who was born 1426 years after Attila's death, is related to the Hun leader in an interesting way. If we consider Attila as the first European representative of the people who broke the human time barrier, Einstein was the first man to understand the relativity of time – an extraordinarily subtle concept. Attila, using 'equestrian dynamics', and Einstein, understanding the physical phenomenon behind it, stand as two important marks in European social, economical, scientific and cultural evolution.

A nomadic lifestyle imposes on its members the need to raid and pillage, in a never-ending cycle, which demand strong leadership and a fine sense of organization. Without intensive planning, hard discipline and perfect cooperation, life on the steppes would be unbearable. The recorded history of the Hun people began in the year 221 BC and their conflicts with the Chinese. The Hun military incursions into northern China and their clashes with Chinese military forces provoked emigration waves in most of Eurasia — towards Europe as well as India. In 128 BC the Chinese Emperor started a powerful campaign to exterminate the Hun invaders – the war lasted a hundred years and finished as a draw. After these campaigns many Hun tribes swept west and successfully invaded Europe.

Attila (406-453) was born in Transylvania, a Hun-conquered country in what is now Hungary, and was crowned king in 433. The first eight years of his reign kept him busy fighting and annexing other equestrian tribes, until he became virtually supreme in Central Europe – between the Caspian Sea and the Rhine. For several years Attila raided the Balkan Peninsula and even threatened Constantinople. But the Byzantine Emperor Martian resisted him bravely, and Attila turned his cavalry towards an easier pray – the declining Roman Empire of the West.

But before taking on the forces of Rome he formed an alliance with the Francs, crossed the Rhine and plundered most of Belgian Gaul. The bishops of the new Roman Apostolic Catholic Church, which has been founded some 400 years earlier, didn't admire Attila's 'blitz krieg' tactics and military success, which ruined their new dioceses, and so they called him *the Scourge of God*. Heading south, Attila besieged Orleans in France, which was saved by a Roman-

Gothic army. The famous battle of the Catalunia fields lasted an entire day, and both sides suffered heavy losses, before the Hun warriors withdrew back to Panonia. In 452, Attila's cavalry rolled down to Italy where they plundered Aquiléia, Concord, Altinum and Padua. (The survivors of these cities, looking for refuge in the Adriatic, founded Venice.) Near the city of Mantua, Attila received the visit of Pope Leo I who supplicated – or more probably bribed – him to spare Rome and go home. During 19 years Attila – the Scourge of God – wrought more havoc in Europe than any other military leader before him. To the steppe people, equitation was a God-inspired blessing – a miraculous shortcut to fame and fortune.

Most contemporary historians agree that, far from being the madman described by legend, Attila the Hun was the leader of a very well organized nomadic Empire. The prejudice against Attila and his people was an understandable reaction of sedentary societies against an almost invincible weapon: the stupendous mobility of the mounted archers, equipped with the dreaded short-bows. (Centuries later, the destructive power of cannons, machine-guns and tanks would raise similar wails and protests from their victims.) Equitation – the perfect union between man and horse, had been turned into a mobile military machine of enormous efficiency.

The *civilizing legacy* of the equestrian steppe people was not magnificent cities and beautiful monuments. Nomads built very little, but they formed a highly efficient social structure entirely sustained by equitation. The Asian nomads' cultural legacy to mankind was *'equestrian dynamics'*, which allowed them to use time in a revolutionary way. By breaking humanity's *biological time barrier* they started a trend of thought and behavior that, ultimately, would shape all victorious societies and shorten history's time span. This subtle dynamic concept of space and time would only be understood many years later, by an uncommon man – *a real Homo sapiens* – born in one of the old war zones disputed by the equestrian Huns and the sedentary Europeans.

Albert Einstein was born in 1879 in the city of Ulm, by the Danube River, in south Germany. Young Einstein would soon reveal his vocation as a 'learning machine'. In 1895 he obtained permission – for he was two years in advance of the minimum age – to undergo the admission exam for the *Polytechnikum* School of Zürich. He went through tests on mathematics, physics, chemistry, literature and political history. He was not approved due to the general subjects – literature and political history.

Perhaps this setback was the cause of the erroneous impression that Einstein was a bad student. He was not. Actually, he liked books but not schools. (He probably found his teachers mediocre, which would be a normal feeling for a genius.) In 1900 Einstein earned a diploma as a science teacher. However, all his

www.horsetravelbooks.com

THE CENTAUR LEGACY

attempts to be accepted as an assistant in several universities were refused. Only in 1902 did Einstein get a permanent job as a junior assistant in the Patents Registration Office in Bern. At that time Newton's universe was still going strong, though it was on the verge of a heart attack.

Nobody knows if young Albert knew about Newton's universe. It seems that he hadn't paid much thought to this matter at the University. It is said that during his adolescence he had already asked himself 'what would our experiences seem like, from the point of view of the speed of light.' The answer to this question is full of paradoxes. And like all paradoxical questions, the most difficult part is not the answer, but to formulate the correct question necessary to establish the paradigm. But, even if we have Einstein talking about *riding a beam of light* or *falling free in space* he always had simple ways to illustrate these principles.

So let's follow J. Bronovski's description of Einstein's theory:

"I go to the bottom of the clocktower and get into the tram that Einstein used to take every day on his way to work in the Swiss Patent Office. The thought that Einstein had in mind in his teens was this: 'What would the world look like if I rode on a beam of light?' Suppose that the tram was moving away from the clock on the very beam of light that brings us the image of the time the clock shows. With the tram at the speed of a light ray, time would have to stop. Let me spell that out — suppose the clock, behind me shows 'noon', when I leave. I now travel 186,000 miles away from it at the speed of light; that ought to take one second; but the time marked on the clock would still say 'noon', because it takes the beam of light from the clock exactly as long as it has taken me. So, as far as the clock as I see it, so far as the universe inside the tram is concerned, in keeping up with the speed of light I have cut myself off from the passage of time. This paradox explains two things. An obvious one — universal time is non-existent. And another even more subtle – that experience runs very differently for the traveler and the-stay-at-home, and so for each of us on his own path."

Now we can finally conclude the reason for gathering these two seemingly disparate characters – Attila and Einstein – in the same chapter of a work concerning equitation. Horsemanship reduced drastically the relation of time and distance for the horseman and brought him enormous benefits, when compared to the *biological time limit* of people tied to their bipedal locomotion. The Central Asian nomads, using only the speed of equitation, conquered empires and did just what their heart desired – a concept today deeply linked to Homo sapiens. Or, as Einstein said, "the values that I get from time, distance, and so on, are not the same for the man standing on the sidewalk."

In a nutshell: the equestrian nomads shortened the distances between today and tomorrow. If you can be in a place today where you normally could only be tomorrow you have changed the values of *time and space* of your existence. This

www.horsetravelbooks.com

differential *use of time* invented by Central Asian horse people is the motor that has inspired human technology up to our days, and Internet may be considered to represent the current breakthrough. Einstein's theory, explained with the example of the tram, was his way of *breaking the barrier* of space and time. The two achievements – the breaking of the human time barrier through horsemanship and the Theory of Relativity – shows Einstein's *direct cultural link* to the successive equestrian civilizations that accelerated and formed Western thought, and from which he and Attila can be said to be exponents. (Although while Einstein's mind was probing the far reaches of the universe you couldn't expect him also to figure out where his *brain wave* came from).

The exhilarating sensation of surpassing the speed of your own physical limit was experienced, for the first time, when man freed his body to navigate in a faster time on the back of a horse. And the liberation of the body liberates the mind. Without this cultural experience, no sedentary civilization could have conceived the Theory of Relativity by 1900. As Bronowski himself stated – "I believe that the importance of the horse in European history has always been underrated."

And to my way of thinking it hasn't been understood at all!

Newton, observing the fall of an apple, formulated the law of Universal Gravitation and Einstein, after two hundred years of man's accumulated intellectual experiences, put himself in the place of the apple and formulated the Theory of Relativity. All this was only possible because horsemen, one day, broke the human time barrier, introduced equestrian dynamics, accelerated the speed of history and impelled mankind to the present. But if equestrian power has been grossly underrated in Western History, the impact of Homo-Caballus on man's imagination, created the most extraordinary character ever to inhabit human mythology – the Centaur.

8. The Rule of the Centaurs

The myth of the Centaur, the fantastic half-horse, half-human figure first referred to by Homer, symbolizes the pastoral nomads that ravaged sedentary villages as early as the III millennium BC, causing widespread social disruption in great parts of Eurasia. The devastating incursions of nomadic cavalry swarming out of Central Asia only abated some five hundred years before the rise of the Greek 'golden age' of Xenophon, horses, and cavalry, leaving in its wake the myth of the Centaur. Therefore Greek mythology is ambiguous toward the Centaur – sometimes showing him as a treacherous enemy and at other times as an intelligent entity, wise in horsemanship, hunting, music and medicine. The reason for this duality is that the Centaur—the mounted warrior of the steppe—when a friend is the most precious of allies, and when an enemy the most dangerous of all.

As the spread of horsemanship and the pastoral way of life was expanding in Inner Eurasia, cyclical incursions of fast riding horsemen looting the peasant villages of Southern Asia became a widespread event. And as the frontiers of horsemanship expanded in every direction of the Old World the "Cortez effect" – the awe of defenseless farmers for the first time spying horsemen approaching and in the next moment being massacred and having their villages sacked by the superhuman predators – left a profound imprint on sedentary societies. This deep-rooted fear of the human-horse combination is the stuff of Centaur mythology and has haunted urban-agrarian people since time immemorial.

In fact archeologists now believe that the Central Asian cavalry raids on agricultural settlements began in the 3rd millennium and provoked the so-called "migration of the peoples,"[10] when uprooted populations, fleeing the areas devastated by the mounted nomads, overran and sacked other communities in their line of flight. The impact of Central Asian cavalry raids and the waves of desperate emigrants settling in other lands greatly changed the ethnic and political map of much of Eurasia.

The storm of the Centaur's thundering hooves only abated in the 1st millennium BC, barely a century and a half before Homer's time. When

---

[10] If we compress the 6000 years that horsemanship is believed to have been in practice into one solar year, the Central Asian Nomads held sway in Eurasia from January to May, the Greco-Roman Empire ruled from June to August, the Huns and Mongols were supreme from September to the middle of November, the last weeks of November were hotly disputed by the Ottoman Empire pitted against a West European coalition, and from the fifteenth to the thirtieth of December the Equestrian Age was ruled by Western sedentary powers, and only in the last day of the year machines tipped the scales of world power.

www.horsetravelbooks.com

Herodotus[11] in the fifth century BC wrote *The History of Herodotus* the sedentary world, after millennia of nomadic oppression, had at last achieved political organizations, walled cities, better arms, and military forces capable of withstanding the "barbarians" attacks.

In the time that Herodotus, the father of History, traveled through Asia Minor, the Middle East, Italy and Sicily to record the historical facts of his day, mounted pastoralism was in decline and sedentary civilizations, now adapted to the horse, were on the rise. And the author's first sentence makes the strife between East and West totally clear: "These are the researches of Herodotus of Halicarnassus, which he publishes, in the hope of thereby preserving from decay the remembrance of what men have done, and of preventing the great and wonderful actions of the Greeks and the Barbarians from losing their due meed of glory; and withal to put on record what was their grounds of feuds".

As you can see, Western historians have traditionally called all types of horse people with pastoral tradition "barbarians". The "barbarians" in Herodotus's time were the Persians who descended from the Medes, a nomadic pastoral people that had settled and formed an empire in the Middle East that reached as far south as modern Lybia and as Far East as Pakistan. Herodotus started writing his annals a few centuries after the last storm of nomadic horsemen had abated and the Greek culture was approaching its zenith.

It can be said that the Equestrian Age, the times when horses and riders held center stage in human affairs, began around 1500 BC when the Scythian nomads occupied the lands north and east of the Black Sea as far as the Caspian. The military supremacy of this hectic period has swayed between nomadic federations and sedentary societies all the way up to the Middle Ages. In Herodotus' day the nomadic societies were going through their "dark ages", an eclipse of their military power, though a thousand years later the Sedentary empires were once again ceding to the unrelenting nomadic pressure and the crisis of the classical world reached its peak in the 5th century with the decline of the Greco-Roman Empire and the ensuing "dark ages" of the West.[12]

But in the Roman Empire's heyday Eurasia was already fully powered by 'equestrian dynamics' and the Roman cavalry had adopted Epona, the protector of horses and the only universal goddess to be worshipped by the Celts. Epona, a female Centaur of sorts, had her image affixed to horse stables throughout

---

[11] Herodotus (c.485-425 BC) Greek historian, born in Halicarnassus, Asia Minor.

[12] The drama in proto history called the 'Migration of the People', when great parts of Eurasia were devastated by Central Asian horsemen, caused whole communities and their navies to seek new places to settle. The decline of the Roman Empire, when the classical sedentary cultures were once again thrown into turmoil by storms of horse peoples, caused the Dark Ages that anteceded the Middle Ages.

ancient Europe. The White Horse of Berkshire, probably a zoomorphic represenation of Epona, was carved fifty years before Caesar's landing in England.

To the Vikings, thunder and lightning was attributed to Odin's war-chariot rumbling over the heavenly stone pavement, drawn by his eight legged horse Sleipnir.

In the Middle Ages the Slavs of Central Europe, descendants from the Huns, worshipped Muromyets whose power over mortals was multiplied, a thousand times, by his fantastic white winged horse. (Horse people obviously had a good collective memory of their past equestrian feats).

But the most fantastic figure representing the Homo-Caballus symbiosis is the Centaur – half man and half horse – that plays an important part in Greek mythology. The word 'Centaur' means 'cattle guard' in Greek, and is an obvious reference to pastoral nomads. But this fabulous creature is commonly thought to have been inspired by the horsemen of Thessaly, the animal herders of ancient Greece. Though I think it more plausible that the myth of the Centaur arose after the third and especially the second millennium BC, when the Central Asian horsemen ravaged great parts of Eurasia with devastating consequences for the sedentary cultures living on the borders of the Aegean Sea, the Near East, the Middle East, and even as far as Egypt.

Nomadic and sedentary societies had been in ferocious opposition since the domestication of animals split humans into two types of societies: sedentary or nomadic, depending on an individual's disposition to live in a closed agricultural community or to range free over the land on horseback in search of nature's varied opportunities. Due to these entirely different life styles nomadic and sedentary economies shaped societies with opposite mentalities that would clash again and again throughout history. Throughout the Equestrian Age horsemanship would tip the scales in favor of whichever society was best adapted to horses and equitation.

"The horseman is more than a man", wrote Bronowski in *The Ascent of Man*. "To ride a horse symbolizes the act of dominating the whole of creation. It is not possible nowadays to recapture the terror of the appearance of mounted men in the Middle East and Eastern Europe. This is so, because there is a difference in the human scale that can only be compared to the coming of German tanks into Poland in 1939, sweeping everything before them" explains Bronowski. The Dead Sea Scrolls also narrate, with deep emotion, the coming of the Roman cavalry to Israel, a hundred years BC.[13]

---

[13] Though I think that the horsemen who overran Israel were probably Numidian mercenary cavalry hired in North Africa to 'soften' the enemy before the arrival of the Imperial phalanxes. The Romans themselves were not fast riders and would not have planned an attack without the support of their infantry.

www.horsetravelbooks.com

"Faster than Panthers their horses, fleeter than desert wolves. Their horses galloping, spread out, from afar they fly as birds of prey toward carrion, all with violent intentions, their faces always turned forwards. The Kittim [Roman cavalry] trample the ground with their horses and beasts. They come from afar, from the coast of the sea, to fodder on the people as insatiable buzzards. With anger, hostility and arrogance... their faces ever forward".

These dramatic words, echoing out of the past, describe the tragedy of the Jewish people being devastated by the most fearsome predator that this world has ever produced: the Centaurs.

To try to recreate the strangeness soon turned into terror of a group of ancient farmers who do not know horsemanship and who are attacked for the first time by a pack of Centaurs is impossible – the horror of death can only be fathomed by one who has faced it. But let's imagine that you and I are agriculturists of yesteryear hacking at the soil outside our village somewhere in Asia Minor, and that suddenly we notice in the distance a group of strange creatures cantering our way, with the determination of purpose that we vaguely associated with predators. We immediately stop the work, lower our hoes, peel our eyes, and start distinguishing some horrifying details of the approaching ogres: each animal has two bobbing heads, four galloping legs and two waving arms carrying weapons. The lower part, which gallops on the ground, looks like a great hornless deer, but over the animal's head, between the ears, a grim painted face takes shape, which undoubtedly looks human! Before we can distinguish more details of these horrifying creatures, they fan out in a line abreast, stretch into a thundering gallop, and like beasts of prey close in for the kill.

And before the full horror of the meaning of these monster's intentions becomes clear to our slow working minds, arrows are flying in search of our tender parts.

The Centaur myth no doubt represents the mounted nomads of Central Asia who for millennia preyed on the settled agrarian communities of Eurasia. Greek ambivalence toward the Centaurs, the *enemy-friend* dichotomy found in their mythology, very probably symbolizes the time *before* the sedentary Greeks adopted horses and cavalry in their cultural progression and were subject to the direct ravages of horsemen, or had to deal with whole fugitive nations fleeing the war-stricken areas.

In Hellenic mythology the ancient Greek heroes always vanquish the Centaurs, which in fact is an accurate version of the nomadic-sedentary disputes in the golden age of Hellenic culture, where the pastoral nomads had been "reduced" and posed no serious threat to sedentary kingdoms. What Herodotus could not foresee was that the future decline of the Greco-Roman Empire would be caused by new waves of Centaurs—Huns, Avars, Alans, Magyars and

Mongols—who in the first and early second millennium AD were again on the rise and the tornadoes of loot and conquest would eventually cause the fall of the greatest sedentary empires on earth.[14]

The Centaur is the archetype of mounted pastoralism that for thousands of years defied the domesticated population's urge to settle and live a "safe" and predictable life. The warriors of the steppes are a symbol of mobility and freedom from urban laws, bureaucracy, overpopulation and environmental artificiality. The state of war between nomads and sedentary societies has been the motive force of the main historical events up to the Renaissance. But in the 1st millennium BC sedentary societies adopted the horse to save themselves from the Central Asian Centaurs and the classical empires ruled almost supreme until the first centuries AD.

---

[14] History confirms the Universal dread of the Centaur: the Great Wall of China was not build to keep out the Huns – it was raised to keep the Huns from passing with their horses – *the enemy was not man, it was the Centaur*, 'the scourge of God'.

www.horsetravelbooks.com

9. 'Equestrian Dynamics' Powers the World

Has humanity been unable to understand the sudden accelerating of the chain of events that occurred after the invention of equitation and that ultimately led to the landing on the moon? Is the general oblivion to the historical importance of equitation just the result of a 'collective reeling mind' after the steep upswing of Western civilizations' rise to fame and fortune, following the Middle Ages? Now anthropology and neuroscience can shed some light on the Equestrian Age when Homo's brain capacity had outgrown his footwork, and he discovered how to use Caballus' powerful motor-system to diminish time and increase his worldly success.

Every living being – from the invisible ameba to the gigantic sequoia – has a life span in which it is born, flowers into adulthood, spreads its genes and withers. But animals like insects, reptiles, birds and mammalians are born with a motor system with which they can annul the distances of time and space between themselves and an *opportunity* – be it a chance to eat a nut, encounter a mate, or to widen the distance between oneself and some encroaching unpleasantness. Legs are the most common strategy for these creatures' displacement, although wings are also popular and even some animals without the least vestige of legs or wings can attain great speed by snaking out of a difficult situation.

The capability of locomotion has also led to the demarcation of the area that the legged creatures feel that they need to survive – the so-called 'vital space'. To move around on its staked-out territory to feed, breed and keep an eye on intruders, many mammalians developed hard hoofs to resist the wear and tear of the daily guard duty. As cloven hoofs are not usually recommended for long travel, the animals equipped with this type of footwear, developed horns to help defend a smaller territory. With the domesticated of the ox humanity's 'vital space' was not much enlarged because bovines do not generally occupy great extensions of land.

But the horse, as we know it, has passed through a long period of evolution, from the animal possessing four, or even five toes per foot – to the *single-digited soliped*, as the experts call Equus. With the old multiple toe strategy the ancient Equidae probably occupied a smaller 'vital space' than modern Equus. Therefore, the new *single digit* footwear, capable of great-sustained speed, also developed in the horse an inclination to roam over vast tracts of land – but, though it has a habit of marking its stamping ground with piles of dung, Equus doesn't seem to have the same attachment to these locations as most other animals.

Horses have a grazing cycle that they will follow as long as there is available grass. But, if the commodity grows short, or if a predator pesters the herd, at the drop of a hat they'll be over the hill and grazing in a friendlier neighborhood. Equus Caballus is a citizen of the world!

When the Central Asian nomads domesticated the horse and discovered that it could be ridden, they acquired Equus Caballus' mobility and also became citizens of the world.

As we have already seen, man was endowed with the worst pair of feet that the Maker had in stock, because Hominids were originally designed by nature to move by swinging with their arms in the treetops and not to stand on their feet on the ground. For efficacious footwork Hominids were built with the wrong side down! Before the invention of equitation, the 'naked ape' would only budge his rump from his native lump if moved by a catastrophe or some urgent business as in J. H. Rosny's *In Quest of Fire*. No wonder—outfitted with two floppy feet, flatfoot walking has never been very popular with Homo Faber.[15] 'Wanderlust' is not generally part of most people's genetic make-up. *But horsemanship would change all that.*

The taming of the horse on the steppe and the human incorporation of its developed motor-system was even more important for Homo's world dominance than to grow a green thumb down in Mesopotamia. Now, the 'catch 22' of equitation (nothing is perfect, there's a *catch* in everything, as Joseph Heller slyly perceived) is that the human *bi-pedal motor coordination* comes from the Maker connected to a *two-beat brain,* contrary to the horse's more advanced two, three, and four beat gaits which comes with a more sophisticated brain-wiring in accordance with the Lord's specification.

To re-wire his neurons, so they could interact with his newly acquired motor-system, the horse-people had to put their famous 'learning machine' to the test. But when they finally did manage to connect and fine-tune their neurophysiological system with their horses' the two symbiotic partners would be able to occupy the horse's 'vital space' that stretches from China to Eastern Europe. And after that the Centaur's clan, and his clan's clan's clan, became masters of the earth and all the goodies that it contained! *Equitation had started a new 'time dynamic'!*

Some sixty centuries ago, the East was the birthplace of a dynamic society organized around the horse, which radiated in every direction of the free steppe – East, West, North and South – changing the *time concept* of whatever culture it

---

[15] History's boat people such as Phoenicians, Vikings and Polynesians would save their feet by following a river or land-coast for longer voyages. But it took the great Portuguese navigators *fifty years* to fumble their way down the African coast from Lisbon to the Cape of Good-Hope in their filthy bug-ridden, scurvy-festered caravels. And it took only two decades for Genghis Khan to conquer an empire that spanned from West Russia to North China.

www.horsetravelbooks.com

touched. Horse breeding was greatly increased with the demand for horses from the urban-agrarian people from Outer Eurasia, eager to catch up with their nomadic neighbors. The forming of cavalry in these civilizations provoked a great demand for horses, which was a strong motivation for all Central Asiatic people to abandon agriculture and start breeding horses. Through trade and warfare the nomad horsemen set the world on the move.

In the Mediterranean, the Greeks and Romans would be directly affected by Persian horsemanship[16] but, as all sedentary people, they would spend most of their time tinkering with their war chariots, and would never attain a *perfect neurophysiological merger* with their horses. This lack of equestran technology would ultimately cost them their empire. In Rome the increasing rumble and thunder of the rising tide of the Centaurs on the frontiers had been heard for many centuries without the magistrates taking much notice. Who could stand up to the might of Rome? But when cavalry — 'equestrian dynamics' in its purest form — smashed through their frontiers and overran the Italian boot – leg, heel and toe-tip – it sucked the greatest empire in the world into its vortex!

In the Iberian Peninsula Portugal and Spain would adopt 'equestrian dynamics' from the Moors, and turn themselves into the best horsemen in Western Europe. In Central Europe the regions that were in touch with the steppes – Poland, Lithuania, Hungary, Bulgaria and Austria – were also greatly influenced by the Equestrian Age and formed good cavalries.

But north-western Europe would for a long time be the backwoods of this equestrian tide that was spreading all over the Old World. Isolated by dark forests, marshy moors and foul weather, an unsuitable environment for brisk cavalry action, the Anglo-Saxon-Germanic draft-cultures would take a long time to come into contact with real equitation. In Europe the stirrup would take 800 years to spread from Lithuania to the northwestern regions of the continent! You see, these people didn't ride much – they mostly walked or rode in carts.

Therefore in the slow European environment news didn't circulate properly, and well into the Renaissance the housebound, land-tied, peasant was almost as ignorant about the world as Paleolithic man. For thousands of years northwestern Europe would not be touched by 'equestrian dynamics' that change people's behavior, transform people's ways of living, and jump-start their neurons to accept an increasing flow of new ideas. The civilizing effect of circulating info didn't give width to the farmer's horizon and depth to their thoughts. While the Duke of Newcastle could study equitation in Naples, most of his retainers would probably not know the outside of their home county. *But, eventually, horsemanship would catch up there too.*

---

[16] Persia had been formed by nomads—mainly the Medes—and consequently had a solid horse culture.

www.horsetravelbooks.com

The diffusion of horsemanship in northwestern Europe in the first millennium AD would slowly take hold of the upper classes, who became mobile and would also hire couriers to criss-cross the land to communicate with nobles in other kingdoms. 'Equestrian dynamics' set modern communication on the move. In the Middle Ages post offices and private riding would start to follow in the noble's footsteps and puncture the bubbles of public ignorance, which persisted in many corners of the Europe.

Once a peasant in Grassington could say "I have a uncle in Gloucester who wrote that if you leave the barley field fallow, the next year you'll harvest in double" it was a sure sign that *news* were starting to flow among *all social classes*. Because the universal circulation of information is important for a fast moving society, because the *poorly uninformed rear-guard* will ultimately be a drag to the *fast moving vanguard*. With the social and economic changes that equitation brought to a society, Europe's old arteries were unclogged and the Western world gained a new notion of time and the transforming power of new ideas.

And though Western Europe's equitation would never attain the speed and agility of the steppe horsemen, all later time-saving inventions inspired by the horse would be a short cut to world domination anyway. Today's eye-popping 'economic globalization' is the most visible consequence of the *equestrian wired brain* capable of envisioning global integration. And of course, in the West it was Alexander and his Ferghana horses that put the concept in motion.

The increase of the speed of information, a wider social cohesion and the strengthening of the economy was the real contribution of 'equestrian dynamics.' The importance of warfare has been secondary. And though equitation had also the capacity of splintering a society, as an instrument of war, the loser would eventually be absorbed by the winner and form a new and more powerful political unity. This ever-growing spin of equestrian power politics would ultimately create the force that propelled the man to the moon. And if this event was not the 20th century biggest technological achievement at least it was the biggest technological show, and a handy milestone to fifty centuries of chronological HorsePower.

www.horsetravelbooks.com

10. The Masters of Speed and the Masters of Space

If it is accurate that human neurons are connected for man to cope with the environment, as modern neuroscientists maintain, then Planet Earth seems to have produced two main types of brain-wiring: the urban-agrarian mind focused on agriculture and architecture, and the nomadic-equestrian brain centered on animal husbandry and equitation. These two types of mentalities made for two distinct life styles, which both became successful and would clash time and again throughout history. The 13th century was to witness one of the great duels between sedentary and nomadic life styles, when the Mongols broke out of their frontiers and conquered one fourth of the world's landmass and called Western Europe out for a showdown.

Agriculture and architecture are two technologies that were developed by the same people with the same type of mentality, as field tillage and house building is the product of a finely developed spatial sense. After inventing agriculture and developing architecture, Homo Faber became the only creature on earth that would be able to adapt his environment to his needs and wishes. This led to the urban-agrarian social and economic livelihood, which would lead to the lifestyle of modern societies. As agricultural techniques developed from the digging stick to the ox-plow, the urban-agrarian architecture sprang from the mud hut to the Gothic Cathedral. But out on the wind swept steppe another way of living had also become successful – animal husbandry and equitation that would produce the nomad-equestrian intelligence focused on perpetual movement and a highly developed sense of global strategy.

Now, it's ingrained in Homo's brain to improve on all things that work well, and therefore the urban-agrarian cultures would develop an ever-growing intellectual approach to architecture. From the adobe hut to Inca masonry, from the Egyptian to the Mayan pyramid, from the straight edged temples of Greece to the Roman arches, architecture, which demands a complex understanding of the division of space for human occupation, would become ever more elaborate, beautiful and grandiose.

However on the great Eurasian steppe the nomad, after adopting the horse's motor system and land roving capacity, was learning to form a repertoire of subtle and complex cooperative movements with Equus, an instinctive feeling for the neurophysiology of equitation, which would turn the Homo-Caballus symbiosis into the most successful predator in history, capable of conquering kingdoms and empires mainly by the combination of physical and intellectual speed.

In the twelfth century the world would witness two of humanity's greatest intellectual accomplishments: the Gothic cathedral and the Mongol Empire. The

www.horsetravelbooks.com

Gothic Cathedral is the product of a fine feeling for spatial sense that can transform a slab of marble into the image of a saint and a pile of stones into a cathedral. On the other hand, the Mongol Empire is the result of a broad sense of global strategy that can convert cavalry action into conquest. Or, as Einstein would later define the phenomenon of speed: "the values I get from time, distance, and so on, are not the same for the man standing on the sidewalk".

No buildings had ever compared to the Gothic Cathedrals that burst into light in the twelfth century. They dazzle scholars – and of course they are really good mason work. The Gothic Cathedrals can be said to represent the apex of the urban-agrarian intelligence, wired to perceive the depth of cubic space and bring it into material form. A freemason, by exploiting the natural forces of gravity, the way the stone is laid naturally in the bedding planes and the brilliant invention of the flying buttress arch, could turn stones into an edifice that initially existed only inside the builder's head! Western culture had definitely become the master of cubic space.

Yet, no conquests can ever be compared to the Mongol Empire that was shaped by the monumental feats of Genghis Khan in the century that the French masons began to erect the cathedral of Reims. In his lifetime Genghis Khan conquered more land and peoples than all the kings and emperors of Rome in almost a thousand years of imperialism! The Mongol Khan built an empire so vast that, in his own words, it was a year's journey from the center to either end of his domain! Genghis Khan had developed a mind wired for strategic thought that could use time in a unique and very successful way. Flying beyond the human time limit, the speed of Mongol cavalry could overthrow any army, and the velocity of the Khan's communication system could coordinate war efforts hundreds of miles distant. In the 13th century the Mongol nomads had become the undisputed masters of speed on Earth.

The building of the cathedral of Reims was started in the 12th century. The walls of the structure seem to have been made of light. The body of the cathedral gives the impression of greater height as it angles towards the domes. The facade is ornate with 2500 statues all the way up to the spires. The pillars are cruciform and crowned with exquisite foliage. In the interior, the oblong stained glass windows reflect colored light on delicate blue-grey walls. The lofty spaces are richly decorated with the finest statuary of gold, precious stones, and tapestries are of the purest wool and silk. The gothic cathedral of Reims is a masterpiece that made the city the center of European art and where French kings were crowned.

But while Jean d'Orbais, Jean Loup and Gaucher de Reims were putting their life's work into this perfection of Western architecture, Ogodei Khan, Batu Khan and Subutai were expanding Genghis Khan's masterpiece in military strategy: the Mongol Empire.

When the Mongols, in 1237, unleashed their amazing cavalry forces on Europe an extensive logistic expedition had preceded the invasion. With characteristic Mongolian thoroughness a plan was drawn so that the great army would not have to move through uncharted territory. After years of careful data collection, the Khans started their mass cavalcade, which spread out along a 900 kilometers line of disciplined advance, with toughened horses and steeled men covering the ground fast and living off the land. This was undoubtedly one of the greatest moments in Homo sapiens military history. The brilliant mind of Homo-Caballus was set on attaining one of the highest goals human intelligence could aspire to after the overthrow of China – the conquest of the Western world. And Equus, nature's great 'running machine', with its fleet agility and hardy resistance, furnished the invading cavalry with the sustained speed it had gained over million years of land roving.

After the Khans' reconnoitering, hundreds of tactical problems had been solved concerning the *time and distance* that the army had to cover. Details of the shortest routes, the watering places, the lowest passes, the river fords, the right season to pass through every region to find good pasture, the expected military opposition, the precise whereabouts of forts, cities and villages that must be sacked to furnish provisions, were part of the grand strategy.

The gigantic army (it was not a horde, as envious Western historians would call it) advanced 90 kilometers a day and the inter-communication of the *ordus*[17] could cover 750 kilometers a day by the use of a combination of fast riding messengers and strategically placed smoke signals. Each rider carried rations for ten days and three horses to change mounts – plus an around-the-clock iron discipline. It was a brilliant strategic move, with hundreds of thousands of Centaurs moving towards a goal set five years ahead: the time that western Europe should receive the 'golden bit', as Central Asian horsemen hyperbolically called a conquest!

Bulgaria, on the shores of the Black Sea, was the first European kingdom to fall to Batu Khan with the assistance of general Sabutai. Then in an astonishing winter campaign, Sabutai attacked the Russian principalities west of the Volga, and before the thaw of 1238 had transformed the ground into a quagmire, the principalities of Ryazan, Vladimir and Moscow existed no more![18] Now firmly encamped in the southern steppes of Russia, Sabutai flung his army against Kiev,

---

[17] *Ordu* means tent, from where the word 'horde' comes.
[18] Batu Khan counting exclusively on *'equestrian dynamics'* managed to conquer Russia in a winter campaign. An achievement denied Charles XII's cavalry forces, Napoleon's war machine and even Hitler's panzer corps in the high mechanical age.

www.horsetravelbooks.com

which fell on December 6. Lithuania, Poland and Hungary were next in line to receive the 'golden bit'.

The army of horsemen moved fast and in March 1241 Krakow was in flames. In Liegnitz the army of Henry II of Poland, reinforced by the knights of the Templars and the Teuton Knights, tried to stop the advance of the nomad cavalry. But the magnificent European armored knights were no match for the eastern horsemen. The Mongol riders, working as one biological unity with their horses, when a whole cavalry unit could maneuver as a flight of eagles, guided by flags during the day and by flares through the night, were unstoppable. Smoke bombs would mask the Mongol attacks, and the bewildered defenders seldom knew where the next charge would come from. The slow defensive tactics of the European knights was no match for the speed and precise horsemanship of the Centaurs. On April 9, the army of Henry II was annihilated, and Poland was taken by the 'devil's horsemen', as western historians would call the superb Mongol cavalry.

Although operating in separate *ordus*, the Khans worked in one concerted war effort. Kuiuk Khan, with his cavalry at Hermstadt in Romania 900 kilometers away, was informed of the victories of Batu Khan in Poland only one day later[19], and was able to destroy the army of Transylvania before moving into Hungary proper.

With Poland conquered, the armies of the Khans then joined forces to take Hungary, the ancient gateway to Europe. Kuiuk had entrenched his army near the city of Gran on Hungarian territory; Batu Khan had crossed the Carpathians and was approaching at the rate of 90 kilometers a day, and Sabutai was racing along the river Tisza at the same speed. On April 11, King Béla's fine army was totally exterminated on Mohi Heath, and Hungary occupied by the Mongols. Bela IV fled. In one month's campaign all the land between the Baltic and the Danube had fallen to Mongol cavalry forces.

After Hungary, the next European kingdom in the line of conquest was Austria, and behind Austria Europe quailed! In the summer of 1242 the 'Golden Horde' marched unopposed to the gates of Vienna. Batu Khan's English envoy was sent to demand surrender. But one morning, while the terrified citizens were awaited the outcome of the negotiations, the landscape in front of the city appeared clear of horsemen! Ogdai Khan had died in Mongolia, and all the Mongol princes and army leaders were summoned to Kharkorin, the capital, for the election of the new Khan. To the astonishment of the Western world the whole Mongol army started homeward. Western Europe was saved by the Mongol's iron discipline!

---

[19] The Mongols' fast communication system was the first to approach the value of 'real time' as we understand it in the Computer Age.

www.horsetravelbooks.com

To ascertain the development of Western civilization in the Middle Ages you have only to observe the Gothic cathedrals at Alcobaça, Trondheim, Wroclaw, Castel de Monte, and specially those in France and England. To comprehend the equestrian technology and the strategic intelligence of the Mongol Khans with no palpable *material proof* of their techniques and brainpower is a matter to be discussed by future anthropologists. However, the modern strategic concept of *'thinking globally* and *acting locally'* is an equestrian heritage that has come down to us from Central Asian cavalry action. And nobody ever did it better than the Centaurs of the Mongol Empire.

The equestrian element in history – the acceleration of human speed and the development of the equestrian intelligence has never been clearly understood. Eurocentered historians insist that the Mongol conquest had no lasting effects and rave against the 'barbarians,' condemning their cruelty against man and beast in their drive for Empire, instead of analyzing the amazing equestrian phenomena displayed by their conquests. Ethics apart, to understand 'how' the Mongol cavalry became the most effective war machine in military history will probably be revealed by anthropologists and historians in the 21st century.

11. Horsemanship Throughout Fifty Centuries of Adventures

For more than five thousand years the horse determined human success. From the great equestrian cultures of the Hittites and Assyrians to the waves of central Asian archers; from Genghis Khan's 'Golden Horde' to the Horsemen of Christ; from Europe's nationalistic wars to their Imperialistic conflicts, the impact of 'equestrian dynamics' caused old empires to be conquered, new empires to be formed. Victory in warfare and the cohesion of new political organizations were sustained by the speed of the horse. The old empires used horse drawn chariots, considered to be 'sophisticated' war machines but as time went by this cumbersome form of combat became obsolete in view of the speed of the nomadic horse archers. After the decline of the Roman Empire cavalry assumed military supremacy in Eurasia and horsemen dealt the political cards almost up to the 20th century.

About 5500 years ago the wheel was invented in Mesopotamia and some centuries later, the invention had spread to India, Iran and the Caucasus, being used in vehicles of bovine traction. The diffusion of the wheel, which was invented by sedentary people in Eurasia's Southern hemisphere, would one day collide with the progression of horsemanship originated by the steppe nomads, which was also expanding rapidly. In this cultural clash, the 'wheel culture' learned that the horse moves much faster than the ox, and don't need to rest twice a day to ruminate – and so adopted the horse. The horse culture, on the other hand, noted that the ox-cart carried a much bigger load than the old travois system, and adopted the wheel. With the horse-drawn cart, the best transport that mankind had yet conceived, the world literally started to roll.

But everything that Homo Faber invents he will seek to further his own interests at the expense of his neighbor's, so once the mechanical problems of transforming the awkward ox-cart into a fast horse-drawn vehicle was solved, the path was clear for the next act of the equestrian epic: the age of the war-chariots soon adopted by all sedentary societies which have always fancied cars – mostly to impress their friends and run over their foes. (Though I greatly doubt if chariots were ever really *war-worthy*.)

The chariot culture was developed some four thousand years ago, at a cross point between the Caspian and the Black Sea, and between the Mediterranean Sea and the Persian Gulf – a frontier area that encompass parts of modern Russia, Turkey, Iran and Syria. This flashy car culture would later spread all over the ancient world, but was initially adopted in Persia, India, and Egypt, the great powers of sedentary societies. Later the fad would also catch on in Greece and the rest of Mediterranean Europe, and at last the fancy vehicles were being built all over Europe – even as far away as Land's End, in Cornwall, they say.

www.horsetravelbooks.com

Everywhere the war-chariot appeared the nobles would consider it their 'divine right' to pilot the dashing military vehicle. But alas, the chariot ended up presenting the same trouble as the modern automobile – it would only drive well on level ground without obstacles. Any impediment, a ravine, a slope, a stone, a log or a river – or another broken chariot in the path (the proto-traffic jam) stopped the gaudy vehicle. With time this limitation turned the chariot as obsolete as a 1959 Lada and with the passing of time gave way to cavalry – the horse being the best off-road vehicle ever known to man. The last people to patronize the old war-chariots were the barbarian tribes of the British Isles, a third rate province anyway.

When Julius Caesar invaded England in 55 BC he wrote – "War chariots remain an important part of the British armory. This is the manner of fighting from chariots: First they (the indigenous Britons) drive about in all directions and throw javelins, and usually the terror inspired by their horses and the rumble of their wheels throws the enemy ranks into confusion. Thus they display in battle both the mobility of cavalry and the steadiness of infantry and with their daily practice they can control their horses at a gallop even on slopes and steep places, checking them and turning them around in a moment".

Now, my steadfast reader, if you're a horseman, would you believe what you just read? About the maneuverability of four thousand chariots in battle? This propagandistic report was obviously made up for the ears of the Roman senate to vote Caesar a triumph over a most 'ferocious' enemy. That the English chariots could throw terror into the faint hearted, blue painted, Celtic aborigines that inhabited the island is of course to be believed (they still do in most countries) – but the maneuverability of these war-chariots must be pure fantasy and would never scare a seasoned Roman phalanx. This pulp fiction was obviously written to impress Caesar's sponsors back home.

In 42 AD, when Emperor Claudius invaded Britain and broke the power of King Cassivellaunus, (with neery a scratch to his person, as he candidly confessed), the symbol of the British *backwardness,* noted and ironically commented by a Roman commandant in a letter home, was the obsolete British chariot formations, which were promptly crushed by the Roman infantry. Now who would you rather believe – Caesar, the man who wanted to be Consul or Claudius, the emperor who had no peers? The disappearance of the chariot started a new era for the sedentary cultures – a time of cavaliers, knights, hussars and cavalrymen.

The complete military transformation from war-chariots to cavalry is the last act in humans' and horses' joint history. The Imperial Army of Rome, at the time the largest military force on the planet, was slowly turning its formidable infantry legions into heavy cavalry brigades in the period between the last Consuls of the

www.horsetravelbooks.com

Republic, Pompeii and Crasso, and the last Roman Emperors of the West (but then it was too late and Rome never caught up). The first true battle of Western cavalry forces was waged in the year 378 when a Roman army, led by Emperor Valens, attacked a Hun stronghold in Hadrianopolis. While the Romans were assaulting the provision train, thousands of Hun and Goth horsemen, returning from their own pillaging, surprised them in the act. With spears and sabers the Goth horsemen supported by Hun archers overwhelmed and annihilated 40,000 Roman soldiers, and Emperor Valens died in combat. It was one of the decisive battles in history, which precipitated the fall of the Roman Empire and started almost one thousand five hundred years of cavalry supremacy in Europe. And so matters would remain until the first decade of the 20th century, when Henry Ford took over and started the age of the bangers.

But, what would have happened if Equus Caballus had not appeared, like Cinderella's six-horse carriage, to save Homo Faber from his bipedal destiny and sweep him to the greatest adventure of his existence? It is a question that deserves an answer. While the anthropologists and other 'ologists', to whom this cause belongs, do not pronounce themselves, let us recollect some of humanity's greatest adventures and pretend that horses did not exist.

12. To Implode History Subtract Horsemanship

It is difficult to estimate how much the cultural clock of Western civilization would have to be set back without equitation, and how much man would have his technological achievements reduced if he had been bound to the speed of his own physical means. Without horses, in what evolutionary stage would the countries of the so-called Western World find themselves today? Europe would probably be organized into strongly armed semi-independent city-states on the Middle-Ages model and had North America been discovered it would most likely have a somewhat similar organization down the Atlantic coast. Undoubtedly, had the horse had the destiny of the mammoth human history would have to be rolled back to an indefinite era in a reverse version of the domino effect.

Some 3200 years ago Moses led the Jewish people's escape from Egypt, *but the Red Sea did not part for Jehovah's children to escape their Egyptian captors!* Why the hurry? Pharaoh Rameses's soldiers are pursuing the Israelites on foot (remember we're pretending horses and chariots didn't exist), and were damning their God-given footwork many hours behind the blasted runaways. Charlton Heston and his protégés arrive at the Red Sea and calmly negotiate with some Arab fishermen – who after some bickering, and a fistful of silver shekels, ferried God's People to the Promised Land. See? Without horses no special effects could have saved *The Ten Commandments* from becoming a blockbuster in reverse.

Now let's get serious. Without horses the first empire in the world, that of the Hittites, would never have existed. Even if the Hittites had got around to conquering Anatolia on foot, it would have been impossible for them to consolidate the great empire without a centralized administration. And that would be impossible without a system of fast exchange of information. In other words: without 'equestrian dynamics' it would have been impossible to govern an empire formed by several kingdoms and made up of scores of cities. Such a huge political pile-up would have crumbled like the little piglet's house of straw.

In 350 BC Alexander the Great invades the Middle East. His army of 35,000 men crosses the Hellespont on board 169 vessels and from there heads for Syria and Egypt. Alexander's battles against the Persians would have happened exactly as Arnold Toynbee relates in *Mankind and Mother Earth*. Then Alexander, *without Bucephalus,* leads his troops over the rivers Tigris and Euphrates, invades the heart of Iran and from that point crosses to the region bordering the Caspian Sea. One battle follows another and Alexander, aided by his steadfast infantry, wins them all – that is, until he crosses the Indus and is literally run over by king Porus' elephants! And so ends the story and the glory of Alex and his dream of uniting the western and eastern worlds, before Guglielmo Marconi actually did it with his wireless telegraph.

www.horsetravelbooks.com

But this would be a rather linear description of Alexander's end without the speed of horses, and this hypothesis has a much more subtle interpretation. Without his Ferghana horses Alexander would *never have had the idea* of forming a Universal Empire – his permanent contribution to history – because he would not have had the necessary means to achieve it. And this is why: the Greek culture was the first to organize the natural laws in sequences of causes and effects, instead of explaining nature's ways as the deeds of *mischievous gods.* Aristotle was the first Greek philosopher to accomplish extensive research on history, biology and zoology. Aristotle's concept of the universe was complete and, despite all its imperfections, universal. Young Alexander had Aristotle as tutor and it is very likely that his ideal of a *unified world* was shaped after his teacher's ideal.[20] When Alexander plunged headlong into his legendary expedition, he had control over the ideological as well as the technological variables of the enterprise. His success was the result of a calculated risk – *and horses were the motors that fueled the epic event.*

Alexander's campaign was primarily a political move. His host was actually a mobile administrative center, composed of scribes, engineers, technicians, administrators, diplomats and the usual soothsayers and astrologers – just in case. His goal was to extend the political influence of Macedonia to the *whole world.* Alexander left in his wake 70 new founded cities and fortified commercial centers. But, as Clausewits once said, "war is politics performed by other means", Alexander wisely brought along these other 'means' – *his cavalry.*

Alexander had five thousand horsemen giving him topographical, military and political support. Groups of equestrian pathfinders sped ahead to reconnoiter the lie of the land and returned to guide the troops. Bands of horsemen rode in all directions to forage for edibles (as the raid covered 33,000 kilometers, and lasted ten years, he had no regular supplies coming from Greece). Equestrian committees composed of diplomats and high-level officials preceded Alexander's arrival in all foreign cities to negotiate alliances before the arrival of the Macedonian army. Without horses Alexander the Great – the pupil of Aristotle – wouldn't have risked this unrivalled social-political adventure. Without horses the project would have been as impossible to accomplish as Neil Armstrong landing on the Moon without Apollo 11.

After Alexander's odyssey, we can also discard the formation of the Persian Empire and the unification of China. None of these political events would have happened without horse communications. Without cavalry, the people of Persia — modern Iran — who were renowned for using horses for communication and

---

[20] Though many scholars don't believe so, I think they should consider the meaning of the word 'osmosis'. Nobody, not even a man of Alexander's charisma, could have avoided being profoundly affected by a man of Aristotle's brilliance.

www.horsetravelbooks.com

war, could have done nothing of the stuff that we read about in the history books: the sequence of invasions and alliances that formed their extended political map.

China's unification was another period of constant wars. Without equestrian communication, the fiscal and legal system developed in the Ch'i Era could not have been imposed on the subjects, which would then have rendered it impossible for the political unification of hundreds of cities spread over such a great dominion.

The history of the Rome's expansion is a different matter. Rome's strategic location in the center of the Mediterranean Sea would have permitted her to conquer and settle the rim of Africa, Asia and Mediterranean Europe by navigation alone. However, without horses, Hannibal's elephants may have stopped the Empire's expansion. But supposing that the Roman army, equipped with newly acquired elephants, could have defeated Carthage and conquered north Africa, the next stage of the Imperial expansion would never have happened: the conquests of Gaul and Germany by Julius Caesar and the subjugation of the British islands by Claudius. The bureaucratic dynamism necessary to give political and administrative maintenance to these distant provinces would have been inconceivable without horses and equitation. And consequently France, Germany and England would not have become Romanized, and *Lex Romana* would not have inspired the *Teutonic Order*, *The Napoleon Code* and *Lex Britannica* – the ideological fuel of the future locomotives of Western Europe.

And without the quarrels between Church and State the religious and political pressure of Renaissance England would not have forced the psalm-singing puritans to flee England aboard the Mayflower and start America's colonization – to the desperation of its music loving native inhabitants. Thus the United States would have had its history hopelessly retarded.

But let's admit that English, Spanish, French and Dutch navigators had really set sail for America and got a foothold on the Atlantic coast in the century that it really happened. Would their continental expansion have been possible without horses? How would the confrontations between the pedestrian English settlers and the Iroquois, Delaware and Cherokee nations have ended? How many years would it have taken to extend the influence of the Anglo-Saxon horseless tribe from the Atlantic to the Pacific coast? We know that four hundred years before Columbus Leif Erickson attempted to settle America without horses. And we know that the brave Vikings were slaughtered on the beaches. Without horses a complicated reversed domino affect would entirely have upset history as we know it.

Without horses, in what evolutionary stage would the countries of the so-called First World find themselves in today? Well, it's difficult to estimate but,

www.horsetravelbooks.com

when Homo sapiens adopted Equus Caballus, he amplified exponentially the speed of his social and economic development and social interaction. So, if humans had not adopted the horse to promote their economic progress, they would have had their social, economic and technological advance reduced to the speed of their own biological means. In this case, Europe today would probably be organized into strongly armed semi-independent city-states in the Aztec model. And if Columbus had really set sail and discovered North America, this region would probably have a similar organization down the Atlantic coast – that is, *if* John Smith with his two-beat brain could have outfoxed Powhatan. And the conquest of the West, to the redskin's delight, would be awaiting Third Millennium pedestrian events.

Had the horse gone with the mammoth we would undoubtedly have no cars, planes, computers and global strategies. But for reasons unknown, the impact of horses in our past and their importance to our future is totally misunderstood. Let us now review what happened historically to the social and economical advancement of some urban-agrarian societies who didn't have the chance to form the Homo-Caballus symbiosis and incorporate the horse's motor system to their social and economic progress.

13. A Slow World Devoid of Horses

Sociologists state that the facility of establishing contacts, the so called transcultural acceleration process, the reciprocal exchange of cultural values – in which the partners are both donors and receivers – is a fundamental mechanism of cultural enrichment, either by peaceful or belligerent contacts. Any type of contact makes changes in a society, and helps to improve and develop it. Horse people were, for sixty centuries, the most efficient creators and diffusers of culture among the Old World civilizations. The impact of 'equestrian dynamics' on a society was overwhelming. Its capacity to circulate new ideas, modify habits, form institutions, inspire techniques, enrich cultures and strengthen economic ties was fantastic. Horses have been the catalysts of the success of the greatest civilizations on Earth, and few societies have ever retrograded from an equestrian to a pedestrian state. But what happens when a civilization has no horses and its biological time remains pedestrian?

We have in the pre-Colombian civilizations a perfect historical example of the cultural delay of Homo Sapiens without the symbiosis with Equus Caballus. As neither anthropologists nor archeologists seem to have given much importance to the civilizing effects of *'equestrian dynamics'* let's look further into this matter by ourselves.

In the Americas some groups of Indians began their *Biological Revolution* about 3500 years ago and the *corn culture* became the base of their lives, shaping a civilization of great similarity with the Sumerians before the introduction of the horse. These agricultural tribes also built permanent villages, and some grew into great cities. Around the year 1300 AD the Inca Empire settled in the Peruvian Andes where it established its capital, Cuzco, the largest of all pre-Columbian States. The Inca Empire was consolidated in 1438, fifteen years before the fall of Constantinople to the Turks, when Inca Pachacuti assumed the throne and implanted a heavily centralized State.

With Pachacuti, the Empire expanded more than 4000 kilometers, from Quito to Santiago in Chile (about half the linear size of the Hun Empire in Eurasia). A very well trained administration controlled each vassal's life, registering his working hours, his spare time and even the clothes that he should wear! As in Old Egypt, government employees surveyed the Public works – mostly highways and temples – which were built by the people as a form of tribute to the State. The Inca government and its work-gangs developed many fine highways that linked secondary roads in a net of approximately 40,000 kilometers – *as amazed researchers would later discover!*

To shorten distances the Incas would dig tunnels in the hills and build suspended bridges that overcame marshy areas and crossed rivers up to 70 meters

www.horsetravelbooks.com

wide. This extensive road-net facilitated the flow of news that traveled up to 170 miles a day, which made possible the arrival of Inca infantry in conflicted areas – *declare the astonished archaeologists!*

But only government troops and emissaries were allowed to use the highways and the more than one thousand *tambos* – shelters – that were built for the couriers' rest. In the 16th century, the Inca highway system was the best in the world; much better than the European roads, which only started to improve in the 17th century, after the invention of the coach – *reveal our thrilled archeologists!*

But with Francisco Pizzaro's arrival, in 1532, the mighty Inca Empire melted away like an ice cream cone in the rain! Why?

Separated from the Inca Empire by a mere 3000 kilometers of tropical forest, the history of the Aztec civilization began while Europeans were engaged in the Crusades. During that great moment of the Euro-Asiatic transcultural process, the Aztecs occupied the central lake of the Mexican plateau, and from there they spread out and quickly occupied Tlaxcala, destroying the Toltecs and enslaving many other primitive tribes. Their militarized society formed a sort of tribal federation headed by the Tenochas, the most efficient tribe of the Aztecs, who founded Tenochtitlan. With a population of more than 200,000 inhabitants (no traffic jams), Tenochtitlan (no air pollution) became one of the biggest cities in the world. The Tenochas increased magnificently their agricultural territory, by creating artificial islands of vegetable fiber with suspended roads linking the plantations. Their creativity and cultural development was comparable to Mesopotamia, seven thousand years ago – *declare excited specialists!*

In 1376, while Europe was suffering another onslaught of the "Black Death," most of Mesoamérica and the central Andes region were civilized. Technologically the Aztecs may be considered a quite advanced civilization: they had an alphabet, the old Olmecs knew the factor 0 of mathematics, and they had discovered many advanced laws of astronomy. But, without horses their communication was tied to the pace of their biological speed. When Hernan Cortez arrived, the Aztec Empire, with its 2 million inhabitants, blew away as the little piglet's straw house.

Anthropologists say that the Americas may be considered by the archaeologists as a *laboratory test* which demonstrates that under similar circumstances two human groups develop the same social structures, economic practices and craftsmanship – even though being completely isolated one from another.

"It is as if the first human beings who spread out in the world had in their brain a prototype of civilization just waiting for a favorable environment to materialize it", they say. This reasoning is correct up to a point. In ancient America, the transition from nomadic to sedentary life, after the domestication of

www.horsetravelbooks.com

animals and plants, demanded 5000 years, almost *twice* the time it took the Near East. And this slowness of technological development created uneven conditions between the Old and the New World that lasted until the European invasion – *affirm the experts without really explaining why!*

It must be said that after this spineless definition the specialists simply admit that they *don't know why the economy of the pre-Columbian Empires was so fragile.* They just can't find the reason why many of these cultures, as soon as they had reached the development of Ancient Egypt, simply fizzled out. The researchers can't explain how the most powerful civilizations of the New World – the Incas and Aztecs – crumbled as sand castles when they had contact with a band of hired soldiers from good old Europe. The specialists suggest as the main causes the lack of cohesion among the Inca social classes, the lack of a well-defined line of succession, and also the impact that the Spaniards caused with their vestments, weapons and horses.

In the case of the Aztec Empire, they point out Cortez's betrayal of Montezuma, and the fact that the king innocently believed that the bearded foreigners were send by Quetzalcoatl, a god from beyond the sea. The experts also generally consider that the deathblow to the American empires was the propagation of infectious diseases by the invaders. But it is difficult to say who are more simple – extant experts or the ancient Indians. Now fellow traveler, keep tuned for a different conclusion.

In the future, sociology will be re-written with the help of neuroscience and then it will probably be explained to us that the pedestrian pre-Columbian Indians were mentally 'under-wired' in comparison with the Spanish invaders from Iberia. The Indian Empires had formed 'cultural bubbles' whose learning process was exclusively comprised of their regional experiences. (The Inca and Aztec Empires, only 3 thousand kilometers distant, weren't connected.) The Indian brain had the same intelligence potential of the European, of course, but for lack of cultural exchanges they were less wired to new possibilities than the Conquistadors, who came from one of the most experienced equestrian nations in the Old World – a country culturally enriched by the merging of many ancient horse cultures.

Spain had been a colony of Greece and Cartage, a province of Rome, a center of Gothic culture, and in 1532 had recently been released from Muslim dominance. The Spanish society was a healthy synthesis of the social-cultural experiences of Europe, Asia and Africa. Its economy had passed from the slave-trade system to the feudal rule and was, at the time, forming an expanding mercantilist economy. And some countries in Europe, in a burst of neural connections, had already founded their first open-market corporations! Knowing that any type of contact makes a culture improve and develop makes it easy to

www.horsetravelbooks.com

understand why 16th century Spain was one of the most developed and wealthy nations in the Old World. The impact of the Spanish equestrian culture upon the pedestrian Aztec and Inca civilizations was that of a people with global cerebral connections wired for strategic thought, pitted against a society with regional cerebral connections wired for local concerns.[21]

The Indian empires were primitive slave societies in the stage of the old Celtic Druid communities. Their social system relied upon the vilest subjection of the individual to slave work and mass murder in the name of scatological creeds. Nothing was done to better the people's lot. All public works were the means to exert greater control over the masses, as Marx would have perceived with a cue from Engels. No information flowed between the people, as the 'flatfoot' communication service was in the hands of the government. The subjected tribes were in constant rebellion against their oppressors – 'Big Brother' had an eye on everything.

When the Conquistadors landed in America, the collision of the Iberian equestrian culture with the native's sedentary culture broke the spirit of the society, and their pedestrian Empires were blown away by Pizzaro's and Cortés' mighty puff. In truth it was the absence of inter-communication that doomed the Incas and Aztecs. As we have now learnt, the continual sprawl of urban centers and growth of populations provokes an increase of urban problems that has to be addressed by technological solutions. The absence of a systematic approach to learning and the circulation of new solutions to increasing problems created by an ever-expanding population were the Amerindian Empire's doom. They had no technological solutions to droughts, crop failure, or improved warfare.

The European invaders, to compensate for their diminutive resources in men, had a brain trained for strategic thought and fast tactical solutions. Thousands of years of cultural exchanges between African, Eastern and Western cultures would give Cortéz and his men-of-arms an 'edge' over anything the Aztecs could throw at them. For, curiously, a social system is similar to an immunological system: if it's not properly exercised – if new ideas and experiences do not expand its natural limitations – it breaks down at the first opportunistic attack.

The Indian empires had their two systems – the social and the immunological – attacked simultaneously by the overpowering mental resources of *Homo-Caballus Ibericus* – and, for lack of biological and sociological antibodies, the Amerindian systems perished.

---

[21] There is most probably a parallel between the Spanish and the Mongol intelligences wired for fast strategic and tactical thought after many centuries of 'equestrian dynamics' introduced by several equestrian civilizations.

www.horsetravelbooks.com

No un-horsed society has ever developed politically beyond a city-state standing. But it is difficult to estimate how much the cultural clock of the Western world would have to be set back without horses and equitation. Though we know for sure that if there had been a delay of a mere 100 years (and it would certainly have been much more) we would not currently be in the Digital Era with all its technological wonders.

14. Horsemanship in Sedentary Civilizations

Through warfare and trade the steppe nomads spread the technique of horsemanship over Eurasia. The first urban-agrarian communities to adopt the horse were the classical civilizations, in order to defend themselves from nomadic cavalry. But the settled lifestyle intrinsically modified the horse/man relationship. In the sedentary establishment the horse participates in more of the economical development and less in the horseman's private life. In this new environment man and horse lost their mutual understanding and this degraded the original nomadic horse culture where the symbiosis was based on the intimacy of daily coexistence. Living with the horse gave the nomad a deep insight of the equine psychology and physiology, which he later transformed into an extraordinary equestrian ability. But this millenary horse culture could not survive in the urban-agrarian environment.

The systematic enslavement of Equus began when urban-agrarian cultures adopted the horse to till their fields and conquer their Empires. The capacity of accumulating wealth combined with the dynamism of horsemanship facilitated as never before the amassing of wealth and the formation of vast Empires. Therefore in order to combat the efficient nomadic cavalry and to consolidate or expand their Empires, sedentary societies started to arm themselves with horses for cavalry warfare. But urban culture changed man's natural relationship with the horse and this fact would shape European equestrian principles.

The urban-agrarian way of life is based on planning and building facilities which give safety, ease and comfort to the citizen's daily life: palaces, public buildings, private residences, chapels, stadiums, fortresses, walls, aqueducts, bridges, storehouses, sarcophaguses, sewers, lanes, streets, avenues and parks – all these features spell out the urban environment.

In his eternal quest to build, sedentary man invented two facilities that would destroy the *consenting relationship* with the horse, as practiced by the nomad herdsman. The offending structures have been the *corral* and the *stall*. In these two places man's approach to horse doesn't have to be friendly – *the horse is subjugated by its confinement.* If the animal doesn't like the looks of the advancing person, and suspects his intentions, it has nowhere to run. This situation is profoundly distressing to the horse.

On the steppe, in the open spaces, the relationship between the nomad and his horse was slowly built on a mutual consensual coexistence that cannot happen with the rough 'breaking' and handling of horses in confined regime. And worse – in urban-agrarian societies the horse's proud owner or his dedicated family did not perform the daily handling. In sedentary societies slaves or employees, who would frequently vent their existential frustrations on the horse of their masters, did the horse handling. (Imagine in ancient times a horse belonging to the *highest level* of the equine hierarchy, condemned to be handled by a violent and rude individual of Homo's lowest rank!)

And in urban-agrarian society's inflexible work division, the professional horse trainer, as always happens in backward societies, would keep his 'horse secrets' hidden as if they were the Coke formula. For this reason, equestrian information did not circulate among the horsemen. And besides that, everything that these professionals didn't know they would simply pretend to know. In sedentary cultures, organized in rigid work categories, no outsider could tell anyway. This attitude would transform the western horse world into a backward cultural bubble, extremely resistant to changes.

In the Army the situation was not better. In the 19th century the horse usually belonged to the State, and was a part of the equipment handed out to the soldier – and as equipment the animal was treated. This forced union between recruit and horse was responsible for the low quality of the average cavalryman's horsemanship – although, among the officers, there were often some good horsemen. This was so because the aristocracy usually occupied the officer's ranks, who in many Western countries were expected to bring their personal military outfit – uniforms, weapons, horses and grooms.

In the rural communities of the sedentary civilizations, the confinement of horses in pastures and pickets, and the construction of corrals, broke down the *consensual relationship* that was the basis of the good horsemanship practiced by pastoralist societies.

Though to understand the degrading of the man-horse relationship in urban-agrarian societies, we must make a distinction between the Eastern and the Western cultures. In the East the relationship had probably deteriorated less than in the West, because eastern civilizations were frequently descended from steppe nomads. The Persian Empire, even though it was an urban-agrarian civilization, received its equestrian culture directly from its equestrian conquerors – the Medes – notorious for their extraordinary capacity to use the horse for warfare and communication. In the East the techniques of taming and training the animals were of nomadic inheritance, and therefore some knowledge of good handling would have subsisted. It was probably for this reason that Xenophon, the Geek cavalry general, recommended *patience* in horse taming and training, in his famous book *The Art of Horsemanship*, written in 400 BC.

It is important to remember that in antiquity the cultural exchange between Greece and the Middle East, chiefly Persia, was intense. Long before the time of Alexander, Greece had been the link between the eastern and western world. So it is likely that the Persians had a more frank relationship with their horses

www.horsetravelbooks.com

because they were, in time and space, closer to the original nomadic equestrian cultures. And certainly Xenophon learned much from the Persians.

Xenophon led an army of Greek mercenaries, on behalf of Cyrus the Great, who was fighting a war of succession against his brother Artaxerxes, the king of Persia. It is more than probable that Xenophon, due to his Greek logic, learned a lot about horses and horsemanship with the Persian horsemen, a highly civilized people, and the heirs of a nomadic culture. Personally, Xenophon made rare references to Persian horsemanship (could it be, excuse the pun, xenophobia?) In his book, he refers respectfully to Simon, a Greek general and contemporary, who had also written a treatise on horses, which did not survive.

Xenophon's famous book was probably the result of an extremely cultivated cavalry officer and his acute capacity of observation and synthesis, throughout a long and rich life lived in two relatively advanced horse cultures – the Greek and the Persian. Xenophon was the first westerner to grasp the essence of good horsemanship. But, as we shall see, his writings were not universally accepted or understood in Renaissance Europe.

The degradation of the nomadic equestrian culture in the urban-agrarian environment is a fact that should be confirmed by anthropologists sometime in the future. It is likely that scholars will also discover that eastern sedentary cultures kept closer to good horsemanship for being nearer to its source – Central Asia. But although Europe's equestrian cultures were the most backward in Eurasia, with Europe's fast economical development after the Middle Ages, much time and money would be spent on improving the noble class's horsemanship – the best shortcut to social advancement, fame and fortune.

www.horsetravelbooks.com

15. The Rise of Horsemanship in Europe

Around the 16th century Eurasia's balance of power began to tip in favor of Western Europe. Despite the fall of Constantinople, and the embargo of overland travel imposed by the Ottoman Empire, Europeans were quick to use their naval forces to overcome the commercial constraints with the Far East. And as a consequence of their overseas expansion and newfound prosperity some Western countries founded their first riding schools. But the new academies gave emphasis on breaking the horse's will instead of conquering its trust. Brutality, which was still the dominant behavior in the Renaissance, produced a violent and unnatural horsemanship of poor technical quality. Later, the attempt to explain equitation by the laws of mechanics further hampered the understanding of the biological basis of horsemanship! Due to all this confusion polemics plagued Western horsemanship well into the 20th century.

In the early Middle Ages Europe's economy was moved by the draft-horse – a type of equine of a large size, native of the northwestern forests. For this reason, European horsemanship seems to have evolved mainly from ancient driving techniques. (See chapter *On Horsemanship and Draftsmanship*). In that age Europe's population knew little of the speed and the maneuverability of eastern equitation.

With their heavier, more powerful and slower-moving horse, European military strategy became of a defensive nature – with everlasting sieges, the battering of city walls and the breaking down of castle gates. Cavalry tactics were reduced to charges performed in a ponderous iron-shaking trot of undisciplined Knights, in heavy armor, mounted on unmanageable stallions, who would try to trample the adversary infantry underhoof and knock enemy riders out of their saddles. All this points to rather rudimentary horsemanship, if compared with the speed and the maneuverability of the oriental cavalry, chiefly the warriors of the steppe.

In Medieval Europe all military strategy converged to the slowing down of the action, probably to tune it to a *slower brain process*. Incorporating the *lymphatic physiology* of the draft horse to their culture, northern Europeans had retarded their social and economic progress in comparison to the fast-riding eastern horse societies.

"The European peasants, and their way of life, were almost as ignorant about what happened outside their districts, almost as blunt, as the inhabitants of the villages," writes Eric Hobsbawn. This mental slowness of men and horses didn't develop a fast and highly coordinated horsemanship, and so the petty barons held on to relatively smaller tracts of land – much like the *territorial occupation* of the 'heavy' horse in a wild state. When the Mongols unleashed their superlative cavalry forces on Europe, these lumbering horsemen simply could not

www.horsetravelbooks.com

comprehend the complete reversal of the type of horsemanship that they considered 'standard' in 'civilized' countries.[22]

In the 16th century, Europe's monarchic wars and the urban and rural expansion began to demand more and more horsepower, as today we need ever more petroleum and electric energy. It has been calculated that as far back as the 15th century the use of draft animals supplied Europe with a motor force five times bigger than of 20th century China. In England, Germany and France only the absolutely poor peasants didn't have a horse for their personal transport. And they say that given time even the Irish peasant was riding to the pub. Western Europe was undoubtedly equestrian, but of a different nature from the fast horse-technology developed on the steppe.

The brutal relationship of the European rider with the horse reveals his harmful attitude to nature in general, and this would once again reflect negatively in his equestrian ability. In Europe the expression 'human civilization' was a synonym for 'nature conquered' – and 'nature' was understood as something that should be submitted by iron and fire. To Francis Bacon, a contemporary of Federico Grisone, one of Europe's first horse-masters, "The objective of science is to give back to men the domain over nature that they had lost due to the original sin." To Francis Quarles "Man is God's masterpiece" and William Forsyth, in 1802, declared – "Nature should be dominated and used by mankind."

In the equestrian treatises that began to appear in the 16th century, to ride a horse was not just a more comfortable way of going. It was described as a demonstration of the rider's domination over a 'cruel and wild animal.' Horsemanship symbolized 'human rationality' dominating 'animal irrationality'! The subsequent irrational 'breaking' of horses – a consequence of that ruthless mentality – became standard practice. Riding untamed horses was turned into a show in itself, where reckless riders were mistaken for good horsemen. "The sight of a gentleman frightening a supposedly 'ferocious and cruel' horse created an impression of majesty and terror in the peasant's eyes. The more the rider made the horse jump, buck, gallop and turn this and that way at will, or nimbly move sideways, the more he proclaimed not only his social superiority but also his domain over the whole animal kingdom."[23]

Horse training was done in an atmosphere of violence and it is comprehensible that European horses hated to be mounted and created dangerous

---

[22] Future neuroscientists will probably explain to us that by using the lymphatic type of horse, Western *Homo sapiens* didn't wire as many neurons as eastern Homo, with his more agile oriental horse – which was probably the reason for Europe's delay in getting onto the international scene, which happened a mere 500 years ago. Don't zap me – if this reasoning is scientifically correct, killing the messenger won't change the facts.

[23] From Keith Thomas' *Man and the Natural World*.

www.horsetravelbooks.com

defense mechanisms that were countered with even more violence. Scruples regarding the cruel treatment of the animals were mitigated by the conviction that 'God had created the world for man'. Europeans actually believed that there was a fundamental difference between mankind and the other forms of life on Earth. (The success of the European 'naked ape' had evidently gone to his head.) All this produced an equitation of poor technological quality that in the Renaissance forced the appearance of two novelties: the riding school and the riding manual – introduced so that the aristocracy and the rich bourgeois could learn what the inventors of equitation, the natural horse people of the steppes, were born knowing: horses and horsemanship.

And, unhappily, the books produced after the 18th century analyzed the phenomenon of equitation, through a mechanical point of view – and so in Europe horses were ridden as if they were mere vehicles! There was no sound equestrian tradition or scientific knowledge to make people understand concepts such as 'sensory motor coordination' between horse and horseman. This, in fact, would be inconceivable in Renaissance Europe. No parallel between the human world and nature was accepted.

"Animal habits must be observed carefully", said Hartley Coleridge in 1835. "We should not describe them as capable of carrying out human doings, for which their natural actions have no likeness or imaginable analogy with ours".

Therefore, if the European rider thought that the human and equine physiology had no likeness whatsoever, it is logical that people would never think of coordinating their movements and senses with the horses' to form the perfect Homo-Caballus combination. But it is also obvious that all the great masters did exactly this – from practice or intuition – but when they put pen to paper – alas, they would describe equitation as a purely mechanical operation performed by the rider sitting on a horse!

In Europe, horsemanship was understood as a man driving a machine, a natural extension of the draft-horse culture. Bits, martingales, multiple reins, and a long list of equipment for the mechanical contention of the horse, was used to give a mechanical advantage to the horseman, which mostly ended by impairing the horse's freedom of movements. Western horsemen would for centuries ride with the philosophy of *harnessing the horse's power*, as steam or water was harnessed to power a machine. Later the riding schools would focus their efforts on artistic horsemanship – hence, moving away from the practical use of the horse for work, sport and even for military functions.

This created an eternal misunderstanding between the 'horse artists' and the 'practical horsemen' who had a job to do or who just wanted to ride for sports sake. Equestrian ignorance was spreading and making victims like the plague, and while Europe's feudal economy opened up to mercantilism and later to capitalism, the old horse world would move from fetishism to mechanisms. European horsemanship was a second-hand technique – removed in time and space from its original birth on the faraway steppe.

In conclusion, academic equitation in Europe can be said to have begun with the discovery of Xenophon's treatise on horsemanship, which taught the finer points of riding. In Renaissance Italy Federico Grisone luckily found the recipe, but burned the pizza with the brutal handling of horses that was characteristic of European horsemen in his time. There was a constant struggle with whips, cudgels, cats, sharp spurs and punitive bits, to transform the European 'great horse' into a light, elegant high-school athlete.

In the 17th century, Monsieur Antoine de Pluvinel, the perfect horseman, understood and applied Xenophon's wise techniques of gentling and training, and gave great attention to the choice of horses capable of doing schoolwork. He had great sensitivity and understood that if an animal was a cold-blooded creature, unfit for high-school training, no amount of beatings and terrorism could modify its nature.

In 18th century France, François Robichon de la Guérinière perfected manège equitation with beautiful performances of ornamental high-school movements. His presentations had the precision of a machine, and due to his work 'erudite horsemanship' attained the peak of its mechanical beauty. In the 19th century, the talented François Baucher helped to spark a civil war in the horse world, which had long smoldered between adherents of equitation as an art form and people who wanted to practice riding as a sport. Part of the French community rebelled against the artistic dictatorship, and this feeling was the eye of the hurricane that raged between the commoner Baucher and Count D'Aure.

By the end of the nineteenth century, European science was in great effervescence and Federico Caprilli, an Italian captain, started to employ a new technique that included the perfect union between the horse's and the horseman's gravity center; he unified the movements of horse and rider; he discarded the need of constant collection by the horse and recognized the individuality and intelligence of the animal. Caprilli seemed to understand that good horsemanship had to be carried out as a partnership between two intelligent individuals and not as a man exhibiting his equestrian prowess at a fair or in a circus. All things taken into account, Caprilli's equitation was very similar to Central Asian horsemanship!

In the 20th century, Academic Equitation finally split into two disciplines: artistic equitation represented by Dressage, and sporting horsemanship in the form of Show Jumping. By understanding the difference between sport and art, a vicious circle had been broken and a virtuous circle had begun. (We'll go into all this in the coming chapters).

www.horsetravelbooks.com

The lack of understanding of the psycho-physiology of the horse, the arrogant attitude in the relationship with the animal, the attempt at explaining neurological matters by mechanical laws, the proliferation of prejudices generated by ignorance and quackery in the closed world of horsemanship, were the main obstacles to the spread of high performance equitation in Europe until the late 20th century.

16. The Working Rider

Of all the inventions and discoveries made by Homo Faber – from the flint-ax to the laptop – equitation has had the biggest impact on man's economic progress. Professional riding – civil and military – are registered historically since the Hittites. No other technology has brought so much benefit, changed so many habits, earned so much prestige and employed so many people as equitation. And of all the uses of the horse, professional riding as a means of communication has brought the greatest benefit to the Western world, besides inspiring the current equestrian sports, which will probably be with us to the Planet's last sundown. To understand the history of the working rider and his role in Western economic growth is to realize the historical importance of equitation.

Once upon a time, my dear riding companion, the leading actors of the film of life were either renowned horsemen or celebrated seamen. The rest of humanity, the farm laborer, the factory worker, the soldier, the sailor and the sales clerk were mere 'extras', as you say in the cinema 'lingo', to be enslaved, shot, or slapped around at random. But the Oscar to the best supporting actors of our economic progress should go to the anonymous horsemen who weaved the enormous communications net which consolidated Western civilization and gave you the Euro (whether you're for it or not). The professional rider spun the web of Imperial Greece, built the Roman Empire, extended the Mogul Empire, gave rise to Medieval Europe, and, with the discovery of the New World, extended *'equestrian dynamics'* to the Americas.

Through the anonymous rider, the Roman Senate administered the provinces in Gaul and Germany, more than 800 miles from Rome, with almost the same ease as King Zoser ruled Upper and Lower Egypt by boat, separated by 700 miles of liquid highway. With Rome's efficient communication system, formed by horse couriers and navigation, Gaius Julius Caesar Octavianus, later known as Augustus, received in Greece, in only five days, the news of the assassination of his adoptive father Julius Caesar in Rome!

With the end of the Roman Empire, came the 'Dark Ages' sponsored by the Germanic "barbarians" with the help of the world's best horsemen – the mounted nomads.

Later on, in the early Middle Ages, tens of thousands of civil and military horsemen, deeply moved by the words of Pope Urban II "Renounce thyself, take thy cross and follow me," formed large Crusades to invade the Holy Land and put the infidels to the saber ("Hang yourself Urban" – would Shakespeare have voiced – "we fought at Antioch but you were not there"! For in the last hour

www.horsetravelbooks.com

good Pope Urban wriggled out of his pledge to send Bishop Monteuil to lead the holy invasion. So "follow me" must have been a Biblical metaphor.)

But, more important than war, this mass migration of horsemen gave great impulse to commerce and formed a *double lane of new ideas* between the eastern and western parts of Eurasia. This was 'equestrian dynamics' at its best.

During the Middle Ages, hundreds of cities flourished all over Europe and many urban centers became densely populated. Homo Faber couldn't stop building. Great shopping malls, then called markets, did a booming business with merchandise coming by boat, wagon and caravan from all parts of the Old World. Italian, Transalpine, Florentine, Milanese, Luquese, Genoan, Venetian, German, Dutch and Provençal merchants circulating mainly by horse were the responsible parties for this roaring commercial activity.

The famous *Hanseatic League,* with its head office in Germany and fortified commercial outposts strung from Holland to distant Russia, was the living example of a strong commercial alliance between powerful equestrian societies. Couriers – professional riders – were the only means of communication able to overcome all kinds of roads, in all sorts of weather, all year round. Fast business communication meant fast riding. In the 17th century, in Basilea, the merchant Andréas Ryff, who made about thirty business trips a year, wrote in his diary – "I've had so little peace that the saddle has never stopped heating my bottom".

The first European country to organize a *public post system* was England, during King Henry VII's reign (the victor of the battle of Bosworth, where his defeated opponent begged to swap the disputed kingdom for a horse, but nobody took him at his word, gave him a mount, and saw him peacefully off to Calais) who inaugurated a string of post offices connecting England, Wales and Scotland by mail. The post riders would cover 200 kilometers a day through rain, snowstorms, dust, sleet, mud and Dick Turpin's stick-ups, to deliver their mailbags on schedule. These *anonymous riders* were the real heroes of the nation who was then starting to build the next biggest empire after Rome, as the British would proudly proclaim.

In Europe in the 16th century, bankers who were then starting to finance big commercial enterprises depended on horse speed for decision making as today's financiers depend on the Internet. The communication web built by the House of Fuggers of Austria, to supply world news, connected all the important commercial centers of Europe. Fast horsemen operating in relays transmitted all vital information which could have impact on banking activities.

News such as: "Venice, the 13th of December 1596. The king of Spain has severely ordered that no gold or silver may be exported from the kingdom, or used for commercial purposes."

Or "Rome, the 29th January 1600. The Papal chamberlain has ordered to evaluate once again all silver coins, local and foreign, with a decree that from now on nobody is to take more than five crowns out of the city."

News also flew from the battlefronts to Paris, Bordeaux, Lyon, Nantes, Geneva, London and Amsterdam, where the fortunes of war could decide the fortunes of the stock market. The Spanish Succession was full of dramatic incidents on which *'all'* seemed to depend.

And did Napoleon, as gossip had it, withhold the news of his victory of Marengo to permit a speculative coup at the Paris stock market? Later rumor had it that the shocking news from Waterloo was certainly a booster for the Rothschild fortune. Then as now, the nervous banking centers of the world depended desperately on fast information to make or save fortunes. In Europe, for the last 500 years, the speed of information has been the *soul of business*, and the speed of the horse was the soul of the economy. (The Yuppies didn't invent the stock market, as you know.)

During the 17th century England, France, Holland and Spain had fast growing mercantile economies and in the 18th century, European economists were finally starting to get the hang of what made nations wealthy.

"A nation is not wealthy because it owns gold and silver mines", wrote Adam Smith in *The Wealth of Nations*. "The wealth of a nation should not be evaluated by the sum of its accumulated merchandise, but by its revenue; not by the size of its stock in goods but by the circulation of its products". Alan Greenspan couldn't have put it better. Adam Smith, though, didn't have the biological insight to understand that these wealthy nations owed their good fortune to 'equestrian dynamics'.

Well, as you can see, then as now, more than producing merchandise, the wealth of nations resides in the circulation of information *and* merchandise. So, the speed of the horse allowed political and economical unity besides helping the flow of products – the three main factors of human progress. The working rider was then the motor of the world wide web of international commerce, which in its modern form is being improved by an army of computers connected by the Internet. (And nowadays the speed of electronic gadgetry and cybernetics is causing the world to reel again and making some people wish that humans hadn't started it.)

The equestrian courier of yesteryear has disappeared from our landscape, but the technology of his profession is still being used and improved upon and is now called Endurance and Competitive Trail Riding. This tough and challenging sport evolves around the idea of riding the longest distance and arriving with the horse in the best condition, which must have been more or less the same rules that the galloper had worked with to maintain his job, as horses then were more

www.horsetravelbooks.com

expensive than most cars today. (See chapter *The Sporting Rider* coming up next.)

But besides the tens of thousands of professional couriers that connected all European cities into a vast political and commercial web there were also, of course, the rural riders who played an important role in one specific economic branch: the livestock business.

In Spain, in the 12th century, wild cattle hunting would eventually develop into cattle ranching. The working of wild cattle on the plains of Spain required a very special technology. Lassoes, branding irons and special riding gear were developed to facilitate this dangerous and difficult work. After the 15th century, the Spanish vaqueros were mostly handling domesticated cattle and the first techniques of bull fighting were being developed in the big corrals built on the 'haciendas'. The rejoneio, horseback bull fighting, turned into a popular spectacle and very sophisticated equestrian techniques were developed as part of the dangerous show. Big arenas were erected in the major Spanish and Portuguese cities and the *rejoneador* turned into one of the biggest tourist attractions in the Iberian Peninsula. Today, bull fighters like Alvaro Domeq offer equestrian spectacles, which are among the most beautiful and daring horse shows in the world. But, of course, they got their equitation from their former Arab and Moorish overlords, who had it from the Central Asian nomads.

All the complex equestrian technology of cattle raising developed in Spain and Portugal was exported to Argentina, Brazil, Mexico, the United States and Canada, forming the know-how of the gaucho, the vaquero and the cowboy and is now the mainstay of successful Rodeos.

The mounted courier has for thousands of years made possible the political unity and economic progress of Eurasia's world powers. But to keep count of history scholars have mainly focused on the war-horse, actually a secondary actor in the great game of economical and social exchanges. To really understand modern history, sociologists should start studying the 'peace-horse,' which fine-stitched the European economic progress and eventually led to Europe's Economic Union. Although the courier will probably be the only equestrian character to disappear in the forthcoming millennium, in his wake he has left us the long distance rider, which is a satisfactory substitute for both horse and rider, methinks.

www.horsetravelbooks.com

17. The Sporting Rider

The desire to show prowess in work and play is ingrained in human nature. It is a way of showing off your winning genes, explain molecular biologists. Ancient equestrian employment started a great number of sports and these high-risk games sprang from the use of horses in civil and military duties. Some equestrian sports like horse racing have probably been around since horses were first domesticated. Others like polo sprang from the military use of the horse. Still others like endurance symbolize long distance riding practiced by professional couriers. No other human activity has originated more sports than equestrian practices in economical and military duties. Therefore it's fair to say that modern equestrian sports are undoubtedly humanity's greatest cultural heritage.

Simple logic tells us that racing must have been the oldest of equestrian sports. Once humans found the way to speed up their daily duties by riding a horse, the second step would be to prove to friends and girlfriends who had the fleetest horse in the neighborhood. These heats, run between the younger members of the pre-historic horse communities, have left no archaeological vestiges but can be inferred as surely as after day comes night, or what goes up must come down, and other such cause-and-effect sequences.

The first historical register of harnessed horse races comes down to us from the more advanced eastern societies, where the war-chariot by 'divine right' had become the aristocracy's Ferrari. The Hittites left us as a complete manual for training and handling horses for chariot races and the first description of a chariot-race can be found in *The Iliad*. Although Homer didn't define the exact period, the poem describes in details the rules and conventions related to the sport and the 1st prize was 'a wench expert in domestic work!' (No wonder chariot racing grew so popular.) As you may know, the first historical register of a mounted horse race is referred to the 31st Olympics in Athens in the year of 644 BC. But of course the Central Asian nomads had raced horses millennia before the Greeks took to horses.

Polo was an old oriental sport and the Persian king Dario is said to have been a notable polo player. Polo, like all other sports that use a ball, does not have its origin in work –it was practiced just for sport, although inspired by cavalry tactics.

In the Middle Ages hunting with falcons was also very popular. The nobles—kings, princes and bishops – practiced falconry until the fall of Constantinople and the final demise of the Byzantine Empire, when it became hazardous to ride in the countryside because of Turkish military incursions in all of central Europe.

Horseback hunting to hounds was already practiced in ancient Greece. Xenophon left us writings about how to teach and select hound-dogs. In Europe,

France has the oldest tradition in hunting – deer and boars were the favorite preys. Hunting on horseback was introduced to England by the French conquerors in the 11th century. William the Conqueror's son, William Rufus, was addicted to hunting, an activity that he took more seriously than his state obligations – that is, until he died from an overdose.

War in feudal times was a symbiotic relationship that involved the aristocracy, second-rate nobles and retainers all the way down the social ladder to the menial servants. The liege lord gave protection to his vassals who, as compensation for his protection, had to fight his dirty wars! On the field the aristocracy occupied the cavalry ranks and the lower classes supplied the arrow fodder.

But for the knights warfare had a lot of drawbacks. It was necessary to take up arms either in the name of 'our Lord in Heaven', or in the name of 'our Lord on Earth', the liege lord. War had the added inconvenience of bringing deaths from enemies or diseases. Besides the long marches, counter-marches, meals of scarce amounts and doubtful ingredients, ill-slept nights, frequently under a starry sky, when it didn't rain, or worse; there was an assortment of very unpleasant situations to be faced by the fortune-seeking knight.

But war, of course, had also compensation in prestige, loot and women. For these reasons jousting as a sport turned into a god-sent diversion to the nobility of the Middle Ages. The knights formed teams of merry lancers and in a simulation of pitched battle, would try to knock their opponents from their horses; just like the real thing, without the aforesaid inconveniences. In these 'tournaments,' which came into fashion in the 11th century, the knight could achieve the glories of war, without the dirt, discomfort, disease and bloody death on the field of battle.

During the Middle Ages jousting became the most popular equestrian sport in Europe. The game was created in imitation of Europe's cumbersome war tactics and reflected the cavalry shock between the heavy-horses and their heavy armored riders, weighing about 300 pounds, trying to knock each other out of the saddle. (The silky riding Salah ed-din Yussuf ibn Ayub – Richard the Lionhearted's buddy Saladin – must have laughed his turban off watching the European rough-riders showing off their sleight-of-hand.) In tournaments the noble horseman would turn himself into a professional rider similar to the modern cowboy. And during pleasant summer days he would plan his participation in the jousting circuits, equip himself with the best of gear and prepare good horses to show off his battering-skills every second or third week of the season.

The tournament was heaven on earth for Sir Justin the Jouster. In the 13th century, the tournaments turned from mock-battles into very well organized 'shows' with scheduled combats between famous horsemen. Jousting became so popular that civil, military and ecclesiastical authorities had to suppress them; because no knight in his right mind would be interested in participating in a Crusade or any other unsanitary war sponsored by Church and State. The cool thing was to stay at home, far from the battlefields and close to the beautiful sex – and raking in prize money by jousting away at the tournaments. The decline of the sport occurred mainly because changes in the rules made the combats less dangerous and oh, yawns... ever so boring.

As everybody knows, fox hunting is the modern version of boar hunting. "But it is necessary to do a proviso on the hunting on horseback," explains Charles Chenevix Trench[24] – "many of the hunters were not horsemen by conviction – hunting on horseback was the only practical way to pursue a fox on an open field, across creeks, over fences, gates, boulders and shrubbery. If a car, motorcycle, bicycle, or roller-skates could have kept up with the fox, some people would surely have preferred those." The horseperson by vocation practices show jumping – the test that simulates the obstacles of fox hunting in the field.

As we saw, modern long distance riding is a simulation of private, public or military intelligence undertaken by professional couriers of the past. The messenger had to attain the highest speed possible without harming the horse's health, as the animal belonged to the contracting company. Each stint had an exact duration, previously calculated, considering the difficulty of the trek. At each relay station, where horses were changed, the manager checked the animal's physical condition to see if it has been properly ridden. Nothing should retard the time calculated by the company – no broken bridges, floods, landslides, assaults or weather surprises caused by 'El Niño.' All these challenges were present in the past long distance riding as they are in modern Endurance Tests.

The equestrian sports are a natural consequence of the duties accomplished by men and horses in the social and economical building of old and modern societies. But, since ancient times some men and horses would reveal themselves superior to other common mortals and have turned horsemanship into one of the noblest of all the dynamic Arts – the equestrian art now called Dressage

---

[24] Charles Chenevix Trench, the author of *A History of Horsemanship*.

www.horsetravelbooks.com

18. The Saddle Artist

Horsemanship as any other activity may be accomplished in a casual or in a passionate way. It is passionate when the ability and aesthetic sense provides a high rating of beauty and originality. Painters, sculptors and poets have left an impressive collection of works that can still be admired centuries after their author's death. Artistic Horsemanship, however, has been an art without a memory. The great masters have not left us their works, which would be their dazzling performances. At most, the passionate saddle artist has left us his printed words. But, alas, a book written by Michelangelo describing the techniques he used to paint the Sistine Chapel would not have the same emotional impact on the reader as a chance of watching his masterpiece 'Creation of Adam.' Artistic horsemanship is shorter than life – but even so it is sublime and it is Art.

In a broader sense, the Greeks considered Art as ability acquired through patient work with a definite goal, aesthetic, ethical or utilitarian. The modern concept of Art embraces only the activities oriented to the aesthetic – that is, Fine Arts. These are understood as a person's capacity to put an idea into practice, or the faculty of dominating and transforming matter. It is a well-known fact that art doesn't age, but it is impossible to say why its eternity is an exclusive product of the artist's ability.

One of the greatest artists of all time is the supreme Leonardo da Vinci. As proof of his great spirit we can still admire the works that he left behind – *La Gioconda, The Last Dinner, and Christ's Baptism,* for example. It is Art, which cannot be explained by ability alone. There is in those paintings a mystery element, as mysterious as the soul itself. Being eternal Da Vinci's paintings will live on as long as mankind survives. Science gets old because it is explicit. Art is eternal because it is shrouded in mystery.

Historically, all artistic activities have been criticized as superfluous and that is the first step to consider them as bound to serve a society's utilitarian aims. In a civilization busy producing consumer goods, artists may be seen as parasites that produce nothing. But, there is nothing better than Art to perpetuate a society. The purpose of Art is to create beauty – but beauty is not a disposable ornament – it is a profound need of human beings and has survived better than most utilitarian work.

Equestrian art is one of the older artistic activities. Ancient Greeks and Romans executed high school movements such as the *piaffer* and the *passage*. In the Byzantine Empire, with the help of saddle, stirrup and curb bit, Artistic Horsemanship bloomed, and was later exported to Renaissance Italy. Artistic Horsemanship, as accomplished in the French, Spanish and Italian Renaissance,

www.horsetravelbooks.com

is dynamic art. It was also the product of an ability acquired during the patient exercise oriented to a definite aesthetic goal. Equestrian art is the horseman's ability of putting into practice his talent – and his ability to understand the horse's deeper motivations and shape his natural movements into choreography of great visual beauty. It is also 'erudite' – as music or ballet. It has music's rhythm and ballet's aesthetic beauty. The saddle artist unites in his coordinated action with the horse the intelligent hands of a pianist and the corporal expression of a dancer.

If it is correct to say that Fine Art does not perish, we cannot say the same about Equestrian Art. In Fine Arts, when the author dies the masterpiece survives to tell about the creator. Equestrian art blows away like dust in the breeze as it is being performed by the horse-man-duet. Antoine de Pluvinel didn't leave us his Art, as did Rembrandt with his *Night Watch*. We know that La Guérinière was a great saddle artist, but his equestrian performances weren't immortalized, as was *The Stealthy Kiss* of his fellow countryman Jean Honoré Fragonard. François Baucher trained his great horses Captain, Partisan and Buridan in Jean-Auguste Ingres' Paris. Admired in great equestrian presentations, François Baucher, Captain, Partisan and Buridan are no more. But Ingres' paintings, *The Turkish Bath* and *The Picture of Bertin* can still be admired in the Louvre.

In history, Art has many times been accused of being superfluous and so ends up forced to serve some temporal government. For this reason many a horseman has tried to justify Equestrian art as martial art. It has often been stated that the croupade, the ballotade, the capriole and other high school movements 'would be useful' in a cavalry confrontation. "The horseman combats with lance or sword and the horse with vigorous kicks," wrote Manuel Carlos de Andrade, an equerry from the Portuguese Royal Horse, to Dom João in the 18th century. Wrote he to his king – "The Noble Art of horsemanship is among all the arts the most sublime, the most important and the most illustrious, and the countless victories achieved in campaigns by cavalry, justifies its usefulness".

To mistake Equestrian Art for martial art (if such a thing exists) was perhaps naïve or, more probably, a way of justifying it to a utilitarian society. In the horse world, as you well know, there has always been much confusion agog and Artistic Horsemanship has frequently been criticized as futile, by 'practical horsemen' – people who use their horses for work, hunting, sports and traveling.

The Duke of Newcastle, who didn't mix art with war and didn't mix his words either, used to say about his critics: "Some wag will ask what is a horse good for that will do nothing but dance and play tricks. If these gentlemen will retrench everything that serves them either for curiosity or pleasure, and admit nothing but what is useful, they must make a hollow tree their house, and clothe themselves with fig leaves, feed upon acorns and drink nothing but water."

www.horsetravelbooks.com

The saddle artists, these strange persons who search inside themselves for the ability to accomplish exquisite maneuvers, to produce beautiful equestrian choreography, and great high-school performances, were also the victims of much misconception. Either they were simply misunderstood or they were 'deified' and summoned to teach their Art in military academies – as if Art, of any nature, could be taught to any person, especially raw recruits doing compulsorily military service. As Robert Hinde observed in his day – "A desire to learn was more commonly attributed to the horse than to the recruit, and the discovery that a 'private' was actually capable of thought, a startling novelty".

The non-recognition of Equestrian art as an artistic expression was directly related to another question – most artists are only recognized after their death – which is quite impossible for the saddle artist, whose art has a shorter life than his own. Equestrian art should be appreciated as an orchid in bloom or a rainbow in summer – it is a wonder that exists for a fleeting moment. Equestrian art could only be imprinted in the memory of the beholder, and memories are ephemeral. (Though, fortunately, today you can immortalize it on videotape.)

The Dressage rider is an artist of the movement — he moulds the energy of the horse into harmonic figures, making infinite combinations of its natural movements — alternating, repeating, sequencing, inverting, accelerating, rotating, decelerating and executing movements even when fixed in the same place. As a magician he produces the unexpected — as a sculptor he produces new forms — as a poet he creates meaning — as a musician he gives harmony to sound.

Horsemanship can be accomplished in several degrees of excellence. Artistic Equitation is the most complex. If the aim of Art is to create beauty, the aim of Artistic Equitation – in our time known as Dressage – is to create an instant of splendor that is turned into an object of memory. But let us take a look at the great riding Masters of the past who left a lasting mark on Academic Horsemanship, and examine with modern eyes in what social and scientific circumstances they lived and practiced their Art. As the history of Western Horsemanship can be said to have begun with Xenophon let's begin by checking out some of his wise words in 'The Art of Horsemanship.'

19. Xenophon, Academic Horsemanship is Born

The ancient Greeks were the first to affirm that the existence of the world was due to the laws of nature, and not to the doings of the gods. Greek thought influenced all modern sciences and it didn't overlook equitation either. The treatise entitled The Art of Horsemanship *written by Xenophon is the oldest surviving work on riding. After 24 centuries, it is still an excellent guide to good horse handling and horsemanship. The book, written in 400 BC, disappeared for 1800 years – during the Dark Ages – and it can be said that European horsemanship only became academic after* The Art of Horsemanship *surfaced in Naples during the Italian Renaissance. Xenophon is to Academic Horsemanship what Socrates is to philosophy, Aristotle to natural history or Pythagoras to mathematics. He established paradigms valid to the present time.*

Xenophon was born in Attica and was above all a product of his effervescent time – Classical Greece – where powerful thinkers like Socrates, Plato, Aristotle, Archimedes, Pythagoras and many others established the intellectual foundation of our logic, metaphysics, ethics, politics, rhetoric, poetry, biology, zoology, physics, psychology and Academic Horsemanship.

Xenophon, a personal friend and a favorite of Socrates, was a sensitive observer, profound thinker, fine synthesizer and comprehensible writer – a rare mind indeed. And, as if by a miracle, his treatise on horsemanship survived the rise and decline of the Greco-Roman culture and the Dark Ages and was somehow discovered by Federico Grisone, a Renaissance Italian nobleman, the director of the Neapolitan School of Horsemanship. Xenophon is usually credited as the author of the first equestrian study (as Neil Armstrong has been credited with being the first man on the moon). But this homage does do justice to his merit. Some authors, however, are beginning to recognize the true value of *The Art of Horsemanship*. This book, in the history of men and horses, stands as the milestone where western Horsemanship would begin to make sense – especially to the horse.

Antoine de Pluvinel, a 17th century teacher of Equestrian Art and an adept of Xenophon's principles, wrote in the introduction of his book *Le Maneige Royal* a meaningful passage on Xenophon's book: "His concept of good horsemanship was based on his acute sense of observation, his refined sense of beauty and harmony and his perception of the horse's mind and senses. His horse training was based on rational methods – gentling instead of breaking. And Xenophon himself wrote – "Light bits are better than heavy ones. If you put a heavy bit in the horse's mouth you should render it light by loosening the reins. What the horse does under coercion is made without understanding, and there is no beauty in that."

www.horsetravelbooks.com

In his treatise Xenophon makes it clear that patient and rational treatment of the horse brings better results in taming, training and riding. Monsieur de Pluvinel wrote that, "The Renaissance recovered 'the humanitarian spirit' and this transformed horsemanship." But it is unlikely that Xenophon, a veteran of the bloody Peloponese War, the commandant of the Greek forces in service to Ciro the Younger, and a seasoned soldier of many a gory battle, recommended 'patience' with horses for lofty humanitarian reasons. All his teachings were practical and he never expressed any type of 'special love' for horses, nor did he ever recommend that the horseman should conquer the horse's affection for any other reasons than skilful horsemanship.

When General Xenophon advocated that you should never work with a horse when it is not in a good mood, it was in the sense of not undoing, in an unfortunate moment, the entire work that had already been done. When he said: "be good to your horse", he would add – "because then the horse will do what you want."

Xenophon made special recommendations for the riding of highly-strung horses: "When you mount it you should calm it for more time than the common horse and, when you make it move forward, use the gentlest possible commands... a sudden action can frighten the horse... never let it gallop at full speed, and never let it gallop alongside other horses... long and calm cavalcades quieten the high-strung horse, but don't think of calming it by galloping far, at full speed... when you hear the battle cries, or the sound of the horns, you should not seem scared to your horse, nor act in a way that can cause it alarm... if the conditions permit, you should bring its meals personally."

Xenophon knew perfectly well that emotions flow between the horse and rider and he also recognized that the horseman needs to calm the horse's nerves (to check the flow of adrenaline) and gain its trust by feeding it personally. But, Xenophon reminds you also that – with a lazy horse you should do exactly the opposite. He was obviously not a humanitarian – he was a damn good rider, with lots of hard gained horse sense. Xenophon knew by instinct the important aspects of the horse's psychology and knew that gentle treatment gives better and more lasting results in horse training than rough handling. And modern science now confirmed his methods (See, *Neuroscience Reveals the Principles of Equitation.*)

With *The Art of Horsemanship*, Xenophon intended to produce a good war-horse and at the same time a fine parade horse – an animal with courage and an impressive presence, which would serve for the army commander to lead his troops in war and victory. Though in this particular I think he was mistaken (see *Are the Echoes of the Past the Music of the Future?*).

www.horsetravelbooks.com

Unaware of contemporary scientific discoveries on neurophysiology, Xenophon and all the great horse-masters of the past understood, through observation and intuition, that rational and patient treatment of the horse would bring better results in gentling and training. That is, all but the first horsemaster of the Renaissance – Federico Grisone. As we shall see, he added to Xenophon's gentle ways many of medieval Europe's cruel habits, some of which have lasted into our time.

20. Federico Grisone, the Painful Renaissance

The intellectual movement that triggered the European Renaissance was also responsible for the renaissance of Academic Horsemanship. Grisone was a contemporary of Nicolau Copernicus who surprised the conventional astronomers by placing the sun in the center of the Universe. At that time there also appeared the first simple technical texts, which represented a big step in relation to the alchemist's and the magician's obscurantism. The 16th century's intellectual turbulence gave birth to the scientific revolution that would spark the Industrial Revolution. It was a time of great events for mankind and also for the history of horsemanship.

The principles of the manège, and the modern cross-country horsemanship, were first systematized and published in book form by Federico Grisone, a 16th century Neapolitan nobleman and the founder of one of Europe's first riding schools. As a historical result of the conquest of Naples by the Byzantine Empire, Grisone's methods was influenced by Byzantine equestrian practices that in Greece and Rome had also included the collection of the horse, the piaffer and the passage.

"Grisone and other Italian horse-masters must have been fascinated to discover that their ideas about horse collection had already been formulated by Xenophon, 1800 years before," wrote Charles Chenevix Trench, in *A History of Horsemanship*. But during the Italian Renaissance, Equestrian art was based on such grotesque collection that the horses risked losing all their capacity of movement.

The Neapolitan Riding School became the 'Mecca' of European equestrian culture and many young VIPs from France, Germany, Spain and England, including the Duke of Newcastle, won their spurs tutored by Federico Grisone and his successor, Giambatista Pignatelli.

The method of Federico Grisone was published in a book, *Gli Ordini di Cavalcare,* The System of Riding, and spread quickly all over Europe. But the first thing that strikes the reader's attention in the book is the emphasis in breaking the horse's resistance and to 'reward' the animal's submission with the ceasing of punishments – instead of winning the animal's trust through patience and dedication – as Xenophon's principles had clearly stated.

According to Grisone, the method best indicated to start a young horse was to whip him in circles until "the devil of disobedience was exorcised from it." Just the way to make the horse look forward to the next lesson, comments Trench, sarcastically. Mouthpieces were devised to enable the horseman to provoke violent pain in the horse. There were seven helps or 'aids' in the manège: voice, tongue, rod, bit, leg aids, stirrups and spurs. It was common to say that you "aid

www.horsetravelbooks.com

the horse to the intent that he may not err; but you correct him for that he hath already erred".

From this old jargon comes the popular term 'aid', one of those words that should be abolished from our contemporary equestrian language, because it gives the student the wrong attitude to riding. In modern equitation the horseman does not 'aid' the horse, because he is *a part* of the horse. During training, horse and rider are *both teacher and student* – the rider is learning to blend into the horse's natural movements and the horse is learning how to recognize the rider's intentions through a code of riding cues. The partners are working to form true unity, which is not done by 'aiding' but by 'being.'

But, surprisingly, Grisone alerted his students about the cruel bits that could spoil the horse's mouth, and taught them to ride with a gentle bit, and bearing a temperate hand '…for, assure yourself, it is art and good order of riding which maketh the good mouth, and not the bit.' (But those who have seen the bits used in the Neapolitan Riding School feel it hard to understand what he meant by *gentle* bits).

Grisone recommended leg cues to change directions, and not only for increasing the horse's speed – which was one of the most important techniques introduced into Western equitation after Xenophon's time. He also taught his pupils that the voice is the best form of correcting the horse without exasperating it, while the whip could intimidate and drive it to despair. But 'just in case,' Grisone's system also included the presence of a footman armed with a whip or cudgel to force the animal to obey his master's 'aids.' Force and pain were the methods of preparing a horse for equitation.

In the Middle Ages, all citizen of the male sex thought that they had been created in the 'image of God', and that women and animals belonged to the lower rungs in the hierarchy of living beings! For centuries European theologians discussed whether the feminine sex had a soul or not! In the 18th century, a certain Nicholas Woodies would have affirmed that women didn't possess a soul, only men! And, of course, all this arrogance, mixed with naïveté, perverted the biological interaction that leads to good horsemanship and marriages.

In Grisone's time *fear* was the only emotion used in the didactic process of humans and animals. At school, the teacher would beat the children to make them good students. In Church, the Inquisition tortured people to make them good Christians, and in the riding school the trainer tortured the animals to make them good horses. In the 16th century, the initiation of a horse for Academic Equitation included much violence and whipping which led to low-tech equitation.

In those rugged times, Europe produced precious few good riders, and Federico Grisone can definitively not have been one of them. "The Devil can quote the scriptures to his own benefit," wrote Shakespeare with his flair for human insight, in Grisone's inhuman times.

Federico Grisone was a man of his time, and his version of the gentle techniques of Xenophon reveals a strong influence of the methods of Thomas de Torquemada and the Inquisition's brutality which still held sway in Renascent Europe. But, even admixing Greek equestrian knowledge with medieval cruelty, Grisone returned us the first book on Academic Horsemanship, for which we must be grateful. We should also recognize the value of the Neapolitan Riding School for having started the training of Antoine de Pluvinel—'the most excellent of all those who had ever donned spurs.'

21. Antoine de Pluvinel, Equitation as the Seventh Art

Monsieur Antoine de Pluvinel, a contemporary of Galileo Galilei, published a book entitled Manaige Royal *in the same year that Galileo published his famous work* Delle Nuove Scienze *where, with his fine ironic style, he mocked the opponents of Copernicus's heliocentric theory, causing a wave of protest and his notorious process by the Inquisition. But despite the philosophical and technological evolution of that period – mainly in physical sciences – academic equitation remained stationary, with the riders performing high school movements to entertain the noble spectators in the galleries. It was horsemanship developed for war (so they said) and horsemen gave emphasis to the complete collection of the horse in all movements and gaits.*

Monsieur Antoine de Pluvinel, according to his contemporaries, "the most excellent of all those who had ever donned spurs," spent six years in the Neapolitan Riding School now directed by Grisone's successor, Geambaptiste Pignatelli. Once back in Paris, Pluvinel did much to modify some practices of the Italian riding school of which he disapproved – mainly the use of cruel bits and 'heavy hands' (for bits are not cruel in themselves, of course) and the brutality with which both Grisone and Pignatelli used to deal with the horses. Antoine de Pluvinel played an important role in the history of Academic Horsemanship – and being rational and humanitarian, he re-approximated the French equestrian practices to the wise and gentle teachings of Xenophon, and so turned equitation into a form of art.

In Paris, M. de Pluvinel commanded the Royal Academy, where young nobles were taught dancing, fencing, art, mathematics, and philosophy — but priority was given for the noblest of arts — the art of horsemanship. Pluvinel, besides being a teacher of equestrian art was also a teacher of values of honor, magnanimity, moderation, courtesy, rationality, courage and all the ethical attributes that composed the academic horseman's formation – the so-called *'honnête homme'* – the honored man. These qualities would contribute to the moral character of the young nobleman – for horsemanship develops the mind and the moral judgment of an individual as well as the body — as learned people were already well aware of in those distant times.

In 1623, the year Galileu published *Delle Nuove Scienze*, which promptly landed him in jail, (lowbrows can't stomach highbrows) Pluvinel, by request of his most illustrious pupil the young King of France, also wrote a book entitled *Le Maneige Royal*. It was written in the form of a dialogue between the respectful

www.horsetravelbooks.com

but authoritarian Monsieur de Pluvinel and his illustrious pupil, His Majesty Luis XIII.[25]

In this fine dialogue we find that all the equestrian topics are still the basis for good horsemanship. The book's frontispiece makes clear Pluvinel's philosophy, and his commitment to Xenophon's principles. On the right side there is a picture of a man named *Robur* (looking somewhat like Clark Kent coming out of a Paleolithic phone booth), with an enviable physique, leopard cape, and carrying a bludgeon in his hand. *Robur* shows visible difficulty in controlling a wildly rearing stallion that he is leading by the halter. On the left side of the cover an elegant young woman called *Scientia,* leads, with her right hand (as easy as pie), an obedient stallion with wings on his shoulder, while in the other hand she holds an open book, which she studies with great attention. (Interesting that Pluvinel chose a woman to symbolize rational horsemanship, isn't it guys?) The picture makes clear the advantages of rational and scientific equitation over the brutal methods of Grisone.

Note in the following dialogues, careful reader, that the principles of good horsemanship have existed written in books since Ancient Greece and Renaissance times – and now, more than ever, to become a good rider is mostly a matter of riding and reading.

"I want to learn," says the little king in the overture, "what is necessary to become a good horseman."

Answers Pluvinel: "The horse should feel pleasure in riding, if not nothing will go right." (A reply that shows an enormous difference from the beatings recommended by his former instructor Mr. Pignatelli).

"How," asks the minute king, "should we treat a horse that disobeys?" (Clever that kinglet – he's put the finger on the wound!)

Answers Pluvinel: "It is better to teach with kindness than with severity. If the horse refuses to obey the good horseman finds out what is impeding it. The horse should only be whipped for laziness. The rider should be parsimonious in punishment and prodigal in affection. It is important to study the horse's individuality. Some of them are stupid, fearful and so weak that they are not capable of walking some leagues. These are better for a cart than for the manège".

Then the kingey asks: "Do you make a distinction between a graceful horseman and a judicious one?"

Answers Pluvinel: "Indeed, Sire, to be a graceful horseman one need only to see what is graceful and what is not. But, to be a judicious and competent horseman that knows how to school horses, each person does so according to his inclination, his energy, and his disposition – and to those traits add sound

---

[25] The son of the reigning King Henry IV.

judgment – a drug very hard to come by for which one receives very little in return considering the amount one pays Apothecaries". (With this fine irony, Pluvinel shows that lack of common sense in the equestrian world was already endemic in his time.)

"Yes, I have noticed this," says the petite king, "and it is for this reason that I wish to learn from you."

Replies Pluvinel: "It will be quite easy for Your Majesty to understand the Art and skill of horsemanship and to put it to good practice – for God has endowed you with a perfect body and a vast and solid mind, as great, if not greater, than of any other prince." (This shameless flattery was normal in the social intercourse in Renaissance courts). "It is important that the student is a real man and not a beast in man's clothes, and that he posses two important things: a handsome and pliant figure and the desire to learn." (As you can see, in equitation, nothing has really changed.)

Further on the little king makes a comment: "In my first class, you started the horses in the 'Voltes' (a circle of 5.5 m diameter at the canter) which I heard you say it is the most difficult movement that the horse can do". To this question the duke of Bellegarde, Grand Chevalier of King Luis XII, answers: "You may observe how the colts run happily after their mothers and how, every now and then, they make a demi-volte, rotating and stopping on their hind legs, sometimes ending the movement with a courbette." (Here we get to know that in the seventeenth century the correlation between the horse's *natural movements* and their correspondence with their *equestrian movements*, had already been noticed.)

The wee king then asks: "Is it, for this reason that you repeat the exercise of the 'Volte' more frequently than the other ones?" Say Pluvinel: "Exactly. Good horses, which nature has given lightness and strength, learn quicker and have a better performance. Each horse has its own vocation, which the horseman should recognize. Horses learn with good habits and not with long speeches" (notice that 'dishing out the crap', or 'bullshitting', was not invented at that time) "and if the horseman rides the horse 'scientifically' he should decrease the use of artificial means, so that the spectators think that the horse is acting on its own will." (A good way of explaining the neurophysiology of high performance equitation. Pluvinel was a genius!)

Says the minute king: "In the way you teach the students I can see that both the horse and the horseman receive lessons." "Right," replied Pluvinel: "I have been trying to reduce the time that it takes to teach horses and horsemen." (It is also evident to him the importance of the systematization of horsemanship to accelerate learning, an argument also used by François Baucher, as you'll see further on.)

The tiny king then starts the following dialogue: "Monsieur de Pluvinel, I can indeed, see that by your method one is able to judge, in a short time, both the horseman and the horse."

Answers Pluvinel: "I see that Your Majesty understands perfectly well what a trained horse consists of. The judicious horseman will always know how to choose the most docile horses to be trained and worthy of Your Majesty. I will not attempt to make distinctions between nations that breed horses, for I have seen good ones and bad ones in all countries. Everything depends upon the judgement of the horseman, to see whether the movements of the horse are vigorous and performed with strength, lightness, sensitivity, grace and speed. I am of the opinion that all horses can be more or less schooled, albeit some better than others. For we know that well built men are not all capable of dancing well, and all horses are not capable of jumping and hopping." (The reason for this phenomenon is the neurological constitution of horses and people; a matter that would only be studied by neural sciences in the 20th century). "One must avoid the use of force, for I have never seen something positive coming out of a horse if such is the case. My objective is to work the horse calmly, for short periods, but during a long time".

The baby king then asks: "Is there any other rule that you want to emphasize?"

Answers Pluvinel: "I carefully verify if the horse has a better response relating to one heel, than to the other, or if it sees better from one side than from the other. Any horse has a limitation, which we have to overcome, gently and patiently and not by use of force. Horses only learn by means of good and repeated classes, so that equitation becomes a habit. Before the introduction of my methods, many horses got old and worn instead of good and well trained".

"What do you have to say about bits Sir?" questions the miniature king, and Pluvinel answers: "I am content about using a dozen mouthpieces.[26] It is important that the bit gives pleasure to the horse's tongue. One must know and be able to judge what it is that the horse needs for his comfort. We should be careful so that the mouthpiece rests properly and only on the corners of the gums. The curb chain should fit correctly in its place. Take care so that the bit doesn't pinch the horse's lips. All those things should be judiciously considered. But the horseman's gentle hand is, in the end, his best instrument."

---

[26] The book *Origins of the Cavalry School of Saumur and Its Equestrian Traditions* published in the 19th century shows the illustration of about 100 different bits, each with a footnote describing its specific use. The bit was thought to be the 'key to the horse' as the mechanical philosophy of Horsemanship of that century postulated. And this preposterous situation only started to clear up with modern neuroscientific understanding of horsemanship.

www.horsetravelbooks.com

Monsieur Antoine de Pluvinel, as all great horsemasters, understood that the bit is just a tool – like a paintbrush, chisel or lancet – which skillfully used does a good job and ill-used results in mediocre work. He also understood that the change of tools has no positive result on a work done by awkward hands.[27]

Pluvinel's Horsemanship was more than a demonstration of the dominion of man over beast, or a proof of his masculinity. And despite the fact that the Renaissance of Academic Equitation had occurred in Italy, it was due to such men as Pluvinel that France replaced the Neapolitan Riding School, founded by Federico Grisone, as the leader in the training of men and horses in Europe. Seventeenth century France gave equestrian art its particular stamp and François Robichon de la Guérinière, in the 18th century, was the heir to Pluvinel's 'scientific' way of teaching Horsemanship.

---

[27] For a clearer understanding, I did some radical editing of the original text of *Le Maneige Royal*, deleting some of the excesses of the rhetoric style practiced by the 17th century French court. The purists will surely accuse me of murdering Shakespeare's language. I hope the horse people of the Internet generation understand and give me a break. B. R.

22. La Guérinière, the Heir to "Scientific" Equitation

François Robichon de La Guérinière was the legitimate heir to Antoine de Pluvinel. In 1751, La Guérinière wrote a book, School of Horsemanship, *which achieved great success in all European courts. Now we have reached a time where modern Physics has been established in all its plenitude and the last traces of the Aristotelian universe, reintroduced in the Renaissance, had disappeared. In the Newtonian universe, mathematics had turned into a tool through which scientific results could be expressed in numbers. The western world had gone through a scientific renewal and was entering the Industrial Revolution. But academic equitation continued to be stationary, with splendid high school presentations performed to a powdered and bewigged audience. After the gigantic leap of man's perception of the universe, the classic 'ecuyer' was still riding as his forerunners in the Renaissance. Despite all scientific advancements there had been no growth in equestrian thought.*

In the 18th century classical equitation gained great impulsion and the rational teachings of Antoine de Pluvinel started to be felt in France. Horsemen of the quality of Louis Cazeau de Nestier from Versailles will be long remembered. And with the work and study of Claude Borghelat, an equerry from the Academy of Lyon, veterinarian medicine was also on the rise. However, in spite of the technical and scientific effervescence of the age of 'Light and Reason, Göethe and Montesquieu', the principles of classical equitation stayed unaltered as in the time of Pluvinel, 100 years earlier.

François Robichon de la Guérinière, in his time, did not see the horse world in a rosy light. As all masters before and after him, he saw himself as the last bulwark of good equitation – "I have done my best to revive the equestrian excellency of the 'golden age' of equitation", wrote La Guérinière in the Preface of his book, *School of Horsemanship.* "It must be admitted that, to our shame, we have lost some of the expertise of earlier times" (he is not referring to the Huns and Mongols, of course). "We are contented with somewhat shoddy performances, whereas earlier excellence was sought in the airs, which were the ornament of our manege and the jewel of our processions and parades". The words of la Guérinière echo Pluvinel's dissatisfaction with riding in the 17th century and anticipate Baucher's discontent in the 19th century and Decarpentry's in the 20th.

None of the great masters were satisfied with the equitation displayed in their time, just as many riders nowadays feel nostalgic about the 'golden age of equitation,' whenever that might have been. While all areas of science advanced for the benefit of the present, in the 18th century classic equitation was humbly devoted to the glories of the past. In 1777, Richard Berenger, a disciple of la

Guérinière, described the position of seat and hands almost with the same words used by the Duke of Newcastle 200 years earlier.

The 'aids' described by la Guérinière in the chapter *Aids and chastisements necessary to the training of the horse* are based on the same principles of punishment and reward used by Grisone. "The 'aids' are used to anticipate the error a horse can make; chastisements to correct an error while a horse commits it; and since a horse obeys only as a result of fear and punishment, the 'aids' are no more than a warning to the horse that it will be punished if it does not respond to the rider's direction." To la Guérinière the whip was both an 'aid' and a form of punishment, although further on he contradicts himself by concluding that "Finally it can well be said that sparing the use of the 'aids' and chastisement is one of the most desirable traits of the rider." In one moment he makes a eulogy of the 'aids' as a method of punishment and in the next he advises against the use of them. What was wrong with horsemanship in the Age of La Guérinière?

In La Guérinière's time, not all horses were schooled for the manege, which was a rich man's pastime and for which few animals were physically fit. Most horses were used for traveling, hunting, racing, war and work. This naturally produced a conflict of opinions between academic riders and other horsemen as how to use and train horses, and it was common to hear the more exalted equerries exchange acid comments or insults about his fellow man's equestrian methods. (Exactly as the classical and western riders squabble today.)

The 'practical riders' argued that the collection of the horse demanded by artistic equitation eliminated the horse's impulsion and made it worthless for outdoor equitation. And the defenders of high school training used the argument of Newcastle, who apparently was a man who could distinguish equestrian art from the use of the horse at work and sport (which his followers apparently couldn't). In his book la Guérinière condenses the chapter on jumping to half a page, where he gives some careless advice on how to make a horse jump (a clear sign of his disregard for the sport). He undoubtedly thought it to be his business to revive the *'golden age'* of horsemanship', by which he meant the grand presentations of 'haute école' and not jumping fences about the countryside.

And the world spun on its orbit with the 18th century 'ecuyer' insisting on the classical 'rigour' of artistic equitation. "The Prussians," wrote Charles Chenevix Trench, "forgot the lesson Frederick the Great had apparently taught them during the war of the Austrian Succession: 'the rider shall overcome at speed all obstacles of the terrain and advance, advance, advance.'" Yet after the hardship of the war, the equerries fell back to the old ways of the manege. Even the magnificent Russian cavalry, including the Cossacks, was instructed to follow the Prussian example.

www.horsetravelbooks.com

"But", explains Chevenix Trench, "as the officers only knew about la Guérinière's book by hearsay, someone translated *School of Horsemanship* into Russian and the fast gaits were eliminated, collection introduced, the horses lost their conditioning and were incapable of any outdoor activities".

In the Russo-Turkish war of 1828, the Turk cavalry had unfortunately also been drilled *à la Française* and the soldiers, with their new techniques and tight tunics, were prone to fall off their horses, which were unable to advance over the debris of war. These cavalry encounters must have been a sight to see. To mistake *equestrian art* for the *art of war* (if such a thing exists) could only lead to the ensuing mess.

The misunderstanding between classical horsemanship and outdoor riding was at the root of the famous controversy that would rage between François Baucher and Antoine D'Aure a hundred years later. But after the French Revolution, it seems as if some prankster had changed the roles of the opponents: the nobles, represented by D'Aure, were now defending the natural and faster equitation and the bourgeoisie, represented by Baucher, was taking up the traditional artistic equitation. The Duke of Newcastle must have turned in his grave without understanding a word of the controversy. Let's take a ride into the 19th century and see for ourselves.

Even though la Guérinière's School of Horsemanship did not bring new thought to academic equitation, it did influence equitation in the 18th century by refining the high school movements and elaborating the equestrian quadrilles. This beautiful erudite art can still be seen unaltered in the Spanish Riding School in Vienna, where men and horses are trained by the exact principles introduced by François Robichon de la Guérinière, more than 250 years ago. In the century after la Guérinière, artistic equitation would have another great, though controversial, master: François Baucher. Don't miss the next chapter.

www.horsetravelbooks.com

23. François Baucher, Civil War in Horsemanship

François Baucher became renowned for his high-school presentations in the manège-circuses of Paris, where he introduced the flying-changes and gave demonstrations of backwards trotting and galloping. A great artist and skilled horse trainer, he was also the catalyst of one of the most bitter controversies in the history of Academic Equitation. The famous horseman wrote a book, Method of Equitation Based on New Principles. *This treatise had the power to split the French public opinion into two factions: the "baucherists" who admired the spectacular results obtained by Baucher and the "d'aurists" led by count Antoine Cartier D'Aure, who accused Baucher's method of being ancient history. (It is said that Honoré de Balzac was a staunch d'aurist). But, after all, who was this man that had the courage to announce a 'new method' of horsemanship in the most developed equestrian nation in Europe?*

François Baucher was born in Versailles and not much is known about his early years – probably because there was not much to tell. Some historians claim that he was born a 'stone's throw' from the Royal Equestrian School of Versailles and Baucher himself declared that as a boy he used to watch the military exercises and parades held there and that he admired above all Count d'Abzac on his comings and goings to the parade grounds.

Baucher's professional life began under an uncle's tutelage, in a manège in Milan. About 1820, when he was 24 years old, Baucher went to Le Havre as the equerry to a Belgian manège. In 1834 Baucher was very unsatisfied as he felt that he was too far from the great equestrian centers, and as he was also guided by a high sense of mission to teach the methods he was developing he moved to glittering Paris. There he associated with a member of an illustrious equestrian family, Jules Charles Pellier.

His new partner was the owner of a manège-circus – where a new type of circus program was becoming popular. Besides the traditional jugglers, magicians, clowns and wild animal tamers, there were also performances of Equestrian Art. At that time the manège-circus was becoming fashionable in Paris and, besides drawing the 'menu bourgeois', the horse shows were beginning to attract the nobility, thus competing with the operas houses and ballets. In that post-revolutionary, post-Napoleonic and post-Bourbonic restoration, France was in an ideological turmoil — with the nobility becoming more and more bourgeois and the bourgeois becoming increasingly noble – if you know what I mean.[28]

---

[28] Now we are in the in reign of Louis-Philippe the 'citizen king', so you can see which way the political wind was blowing in 19th century France.

But, the growing popularity of Baucher – the bourgeois riding marvel – put him on a collision course with another famous horseman, the count Antoine Cartier D'Aure. D'Aure was a defender of a *new-wave horsemanship* – less oriented to the manège and more devoted to the equestrian sports practiced outdoors – in consonance with the current English and Prussian trend. The Count introduced to France the English saddle, the short stirrup, and the rising trot. D'Aure's *'method'* can be summarized as *"forward! always forward! And once again forward!"* as he liked to say. Since Newcastle's time, many people favored equestrian sports practiced in the open, compared to artistic horsemanship displayed in the manège, as you may remember.

In 1840 Baucher and D'Aure were like two locomotives approaching full steam on the same track. Sooner or later there would be an ideological collision. The publishing in 1842 of his fatalistic book and an official invitation made to Baucher to teach the *'nouvelle method'* in the military academies of Paris, Saumur and Lunéville, precipitated the collision.

Baucher taught his new method in the French army from 1842 to 1845. But with the death of his sponsor, the duke D'Orleans, and the ascension to the French cavalry committee of his brother the duke of Nemours, a staunch d'aurist, the inevitable happened – Baucher's fall and D'Aure's rise. After the defeat, François Baucher left Paris and traveled across Europe presenting himself in circuses to enthusiastic audiences. The two horsemen, the commoner and the nobleman, became mutual critics for the rest of their lives, each one attacking the other in several books and brochures. And Frenchmen, always quick to pick sides in a brawl, backed their champions with heated debates in poor taverns and rich parlors all over Paris. Yet, in the war of communication Baucher came out victorious, though a bit scorched.

After the publication of François Baucher's *New Method of Equitation* Count D'Aure wrote a comment entitled *Observations on the New Method*, where he affirmed that the use of the horse, and the means of controlling it were too well known for 'someone' to come along and announce the discovery of a 'new method'. He also declared ironically that in order to interpret horsemanship the way Baucher did, this person must never have used a horse outside a circus.

"Unfortunately" – commented D'Aure – "when the techniques of Grisone, Pluvinel, Newcastle and other great horseman of the past were reintroduced into Academic Horsemanship, they were used to train circus horses. Now when 'somebody' starts talking about *'ramener'* and *'rassembler'* people think they are hearing about new things. All the fuss has only succeeded in hurting the feelings of some people, and dividing public opinion."

Although it is important to notice that in his attacks on Baucher and the *New Method* D'Aure, unlike other critics, avoided deprecating the talent and the artistic value of Baucher's horsemanship. What was in discussion was the *efficiency* of Baucher's method for the use of the horse in jumping and cross-country competitions. After exploding, the French civil war in horsemanship was hotly fought.

Baucher, to defend himself, attacked his aggressors: "As regarding my presentations in circuses, Shakespeare and Molière also did so, for the enrichment of the English and French theatre. If my method was known before me, then why did they not practice it in all its fullness? There is not a single equerry who would not prefer to obtain results in one day than in a month nor obtain results in a month than in a year." And he adds sarcastically: "Either they did not understand me or pretended not to, because they could not find the proper words that correspond to this kind of work in the manuals of the past."

The *'truth'* is that Baucher was the first academic horseman to write a 'modern' treatise on horsemanship. The novelty was not so much the type of riding described, as the language used in the book. Baucher, thanks to the great technical advance of the Industrial Revolution, was able to write a book on Equestrian art with great technical accuracy – but unfortunately from a strictly *mechanistic point of view*.

The real problem, though, was that neither Baucher nor D'Aure could distinguish equestrian art from sporting horsemanship. Baucher was clearly the artist while D'Aure was obviously the sportsman. Both were devoted to equestrian disciplines of different natures for different purposes. The result of this controversy would be the birth of dressage and show jumping as two independent disciplines. Federico Caprilli would continue the work of D'Aure and Alexis L'Hotte followed Baucher.

In the end the winner was Academic Horsemanship that with the imbroglio had the two disciplines definitively sorted out. But even though they both introduced some new techniques to horsemanship, neither brought any meaningful philosophical insight to Equitation. The horse was still thought of as being a mechanical device, harnessed by mankind to pull a wagon or accomplish artistic movements and sporting feats, whatever.

Was François Baucher the Leonardo da Vinci of Academic Horsemanship? He certainly had an inventive genius and was the author of a system which greatly influenced riders in his time. However, despite all the 'ado', Academic Equitation was only modified in its essence by Captain Federico Caprilli's revolutionary concepts that could have ended the Mechanical Age of Horsemanship in the 20th century if... but that's another story.

www.horsetravelbooks.com

24. Gustav Steinbrecht – The German System

The Gymnasium of the Horse was the most detailed equestrian manual yet written and it surpassed in technical precision all the classical works on dressage published before it. Gustav Steinbrecht, though working in an empirical way, describes before the scientists of his day many important neurological questions about the connection of horse and man during equitation; problems that would only be unveiled after the development of physiology and neurology in the second half of the 20th century.

It may be said that *The Gymnasium of the Horse* represents the collective wisdom of many generations of German horsemen that formed the Prussian state that was founded by the Order of the Teutonic Knights in the thirteenth century.

The author, Gustav Steinbrecht, was born in the tumultuous times of the Napoleonic wars and through his life he was to see the unification of the German state and the forming of the *Deutsches Reich*, one of the most brilliant eras in the history of Germany. Let's gallop back in time and pay a visit to the political context that Steinbrecht lived and wrote his treatise in.

Of all the 360 petty kingdoms that would form the first Germanic confederation, Prussia was the leading state through the power of her military cavalry dynasty – the Junkers – which formed the dominant class. Horses, equitation, and cavalry were, from the very beginning of Prussia's history, the three pillars of that state's military power.

Yet, the nineteenth century did not start well for Prussia. In 1806, two years before Steinbrecht's birth, Napoleon Bonaparte defeated the Prussian forces in the battles of Jena and Auerstädt, where the Prussian armies were completely routed and quickly fell to pieces.

Gustav Steinbrecht was born in 1808, at Amfurt in Saxony, in a Germany recently crushed by Napoleon, but now taken by great patriotic fervor. The German nationalist movement was once more centered in Berlin, the capital of Prussia.

Young Gustav, the son of a Lutheran pastor, was not attracted to the 'faith' and chose to study veterinary medicine in Berlin. The daily routine with horses seduced Gustav into equitation, and through the friendship with an outstanding horseman Lois Seeger, the German riding master, the young veterinarian started his equestrian career. In those times the Prussian army had been reorganized and at the battle of Waterloo had helped complete the victory of the Allies that definitively defeated Napoleon's army. The German star was on the rise.

Steinbrecht stayed eight years with Louis Seeger, the time necessary to turn himself into a good horseman and gain the hand of the boss's niece (always a good way for a young ambitious man to start his career). But in 1834, the same

www.horsetravelbooks.com

year that François Baucher moved to Paris, Steinbrecht decided to accept an offer to manage a private manège in Magdenburg, 160 kilometers from Berlin. After spending eight years in the "provinces," however, Steinbrecht decided to return to Berlin and once again work with Seeger who was now at the height of his fame.

After the liberal and nationalistic revolution of 1848, Germany had resumed her economic growth and was on the way to turn into a great European power. In 1849, Steinbrecht was nominated director of Seegerhof, Louis Seeger's manège, and in those days he started to write the notes that would turn into the book *The Gymnasium of the Horse*.

But in what respect did Steinbrecht's work differ from the books that had been written in France, Italy, and Portugal before him?

The Gymnasium of the Horse is dedicated exclusively to dressage and high school work and doesn't address subjects such as horseshoeing, feeding and the handling of horses. It is the most complete book written on the training of horses that had ever been produced.

Steinbrecht describes minutely the action of the horseman in the schooling movements and airs above the ground, explains how to start a young horse, develop impulsion with a natural carriage of the head, flex the neck, the poll, the dorsal column. It's a system of progressive training and doesn't leave any aspects of the art without a detailed explanation.

In the chapter "the Driving Aids" Steinbrecht describes the horseman's sense of 'proprioception' without knowing that this as yet unknown animal sense would be discovered in the following century – (...) 'so it is the rider's first obligation to keep soft and natural those parts of his body with which he feels his horse. If his seat meets this requirement, he will soon feel the movement of the horse's legs and will be able to distinguish each individual one; he will thus have the means at his disposal with which to control them as if they were his own.' I know of no other author who has described the sense of proprioception with this clarity of mind. Steinbrecht also describes **How** to school the horse and make the best of the qualities of a good horse although, like the other masters of his time, he had no way of knowing **Why** his method worked. This is because in his time psychology and the sciences of life were still in an early stage of development and cybernetics would only appear as a scientific subject in the 20th century.

In his book Steinbrecht severely criticizes his contemporary, François Baucher: 'the biggest example of charlatanism is Mr. Baucher who with the audacity of his affirmations and the enormity of his promises, has brought the entire equestrian world into uproar and confusion. His method consists of gradually and cunningly robbing the horse of its natural power, which Mr. Baucher considers to be the enemy, and thus make it subservient. He renders his horses so wilted and

www.horsetravelbooks.com

limp by unnatural bending and twisting in place, and so thoroughly robs their hind quarters of their natural forward action, that the poor creatures lose all support and are no longer good for any practical purpose. His method should be called the backward system. Having haunted the equestrian world long enough, it has finally, to the relief of all horsekind, been banned to where he really belongs: the circus. (Steinbrecht and Count D'Aure obviously held the same viewpoints.)

The truth seems to be that some of the old masters did use equestrian techniques contrary to the nature of the horse, but with time and training the animal would learn to overcome the unnatural action, leaving the trainer with the illusion that his techniques were correct because the horse had learned to respond to them. (We frequently see horses that are smarter than their riders.)

Steinbrecht, in his turn, is extremely precise in the definition of his system of schooling horses, in the description of techniques and the movements of high school, and is capable, even without knowing the scientific paradigms that rule biology, of presenting with great accuracy certain neurophysiological questions that would only be revealed in the following century. This is the case of proprioception, that Steinbrecht describes with a mechanistic precision without knowing that this sense would only be discovered scientifically in the nineteen seventies. (See chapter "Cracking the Centaur Enigma" in the second part of the book.)

In 1859 Steinbrecht left Seegerhof and acquired his own manège in Dessau, 100 kilometers from Berlin. This was also the time that Wilhelm I ascended the throne of Prussia and had the army reorganized, and after two military victories over Austria and Denmark raised Germany to one of Europe's great powers. And the Prussian cavalry was the decisive military factor that guaranteed both triumphs.

In 1865 Steinbrecht, now 57 years old, decided with his wife to return to the social life in the capital Berlin. Four years later Napoleon III declared war on Germany and, in the battle of Sedan, Prussia showed once more its military genius by thoroughly defeating the French armies. After this victory Wilhelm I was proclaimed Emperor of all the Germans, now again led by the state of Prussia.

Historians attribute the defeat of the French in the Franco-Prussian war to the endemic disorganization of France's institutions, to the lack of leadership in Napoleon's army and to the superiority of the German artillery. 'The German artillery conquered and the infantry occupied' exulted historians, completely forgetting that before the telephone and the airplane there was no way to coordinate the action of artillery and infantry without the participation of cavalry in all tactical maneuvers and crucial moments of the campaign. In the 19th century cavalry was the nervous center of the army, as the Internet is today. Therefore, in a more accurate analysis, the importance of the Prussian cavalry should not be underestimated in the ascension of Germany to the leading powers of Europe. While industry and commerce of the unified German states helped to form a strong economy, cavalry held the political balance pending favorably towards Prussian hegemony.

Gustav Steinbrecht lived through this brilliant political, economic and military rise of Germany, and had the opportunity to see, in the battle of Sedan, the German horse assure the most crushing victory of the history of Prussia, and the greatest military triumph of modern Germany. A victory assured by the best cavalry in Europe and its secular tradition in equestrian excellence. In the year of the battle of Sedan, Steinbrecht, now sixty-two years old, had turned into one of the greatest horsemen in Germany, and, living in Berlin, he kept training horses until his death in February 1885.

As Hans Heinrich Brinckmann writes in his preface of *The Gymnasium of the Horse*, 'Steinbrecht's teachings will always be the soundest and the most reliable foundation because he builds on the laws of nature on which any true art must be based.'

The Gymnasium of the Horse united the best in the German system of riding and in 1912 an army manual based on the theories of Gustav Steinbrecht was published and formed the basics of German riding instruction, and it has also been a fountain of inspiration and instruction to all the German riders and for the spectacular results of their dressage and show jumping in International competition.

Gustav Steinbrecht brought to classical riding, and especially to dressage, a minute, progressive and precise description of the biomechanics of equitation. His book **The Gymnasium of the Horse** *has turned into a source of reference for all German riders who have become great winners in dressage and show jumping. Steinbrecht was the only author to focus on 'proprioception' which, more than balance, is at the root of all advanced equitation.*

25. Federico Caprilli, the Unfinished Revolution

Xenophon can be considered the father of Academic Horsemanship; Federico Grisone had the merit of discovering his treatise in the 16th century; Antoine de Pluvinel turned equitation into a form of art; la Guérinière is accepted as the father of 'scientific' Horsemanship; François Baucher, with his 'Nouvelle Method,' created an enormous strife in the 19th century. But it was Federico Caprilli who introduced a really revolutionary concept in equitation – he elevated the horse from an object to an individual actually capable of intelligent cooperation with the rider – thus greatly extending his efficiency in Horsemanship. But this extraordinary concept was, for historical reasons, forgotten for a very long time.

By the end of the 19th and in the early years of the twentieth century, European horsemanship was still fixed on traditional military concepts: extreme collection, with the frontal line of the head perpendicular to the horizon, established by the Neapolitan School of the 16th century. But this artificial head bearing was obviously becoming irrelevant in an age when firepower was completely changing the strategic use of cavalry. At that time an Italian cavalry officer introduced a completely new attitude towards horses and equitation: the unfetted extension, with natural head carriage and neck, that people today call 'natural' equitation.

Captain Federico Caprilli, an instructor of the Pinerollo Cavalry School in Turin, recognized that in the new reality of war the old cavalry assault was (at long last) fast becoming obsolete. The cavalryman's new duties, he thought, would be carried out in the division of topographical reconnaissance by flying equestrian formations capable of overcoming any kind of natural obstacles, an impossible task for any mechanical vehicle before the airplane (which, unfortunately, was just around the corner).

With this intention, Caprilli trained his horses and horsemen– instead of riding 'collected' as was the practice in academic schooling – to obtain free movements of the 'elongated' horse (as had been pointed out by Frederic of Prussia and Count D'Aure). And the rider should, in all circumstances, adjust himself to the animal's gravity center and natural way of going. Federico Caprilli foresaw the changes that inevitably would affect the cavalry in his time. He introduced modern concepts in horsemanship that would adjust perfectly to show jumping, a sport already practiced in England, and which was later adopted internationally.

Caprilli, however, did not know that the military usefulness of the horse would disappear less than 40 years after his death. Neither could he imagine that modern horsemanship would be reborn in the second half of the 20th century and consolidated in the 21st century *as the most extraordinary sport ever conceived by mankind.* Caprilli had only worked for the reorganization of military cavalry to introduce a more efficient riding style, from a military tactical-strategic point of view; a means of getting cavalry across country with the least possible strain for both men and horses. This economy of the horse's physique and strength was Caprilli's unceasing preoccupation and one of the most vital precepts of his system.

Modern equitation is founded upon the need of uniting the human and equine neurophysiology and transforming the rider into a fluent part of the equestrian action, with a perfect synchronism of movements between horse and rider. The bond between the partners is brought on through systematic training, when the combination's united performance is organized into a chain of interactive conditioned reflexes. This sensorial coordination is easier to describe than to accomplish, and to make it understood neuroscience, biomechanical science and the physiology of exercise is daily supplying more data and information. But, let's return to Captain Caprilli and his revolutionary ideas at the dawn of the 20th century.

The Italian Captain used to teach his students that the horse was perfectly capable of re-balancing itself during changes of speed, changes of gaits, changes of direction and over the fences, without the horseman's intervention, if only the rider would maintained his center of balance in perfect continuity with the horse's. In plain English: if the horseman would refrain from disturbing the horse, hampering its movements and unbalancing it with a lot of unnecessary 'aids.'

Caprilli would say, for example, that the horse didn't need a leg cue three strides before, or any other specific 'aid,' as it approached a fence.

"The horse that has been trained to jump with a horseman on its back, in the beginning with low obstacles, will be perfectly capable of estimating the distance and decide if it should increase or decrease its strides and decide upon the moment of taking off for the jump. Horsemanship should be performed without those instructions to the horse, without 'aids' or other theories of weight distribution – but with the rider continually adjusting his weigh and movements to the horse's center of gravity," argued the great horseman.

"I therefore maintain that we must strive to leave the horse as nature fashioned him, with his balance and attitude of head unaltered, because we shall see that the horse, in the course of his schooling, is perfectly able to do so himself if allowed the necessary freedom. When the rider is capable, throughout the entire course of a jump, of smoothly conforming to the movements of the horse, he will have developed more than sufficient dexterity not to disturb him in anything else he may do. Therefore the first rule of good horsemanship should be that of redu-

www.horsetravelbooks.com

cing, simplifying and even, when possible, altogether eliminating any action on the rider's part. By the strict application of the principle of invariably conforming to the horses' natural instinct and attitudes, carefully avoiding the infliction of all pain – a principle easily applied because of the extreme simplicity of our method – the horse, naturally submissive, not only will not rebel but, on the contrary bring into play those qualities which have for centuries made him man's most helpful comrade."

(All Caprilli's extreme postulations will be discussed in the second and third part of this book in the light of modern science.)

Caprilli was radical and discarded the traditional concept of 'collection' because, as he said, it inhibited the horse's impulsion forward. "The hand should follow the rein and the rein accompany the horse's movement. All that is necessary is for the horseman to interfere as little as possible with the natural balance of the horse and to adjust himself to the horse's way of moving."[29]

Caprilli didn't ride with a free rein but maintained, with the help of the snaffle, a soft contact with the horse's mouth, without demanding the bending of the column, neck and the head of the animal. Caprilli taught his pupils to elevate their body in the stirrups and to lean forwards when jumping. In this way the rider would be poised exactly over the horses' gravity center when taking the hurdles. In order to lean forward, he recommended the shortening of the stirrup leather, in the oriental fashion – or *'a la gineta'*. In spite of the teachings of D'Aure the common practice was still the opposite – people rode with a long leg, as medieval horsemen, and over the jumps would lean backward, to 'relieve the weigh on the horse's withers at the moment of impact,' they argued. (This practice was actually an 'unconditioned reflex' of the horseman that threw his body backwards in fear of being unhorsed.)

In the presence of this admirable simplicity we may well wonder what Caprilli, to whom dropped nose bands were as alien as standing martingales, would have said about the muzzles and pulleys that, from the show-ring, have at present invaded even the hunting field and race-course. He was irremovably opposed to anything even distantly savoring of artificiality. As anyone can guess, the ultra-conservative society of the *fin du siècle* ignored Caprilli and his pupils until the year of 1904– when they astonished the world by easily winning the show jumping trials of the International Horse Exhibition in Italy! After Caprilli's premature death his riding system was dubbed (you won't believe this) the *forward seat*, and was again mixed with the traditional military concepts of incessantly interfering with the horse's movements.

The horsemanship proposed by Caprilli was so revolutionary that for it to be understood it would be necessary to accomplish a revolution in the rider's mind,

---

[29] *The Caprilli Papers,* translated and edited by Piero Santini.

to elevate the horse from a vehicle to a sporting partner. This new way of thinking would only start taking hold one hundred years later, in the nineties, considered by scientists as the *decade of the brain*.

We owe the daring Italian captain Federico Caprilli the understanding of the importance of the horse's cooperation, not as a vehicle but as an *intelligent sporting partner*. By challenging the *mechanical conception* of equitation and recognizing the horse's individuality, Caprilli conceived modern equitation – which was in many ways similar to the highly efficient Central Asian horsemanship of antiquity! The Shakespearean wheel had almost completed its turn.

However, no one really understood the extent of Caprilli's teachings. But neither did most people understand Pythagoras, Socrates, Copernicus, Galileo or Newton. The 'forward seat,' the 'Italian seat,' the 'independent seat,' 'the natural seat,' 'the deep seat,' and other variations of the theme, only go to show that to most people 'science' is what they can see 'with their own eyes'. In Horsemanship the *bottom line* has always been the rider's seat, though now neuroscience will change all that.

Caprilli's 'forward seat' was just the 'tip of the iceberg' of a new perception of equitation, which promoted the horse from a mere object to a sensitive individual. After many centuries of a stiff mechanical use of the horse, Caprilli perceived the value of the motor-sensorial connection between horse and rider – even though he didn't know the scientific terms that would later be used by modern neuroscientists.

Now, have you also noticed that throughout time most western horsemen have suffered from a strange longing for the past – a feeling that in some former time horsemanship had lived its 'golden years'? Let's look into this!

www.horsetravelbooks.com

26. The "Golden Years", Where and When

Western horsemen have always felt nostalgic about the past – riders have nurtured an inner feeling that, in some previous time, horsemanship 'must have lived its Golden Years.' La Guérinière lamented the way of equitation in the 18th century. General Decarpentry showed a deep concern for the 20th century's Horsemanship. Current riders look back in time for inspiration. But has there really been a time in the past which could be called the 'golden years' of horsemanship? If so, could it have been in the 17th century of Antoine de Pluvinel, the 'most excellent of all those who has ever donned spurs?' Or was the apex of equestrian excellence in François Baucher's lively days? Or yet, might the horseman's paradise on earth have been the Old West *of Buffalo Bill Cody, Wild Bill Hickock, Crazy Horse and Sitting Bull?*

I would like to apologize outright for disagreeing with people who believe that horsemanship's "golden years" might have been situated in any century during or after the Italian Renaissance. Despite my undeniable enthusiasm for the progress of classical equitation in the last decade of the 20th century, and my conviction that the development of neuroscience and computer science in the 21st century will lead to better horses and horsemanship than in any other time in our history – I must admit that, in my mind, the equestrian paradise on Earth lies much further back in time.

I believe that the near-perfect past of horsemanship was probably lived by the horse herders of the steppes and later by the nomads of the deserts. Don't zap me, I'll explain.

The indefatigable work of paleontologists and anthropologists has begun to reveal how the domestication of the horse by the nomads happened, and scholars have also uncovered many details of the development of equestrian technology with which the original Centaurs formed their incredibly successful mobile economy.

Life on the steppes was undoubtedly the most favorable environment for humans to gain full biological comprehension of the horse's psychology and motivations.

In the nomadic societies of Central Asia, all the community members were in some way involved with horses. The intimacy of the man-horse relationship was total and the psychological and functional knowledge of the animals was the base of good horsemanship. There were no 'professional secrets' – horses and equitation was an open book that the whole community understood. For a better comprehension of the natural man-horse relationship on the steppe let's ride back to Roman times and watch the Huns living on the plains of Hungary.

www.horsetravelbooks.com

After he is born Allita, the nomadic boy, first learn to recognize his mother, then his father's horse and, at last – oh, hi dad! When Allita reaches the age of 15 he will already have known three generations of the community's horses – all the way back to the grandfather of the colt that has just been born. Allita's childhood and adolescence is enriched by equestrian games that imitate his father's, uncles' brothers' and sisters' adventures on the wide steppes. In these games and contests, Allita learn to share the pleasure and the adventure of horse speed.

One day, in the passage from puberty to adulthood, when Allita reaches the age to own a horse he is invited to participate in his first raid against an agrarian people's horse herd. It is an honorable invitation, which shows that his seniors have already noticed his equestrian skills. His pride is unbounded. The strategy of the raid is minutely discussed at council meetings held in his father's yurt at night. For his participation in the coming event Allita chooses the horse with which he has already played in many daring hunting and war games. The empathy that is at the root of their relationship is an established fact.

On the night of the incursion, the excitement of the horses and the younger warriors is huge. Everybody is impatient to start the adventure. Allita is agitated and, as always happens, he passes his feelings to his horse that hops about in its eagerness to be off. The attack happens as planned by the nomad warriors who with great speed and ability manage to circle and gather the enemy's horses on the plain outside the village.

During the retreat, some horses break loose from the herd and Allita immediately turns back and at a breakneck gallop overcomes the horses and, in a fast maneuver, turns them back to the main herd. The precision of the horse and the boy's equitation is so great that it seems that Alitta's horse is *commanding the action*.

But enemy sentinels also see Allita's exploit and rush in his pursuit. With the hostile horsemen's fast approach Allita leans over his horse's neck, which is a sign for more speed – his intentions flash to the horse's brain, the smell of his fear invades the horse's senses, and in a strong reaction of alarm the horse stretches out in a dead gallop as if it is being pursued by the devil. With *fine-tuned emotions* the horse and the boy disappear in a burst of speed into the silvery night, leaving behind them their awed city-bred pursuers.

With the triumphal return of the warriors to the camp a strong bond has been tied between Allita and his horse. Now Allita, the new warrior of the tribe, *owes his life to his horse*.

But this would just be the first of a series of equestrian feats that would mark Allita's adult life. Later when he becomes the tribe's war leader, and commands faraway raids, a lifelong union with his war-horse will have been formed. And when one day God calls Allita Khan to gallop with him on the steppes of afterlife

www.horsetravelbooks.com

– his old steed, in an elaborated religious ceremony, will be buried with him. *On the steppe, the Centaur's union, besides being perfect, is eternal.*

The great intimacy between horse and rider was the key of the Central Asians' horsemanship.[30] Man and horse kept together because they both found advantages in the relationship. It was an example of perfect animal symbiosis, which has many other examples in nature, though not with such amazing results. Through mutual acceptance human and equine reflexes and emotions were easy to unite. This attachment process began with the difficult selection of a horse whose natural temperament was well tuned with the horseman's. An animal that presented any incompatibility would surely not be chosen for a mount. It would be very risky for a warrior to entrust his life to the legs of a horse that didn't like or trust him. Lack of empathy would disable the neurophysiological bond needed for high performance horsemanship. The Centaur merger was formed after some time of reciprocal observation and shared equestrian experiences. *The partnership was born by mutual consent.*

We know that in ancient times the nomad horse herders developed the fetter for their favorite horses. That would prevent the horse straying and become subject to robbery. We know that nomads preferred to pasture their animals in narrow valleys where they would be easier to guard and to handle. But these – the fetter and the pasturing in closed valleys – were only *auxiliary techniques* for the control of the horse herd. On the free steppe the real basis of the man-horse relationship was trust, which *empathy* facilitated.

All horse people from the steppe, the desert, or the prairie, have developed a high esteem for their horses from which many stories have reached our times. In the 20th century a holy man from Arabia told an American researcher: "Horses are our wealth, happiness, life and religion. The prophet said: The blessings of this life until judgement day are hung in the crest between your horse's eyes."

This communion founded on deep personal friendship between horse and rider explains the quality of the Central Asian nomad's equitation. In ancient times, several Roman witnesses affirmed that the nomadic horsemen only used a rod to guide their horses. In the Flanders war of 1793, general Morand, a French officer commented, astounded, on the Cossacks equestrian performance: "These rude horsemen maintain their horses close to their legs. They change from

---

[30] Don't ever believe in the wanton cruelty of the Central Asian nomads towards horses. The stories of 'unimaginable cruelty' must be discarded as pure ignorance, spun by people who could never understand the full symbiotic relationship of humans and horses. Had the mounted nomads been cruel to their horses they could never have attained the *total reflexive cooperation* that eyewitnesses describe, because that can only be attained with a confident and relaxed horse, as any advanced rider knows.

www.horsetravelbooks.com

immobility to gallop and from gallop to immobility in seconds – the horses are as skilled as the horsemen, and they seem to make part of them!"

No Western society was ever able to form such fine cavalry. The artificial urban-agrarian environment wouldn't allow for it. The Indians of the North-American prairies, after only 200 years of horse culture, developed many of the equestrian qualities of Eurasia's shepherds: patience in taming the animals; a very well adjusted center of gravity, perfectly tuned body movements, and complete control at all speeds.

By all descriptions, a nomadic horseman was a fluent part of the equestrian action. Though to reach this excellence in equitation the nomad's training took longer than the modern rider's. His equestrian perfection was the result of a relationship that began with his birth and ended with his death and was the reason of his whole existence. So if there ever was a 'Golden Age' in the long relationship between man and horse it must have been in the Era of the free steppe horse-societies. They built the greatest horse cultures, ever, harvested the greatest success, which lasted the longest time. *The steppe was the time and place where it all began.*

When the urban-agrarian civilizations adopted the equestrian dynamics, a breach of physical and emotional distancing between man and horse was opened. This resulted in the loss of the understanding of the physiology and psychology of equitation, which ended in low-tech mechanical riding. The urban environment generated new social pressures and these completely modified the horse-man relationship – although the 'Golden Years of horsemanship' did flare up for a brief moment on the central plains of North America.

27. The Last Myth

The second half of the 19th century gave birth to the biggest equestrian myth in Western culture. And, surprisingly, it was not the great masters of Academic Horsemanship – Baucher, L'Hotte or D'Aure that captured the public imagination. It was a simple character that with his horse helped to build the most powerful nation in the world: meet the North American cowboy. This mostly ill-paid, rude horseman, responsible for the large bovine herds necessary to feed the great emerging country, became a more powerful myth than Saint George, Roland, King Arthur, Sir Lancelot, Dom. Sebastián and El Cid. Why? The cowboy is probably the last Western horseman to have lived free as our nomadic ancestors on the steppes. An emblem of human liberty that from time to time haunt city-bred people's nostalgic imagination.

In the 19th century, the American cowboy fired the imagination of people in such a way that the myth of the Far-West extrapolated national frontiers and became the only world-wide symbol of an equestrian world where most people – civilians and military – depended on the horse in their daily life. The idolatry of the free roaming cowboy of the American plains is certainly a powerful reaction by urban dwellers against the negative effects of the Industrial Revolution. An unconscious repulse of the dirty and artificial big city which enslaves man and restrains his aspirations and respiration, limits his physical movements, and impedes his free circulation.

On the American prairie occurred the last confrontation between nomad cultures and sedentary civilization in the history of mankind. The *frontier* was not, in fact, the divide between the Union of the American States and the lands still dominated by the American natives, but the long-forgotten frontier disputed since the invention of horsemanship by nomadic and sedentary people. Probably the American West represents the last time when a man and his horse was the master of all the horizons, and his fatherland was the land occupied by his horse. It is a nostalgic feeling that blows cold in the human soul, vivifying long ago-images from the ancient Eurasian steppes dominated by the extraordinary Centaurs – the catalysts of history. *In this sense, the American West was in fact the last frontier on earth.*

The role of the horse in building the United States is not underrated as much as it is in European history. The image of Homo-Caballus is the very essence of the *American way of life*. The horseman's freedom of action finds great resonance among Americans, whose cultural identity is permeated by the individual's natural right to freedom. The cowboy represents the human dominion over nature and the uncertainties of destiny by a fearless horseman who, with a good horse under him, a revolver in his hand, and a sense of justice in his head, writes the script of his life the way he thinks it ought to be written. By the laws of the American West, the union between man and horse was so strong that the robbery of a horse was punished in the same way as the murder of a person: the culprit was summarily hung by the neck until declared dead. As the law of the steppe, *the horse was wealth, happiness and freedom* – it was the reason of life – so a horse theft must be paid with a life. (I'm all for it, you know.)

Incredible as it may seem, even the Archduke Alexis, third son of the Czar Alexander II of the Russias, caught the fever of the great American myth and in 1872 traveled from the Russian steppes – the birth-place of the Centaur and center of the rich equestrian culture – to hunt bison in Nebraska with the notorious Buffalo Bill Cody and his horse Brigham, or was it Bucking Joe? I can't quite remember.

Buffalo Bill, one of the sacred icons of the American West, had his adventures greatly enhanced by a novelist called Ned Buntline. They say that this story-monger arrived one day at Fort Kearney in Nebraska with the intention of interviewing James W. Hickock for some woolly 'Wild-West' stories. Wild Bill refused to grant him an audience – he probably had a more important duel to fight – and told the journalist to speak with Billy Cody, a famous and courageous scout of the day. As the name of the actors doesn't alter the factors, Buntline changed Hickock for Cody, and the rest is history. But let us return to the Russo-American safari on the American plains.

The Archduke Alexis and his retinue of 'rough riders' was followed by a support-train with a real live steam-puffing locomotive, bed-wagons, a wagon-restaurant and a wagon-refrigerator, well supplied with quail, champagne and caviar (the Bolshevik revolution is really quite comprehensible). As a guide, the Archduke hired none other than Philip Sheridan, a general of the American civil war, who has to his credit the immortal adage *"The only good injun is a dead injun"*, and in his hunting-cast he included the notorious George Custer (who would try to abide by Sheridan's epigram, but somehow got on the wrong side of the shooting irons), and for good measure Alexis hired around 1000 Sioux extras to enliven the proceedings.

What the members of the noble Russo-American safari couldn't foresee was that those same redskins would de-hair General Custer, and all the 7th Cavalry, in the ominous battle of the Little Big-Horn. An innocuous little cavalry skirmish where everybody was a loser: the white soldiers lost their top-notch, the red soldiers lost their liberty, and the United States lost their human rights credibility. Of the 7th Cavalry, only a horse called Comanche was to die from old age, and it is now happily stuffed in the Smithsonian Institute... but I think I'm wandering.

The myth of the American West is forever consecrated in Western mythology. I believe that a thousand years from now these equestrian idols – both cowboys

www.horsetravelbooks.com

and Indians – Buffalo Bill, Kit Carson, Wyatt Earp, Crazy Horse, Red Cloud, Geronimo, Calamity Jane and Wild Bill Hickock will have the same mythical power of Zeus, Poseidon, Apollo, Artemis, Peleu, Achilles, Ares, Aphrodite, the Centaurs and the rest of the Aegean pantheon. As an 'old-timer' of Montana used to say – *"Ah'long as thehs a sunset, there'll be an Ole West"*.

The legacy of the 19th century's equestrian adventures cast such a powerful mythical spectrum over twentieth century equitation that modern riders passed almost one hundred years suffering from a acute inferiority complex, an equestrian identity crisis, which has deeply affected the development of modern horsemanship. The 19th century, with its great European wars, colonial conquests and the independence of ten South-American countries, had thousands of historical incidents full of fantastic equestrian adventures.

It was a time when the horse was industry, trade, pomp, fashion, sport, leisure and ostentation for the rich and well born, and profession, work, drudgery, grind, toil, moil and opportunity of advancement for the poor and low born. It is natural therefore that to future generations the 19th century will seem to be the apogee of mankind's equestrian culture. But if you believe that, you'll believe anything – Western riding has in reality just begun.

The legend of the Old West helped Homo-Caballus to cross the border into the third millennium. The cowboy and his horse certainly helped to keep alive the equestrian flame during the worst crisis of horsemanship since the Asian horsemen were called 'Centaurs' by their wary Greek pedestrian neighbors. Now, let's recall the adventures of Homo-Caballus in the 19th century and try to understand why to the 20th century, those one hundred years seems to so many the moment of glory in all equestrian History.

www.horsetravelbooks.com

28. Horse Power Supreme

Never in European history had horsemanship been the means to conquer so much wealth and political power as in the 19th century. 'Equestrian Dynamics' that had become the touchstone of Europe's Industrial Revolution would in that century become instrumental to maintain the delicate political balance between the Western powers. The difference between victory and defeat was intimately connected to the civil and military horsepower of Europe's leading nations. In South America ten new equestrian nations were formed, and in North America, the pounding of galloping hoofs would shape Mexico, Canada, and the United States. European Empire builders carved up Africa and Asia and everywhere horses and equitation were the means of gaining political and economical leverage.

The roaring of Napoleon Bonaparte's cannons in the battles of Marengo and Hohenlinden inaugurated the 19th century. With these victories over the Austrians, France began its continental supremacy in Europe and extended its domains by successive battles – Ulm, Austerlitz, Friedland, Eylau, Essling, and Wagram – conquering the lands from Naples to Warsaw and from Lisbon to Vienna. (After Caesar Napoleon was undoubtedly France's greatest Italian warlord. No ethnic Gaul could have united the country around the same grand ideal. De Gaulle, the greatest French general ever (six foot five inches) tried but gave it up with the celebrated comment – "Nobody can unite a country that makes 265 types of cheeses.")

In Europe's expanding economy the horse was the motor for circulating all agricultural and manufactured products. It furnished horsepower to move the barges along extensive channels; in the cities, the horse distributed the beer, the milk and the Lord's daily bread; horses also pulled carriages, couches, cabriolets and tilburis. Equus Caballus was the axis of the urban commuter service. In Ludgate Circus, in the first half of the century, horse drawn traffic snarls were almost up to modern standards.

Equitation gave speed to national and international mail service, as well as to private courier systems. In the United States, the Pony Express could cover 375 kilometers a day – crossing the American continent from New York City to San Francisco in only ten days! In London and Paris magnificent manège-circuses offered shows of Dressage and were among the great attractions for noble and not so noble audiences. In Astley's Amphitheater Charles Dickens "was enthusiastic for all the paint, gilding and looking-glass, the vague smell of horses suggestive of coming wonders!" Buffalo Bill's Wild West Show toured the United States and Europe and had among its many attractions Chief Sitting Bull,

www.horsetravelbooks.com

the fastest gun at Little Big-Horn, and little sharp-shooting Annie Oakley from Deadwood city who enthralled the city crowds.

In the rural areas the horse tilled the fields, pulled the reapers, threshed the grain and transported the produce to fluvial and oceanic ports for exportation. Western civilization was a grand horse-powered world. In 1872 a quarter of the equine population of the United States died due to a virus epidemic, and left American life and its industry deeply affected. In the 19th century horsepower did most of what electric energy and petroleum would do for the economy in the 20th century. And that's an awful lot.

In military operations the ever-growing artillery cannons were pulled by an ever-growing number of draft-horses. In military affairs light cavalry had strategic functions in attacks, and tactical functions in supporting the infantry. In case of defeat the horse-brigades gave protection to the retreating soldiers and, in the case of victory, did the final mopping-up of the last pockets of resistance, as well as pursuing the enemy's escaping soldiers. The heavy brigades performed the standard European cavalry clashes forming the impossible melee, where flashing sabers would do a good job of hacking off the horse's ears. All cavalry officers came from Europe's elite and the Hussars influenced fashion, the bourgeoisie's mannerisms and were the center of the attentions in elegant balls. Cavalry officers were also an obligatory presence in military parades and diplomatic affairs. The main equestrian sports practiced today began in the cavalry schools and military garrisons of that century. Polo, pig sticking, tent pecking, show jumping and cross-country heats made life bearable for the non-com officers from Capetown to Cawnpore.

Great cavalry feats and greater strategic blunders made head-lines of living legends like Marshal Ney 'the bravest of the braves', Hodson, Murat, Garibaldi, Kitchiner, Nicholson, Gordon, Roberts, Cardigan, and Waterloo's champ, the Duke of Wellington. All these horsemen were household words in the powerful European horse-driven culture.

The 19th century was also agitated by the daily conflicts of the British Empire and her multiple colonies which produced some notorious equestrian conflagrations. Some of the most amazing adventures happened in the Crimean War culminating by the surprising victory of the British Heavy Brigade which, outnumbered by 1 to 50 by the Russian cavalry, held the Balaclava front until the arrival of the Light Brigade, and the charge to the 'valley of death', the ensuing carnage and court-martials. As everyone knows, the 'Charge of the Light Brigade' became the most extraordinary feat of heroism, or the greatest tactical blunder, in the history of the British or anybody else's arms. During the insane charge against the Russian cannon Marshal Bosquet, a French officer, was overheard muttering below his field glasses *"It's magnificent but it is not war!"*

www.horsetravelbooks.com

In the Franco-Prussian war Germany's bid as a continental power, led by the State of Prussia, was unequivocally decided at the battle of Sedan. This famous cavalry battle was to be Napoleon III's personal Waterloo which ultimately led to the victories of German horsemanship all the way up to the Olympic Games of Athens.

Oh, and there was also the last British colonial wars – the Boxer Rebellion and the Boer War – which ended in the 20th century because with Gordon in Sudan, the French in the Upper Nile, and the situation in Nigeria there wasn't room for them in the Foreign Office's loaded military agenda. In case you don't remember, in the infamous Boer War fought in South Africa, the cavalry of the greatest empire in the world, after the Roman, was thrashed by a pack of Dutch hillbillies mounted on a handful of Boer nags. But even the impressive string of British military defeats at Kroonstadt, Stormberg, Magersfontain, Colenso and Spion Kop can't compare to the blazing defeat of Valens by the Goths in Adrianópolis, which precipitated the fall of the Roman Empire. The Queen of England died *during* the Boer War, but not *in* the Boer War, so there was no heroic scenes like that of Boudica, *'the warrior Queen'*, hurling chariot-charge after chariot-charge against the Roman invaders of the British Isles. The Boer War turned into a faraway, jingoist, slapstick cavalry adventure that needs to be read because it was just so unbelievably inept. The venerable Winston participated in it as a war correspondent and reported the daily foot-dragging, paper-shuffling and corruption-soaked details in the London Morning Post. But, of course, in those times cavalry made everything look magnificent.

By the end of the 19th century the world's great equestrian powers had reached their zenith and the 20th century was saluted as probably being an even more glorious version of the one gone bye. But now, just you wait and see what the 'naked apes' whiz-bang brain was capable of scheming in that appalling century. You won't believe it. Don't miss the next part of your book.

The 19th century seemed to many as the summit of the fifty centuries of Homo Faber and Equus Caballus' common History. It was the stage of some of the greatest equestrian adventures of the Western world. Its wars and revolutions generated tales, heroes and myths of such magnitude that the poor Academic Horsemanship of the 20th century suffered from a severe inferiority complex; an identity crisis, which only began to fade in the last decade of that century. But, with the help of neuroscience and computer wizardry, the best of Western Horsemanship is yet to come.

www.horsetravelbooks.com

II—IN SEARCH OF THE CENTAUR

1. An Auspicious Beginning

The 20th century was hailed by the world as a bigger and better edition of the nineteenth. The Industrial Revolution was thought to be definitive and nobody could imagine that the next hundred years would be the crossing point from an industrial to an electronic age and that this would change the way riches would be produced and life would be lived. "The horse is definitive but the automobile is only a passing fad," predicted the Michigan Savings Bank president to his investments customer Horace Backam, who planned to buy shares of the Ford Motor Company, a new corporation formed to manufacture 'horseless carriages.' This optimistic opinion was emitted in 1903 when the 'old horse world' was opening another century for 'business as usual.'

At the dawn of the 20th century the great equestrian empires of the world, Britain, Germany, France, Austro-Hungary, Russia and Turkey, felt as safe and sound as the Pyramids in Egypt.[31] As the new century was chimed in, *the extent of British power had never been greater*, wrote one passionate English reporter.

In 1901, after the death of 'The Mother of Empire,' Queen Victoria, Edward the Prince of Wales, conveyed in a magnificent eight span state coach, was acclaimed on his way to open his first Parliament by cheering crowds. In 1902 Edward was crowned King and departed on an international tour of pomp and equestrian circumstance that included visits to Lisbon, Naples, Rome and Paris – all festooned with glittering military parades and equestrian super-shows.

At the dawn of the twentieth century horses and equitation were as 'in' as cell-phones and private jets today. In the rock-solid Austro-Hungarian Empire Franz Joseph was promoting memorable High School performances in his centennial Spanish Riding School in Vienna. At that time horses and riders dominated sports, military strategy and the glittering ceremonial rituals of the Great Nations – and cavalry officers added glamour to society events. The horse was also the motor of urban transports and in London a horse-drawn coach was more expensive to hire than a motorized taxicab.

But a 'revolutionary high-performance car' had just been made for the Consul General of the Austro-Hungarian Empire! 'The appearance of this striking new car is quite unlike a horse-drawn carriage,' announced one excited reporter, and the wonderful contraption was named after the Consul's daughter Mercedes.

---

[31] Eighteen years and a World War later only the British Empire was still on its feet.

High performance? Striking new car? Something odd was definitely going on in the 'old horse world.'

However, in 1902 horse-drawn fire squads were still used to fight the blaze that gutted the Barbican in London, and the tour of Buffalo Bill's Wild West Show was a powerful crowd-puller. In 1903, a time when scandalous parties were in fashion, the dinner on horseback thrown by the American millionaire C.K.G. Billings at the Sherry's in New York, was an affair in which the nabobs ate, drank, and chatted all night mounted on their horses and the event was 'well commented' in the next day's tabloids.

To possess a 'motor' – an automobile – was more of an extravagance than an indication of good taste. His Majesty, King Edward, owned one of those 'Mercedes' cars, which he mostly used for picnicking in the countryside. It was practical to carry his great lunch basket. On official duty he would ride a horse or a coach, as decency and protocol demanded.

But, in 1903, Henry Ford formed a motor company in America and the next year Mr. Rolls and Mr. Royce started a partnership to sell their cars under the name of Rolls Royce in London. Something odd was definitely underfoot in the 'old horse world.'

"The airplane is an interesting toy, although of no military value", declared Marshal Ferdinand Foch, a French cavalry officer and the future commander of the Allied forces in the First World War. In homage to the novelty, English cavalry officers invented a new sport – aviation pushball – that was hotly disputed with four horsemen on each team handling tennis rackets, a tennis ball, and with a goal on each side of the field (a remarkable sporting feat by any standard).

During World War I the belligerent nations summoned their best cavalry officers to pilot the newly invented aircraft, because horsemen were considered to be the only 'men' with the courage and the ability to 'tame' the dangerous flying machines. The most notorious case of a successful horseman-pilot was that of Manfred Freiherr Richthofen, a German cavalry officer, who commanded the 11th Squadron of Fighter Planes – also known as The Flying Circus. The Red Baron – as Richthofen was to be known – became the greatest aviation ace ever, with eighty allied planes shot down in combat! When he was finally downed in the Battle of the Somme, a British pilot commented dryly: "I hope he roasted all the way down" (so much for corporate feeling).

Soon Neuroscientists will explain to us that the neurons of the horseman's brain, wired to cope with the uncertainties of a horse, will give him 'an edge' to operate the relatively fewer operational uncertainties of a machine – even a flying machine. (Don't miss the third part of this book *Odyssey in Science*).

But, the future was not catching up at the gallop — it was coming around the

www.horsetravelbooks.com

corner in a jet plane. In 1901, fifty-four years before Bill Gate's birthday, Marconi had demonstrated the viability of uniting the Globe through a telegraphic apparatus, and this was the birth of a technology that will probably change the life on this planet as much as the invention of equitation had done in antiquity.

Now let's hear the opinion of the 'Intelligentsia' of the day about the inventions that would transform the world: "The radio has no future," declared the Royal Society's former president, Lord Kelvin. "What can this company do with an electric toy", said the Western Union president – William Orton – as he rejected Graham Bell's offer to sell him his money losing Telephone Company.

Charles H. Duell, a specialist on inventions, affirmed categorically, "Everything that could be invented has already been invented."

"Man will never reach the moon, regardless of all future scientific inventions," professed Dr. Lee De Forest, a radio pioneer, barely one year before it actually happened.

"There is no reason for any individual to have a computer at home," avowed Kenneth Olsen, founder of Digital Equipment in 1977.

"Television has no way of holding any consumer market for more than six months – people will be bored to sit looking at a plywood box every night", foresaw 20th Century Fox's CEO Darryl F. Zanuck, in 1946.

"In the future computers will weigh, maybe... only one ton", prophesied Popular Mechanics in 1949.

Nobody believed in the future.

A few years later, Norbert Wiener alerted that, "While the Industrial Revolution changed society, the Computer Revolution will change the very nature of the changes."

So, just as 'equestrian dynamics' had accelerated human speed and technological progress in the past, the computer technology is also a qualitative phenomenon, which is now changing the very nature of the changes. However the 20th century, which would be shattered by all kinds of catastrophes, crises, uncertainties, ideological, economical and social collapses, began with an unshakable trust in itself... and in horses.

In 1910 the London papers warned 'that Britain could face a serious shortage of horses should war break out. The National Horse Supply Association was told that 170,000 horses would be needed immediately on the outbreak of hostilities, the same number being replaced every six months.' There was no business like horse business.

In Europe horseracing was a predominant matter in peoples lives. The elite bred the horses and the commoners gambled on them. Fearless horsemen and determined amazons were galloping in the best prose and romantic poetry of the time. In his book *Ulysses*, James Joyce's characters discuss intensively the pro-

www.horsetravelbooks.com

bable winner of the Ascot Gold Cup that would take place in Berkshire on the afternoon of June the 16th, 1904. Would the winner be Maximum or Zinfalder, or Scepter, or perhaps the outsider Throwaway?

In *Madame Bovary*, Flaubert had Emma (the adulteress) dreaming of being kidnapped and tumbled in a coach at the gallop by her lover Rodolphe Boulanger. Horses and equestrian scenes gave color to romances, operas and circus presentations. But in 1908, Ford's new Model T, now rolling smartly off the assembly line, was hailed as 'a motor car for the great multitude'. (Aha... are horses and equitation to die out from social life?)

But in the beginning of the new century to be equestrian was to be modern, though there were also serious horse related urban problems: in London, a Member of Parliament warned that the city would soon be buried under a mountain of horse-dung! In New York the streets were daily cluttered with 150,000 horses pulling coaches, sedans, tilburys, gigs and a host of other rattletraps that, naturally, provoked some collateral damage on 5th Avenue and the neighborhood. A sea of dung, myriad potholes, and dead horses made for colossal traffic jams. During dry days in London, Berlin, Paris and New York a fine layer of manure dust would descend and cover the buildings and passers-bys' overcoats.

And in 1913 the automobile's in-built stupidity provoked the first notorious auto-related tragedy in the world. In Paris, as Isadora Duncan's sons were being driven home from a visit to their father, the car stalled on an uphill gradient. When the chauffeur got out to crank the engine the dumb beast began to roll backwards and plunged into the Seine. The children and the nurse were lost. Twenty-four years later Isadora's unreliable Bugatti broke her neck when her flowing scarf got caught in a hind wheel! In those times people had no idea of the tragedies that the new conveyance would cause in motor related accidents.

In 1916, the Ford-led automobile revolution had already produced vast social changes in the United States and the construction of hardtop highways, garages, and filling stations were doing almost as much to stimulate the economy as the war-boom. In that year an American car dealer commented to a prospect buyer "an automobile beats a horse and buggy any day. It's quicker and it's cheaper." At the dawn of the twentieth century, a group of enthusiastic American scientists, in an article published in Newsweek, hailed the development of the automobile as a 'clean and efficient form of transport.' As my reader of the dot com generation may attest to, forecasting the future is not and will probably never be among the exact sciences.

But in the opening days of the old century, philosophers, artists and scientists were making incursions into the disturbing universe of the human mind. Sigmund Freud was working to unlock the secrets of dreams and physiologists were searching for the source of life. How will all this affect horses and equitation?

www.horsetravelbooks.com

Let's try to find the sobering facts.

The 20th century saw much suffering, as have all ages of great technological renewals. After thousands of years of 'horse power' the Computer Age superseded the Mechanical Era, and this technological upheaval has caused, and is still causing, a great number of victims – now on a global scale. But, the first casualty of the 20th century's new technologies was undoubtedly horses and equitation.

2. The Centaur's Last Stand

In the second decade of the 20th century, it became clear that the old society, the old political system, and the old horse world had to go. In the new economic model, electric energy and petroleum would substitute horse muscles. For commuting, even the ridiculous bicycle, horror of horrors, was more practical than a horse, and in warfare airplanes proved to be superior for spying on the enemy. After six thousand years of decisive contribution to the social, economical, military and mental development of the world's civilizations, horses and equitation quickly withdrew from the international scene to inhabit faraway places, where modernity had not yet come or nostalgia had not yet departed.

If you examine pictures of the big capitals of the world, photographed during the first two decades of the twentieth century, you will find that the city traffic had a few isolated automobiles bobbing amidst a sea of horse-drawn vehicles. An advertisement by the Lincoln Motor Company published in 1928 announced that 'To ride a pure bred, agile, docile horse and feel it obey, without hesitation, the most sudden demands, instinctively understanding the horseman's will, and to make it gallop and suddenly stop, with only a light pressure of hand or foot – is an identical pleasure to that of driving a Lincoln automobile.' This ad obviously indicates that, in the third decade of the century, the emotions of horsemanship were still sufficiently vivid to attract customers to buy automobiles!

But this multi-vehicled scenery changed radically in the photos you see after the third decade. You'll notice that, in the streets of Chicago, Liverpool, Frankfurt and Lyon a few vehicles of animal traction are lost amidst an ocean of automobiles, trams and electric buses. In all major capitals, electric buses were fast substituting mule-trolleys.

"There were trucks, tramways, electric buses, advertisement lights, street clocks, neon lights, radios, motorcycles, telephones, tips, posts, chimneys... There were machines and everything in the city was only machines", complained the Brazilian poet Mario de Andrade about the City of São Paulo in the 30's. (He was lucky to have departed in the nineties.)

It was around that time that the British Royal family and cavalry horses were demoted to mere decorative office, both in war and peace. During Great Britain's military reorganization, which started in the last years of the thirties, the Hussars of Enniskillen were one of the last cavalry regiments to be mechanized. In a touching photograph, published in Life magazine, you see a young ornate cavalry officer giving a light farewell kiss on the nose of his departing war-horse. The world without horses? What was the future coming to?

But in no other country was the military reform faster than in the United States of America. By the summer of 1940 all cavalry brigades had been

www.horsetravelbooks.com

automated. Even Custer's 7th Cavalry, which had been entirely refurbished after the unfortunate accident under Sitting Bull's steamroller, suffered the indignity of being transformed into a helicopter unit! (Maybe to enable the troopers to make a faster departure from Greasy Grass when they hear the war whoops.)

Caprilli's forecast had proved correct – the military usefulness of cavalry had come to an end and the Second World War was essentially a mechanized conflagration. However, amid the scenery of destruction of the Great War, Life magazine also published a peep into the future of horses and equitation: the participants of the annual Aldeham hunt, led by Major Sir Jocelyn Morton, dressed in red tuxedo and black helmets pursuing – tally-ho, through the ruins of a bombarded English village — a red fox! "The unspeakable still in pursuit of the uneatable," Oscar Wilde would spitefully have exclaimed. "A horse culture, will be a horse culture, will be a horse culture," would the 'great bard' have replied in turn.

But in 1942 the German army wobbled along the 3 thousand kilometer Russian front, pressured by attacks of the red infantry, artillery and horse brigades. These cavalry offensives were to be the last equestrian assaults to have a victorious participation in a major war.[32] But the end of the warhorse was not to come – it had already happened.

Let's have a look at the last scene of the lifestyle that the horse had afforded Homo sapiens for sixty centuries of fruitful coexistence. A dramatic sight that lops off, with a single blow, the participation of Equus Caballus from mankind's civilization process, leaving humans alone in the chilly company of machines.

September 1, 1939 – Hitler's design on Danzig unleashes German armory and assault troops on Poland that surround the city of Kutno. The Polish war minister orders an immediate attack by Poland's magnificent cavalry against the 'Huns of the Third Reich.' The daring Polish hussars and their noble warhorses, charge the enemy line with bared chests, manes to the wind, pointed lances and sabers, proud fluttering banners – in the manner that cavalry had fought throughout fifty centuries of civilization. Suddenly, above the deafening pounding of the galloping horses, a thundering sound like a long and intense roll of death-drums is heard along the German lines. The fire of panzers, mortars and machine guns destroys – with one long murderous volley – the whole Polish squadron.

Dead are horses and horsemen – on the earth the slaughtered Centaurs.

---

[32] The Pentagon's most celebrated tactic in Afghanistan was its deployment of small groups of special-ops commandos to ride horseback with Northern Alliance forces and call in air strikes using handheld lasers and target spotting binoculars. The combination of high-tech gadgetry and the speed, agility and silence of good mountain horses made these commandos irresistible.

www.horsetravelbooks.com

Finished is the Equestrian Age and the Centaur's era of military supremacy.[33]

In the 20th century transports and commuter systems had reached such skyrocketing speeds that horses and equitation, its forerunners, were discarded like a burnout stage of an interplanetary rocket. With a specialized machine to facilitate all areas of human needs, what will the future reserve for horses and equitation?

---

[33] Many similar incidents surfaced after World War II, some set in Mongolia, others in Russia, Yugoslavia and other parts of the war theater. I set this sketch in Poland as a way to pay homage to this country's long-standing equestrian tradition.

3. A World Without Horses?

"The horse has disappeared from modern life because it has become unnecessary and its future will depend on how much modern man will continue to desire the unnecessary. This book is in reality a book of memories". With these dramatic words Harald Lange and Kurt Jeschko ended their book The Horse Today & Tomorrow? *published in 1972. Poignant sadness of a lost world had worked into the mid 20th century's horse people, and this book sums up the mood that prevailed in those dreary times.*

The 20th century was not, of course, the first time in human history that the horse world had faced a crisis. In the 14th century, after one of the worst onslaughts of bubonic plague in Europe, when England's population decreased by 50%, horse breeding and the horse market were greatly affected. And in the 16th and 17th centuries, after the invention of the coach, the practice of horseback riding greatly diminished. (Sedentary people have always fancied cars.) Wars and revolutions has also taken their toll on horse breeding with the destruction of property and the theft of breeding stock, perpetrated by hundreds of conquering armies. But, the real difference between the crisis of the past and the crisis of the twentieth century was that for the first time in history, horses and equitation were definitely believed to be doomed! As Ford's 'vehicle of the multitude' had finally taken over human transportation, nobody could see what further use horses and equitation would have in the future of mankind.

From the equestrian point of view the twentieth century started full of zest and zeal for horses and equitation, but this mood waned fast after the first two decades. We could divide the equestrian cycles of the century in four phases: 1900/1925, zest and zeal; 1925/1940, waning interest; 1940/1950 eclipse; 1950/1990 moderate crescent. (The next equestrian upswing will start in the first years of the 21st century, when the understanding of the biology of equitation will rapidly change people's view of the horse and the intellectual and physical importance of riding, though a hundred years overdue.)

General Decarpentry, who from 1933 to 1947 acted as a dressage judge for the International Equestrian Federation, published *Equitation Académique* in 1949. This work, written during the eclipse, is regarded as one of the few classics on equestrian literature written in that century, and in the book the author frankly exposes his worries about the destiny of equitation and dressage. In the foreword E. Schmidt-Jensen writes, "The eclipse in the interest of equitation as an art form, formally so illustrious in France and reflected through a rich and important literature, was a reason of great worry and disappointment to General Decarpentry".

In the introduction Decarpentry himself writes – "This book is an attempt to remedy and revive this literature to the modern equestrian community." (As you can see his tone reminds us of la Guérinière's preface in his book 200 years before.)

General Decarpentry was a member of the 'Cadre Noir' in Saumur and a disciple of the methods of D'Aure, Baucher and L'Hotte. The General was considered to be one of the last great masters of equitation – a species, which in that bleak age, was considered to be on the Green Peace list of creatures on the verge of extinction – such as the Blue Whale, the African Dingo and the American Bald Eagle. In mid 20th century, Academic Equitation besides being practiced with the eyes on the rear mirror was obviously thought of as being in the process of extinction. But why should this be so?

After World War II, and the horse's loss of military status, the survivors of the old equestrian establishment started to re-build their world as it had been before – in the 'good old times'. In other words, most of the 20th century was lost in the attempt to rebuild the old equestrian order that couldn't fit the pattern of post-modern society. Almost 40 years were spent with the fumbling attempt to fit a medieval key into a photo-electronic slide door!

No one seemed to look for solutions for a 'new horse world' where equitation could fit into the lifestyle of riders who had homes to run and jobs to hold. For this reason the horse still carried the public image of its old role: the universal transport; the powerful weapon; the seat of the noble; the mythological beast that most inspired human imagination. And then we are really faced with a paradox – everybody knows that more efficient vehicles now do modern transportation; that in order to wage war deadlier weapons exist; that with the advent of democracy the remaining nobles tend to drive democratically around in automobiles; and besides that, in current times, the place of mythology is in CD encyclopedias and video games.

To ordinary city dwellers, what are horses really for? In much of the 20th century horses and equitation suffered from a severe 'marketing problem' known to professionals as a 'blurred image.' With the end of horse transportation public opinion could not fathom what other purposes horses could be good for!

So, how should we answer the pessimistic Socratic question – 'all the things I can do without' – posed by Harald Lange and Kurt Jeschko? Will man continue to desire the unnecessary to live? To reply to that and other such questions we could paraphrase Newcastle and his sarcastic rebuttal to the wags of his time, or we could answer by posing other questions.

What is necessary and unnecessary to people in the world of cyberspace, telecommunications and robotics? Is art necessary? Are books necessary? Is a trip to Paris necessary? Are sports necessary? Of course, all these thing are definitely 'in' for whoever can afford them.

www.horsetravelbooks.com

The Centaur Legacy

But especially sports will be open to everyone, everywhere, because, sport is in fact older than culture itself. It is a physiological need to most healthy people. In case you haven't noticed, sports have stealthily spread their influence at a greater rate than electronics and have conquered vast new territories on a national and international scale. Why?

Not counting the explosive Balkans, the burning Middle East and some African hot spots, the lasting state of peace among the great powers has turned sports into a fine opportunity to establish national sovereignty and make people proud of their country. There is something in sports which transcends the immediate necessities of life and gives meaning to bold action. A game is an exercise in self-control and of group control indispensable to the individual. Sports have a biological objective, when testing the physical and psychological limits of the individual, besides having a profound aesthetic character. For this reason it sparks passion, and the capacity to stimulate, fascinate and excite is the reason for its universal practice. Nothing substitutes the tension, the joy and entertainment of a game.

Johan Huizinga[34] puts it well – "For many years I have had the growing notion that it is in sports and for sports that civilization appears and develops. Sports started before civilization and if civilization fails us, we can still have sports". (Don't miss *Sport is War by Other Means* in the third journey of our ride.)

Horses and equitation have ceased to be the hub of industry, commerce, and the path to military glory. Nowadays horsemanship belongs to the world of dreams, of leisure, of victory in sports. This is one empire where the sun will never set. Horses and equitation have retired from their military role and a new age has started: the Sporting Age. And you, modern rider, are not the last survivor of a dying breed of horse people – but a pioneer of the brave new world of biologically sound equitation. Mark my words – the best in Western equitation is yet to come.

---

[34] Johan Huizinga (1872-1945) a Dutch historian and dean of the university of Leyden was noted for his work on the history of Middle Age Culture. We will visit his treatise on games as an important element in culture in the forthcoming chapter *Equus Ludens*.

www.horsetravelbooks.com

4. The Centaur Spirit Lives!

After having invented a great number of cars over a more than three thousand years time-span – carts, chariots, coaches, carriages, buggies and innumerable other horse drawn vehicles – about one hundred years ago Homo Faber, urban and sedentary, finally managed to build the vehicle of his dreams! This new conveyance was able to function without a horse! The advent of the 'horseless carriage' was hailed as an extraordinary contribution to world progress and the horse was of course declared irrevocably obsolete. But today equitation is once more on the upswing and new generations of horse people are forming in all developed nations. Why?

The invention of the automobile was hailed as the end of the Equestrian Age because everybody knows that it is much better to drive a car than to be caught in the rain on horseback. As to this, everybody is absolutely right. The invention of the automobile broke definitively the dorsal spine of horse transportation, just as the telegraph robbed Butch Cassidy and the Sundance Kid of their livelihood.[35]

With the end of horse communication, it really did seem as if the usefulness of Equus Caballus had come to an end. But why were equitation and equestrian sports reborn exactly in the developed nations, the first to decree their demise? Let's look into this.

After World War II, won by the grace of God and mechanical science, the horse was also found to be on the casualty list. It is said that in the fifties even some buckaroos in America were starting to think that pickups looked prettier than horses!

But surprise! In Europe, in the early fifties, the first signs of an equestrian revival could be seen timidly blossoming among the debris of the Great War. During the European reconstruction, in many countries, a discrete comeback of horses and riders could be noticed. In England, equitation grew so fast that the government had to start sending out vans with professional farriers to teach people how to shoe horses. After the Great War the blacksmith of yesteryear seemed to have gone with the wind.

In the seventies, the city was consolidated in the urban pattern known to us today. All buildings had elevators, all radios had transistors and all apartments had televisions. The mechanical world had become electronic and the city streets, once clustered with sweaty draft-horses, were now congested with polluting automobiles. Instead of the deafening din of cart wheels on the cobble-stones and the swearing of foul mouthed cads, city streets had been transformed into an

---

[35] As the telegraph was the first means of communications where news traveled faster than horses, the news of Cassidy's train robberies spread faster than he and his buddies could make a safe getaway.

www.horsetravelbooks.com

infernal roaring of motor-cars and the honking of neurotic drivers – the same road rage, missed appointments and late deliveries; the post industrial version of the age old traffic-snarl. The fine haze of horse dung on dry days had turned into a dark cloud of pollution all day. The big city that did not get along well with horses had also shown its incompatibility with automobiles!

But already back in the seventies, the automobile started to lose its aura as the all-time symbol of social status (the 'vehicle of the multitude' could obviously not retain for long its image of the ultimate status symbol). In the 90's new environmental activists deplored driving as an anti-social activity, the physical restrictions on car access were on the rise, and the social cost of driving frowned on.

Besides that, the last technical innovation to come from Detroit had been the automatic transmission – way back in the forties. Since then, the auto industry had stuck to the same old recipe trimmed with different icings. The color, the shape and a myriad of small details were advertised with great pomp as 'major breakthroughs' in automobile engineering. But, as we shall see, the automobile that was invented to substitute the horse was also destined to be the main tool for Equus's resurrection. As horses proved to be irreplaceable, horse and auto made their peace and became allies. And this is how it came about.

Back in the seventies, in the high-rise city, dwelt a dispersed tribe. In the chests of many urban men, women and children a heart was beating with a different rhythm: the cadence of the galloping horse. Deep in the unconscious mind of Homo the soul of Caballus had survived – and was starting to give signs of life.

Babies were born and before they learned to speak they would point to the pictures of a horse with great excitement. Small experiences with horses as a child would linger as sweet memories of the adult. Tack shops, horse books and horse films fascinated people of all ages. Horses were talked about on airplanes, at conventions, social meetings, saunas, tennis courts, cocktails and hotels. The horse traveled in daydreaming minds and inhabited the nights of the horseless riders. And then at last something new happened.

In the eighties, highways, viaducts, tunnels, bridges and turnpikes sped up traffic to over 150 kilometers an hour, which allowed city dwellers to populate at weekends summer houses, small farms and villages up to 400 kilometers from their home-town. In the nineties, better freeways made people move further away from their workplace – and nearer to their horses. Right now, intelligent transportation systems in America and telematics in Europe, besides many other separate projects, are under way to apply advanced computing and telecommunications to the workaday task of motoring around.

Jobs and housing keep moving away from the hub of the big cities. People's

www.horsetravelbooks.com

motoring habits are fast changing where they live, and the way they live. A modern society is being born and organized around the speed of the car. Not for the speed in itself (a mere thrill to jump-start the brains of lesser primates) but for what speed can bring you. Just like the Asiatic horse herders of yesteryear, Western society has learned that speed opens life to new dazzling options.

With a Pony Club in almost every county, the sporting horse and the leisure horse is once again on the rise. Sedentary people that in the seventies rediscovered their legs and started jogging, in the eighties rediscovered the horse and started riding, and as in the past the new horse-people have begun to reorganize themselves into tribes and to occupy their place in the post-industrial world. The Centaur lives, and a new high-performance horse culture is being born in the West that will probably influence the old horse world in the East, the very birthplace of the Centaur!

Good horses and good equitation are more than status symbols. Great equestrian performances are actually superb displays of human body and mental intelligence. Equestrian sports are played beyond human biological means, but within people's ability to develop physically and mentally to cope with the challenge. Horses are back to stay.

All modern societies have taken up riding. And sociologists, once they become aware of it, can explain why. This great equestrian revival will spearhead a technological revolution where, for the first time in history, riders will be able to understand the psychology of the horse and the physiology of equitation, and learn to ride as our forefathers have never ridden before. Let us open our eyes and minds to the future, because a new Western horseman is about to emerge from the recesses of the Dark Ages.

www.horsetravelbooks.com

5. On Horses and Automobiles

The faster the vehicle the more the driver has to be protected in case of an accident, and the more he is protected the less his neurons will receive information to understand the environmental factors of the speed he's traveling in. When riding an automobile the human brain will become disconnected from the feelings of speed, and over 45-55 kilometers man's primeval brain loses its capacity to cope with the car's un-biological velocity, and this automatically decreases brainwork. But when riding a horse the rider will be traveling at a greater speed than his original motor program, but the plasticity of the human brain can be wired to cope with the new biological task.

The greatest difference between automobiles and horses is the way that human neurons interact with automobiles and horses. The car is built to bring the biggest possible comfort to its driver. The rain won't drench him, the wind won't bother him, and the sun won't scorch him. The windows and doors open at a touch and a computer checks the electric system, the gasoline level and makes a host of other safety operations, to insure good working conditions during the ride. Inside the car the driver is protected by an all-cushioned and air-conditioned cabin, which is outfitted with a telephone, and will soon be enriched by other multimedia gadgets, which are, right now, on the car-makers' computerized drawing boards. Everything is designed to give the driver the agreeable sensation of well being, and driving a car can be almost as comfortable as being at home.

'At 60 miles an hour the loudest noise in this new Rolls-Royce comes from the electric clock,' announced an advertisement back in the sixties. "Cars ought to be entertainment," said Ford's vice president J. Mays in an article in Time. So to the rather stout driver, the landscape outside, framed by the windshield, rushes by in an unreal and distant way, rather like the image on his television set at home. When the CD plays a favorite tune, the driver's feeling of well-being is complete (at a hundred miles an hour – God save the 'naked ape' from his own wizardry) and he will feel as snug as if sitting in front of his television set. And when his senses are cut off from the stimulus of speed, what does Homo's neurons read from this situation? ALL CALM, NO DANGER, and the unwary driver's biochemical system will produce soothing serotonin, a substance that produces a sensation of well being. If tragedy eventually explodes through the windshield, it will catch the driver completely by surprise – as if the television set had exploded in his living room! *Cars are not horses, and the difference is the way human neurons interact with cars and horses.*

The greatest problem with automobile driving is that Homo sapiens' brain probably can't be wired to cope with speeds much over 45 kilometers an hour, and so driving doesn't contribute to mental development. Automobiles are speci-

www.horsetravelbooks.com

fically built not to challenge the human body and mind – and with racing cars the problem get even worse. Let's look into this, and speculate on how Homo's brain works on the fast track.

Car racing technology, for the most part, is monkey-see-monkey-do business. That is, racing crews ape what other crews are doing right to prepare the cars for the racetrack. But even so the mechanics will acquire some specific brain wiring. But not the poor Pilot. The hot-rod racing star is harnessed tight in the cock-pit, where his graphic designed custom paint crash helmet, smart professional nylon racing suit studded with famous logos, zipper-closure pockets, fly front with Velcro tabs, adjustable elastic cuffs and split-fit gloves will help to protect his body and hands from heat, cold and abrasion.

The windshield will safely provide that his senses are also cut away from most of the sound and feeling of speed. The helmet also impairs his eyes, which could help substitute some of the cut-off senses and the poor visibility afforded by the car's body. Actually the pilot can only see clearly straight ahead. The trick on the track is to keep up with the 'pack', and try to leapfrog the front-runner during the laps whenever a chance appears.

The long-runs are quite monotonous and the pilot's brain-work is resumed to try to position himself so as not to be 'frog-leapt' by the car behind him, as he's stepping on the speeder to keep up with the forerunner, while grasping the wheel with stiffened hands. On the turns, in the middle of a corner, the tension grows, but even the action to improve the forward bite of the rear tires when exiting the corner is relatively slow business. The hot-rod-racing star cannot fathom the speed of 300 kilometers an hour so he tackles the curves as a kid maneuvering a joystick – through a very simple visual-motor program. The only strategic thinking he'll be doing is to try to find an opportunity to 'go underneath' the front car, if he can get the chance. Many *whole seconds* will elapse without anything happening at all.

But while the driver's tension from watching his butt and fore is undoubtedly real, the situation is not favorable for strategic thinking and brain development – because the driving ace is not being fed by his senses with all the facts that spark fast actions and trigger fast thoughts. For this reason emotional and physical burnout takes its toll in the ranks of the 'hot-rods.'

While the winner of real physical sports will be elated by his performance, the auto-racing pilot works in an anthropologically modified environment that mostly produces stress. The fast action in car racing comes entirely from the TV commentators who, with great imagination, spew into the microphone the fantastic performance of the tires, suspension, engines, throttles and the dramatic battle of the auto heroes challenging each other's motor strategies!

From the physiological point-of-view car racing cannot really be considered a sport, and a pilot is not a sportsman – it's a media event geared up for public consumption. And all that the driver will get out of the event is the money – when he has a good season.

Let us have a look at some physiological details of this process and try to understand why automobile driving doesn't benefit the human physiology and probably does not concur with significant mental development.

Homo's brain functions in the same way his body does – it has to be fed with a certain number of experiences to stay fit. Neuron connections, which don't get regular exercise, will be disconnected. To maintain its vigorousness the human brain, like the human body, needs a varied diet of interactive experiences – which occurs best when the body interacts with the brain. The more areas of the brain that are connected to cope with the body's sporting challenge, the more intelligent mental and corporal answers the body will be able to deliver in any given situation.

To the human brain, a 'diet' of automobile driving will exercise mostly the viso-hand-motor system (the coordination between the hands and the eyes) – which to the brain would be the same as the ingestion of great amounts of macaroni to the body.

The healthier the sport the more it will challenge sight, touch, hearing, equilibrium and the body's flexibility and movements. A professional pilot will drive with most of his neurons unchallenged – and with time, millions of neurons may be disconnected. So in reality the 'fast-track pilot' is not a sportsman in any physiological sense, but only a man carrying out a dangerous task for the money value. And although automobiles can also be a path to fame and fortune, they are poor neuron stimulators and drivers shouldn't count on turning into great leaders and the catalysts of history, like yesteryear's horse people. (A motorcade doesn't create the same glory and majesty as the equestrian pageant. The sight of a general waving a machine-gun from a Land Rover would not produce the same emotions as a field marshal on his war-horse flourishing his saber. Cars are not horses in any circumstances whatsoever.)

Humanity has known intuitively, for thousands of years, that equitation is somehow connected to leadership. Not only as a symbol of leadership, but as a means to achieve leadership. Homo sapiens is probably right. In equestrian sports all human senses have to be connected to help strategic split-second action, and sharper senses makes sharper thoughts. Horsemanship challenges the activity of body and mind in a fast, tough, but otherwise equilibrated way. As brainpower is what determines the position of the individual in human hierarchy, due to its unique capacity of stimulating the senses to cope with the powerful physiology of Caballus, equitation can be turned into the catalyst of leadership.

If modern neuroscience is on the right track, the past elites – the nobles –

www.horsetravelbooks.com

promoted the increase of their hard-brain wiring and those of their heirs, mainly through equitation. So to the general stimulation of the human neurons, car driving cannot be compared to horse riding. As we now know, modern cars are built to under-stimulate the neurons of the driver, with tragic daily consequences. A driver is physiologically an immobile person being conveyed from one point to another. A rider is an active person in full control of all his senses, which are continuously being challenged by the horses' powerful sensory motor system.

Automobiles are not horses under any circumstances – though autos and horses are here to stay. They fulfill different roles in human affairs and are complementary in a fast living society. (See more in *Why Ride*, in Part III).

The technology developed by neuroscientists in the last decade of the 20th century could have detected the amount of brain wiring that separates horse riding from car driving. That is, if the specialists had got wise to it. The other day I read that scientists are working hard on a project to produce the 'exercise pill' – a drug that can make the sedentary pill-pusher burn calories without doing any exercise at all. What happens to brain and muscles that get no maintenance, the sedentary scientists didn't comment in the article.

In all advanced societies, marked by rapid technological changes, the equestrian sports will certainly be recognized as highly efficient in sharpening the psychophysical power of men and women, and helping people cope with a fast-moving world. A thesis that has been proved time and again in the many dramatic chapters of history when sedentary societies had to deal with the fast thinking, fast-riding, nomadic horsemen, and cavalry proved to be the road map for survival. Therefore from this chapter on we'll be hot on the trail to use modern science to crack the ancient Centaur enigma: what is equitation really about?

www.horsetravelbooks.com

6. Scientific Equitation in the 20th Century

The mounted nomads of Central Asia, with no scientific background, were probably the best horsemen the world has ever produced. In the West, Xenophon, propelled by Greek scientific insight, published his equestrian knowledge in book. Pluvinel, influenced by the advance of science in his time, raised equitation to the level of art. Baucher in the mainstream of the Industrial Revolution wrote a manual with a precise mechanical language. Federico Caprilli didn't write much, but in his time humanity had produced men like Ivan Pavlov, Charles Sherrington and Sigmund Freud, who started unveiling the world of physiology, biochemistry and psychology – life's three dimensions. Caprilli elevated the horse from an object to an individual – which was in perfect harmony with the advance of science in his time. But what was scientific equitation really like in the 20th century?

In the West it is said that science is knowledge obtained from systematic observation and experimentation. For this reason most city-bred scientists have had great difficulty in understanding the natural knowledge of 'primitive' people, who obtain knowledge, not through methodical research but simply by being a natural part of the ecological machinery.

"As the world is governed from the cities, where men are detached from all forms of life but the human, the feeling of belonging to an ecosystem is not revived," wrote Bertrand de Juvenel.

Another problem which has obstructed Western understanding of the high-tech environmental knowledge of primitive societies is that, as our science is considered a 'secular ideology of progress,' an Indian possessing a 'stone age' technology is not supposed to know more about nature than a scientist. Yet, for example, in Brazil a Kayapó Indian has a deep and sophisticated understanding of the environment he belongs to, and will thrive and raise a family in a rain forest where Claude Levi-Strauss, with his wealth of scientific knowledge, would roll up and deliver his soul to the Lord!

All this is to say that the steppe nomad and his horse formed one integrated biological mechanism – tuned to perfection by centuries of bilateral learning (man learns equitation with horse and horse learns equitation with man). A Scythian rode his horse as Dame Margot Fontaine dances ballet or Leonard Bernstein conducts an orchestra – with the knowledge of the soul. For this reason the horse people of the steppes didn't need books to pass their equestrian knowledge to the new generations. Everybody in a nation on horseback started to learn about horses and riding as soon as they were born.

Now, in sedentary societies, organized into hundreds of specialized professions, learning to ride is a complicated matter. As, unfortunately, many urban children get the idea that eggs come from refrigerators and horses come from stalls, books have to be written about equitation to teach each new generation how to understand a horse's individuality, motivations, and especially how to ride it. As McLuhan once said "The restructure of work and the association of men was shaped by the fragmentation of technique, which is the essence of the machine technology."

This can be exemplified by the assembly line, where every worker knows to perfection his part of the job, but no worker understands the whole operation. And this is the problem that has haunted scientific equitation up to the 20th century: if science has not yet unveiled the riddle of the equine psychology and physiology, and if a person has not grown up in intimacy with horses, how can one understand the horse's priorities, which constitute an important part of the psychology of equitation?

But even so, in the past, some great masters tried to give a 'scientific' direction to their work. Pluvinel, without going into scientific details, is clear about the advantages of rational, or 'scientific' equitation as he called it, as opposed to stupid, violent and irrational methods. As we know, throughout the 19th century, science progressed with great celerity and topics which were distinct matters started to converge, creating new syntheses and new discoveries.

But today, Baucher's writings echo as a purely mechanic description – *"Each movement is the consequence of a specific position, which in its turn is produced by the forces transmitted by the rider. The horse in our hand will be no more than a machine in waiting."*

Baucher, the great saddle artist, sound like James Watt describing his steam engine. Equitation was transformed into a metaphor of mechanical science and the masters, great horsemen in themselves, were unable to teach their art through their writings. *"There have always been fewer outstanding men in the equestrian art than in other arts"*, wrote L'Hotte in his book *The Quest For Lightness*.

And one of the reasons for this is that the old manuals on riding and their methods are practically useless to people who cannot ride. The classical author's description of equitation covers only the mechanical part of what really happens in equitation – and that's not even the most important part. We'll talk more about this matter in Part Three of this book.

In the twentieth century, Caprilli elevated the horse from a mechanical object to a sensitive individual – which is a monumental leap over past psychological blindness. By incorporating the horse's sophisticated mind to his riding philosophy, suddenly he and his horse became *partners*. To him, the union of the senses and the harmony of the gestures were important factors to good equitation. Caprilli's techniques were adopted with great success and Academic Equitation was ready for a spectacular leap from the Mechanical Age into the era of

www.horsetravelbooks.com

Neuroscience – when warring human apes once again bungled the century!

Early in the twentieth century the world stopped worrying about horses and all scientific research in neurology, psychology, and chemistry – subjects that nobody in the horse-world had associated with equitation – was concentrated on solving the social, political and economical problems which abounded in that tormented century.

Suddenly, the horse was decreed as obsolete as the quill after the pen, the pen after the fountain pen, the fountain pen after the typewriter, and the typewriter after the word-processor. Ardent horse lovers stopped caring for their horses to live a torrid romance with the automobile. One third of the world's population was raked with the fever of communism, which was only cured with massive doses of consumerism. And for their entertainment sedentary people turned to electronic gadgets of all sorts. After the War God was dead, Marx was dead and the Centaur was listed among the missing.

With the discrete comeback of equestrian sports in the fifties, the 'horse enthusiasts' fell back to the old academic equitation of the past, as medieval society turned to the Greek classics during the European Renaissance. The Mechanical Age was restored to power as if the technological revolution had never happened. Therefore it must be said that scientific equitation of the twentieth century was no more than a blurred daguerreotype of the unscientific equitation of the 19th century. The best riders could do it, but they still didn't know why it worked. And this is where I propose that we start the search for the Centaur.

Let us begin an equestrian revolution by breaking some of the dogmas of the Mechanical Age which still survive in many grottos of ignorance and prejudice and which have blurred Western riders' vision of advanced equitation. Let's start a trend of thought on horsemanship whose principles can stand up to the light of modern science. As Abie Hoffman once said 'Sacred cows make the best hamburgers!' Saddle up and let's be off!

7. Horsemanship on the Rise

During a chess game, on board an ocean-liner, Einstein once asked his opponent if he could see any movement on the chessboard. When the puzzled friend answered no – the pieces were immobile – Einstein, with his customary sense of humor, reminded his friend that everything was in motion: they were both on board a ship going to Europe, the earth was moving around the sun and spinning around itself, and everything was part of the universal gravitation! Horse people hardly notice in their time that equitation is not static and that it is, or should be, in permanent evolution. This realization is of great importance for horsemanship to become more efficient, beautiful and fulfilling for horse and rider.

Riding in the ancient sedentary civilizations consisted of being transported by an equid – donkey, mule or horse – in the daily comings and goings, with no concern about ethics and aesthetics. Besides transporting people, equids also carried water, firewood, foodstuff and other heavy loads. Riding was a synonym for transportation, and a rider was nothing more than a passenger mounted on a horse to save his weary feet. Throughout the centuries, sedentary horse passengers watching or hearing about nomadic horsemanship thought that by adopting equitation, they could also form invincible cavalries and excel in the art of vanquishing their neighbors. However, as they were city dwellers and hadn't been brought up with the horse herd, these people didn't understand the nature of the horse and so would never learn to ride a horse as completely as a nomad of the steppe.

When ancient civilizations transformed the horse into a weapon of war the systematization of horsemanship in book form became a necessity for city-bred soldiers to learn how to ride by 'the book.' But military equitation was mostly resuméd to the simple view of a horse carrying a load. In early medieval Europe, in the first stages of the development of cavalry, the soldiers were transported to the battlefield on horseback where they would dismount and do the fighting on foot. Such military troops were called *mounted infantry*. Only in later centuries would Europeans develop horse soldiers capable of wielding arms effectively from the saddle.

With the invasion of England by William, King Harold's 'housecarls' arrived at Hastings on their horses, but dismounted and fought on foot. And William, who had set sail in Normandy sporting the crude handle 'The Bastard,' fought on horseback and sailed back with the smart sobriquet – 'The Conqueror.' William's use of the horse, as you may verify on the Bayeux Tapestry, was more advanced than Harold's, so the fruits of victory was his to pluck. The slow step-by-step domination of the various neurophysiological links that leads to good horseman-

www.horsetravelbooks.com

ship can be said to be the secular ideology of equestrian progress that conducive to highly sensitive, or high performance equitation.

Modern equitation is based on the preliminary need of uniting of the horseman's sensory-motor system with the horse – of transforming the human load into an interactive part of the equestrian performance. But most riders seldom fully assume this proposition. As we know, Western horsemanship owes Captain Federico Caprilli the adoption of this concept in show jumping a mere 100 years ago. But Federico Caprilli's revolution was unfortunately interrupted by his untimely death at the age of 39.

Tod Sloane, an American jockey and a contemporary of Caprilli, also made a contribution to modern equitation by introducing to horse racing a 'new' style of riding; by standing up in the stirrups and crouching over the horse's neck in a seemingly precarious position he obtained great speed from his horses and broke new records in horse racing.

"The essence of Tod Sloane's crouch was to bring together the horse's and the rider's center of gravity. Since at full gallop, the horse's center of gravity is well forward, the jockey's must be also, a position achieved by riding very short, the seat right off the saddle, body lying almost parallel to the horse's neck, arms stretched forward. Besides advancing the rider's gravity center to conform it with the horse's, this seat reduced wind resistance and, by freeing the horse's loins, allowed him to reach well forward with his hind-legs, thereby lengthening his stride" – wrote Charles Chenevix Trench about Tod Sloane's riding style, in his most excellent book *A History of Horsemanship*.

All the literature that one comes across compares Sloane's riding technique with the principles of mechanical dynamics – the uniting of the horse and horseman's gravity center, better distribution of the rider's weight, decrease of the air impact, etc. The horse world has not yet adopted the laws of aerodynamics to equitation.

Now, I will ask for your permission, faithful traveler, to take a step in a different direction: the jockey standing up in the stirrups receives the air pressure in the same way that the principle of aerodynamics act on an airplane's wings; the air passes over the horseman's back and under his body, creating a differential pressure similar to that which annuls the airplane's weight and makes it fly. Or, yet – the air which passes over the jockey's body accelerates faster than the air that passes underneath him, increasing the dynamic pressure on his body and decreasing his body weight.

In the case of the airplane, when it reaches 'lift off speed,' the plane is 'sucked' into the air and flies. In the case of the racing horse galloping at about 70 kilometers per hour the speed doesn't allow it to fly, but the principle of the pressure differential will act on the jockey's body, drastically reducing his corporal weight. So, the jockey's crouched half-standing position on the horse's back makes him partially *airborne*.

"In the 21st century scientific equitation there will be more things between heaven and earth, than supposes your vain philosophy", would Gabby Hays[36] have said to Shakespeare were they riding in the same heat.

Now let's ride ahead on our journey of discovery to search for more scientific facts behind advanced horsemanship. Let's backtrack in Western scientific thought and try to solve the millennium-old Centaur enigma that has haunted man from the beginning of time: how do human and horse blend into one galloping being? A trip that may take us to the very source of the ancient symbiosis: the union of Homo's and Caballus' nervous systems and inner feelings – where the human brain in perfect cooperation with the equine body, blends effortlessly into one biological unity. Come on, we can do it!

A scientific concept of equitation is important as a means of establishing a biological paradigm for the rider. No amount of reading and riding will ever help the novice rider to understand equitation if he or she believes that the horse is nothing more than a vehicle. The first lesson of anyone who wishes to learn equitation should be to understand that a horse is not a car under any circumstances. To lead the horse into high adventure requires a complex task of communication and negotiation where all human senses will come into play with the horse's sophisticated neurological system. Above all, high performance equitation is a revolution of the mind.

---

[36] Publisher's note: Gabby Hays is the ultimate side-kick. His toothless, goofy grin, rumpled clothes and mild confusion added comic relief and humor to many cowboy movies. He even has a magazine devoted to him! The author uses Gabby as a *nom de plume*.

www.horsetravelbooks.com

8. In Search of the Centaur

On the trail to a biological understanding of equitation we must start by following the tracks of the early 20th century scientists who were searching, themselves, for the third dimension of life – the 'magic puff' that animates living beings – which had never been understood in the past. And from there, with the help of contemporary science, pave the way for modern horsemanship to be performed in all its dimensions – the harmonious fine-tuning of man's and horse's psychology and the complete connection of their sensory-motor system – the way equitation must have been performed in man's remote pastoralist life.

In the first part of this book we sped through the horse's sacrifice to work, toil, and military glory, and naturally the day and chapter would come when science would make it possible for riders to make better use of their horses – in body and mind. And to support such an auspicious circumstance a startling scientific truth has recently emerged: Homo has much more in common with Caballus than was ever dreamt of before, and neither is man as rational as was formerly thought, nor is the horse as irrational as considered it in the past. I think this should be further investigated. So let's turn the horses and ride back to the 17th century to see where our misunderstanding of horses was definitively consolidated.

René Descartes, a contemporary of Antoine de Pluvinel, was the product of a society that was beginning to feel the impact of mechanization. In his day clocks, automatic puppets and mechanical games and gadgets amused the nobles and bedazzled the bourgeoisie. As you know, a common mind marvels at uncommon things and an uncommon mind marvels at the commonplace.[37] So, in his treatise *Discussion of the Method*, Descartes wrote that "animals are mere machines lacking in soul and mind" – a thesis which was to become the basis of the future mechanical psychology, which explained all animal behavior through mechanical dynamics. But science began to progress rapidly in Baucher's time and even faster in Decarpentry's 20th century. New research supplied a vast amount of scientific data, which led to some complex concepts about the natural world – such as Einstein's Theory of Relativity and Quantum.

There was also the prodigious development of biology concerning the human and animal physiology, the evolution of the species and genetic heredity. All this scientific progress helped to create a new discipline – molecular biology, a subject where physics, chemistry and genetic theories linked in a way that would be extremely important for the future. (And though nobody thought of it, also for the

---

[37] Can't remember who said this – if anyone knows please send the editors an e-mail for the next edition.

future of horsemanship.)

However, in the first decades of the 20th century, a strong belief that every phenomenon of life may be reduced to chemical and physical laws gained great scientific support in academic circles. This may be said to be a simple two-dimensional view of life. Jacques Loeb, a Prussian, was the leader of this 'new mechanical school, an extension of the old Cartesian mechanistic physiology. Loeb emphatically announced his point of view in a treatise entitled *The Mechanistic Concept of Life*. This two-dimensional theory was totally accepted throughout the twenties.

But ten years later, Loeb's theory would clash with the view of some English and French biologists who were trying to find relations between behavior and the physical organization of the different parts of an organism – the *third dimension* of life. To study the isolated parts of the body, for them, was not enough.

"Living systems are not merely groups of molecules, but rather systems with a highly organized behavior", argued the Anglo-French scientists. These two viewpoints – Loeb's two dimensional 'mechanistic concept' and the three-dimensional 'integrated,' 'holistic,' or 'systemic concept' – are of course both present in the studies of the nervous system – but Loeb's theory was only a piece of the life science puzzle and not even the most important part. The scholars who adopted a mechanical or materialistic conception of life were inclined to reduce everything to simple physical reactions.

But another academic reaction was already forming to dash the mechanistic conception of life. The 'systemic concept,' adopted by English and French researchers during the 1950s, considered the nervous system as a whole. This view led to the perception of a difference between the nerves that *go* to the spinal column and the ones that *come* from it. This was science's first clue to understanding the neural-motor circuit in highly developed mammalians, like Homo and Caballus. (Even if you think all this palavering rather weary, don't ride away! You'll regret it in this life and the next!)

The scholars who adhered to the 'systemic concept,' made an interesting study of the reflex system (responsible for such involuntary actions as the beating of the pulse, of the movement of the knee when it is hit below the kneecap and other (unspeakable) physiologic reactions). And the Russian Biologist Ivan Pavlov had already made remarkable approaches to this matter. (Although the discovery of the reflex responses of his drooling dogs was purely accidental, this doesn't diminish the scientific breakthrough.)

Pavlov began to interest himself in this subject when he noticed that during the routine of feeding the dogs in the laboratory, the animals began to salivate at the ringing of a bell before the presentation of the dog biscuits, or whatever. Aha! thought Pavlov, and with careful research he concluded that not only was an automatic learning process taking place, but also that the learning was being made by the organization of *chain reflex* actions: the repeated use of a certain stimulus created a determined response – a classic example of a conditioned response – which the researcher could produce at will.

If you are still with me, shrewd reader, you are naturally beginning to see the consequence of all this for equitation. With his extensive research, Pavlov discovered the important relation between the nervous system's behavior and physiology, a *non-mechanical concept* of the science of life! (A shame that he didn't exchange ideas with his contemporary – General Alex François L'Hotte, the most learned horseman of his time. The two might have found something.)

Our man Sherrington published in 1906, one year before Federico Caprilli's death, a treatise *The Nervous System's Integrated Response*, that incorporated the more than reasonable opinion that there are three levels in which we should study human and animal behavior: the physical-chemical, which makes people and animal action look like 'machines;' the psychological, in which the neurological processes converge to form a thinking and perceptive creature, and thirdly a mind-body relation. In the horse world Caprilli was then introducing an argument surprisingly in accordance with the new philosophy and recognizing the horse's individuality and capacity for intelligent interaction with the rider!

We have now finally arrived at a crucial crossroads in the scientific history of horsemanship: until the 20th century, science had only understood the two dimensions of life – the physical-chemical part of physiology – which gives the animal the machine aspect, which led people to ride horses as if they were machines. The psychological part, the third dimension of life, in which the neurological process forms a thinking, sensitive, and perceptive creature, was unknown. The phenomenon that subordinates all vital functions to the brain through the nervous system had also been unknown.

With Sherrington's and other physiologists' research to unveil the working of the nervous system, the thread to life's third dimension had at last been found! But unfortunately when these neurophysiological discoveries were being disclosed to the world, Western society began to lose interest in equitation, and so the relation of this extraordinary scientific breakthrough – the essential mechanism of life – was never connected to equitation. (If many people are not liable to understand what they can see, imagine what they can't see.)

Now, with the great equestrian renaissance occurring all around the world, it is time to retake the studies of the neurophysiology of equitation and to make a spectacular leap in Western horsemanship. With this knowledge all riders can learn how to distinguish the mechanical and physiological aspects of equitation and understand their specific roles in the *neurophysiology of equitation* and the part played by the horse – the long lost links, which lead to biologically sound horsemanship.

What Caprilli instinctively felt, and tried to explain to his generation, is that the horse possesses a developed neurological constitution and therefore is perfectly capable of taking decisions on balance and other relative matters. Therefore a horse should not be trained as an 'irrational object' (mainly because irrational objects cannot be trained at all), but as a true sporting partner. For the understanding of the psychology and physiology of equitation modern scientists have a lot to offer, and therefore in the forthcoming chapters we'll continue following in their footsteps.

9. The Miracle of the Physiology of Equitation

To blend into one biological unity Homo and Caballus must form a psycho-neurological cooperation chain. The interaction between the human's and the horse's nervous systems may be achieved in different degrees of intensity depending on the difficulty of the task and the quality of the equitation displayed. It can be said that equitation is a miracle of psycho-physiological coincidences that common-sense would consider far-fetched – because only a miracle would allow two creatures programmed by nature to accomplish very different vital tasks to unite their physical resources and carry out the same chore, with the high degree of efficiency verified in some equestrian performances. Let's stop our horses and wonder at the workings of this miracle.

The utilitarian cooperation between humans and animals is not a novelty in itself. Since times immemorial Homo has formed symbiotic alliances with animals that could help him to survive his daily drudgery and sometimes even assist him to prosper. In India elephants did, and in some places still do, the job that cranes and tractors do in most other countries. Throughout the world oxen pull plows, donkeys transport burdens and in nomadic societies, the dog, the reindeer and the camel have been used for centuries for the transport of passengers and cargo.

All these tasks performed by animals demand some degree of psychological and neurophysiological cooperation between the human masters and their animals. What differentiates equitation from the other uses of domesticated animals is the intensity of the neurophysiological bond necessary for Homo and Caballus to accomplish a good day's work on the ranch or excel in a sporting competition.

But man and horse have such great biological differences that at first sight horsemanship would seem to be an unbelievable accomplishment. The theoretical impossibility of equitation has been confirmed by every occasion in which unhorsed cultures were confronted for the first time with the sight of mounted warriors. The pedestrians would view the fast riding horseman with the same disbelief as if you, on a Sunday morning, saw a chimpanzee flying over Central Park riding on a real live hippopotamus headed for the Yankee Stadium.

However, if we look carefully into the biological phenomena of equitation we can distinguish how most of the psychological and anatomical characters Homo sapiens and Equus Caballus ultimately fit in. If the differences between the two species are colossal, the similarities are even more so.

For a better insight into the anatomy of the Centaur let's start by examining humanity's main physical contribution to equitation: the human body. To start with, humans are divided into three parts – head, body and members, just like the horse. But the human body, unlike the horse's, has great flexibility and human limbs have a great capacity of inter-coordination. The 'naked ape', before putting airs on, was programmed by nature to move from branch to branch propelling himself with the arms and using his legs as pendulums to impel his jumps. This is probably from where human flexibility evolved.

Therefore, one of Homo's main contributions to equitation is his great sense of balance, two legs to grip onto the horse's rib-cage, which also produces some of his most important riding cues, and great ability to coordinate his arms independently from the use of the legs, useful to produce auxiliary communication cues. And even humanity's un-dynamic vertical body posture is an asset that allows the rider to rapidly sway his gravity center to follow the horse's shifting gravity center when altering speed and changing gaits.

Besides these positive features humans, throughout their evolution, have developed a great number of movements, which in some people can be schooled into a chain of riding reflexes, and a large number of sensor-nerves and specialized muscles that allow for an excellent coordination between eyes and hands.

And now please note one more amazing feature: remember those two awkward floppy feet, which were tenderfoot's weakest points in the African savanna? They fit perfectly into the stirrups (you can look all over the animal kingdom and never find so perfect a foot to fit a stirrup!) which will give the human body the 'ground feeling' necessary to coordinate his equilibrium to near perfection. In horsemanship, every part of the human oddly shaped body can be turned into an asset! Equitation can turn Homo sapiens—nature's ugly duckling—into Andersen's beautiful swan! (There's no limit to the wonders of the Lord!)

And, from the neurological point of view, humans have developed one fundamental organ that makes possible the miracle of equitation: a multifaceted brain capable of establishing enormous sequences of relations between the natural phenomena which transformed Homo Faber into an extraordinary 'learning machine.' Notice then, my traveling companion, that good equitation springs firstly from the rider's ability to learn from the horse and not from teaching the horse – a seemingly hair-splitting difference that urban-agrarian civilizations have had a hard time understanding. People have mostly thought that any upstart rider should 'aid' the horse to be a horse, and heaven knows from where they got that mixed-up idea.

Hominids, throughout millions of years of evolution, many of them spent up in their green haven, developed a series of successful unconditioned or involuntary reflexes that were passed from one generation to the next. Humanity's other behavioral characteristics, conditioned by environmental stimulus, are developed during the individual's life-long learning process.

In equitation, these two types of natural reflexes – the unconditioned and the conditioned – must interact with the horse's unconditioned and conditioned

www.horsetravelbooks.com

responses, which were also acquired in the natural habitat under environmental pressure. All equestrian movements are started by the rider and instantly sensed by the horse's receptor nerves and acted upon by its motor system. That is: the horse's chain of riding reflexes is initiated and sustained by the rider's chain of riding cues. It is a feed-forward and feed-back system connecting all human and equine sensory motor responses. The decision to initiate or maintain each link of the chain of riding reflexes, and the capacity to monitor the horse's chain of riding responses, may be said to be the rider's principal role in equitation. Now let's see how this fits in with the horses' role in equitation.

Compared to Homo sapiens Equus Caballus is an animal with notable morphologic and functional differences. As we have already seen, the horse's body and motor system were developed to attain instant speed, under any circumstances, and over any type of terrain. The horse's skeleton has a construction similar to the human frame; however it is conveniently horizontal in order to be more aerodynamic. On the other hand, the horse doesn't have the same agility as man.

"There is a common misconception that the horse is a natural jumper with a flexible and supple body capable of maintain balance at all gaits and speeds," writes R. H. Smythe in his book *Horse Structure and Movement*. "The reality is very different. In fact, of all athletic animals, the Horse has been provided with a very inflexible carcass of great bulk and weight, which is solely propelled by the limbs, over ground and through air, as so much ballast. Apart from the trunk providing anchorage for muscles responsible for the movement, its weight is a serious handicap to rapid and flexible progression, like a motor car with a very heavy chassis," asserts the author.

Further on R. H. Smythe continues: "Now however on firmer surfaces, it balances on four feet of small diameter, whose foothold is made even less secure by the addition of iron shoes. These feet have to support and balance the animal on the flat, up and down hill, when landing after a jump and as brake to slow the pace. On corners they hold balance, often at great speed, and must even contend with the interference [by the rider] that may occur, normally, in competition. A closer examination might suggest the specie is quite unsuited for all these tasks. However, whatever limitations, the horse of today manages to carry out most of them very well", concludes Smythe.

Note, fellow traveler, that the analysis of Mr. Smythe is entirely mechanical – that is, from a mechanical point of view the horse is not considered suited for equitation. What overcomes this limitation is the horse's third dimension – his sophisticated nervous system, which Mr. Smythe doesn't mention in this book.[38]

---

[38] R. H. Smythe is also the author of another book, *The Psyche of the Horse*.

www.horsetravelbooks.com

In conclusion: just like man, the horse's most important contribution to equitation is his nervous system, which enables the animal to do all the things that mechanical laws say it is not capable of doing! So, the age-old adage 'no foot no horse,' very popular in the mechanical age, should be changed to 'no brain no horse,' which is much more in accordance with the equestrian reality revealed by contemporary neuroscience.

And now a surprise! The horse's inflexible carcass so well described by Mr. Smythe is in reality the main element to favor equitation! Look here: if the horse had the flexible body of a cat, not even John Travolta would be able to ride it. If it had the loose skin of a dog, no man could safely sit it. If it had flexibility of a tiger, the human nerve-system would be unable to connect with it and form a smooth chain of riding reflexes. Under any of these circumstances there would be no way for horse and rider to join their physical constitution and form a working partnership.

The coincidence of Homo sapiens and Equus Caballus' harmonious chain of reflexes is also a factor that allows for their good neurophysiological merger. The entirety of the horse's natural motor system can be used in equitation and can be fully controlled by a rider who has had his brain wired for this purpose. Such a person, like the horse, can instantly spring from thought into action and coordinate the changes of speed and direction through an automatic chain of riding cues clearly understood by the horses' nervous system.

If we consider the psychological structures of Homo and Caballus there are also inconceivable coincidences which help produce the miracle of equitation. Feelings such as fear, pleasure, trust, curiosity and determination are part of the horse and rider's emotional make up – which are greatly responsible for the success of their psychological understanding and the merging into one single biological unity. And perhaps other as-yet-undiscovered 'neural waves' or magnetic fields may also play a part in the spectacular ability to coordinate the sense of direction and speed verified in every great equestrian performance. In this century, the growing understanding of neurophysiology will surely bring us more information about this. (Don't miss the third part of this book.)

After this brief analysis of humans' and horses' anatomy and behavioral coordination we may conclude that God's remarkable 'learning machine' and his astounding 'running machine' possess a number of extraordinarily matching psycho-physiological characteristics. These two superior animals are possibly the only creatures on Earth who could merge their behavior and form a third organism, more efficient than the two partners individually. It is a miracle of physical coincidences, which has worked for thousands of years and, for better or for worse, has given our civilization much of its present outlook!

---

www.horsetravelbooks.com

The capacity to interact with the horse's complex nervous system, which produces a 'neurological feedback chain,' demands instantaneous reflexive cues from the rider to produce incessant reflex responses from the horse. To administer the performance of a horse – an animal on the average at least six times heavier and three times faster than man – is an enormous challenge for the 10 billion nervous cells that compose Homo sapiens cerebral, cerebellum and brain system. Fortunately neuroscience can now give us some interesting data from which we can infer the complex brain wiring needed to connect the equine and human motor programs for advanced equitation.

10. Neuroscience Reveals the Principles of Equitation
With the involuntary help of Dr. James Rooney

In our first view into the inner workings of the Centaur we'll have the guidance of the research of an extraordinary man: Dr. James Rooney, the famous veterinary, who in the seventies performed research on the nervous system of the horse and found the very first clue to unraveling the Centaur enigma: why a horse obeys subtle cues rather than forceful methods of riding, which are always self defeating.

In our journey in search of the biological foundations of equitation it is advisable, more than to consult the existing manuals, to search for new facts in modern science which might help to extend the limits of human perception of the horse's psychology and physiology. To contribute effectively to current knowledge it is not sufficient to translate, transcribe and agree with the existing bibliography. To help bridge the troubled waters between old equestrian practices and a modern view of equitation it will be necessary to do a lot of riding, reading and researching. So let's continue to struggle along this narrow, stony and dimly lit path that may lead us to disillusionment or perhaps to enlightenment.

But before plunging into a more advanced philosophy of equitation, let us analyze the horse's neurology, which permits equitation in the first place and is well described in the research done by Dr. James Rooney, Professor of Veterinarian Pathology at the University of Pennsylvania.

This amazing study, published in Equus Magazine, in 1974 under the title *Riding Reflex Chains*, made a most important revelation: the horse reacts to the cues of the rider through a chain of natural reflexes called 'classical conditioning responses.' Through systematic schooling, the horse learns to associate the rider's cues with the movements required, and more: through training the horse automates these cues so profoundly that they obtain the same involuntary response value as unconditioned stimulus (as we involuntarily blink in the face of danger or salivate when confronted with a fried chicken). If you have a good relationship with the horse and perform biologically correct cues, under favorable circumstances, the horse can't help but obey!

This extraordinary information, coming from scientific research, has the power to establish a new and solid basis for a complete merging of the horse's and rider's sensory motor-systems – which should lead to biologically sound equitation, which was probably instinctively practiced by the Central Asian steppe nomad, after thousands of years in close communion with the horse.

These facts also agree with Caprilli's revolutionary postulations, euphemistically called the 'Italian' or 'forward seat'. And due to the facts already discussed, only show jumpers adopted Caprilli's new philosophy – but for a

www.horsetravelbooks.com

general lack of scientific knowledge his ideas about horsemanship in general were not understood and later mostly forgotten.

From Dr. James Rooney's research it becomes clear that there is much more behind equitation than the use of hands, legs, seat, spurs and whips – the notorious 'aids' which when used as a means to 'drive' the horse forward or to restrain its movements provokes the often-seen shows of poor horsemanship. To obtain a fluent performance, as Dr. Rooney aptly explained, it is important to understand the motor coordination of the horse and to be able to take advantage of it. And from this point on, the rider must learn to unleash a chain of riding cues, which will spark the horse's chain of riding responses – a neurological process similar to, though infinitely more complex than, working on a computer and not at all like the laws of conventional mechanics, as most people thought in the past, and many people still believe today.

As we have just seen, to obtain a certain reaction, or a chain of movement, the rider will have to stimulate the horse's automatic responses (even if he or she doesn't know about them), which is a 'program' of the nervous system that the animal uses in its natural life. These responses must have been organized in a sequence of 'riding reflexes' throughout the horse's schooling. This means, unequivocally, that equitation is a process of bilateral learning. The rider must learn how to stimulate the horse's chain of 'riding reflexes,' and the horse must learn to respond to the rider's code of riding cues.

Let's follow further along in Dr. Rooney's footprints. "The stimulus of the horse's natural reflexes is linked to two points in the horse's spinal column called cervical dilation and lumbar dilation. The cervical dilation commands the movements of the front legs of the horse, and the lumbar dilation coordinates the posterior legs. These two points are enlargements of the central nervous system, which begins in the brain and runs down the spinal cord to the horse's croup and tail. When stimulated by the sensor nerves, this sets the chain reflexes that determine the horse's gaits – the walk, the trot (or the running walk in multiple-gaited horses), the gallop – and also all changes of direction and speed," explains professor Rooney. But how does this fit in with the rider's reflexive cues that must trigger the horse's responses?

Humans have a similar reflexive system – or motor program – that allows a person, for example, to walk and talk at the same time, or to drive an automobile and simultaneously discuss yesterday's rotten soccer game with a friend, while maneuvering the steering wheel with his left hand, handling the gearshift lever with the right hand, stepping on the clutch with the left foot, accelerating with the right foot, while checking with a glance the oncoming traffic through the rear-view mirror, without missing a word of his story.

This chain of actions can be set in motion without the need to concentrate

www.horsetravelbooks.com

directly on each independent movement (on the contrary: if you concentrate on the details you will surely mix up the performance) and all these mechanical operations can be performed while the driver's intellectual focus will be on the details of the awful soccer game. We could name this sequence of movements the chain of 'conditioned automobile driving reflexes' – and they are also organized through a certain time-consuming learning process (and if you haven't practiced properly your car will show it).

Now take a deep breath and let's examine a practical example of the operation of the 'Chain of Riding Reflexes': with a slight pressure of the legs you induce the horse to start moving. The horse's receptor nerves located along the rib-cage, which transmit an electric signal to the cervical dilation, capture this cue, indicated by your legs. From there, a nervous stimulus flashes back to the protractor muscle of the legs liberating a chemical substance that makes the muscle contract and move the limbs forwards. The neurons that move the legs are called motor nerves. To set a regular walk in motion, this process is repeated alternately, with the protractor muscles impelling the legs forwards and the retractor muscles pulling the legs backwards, and so on. The whole series of muscular reactions, that determine the coordination of the gait, is called 'reflex action.' (Attention please: do not even think of skipping this page because this part of the neurophysiology of equitation has the same importance for horsemanship as Aristotle's observations of the 'motions of the spheres' had for physics! So hang onto your hat and follow the story.)

Well, you must have noted that the horse's receptor nerves feel the cue of the rider's legs, and send the information to the lumbar dilation, which transforms the command into a reflexive response movement – which start the chain of walking movements. This means, as Dr. Rooney explains, that the protraction and the retraction – the forwards and backwards movement of the horse's legs – the action of walking, trotting and galloping – may be governed exclusively by the cervical and lumbar dilation, without the direct participation of the horse's brain in the process; which means that the action is automatic.

But how and why can the horse's brain interfere in the automatic coordination of its movements?

Dr. Rooney continues: "In an area of the brain, below the cerebellum, there is a group of nervous centers responsible for the coordination and adjustment of these movements. They determine the gaits [walk, trot, and gallop] and determine the sequence in which the legs will move." For example, if a horse is out grazing, and for some reason decides to walk in another direction to have a drink, the new course decided upon will be repeated automatically until he decides for another change of speed, a new change of direction or to stop altogether. Each new decision is taken with the help of the brain, and the continuation of the act is

www.horsetravelbooks.com

automatically maintained by the cervical and lumbar enlarged nerve centers. Whew!

In my opinion Dr. James Rooney, who is a veterinary, did not go into an important link between Homo's and Caballus' joint performance, the neurophysiology of equitation, because the complete physiological interaction between horse and rider is probably not within the area of the distinguished veterinarian's field of research and the phenomenon is probably not yet part of the curriculum of human neurophysiology either. At the moment the neurophysiology of equitation seems to be a no-man's land to the scientific community. Vets do research on horses and Docs do research on humans and nobody has yet set his or her mind to research the neurological relation that connect horses and humans in equitation that in this work we are calling the 'neurophysiology of equitation'.

For this book I have transcribed the parts of Dr. Rooney's observations that I thought were the most important, in view of the interactive reflexes produced by the partnership of Homo and Caballus. For the time being it will be up to the horse people of the world to try to untangle the equestrian phenomenon that more than any other has been responsible for mankind's history of success and that, in today's ever faster moving societies, will have other important roles in the future.

From now on, in our search for the human role in the Centaur's anatomy, we won't have Dr. Rooney's clear footsteps to guide us, so we'll have to strike out on our own.

The research on the 'riding reflex chain' performed by Dr. James Rooney is to equitation what Kepler's law of planetary motions was to astronomy. Dr. Rooney gave us our first scientific insight of an entirely unknown world: the inner workings of the horse's equestrian performance – a universe traditionally inhabited by myths, mistakes, conflicting opinions, cruelty, stupidity and plain charlatanism. The understanding of the 'neurophysiology of equitation' will help modify the ancient mechanical riding methods and horse training techniques which have been in use since the Middle Ages. Let's move along the trail of scientific discoveries and see if we can find more traces of the Centaur.

www.horsetravelbooks.com

11. Organizing Equitation into Conditioned Responses

In its private life the horse uses its brain to activate its natural gaits, but not to sustain its action after starting a chain of movements. In the horse's equestrian life it is the rider who must spark and sustains the animal's 'riding reflex chain' and determine the direction that the horse will take, the exact speed and how far they should go. To achieve a more precise equitation, it is essential to understand how this system works. Let's be off and see how the Centaurs do it.

When the horse is well schooled and competently ridden, the experienced rider can easily assume the decisions for the changes of speed, direction and maintenance of the gaits (which is basically what equitation is all about). Or, in other words: the rider's mind substitutes the horse's decision-making and activates its reflexive system, which will start the chain of riding responses when the animal's legs begin to move automatically, like an airplane flying 'on automatic pilot.'

The important matter to remember here is that the rider's decisions guide the horse's sequence of movements and are automatically maintained in operation by the part of the horse's nervous system situated in the cervical and lumbar dilation. But the horse is perfectly capable of trying to take matters into its own teeth if something disagrees with its sense of security or with the way the rider behaves upon its back.

For example, if it does not enjoy the ride the horse may decide to go home or it may momentarily forget the rider and try to approach another horse, or simply freeze on the trail in fear of something it sees or hears. At such moments there often arises a dispute between horse and rider for *decision taking*. And this is when the inexperienced person will do all the wrong things – like trying to regain control by using spurs, whip, voice, and angry manners. This attitude will activate the animal's full consciousness, spark its rebelliousness, and trouble will be at hand, which is a film we have seen hundreds of times before.

The experienced rider, on the contrary, will regain command without being much noticed by the horse – the animal will be aware of his soothing presence as he transmits his 'forward' cues through firm but smooth coaxing movements – an attitude which is the attribute of a true leader. If the rider is a reliable partner and has never ridden the horse into trouble, the horse will be persuaded to move forward and resume the enjoyable ride. Therefore, to understand the horse's chain of riding responses is very important for the thinking rider. And thanks to Dr. Rooney's pioneering research people can now finally count on real scientific evidence to supply sound orientation of how to organize their equitation into an efficient code of riding cues, and learn how best to communicate with Equus Caballus, one of the world's most complex animal species.

www.horsetravelbooks.com

Therefore modern training techniques should start with the organization of all equestrian action into a chain of riding responses that must be automated by systematization. This organization of the riding reflex chains begins with the groundwork in which the horse learns how to walk, trot, gallop, stop and change direction, through specific cues emitted by the trainer. The groundwork should be understood as a 'simulated flight operation,' where young pilots learn to fly without the risks of the real action. It is when the young horse learns, step by step, all the riding maneuvers without the risk of the stress and accidents of the real action. The horse, during ground training, will learn the stages of speed and maneuvers administered in a biologically progressive and understandable way, before it receives the rider on its back. Step by step the horse, with his infinite memory, will learn how to move with balance and dexterity in all gaits and in all maneuvers of equitation with a human guiding its steps. (See more about this in Book Three.)

The equestrian discipline that most depends on the organization of the horse's natural reflexes into an extensive chain of automated responses is by a long way Dressage. All the High School gaits, passages, pirouettes and lateral movements, depend on a long training process undergone by the horse and rider to reach perfection in the merging of their senses and to sort out their roles in the mutual riding reflex chain. In show jumping, the approach to the obstacles and the adjustment of the horse and riders to accomplish the perfect height and curvature of each jump, with totally united movements and balance, also requires long training. It could be said that the ideal show jumping technique should be performed with the same view for detail of a Dressage movement.

In western horsemanship (in this case I mean cowboy riding), the pole bending and the three-barrel race, for example, are also performed by automated movements, which depend on practice to attain perfection.

However, for the cutting horse in the cattle pen most cues don't spring from the horseman's brain. The cutting horse's reflex action is sparked by the cow's nervous system. It is a personal duel between horse and cow, where the rider's job is to point out which animal is to be parted from the herd and then cling onto the saddle horn and keep out of the performance, while the horse does the cutting. In this interesting action the horse shows it is able to reverse its natural reflexes: the cutting horse will move with the aggressive lightning reflexes of a predator cornering its prey!

To organize all equestrian action into chains of conditioned responses without causing pain to the horse (because this can arouse its rebelliousness) is the secret of advanced equitation. With this new perception of the equine neurophysiology the old rivalries between the various schooling systems, which have been fought throughout the centuries, should also cease. Because the best system is the one

www.horsetravelbooks.com

that makes the most sense from the equine point of view, and this sensory-motor stimulating pattern can be rationally worked into a system, as we'll see further on.

And now we can also understand why most of the great academic masters, the men that made the history of European horsemanship – Xenophon, Pluvinel, Newcastle, Louis Cazeau de Nestier, Eisenberg, Jean-Elie Ridinger, la Guérinière, Baucher, L'Hotte, Gustav Steinbrecht, Fillis, Caprilli and Decarpentry recommended gentling and training with patience, without inflicting pain on the horse, with short but frequent classes in order not to stress the animal.

"My goal is to work the horse calmly, for a short time, but constantly," wrote Antoine de Pluvinel. "The horse should be returned to its stall in the same good mood in which he left it," advocated la Guérinière. These recommendations were, of course, favorable for organizing the riding reflex chain in horses and riders with more success and less stress. Although I wonder what these masters would have said about biological equitation had they been told about it. To change a deeply ingrained mechanistic methodology for a natural biological philosophy can be a most difficult business.

To organize the horse's 'riding reflex chain' demands knowledge, time, and patience. But this scientific data is certainly great news to 21st century horsemanship that promises to become increasingly spectacular and more satisfying for both horse and rider than ever before. Now let's have a look at a part of the 'neurophysiology of equitation' that Dr. Rooney, as a veterinarian, had no way of going into: the human 'riding reflex chain', which in connection with the horse's chain of automated responses produces high-performance equitation.

12. The Code of Riding Cues

Now that we have ridden the narrow path that led to the neurophysiological bond between horse and horseman, we can proceed on the rocky trail that led to the understanding of how the rider should manage these reflexes by transmitting his riding cues to his partner in a clear and efficient way. Advanced equitation is attained with the perfect adjustment of the rider's cues to the horse's sensory motor-system, and all matters concerning horses and riding should spring from a scientific understanding of the animal's movements, priorities, and habits. If a person is not born with the horse herd, understanding the laws of biology can also lead to good riding practices. Let's follow this lead.

The horse is a great reader of intentions. It has survived for millions of years by the accurate reading of other animals' designs on it – both within its own social order and also from external threat. The capacity for accurately reading the horseman's intentions is probably the horse's greatest contribution to equitation.

As we have seen, the secret of equitation is to induce the horse to respond to the rider's cues, which automatically stimulates the horse's natural reflexive system, without provoking negative reactions. These cues should clearly represent the rider's intention – for the well-schooled horse will, with time, respond to the rider's intentions, rather than to his cues. So, these subtle cues should be biologically logical – which might sound funny but is a dead serious matter.

The cues should stimulate the horse in the same way as the environment activates his mind and senses – basically to give the horse a 'reading' of the rider's intentions so it can answer through automated reflexive responses. The rider's cues should not have conflicting aims: such as using the same cue to obtain opposite responses. For example, using the spurs to back the horse. The firm use of legs and the light use of spurs should stimulate a forward movement, only. The code of riding cues should induce the horse to perform automatic *unconscious* responses.

Now, the word 'induce' means to inspire, to instill, to instigate, to incite, to suggest or to persuade – it does not mean to use force, or to cause pain to the horse – which, as we now know, would be counter-productive, as the horse could choose to get nasty (especially the good ones). Physical punishment arouses the animal's full conscience and it may show its indignation by bucking, rearing and running away – a fantastic show in rodeos but a deplorable sight otherwise.

Of course Robur – Pluvinel's primitive horseman – would endorse, in the case of a rebellious horse, the old Grisonian expedient: a good whipping to exorcise the devil of disobedience from the horse's body – which, for a rudimentary training, will work to a certain degree. But neither this horse nor this rider will qualify to a superior equestrian performance, the subject that we are discussing here.

Let us remember what Xenophon wrote – "What the horse does under coercion is made without understanding, and there is no beauty in that." In modern equitation, which is usually practiced before a crowd of spectators, and may also be aired on television to an ever-increasing audience, the harmony and the beauty of the performance is the most important element of the presentation. A stressed horse, ever in fear of the whip, cannot streamline the beautiful movements necessary to high performance equitation – because graceful movements will spring from the horse's pleasure of moving. Or as Monty Roberts wrote – "If a horse is started off right you should never have to use discipline at all".

To administer the horse's chain of riding responses you have to work with a code of riding cues transmitted by hand-touch, leg-pressure, body-weight and sounds which are alternated, repeated, superposed, but never cease while you are in action – they are not 'aids,' because you are not helping the horse – you are merging your senses with Equus, which is more like a pianist who throws his body and soul into his music, alternating, repeating and orchestrating the notes in a cascade of soft touches on the keys. Much more than your hands you will use all your senses to stimulate the horse's senses into a fantastic chain of smooth unified movements.

Let's analyze a simple example: as you mount, and adjust your position in the saddle, you activate the first link of the horse's chain of riding responses: the animal starts a series of muscular contractions of its legs, predisposing it for eventual action. Then, with a soft pressure of the legs, you 'cue' the horse to move forward at a walk. Then a light leg pressure will start the trotting chain of reflexes. To strike into a gallop you carry out a combination of movements such as a new pressure of the legs, a slight onward movement with your body, a discreet backward movement of the reins, to lightly connect your hands with the horse's mouth – and the animal (schooled this way) will strike into a gallop.

Now you guide it, with a light pressure of the right leg, towards a pole on the left. When the pole is at the height of your left leg you subtly incline your body to this side followed by the touch of the right leg and rein which will lightly press the horse's flank and neck, so the animal (trained this way) will understand your intention and make the curve to the left, naturally balanced. The inclination of the body, the pressure of legs and heel are so subtle that the audience will not notice them.

The capacity of the horse to feel the rider's intentions and cues is fantastic and visually it will look as if the animal commands the action. In high performance equitation, the reins are basically used for softly curtailing the horse's speed – for precise timing – and, most of all, to establish a connection of neural-communication of your intentions to the horse. What makes a good rider is not 'good hands,' but a sensitive attitude that produce a soft touch. (See chapter *The Bit, a Connection to the Mind.*) The rider's legs are the cues for the horse's impulsion and to change direction, or in other words: you produce impulsion with your legs and discretely manage the forthcoming energy with your hands.

But, Dr. Rooney also reminded his readers that it is not possible to teach the horse new reflexes; it is only possible to use his existing repertoire of reflexes, and for which the horse's natural life was programmed. However, all the possible reflexive combinations that the horse offers can be turned into hundreds of combinations and a score of equestrian disciplines, therefore we need not try innovations in that area. The great masters of the future will have Pluvinel's vocation, plus a perfect knowledge of equine psychology and physiology. And that is of course a winning combination. But let's move on to the next challenge – to understand the power of the horse's pleasure in riding.

To a writer, the alphabet, the words, the syntax and all linguistic resources are used to give clarity to the reader. The rider, in his code of riding cues, should also look for the clarity of his communication so that it can be automatically de-codified by the horse. Therefore it is essential to understand clearly how the cues affect the conditioned responses of the horse. If clarity is the author's courtesy to his readers, then clarity of the riding cues is the courtesy of the rider to his horse. And as we are now penetrating deeper into the land of the Centaur I hope that we may soon have a glimpse of these wondrous creatures.

13. The Merging of Homo and Caballus

Greek myth clearly depicts the Centaur as a man with a horse's body. In those distant times Hellenic civilization did not have the scientific reach to probe the recess of the human brain with its trillions of neurons, connected to a nervous system which rules all movements and behavior. And to investigate the synergy of two brains belonging to two different species, working through an integrated circuit of sensory feedback that allows for a perfect coordination of movements and behavior was an adventure of the intellect beyond Aristotle's science. With the progress of modern science and the interface of each subject creating new fronts of research, we may now start envisioning the contribution of 20th century science to the Third Millennium Centaur.

When, some six thousand years ago, the first human mounted on the back of the first horse and rode it, the frontier between the inner-self and the external world of the horse was suddenly invaded. With man placing himself on and above the horse and assuming a position of leadership, Caballus' private world and natural sense of hierarchy was forever altered. But why did the horse suffer this invasion, and how could man control the horse from a precarious position on its back?

The first neurophysiological merging between horse and rider in Central Asia must have begun by the union of the symbiotic partners' gravity centers, so that the two species could acquire total balance in all equestrian actions. Though in ancient sedentary societies like Mesopotamia and Greece you can see on vases, sculptures and bas-reliefs that riders sat much behind the horse's gravity center. In Goya's paintings it is also clear that, due to the incapacity of finding a common gravity center, the Spanish riders collected the horse excessively by pulling the animal's gravity center towards his own.

The complete interaction of Homo and Caballus' nervous systems can now be envisioned through modern neurophysiology. Understanding the working of the horse's nervous system, organized by nature in receiver and transmitter circuits and coordinated by visual, auditory, olfactory and tactile information, the rider can, like a maestro, learn to adjust his motor-system to the horse and conduct the perfect equestrian performance. Just as the ecologically well-adjusted Asiatic nomads probably did in the past (and were scorned by sedentary horsemen who would call the nomads 'natural riders,' which was meant to sound as rough and unsophisticated!) modern horsemen can now, through new scientific discoveries, understand the neurophysiological part of equitation, in which the horse becomes a thinking and perceptive partner capable of successful interaction with a skilled rider.

The old fashioned mechanical equitation, by which the horse is subjugated by

www.horsetravelbooks.com

the mechanical leverage of the bit, and is prodded with spurs and whacked with whips to make it react from fear of pain, may be considered as an aggression to the horse's life. Biological or natural equitation, which implies the understanding of the physical-chemical-physiological facts of horsemanship, should be understood as a reorganization of the horse's nervous system for the practice of high performance equestrian games, which mobilizes the interest of both horse and rider. Now with the guiding hand of modern science we cannot only understand how the horse's neurons work – we can link our synapses to the horse's muscle cycles and become one galloping unity. With this new understanding of the phenomenon of equitation, the neurological systems of horse and rider can be totally connected thus forming a life connected and well adapted combination.

A really good rider is actually a paradox to the horse. At some moments the horse will be unaware whether he or the rider is leading the action, in other moments the rider must emerge as the leader and in the next submerge into the central flux of emotions formed by the intercourse of the two nervous systems, which compose the horseman's intentions expressed by a chain of riding cues and the horse's automatic reflexive responses. The feedback between the two partners' senses travels with the speed of their synapses, the correction of speed or direction of an imperfect movement happens in a tenth of a second and sporting victories are gained by a tenth or even by a hundredth of a second. The Centaur combination is undoubtedly an entity of great complexity.

In show jumping, for example, the horseman's rational mind administers the strategy of the course, the tactical complexities of the obstacles – everything that needs solutions within the space of seconds. From this time fraction onwards, to the tenth and a hundredth of a second, the horseman's mind loses the ability to process the information and his chain of riding cues, connected to the horse's chain of automatic responses, will be automatically performing the chain of riding reflexes stored in their memory during the training sessions. In the space of up to a millisecond all movements are automated into such a fast chain of events that the human eye cannot distinguish the micro-details of the action and the horse and rider who have developed the best sensory-motor coordination – whose interactive and automated reflexes are the most fine-tuned – will present the best performance.

During such displays of perfect interactive performance the rider's intentions are flashed from his brain and travel through his motor nerves to the parts of his body that must operate the riding cues — the tensioning and displacements of the body and limbs, following the horse's rapidly changing gravity center, and by the subtle use of legs and hands cues to indicate the degree of collection and direction. These combinations of cues executed through a code of natural

www.horsetravelbooks.com

corporal language indicating speed and direction are captured by the horses' receptor nerves – present on the skin surface and inside its mouth – and are transmitted through the synapses to the cervical and lumbar enlargements that sends back reflexive responses to the animal's motor system, which immediately complies by performing the correct movement. Each movement executed with perfection may give a sporting advantage of a hundredth of second. Actually, in this fast chain of events the horse cannot distinguish from whose nervous system the cues are springing and will perform as smoothly as if he was acting on his own volition! (Which should be the aim of all well schooled horses.)

In the words of M. de Pluvinel, "If the horseman rides the horse scientifically he should decrease the use of artificial helps until the spectators think that the horse is acting on its own will." And 21st century science agrees with the old master's judgment.

The inspired rider performs on the border of the senses where human intentions become the horse's goal. The great masters of the past knew how to do it, but they didn't know why their methods worked. And for lack of scientific insight each generation produced very few outstanding riders. There were no biological paradigms to be observed and each person had to discover, almost single-handedly, the narrow path that leads to equestrian excellence. No wonder that in this chaotic world the majority would founder in the swirl of misinformation, and in the process ruin their horses. But, maybe all this could have been understood a hundred years earlier, if two important men had met and talked about their work. Let's backtrack into history and imagine an encounter between Dr. Pavlov and Gen. L'Hotte at Queen Victoria's jubilee in London.

www.horsetravelbooks.com

14. Doctor Pavlov and General L'Hotte

Even though the world had entered the era of electric energy, transcontinental railways, gigantic oceanic steamers and was living a troubled romance with mass-production, the closing years of the 19th century are considered to be the climax of Western horse culture. And, as we have seen, Academic horsemanship had reached the pinnacle of international prestige and some of the best horsemen in European memory were in command of the riding schools of Saumur, Pinnerollo, Weedon, Warendorf, and the Spanish Riding School of Vienna. In those years two famous men were working, one with physiological research and the other with the schooling of horses, not knowing the intrinsic relationship that exists between these two subjects. It is tempting to imagine an encounter between Dr. Ivan Petrovitch Pavlov and General Alexis François L'Hotte and the consequences that an animated chat between the doctor and the general would have had for modern equitation.

Fifty thousand imperial troops, coming from all over the British Empire, the largest military force ever assembled in London, paraded through the city to converge upon St. Paul's Cathedral for the thanksgiving service of Victoria, Regina et Imperatrix – for the commemoration of the sixty-year reign of "ole Queen Vicky," as any butcher boy would have explained to the astonished tourist. "Such a pageant with the splendour of appearance and especially for splendour of suggestion has never been paralleled in the history of the world," wrote a mesmerized reporter from *The Daily Mail* of this grand display of the 'Heirs of Rome.' (Obviously the reporter had missed Caesar's Triumph in the old mother country back in 46 BC.)

One half of the procession was led by Field-Marshal Lord Roberts of Kandahar, mounted on his beautiful steed Vonovel, and followed by the Sudanese Horse, New South Wales soldiers, Hussars from Canada, Carabinieries from Natal, camel troops from Bikaner and Dyak head-hunters from North Borneo, the Indian Imperial Service Troops, Hong Kong's Chinese Mounted Police, Malays, Singhalese and Hausa troops from Niger, the Gold Coast and Jamaica, Cypriot Japheth, Turkish horsemen and the famous Indian lancers. The other half of the parade was led by Captain Ames of the Horse Guards, at six foot eight inches the tallest man in the British Army, and looking more stupendous still wearing his high plumed helmet, swelled out with breastplate and cuirass, and astride his tall charger, and followed by ...hey! James, or rather Jan Morris,[39] my historical source, in his or her excellent book *Pax Britannica* doesn't seem to recollect who

---

[39] During the writing of the excellent *Pax Britannica* trilogy the author James Morris completed a change of sexual role and is now living and writing as Jan Morris.

or what came after the gorgeous sight of this splendid horseman!

The two impressive columns of horsemen, magnificently turned out, marched down Fleet Street all day long, waving banners, fluttering handkerchiefs and thousands of Union Jacks, on their way to Her Majesty's Jubilee ceremony.

In those days, a Russian physiology teacher of the German Military Medical Academy was researching the conditioning of dogs. Through his experiments Dr. Ivan Petrovich Pavlov discovered the physiology of conditioned reflexes. And more: that the learning, training and domestication of animals, and humans, are the consequence of organizing all action into conditioned reflexes by the trainer!

It is most surprising that in a world inhabited by splendid horses in the highest degree of schooling, trained by great equestrian masters like General L'Hotte, Dr. Pavlov hadn't even thought of researching Equus Caballus to prove his most famous theory. This could only have happened because Dr. Pavlov didn't see Academic Horsemanship for what it really was: a sophisticated organization of the horse's natural reflexes into a chain of riding responses, accomplished by true artists of equine training.

On the other hand, it is remarkable that General L'Hotte had not realized that his equestrian training was directly connected with Dr. Pavlov's research. As a learned man, it is probable that L'Hotte followed the most important news of the world in the French press. Especially such significant experiments as those of Dr. Pavlov that in 1904 would deserve the scientific community's greatest homage: the Nobel Prize.

Which only goes to show that Homo and Caballus live in a closed society — in a world, how should I say... occult, maybe. Let's see what the dictionary says: *Occult. Adj. Any teaching ministered to a restricted and closed circle of listeners. It is said of the teachings related to occultism, understood by few, obscure, hermetic.*

Exactly! The horse world is occult, obscure, dimly lit and hermetic. Its closed character marks the equestrian community. It maintains a certain magic and occultist aura, as if equitation is a matter exclusively for the initiated. Dr. Pavlov in his laboratory hadn't associate the magnificent horses with his physiological experiments with dogs – and general L'Hotte didn't see any relation between the research accomplished with simple dogs and the beautiful horses that he trained in Saumur, and that his teacher and friend François Baucher had presented with so much success in the manage circuses of Paris.

You can well imagine the progress that Academic equitation could have had if, by a fortunate coincidence, Dr. Pavlov and General L'Hotte had met at Queen Victoria's Jubilee, and animated by the splendid cavalry pageant had struck up a chat about their ideas and work. Let's imagine that by a lucky chance the two eminent gentlemen had been presented by a common friend as they stood, on

www.horsetravelbooks.com

Constitution Hill, watching the grand parade clattering by with all those beautiful horses and gallant horsemen. Maybe they could have started a dialogue like this.

"Dr. Pavlov?!" exclaims the surprised general as he is introduced to the doctor.

"Pleased to meet you monsieur General L'Hotte", replies the doctor with a Russo Germanic slur.

"Dr. Pavlov," says the general, "I just read in the papers this morning, about your interesting experiments with dogs and the conditioned reflex response, as you call it. Do you see any relation between this learning process and the techniques that we use to train men and horses in Saumur, Weedon and Saugur – do you think that...."

As in *Treasure Island*, one man had the map of the location and the other had the key to the treasure chest. General L'Hotte knew how to train men and horses and Dr. Pavlov was beginning to understand the inner workings of how men and horses learn! But regrettably for the old horse world the two masters never met to talk about their life commitments: science and horses.

If the two eminent teachers – the horse-master and the physiologist – were among the thousands of distinguished guests at Queen Victoria's Diamond Jubilee on June 22nd of 1894, they certainly didn't meet, and equitation had to live in a hermetic and pre-scientific world for another hundred years.

www.horsetravelbooks.com

15. On Horsemanship and Leadership

Good horsemanship is chiefly an exercise in leadership. And leadership, as everything else in life, may be exercised in an intelligent or a stupid way. Intelligent leadership produces a high degree of satisfaction for the leader and the led. And stupid leadership is solely held for the leader's personal fulfillment and to his or her inevitable fall from power. Horsemanship is a metaphor of life and the fall from power and the fall from a horse generally reveal a person's incompetence in understanding people and horses. Let's stop our trek for a moment and look at these psychological findings.

Thousands of years ago, Homo Faber's ancestors began to organize cooperation systems that would allow them to accomplish vital tasks for the common survival of the group. In each hominid gathering a hierarchy was formed where the alpha males and the dominant females took decisions concerning the strategy of hunting, the collecting of victuals and the meting of justice. They also decided about strategies for the group's defense to external menaces.

For the same reason wild horses form hierarchies where each animal has a place in the social order. The dominant male is responsible for the group's defense and for the fertilization of the mares and the dominant female helps organize the group's behavior – that is, she will show an antisocial individual the way to the door[40] and may even determine the order in which the horses will drink in narrow watering places, and who will graze in the best spots of the pasture and so on.

When a man and a horse, coming from two social organizations with similar hierarchical structures, join forces to merge into a Homo-Caballus combination, the most important element for the success of this enterprise is Homo's capacity to understand which are his duties as a leader. In other words: to make the horse work willingly with him, it is imperative that man understands the principles that rule the equine hierarchy. For example, Equus has a limited comprehension of the concepts of freedom, equality and fraternity. About this famous human ideology the horse only understands the first and the third concepts.

Considering that identical individuals don't actually exist in nature – that every creature is unique – equality is pure utopia and therefore the horse is right: in equitation somebody has to lead. The hypocritical 'naked ape,' with his natural inclination for demagogy, also knows that there isn't really equality in the exercise of power. For this reason man has invented words such as 'monarchy' for the government exercised by one person and 'triumvirate', for the case when

---

[40] As described by Monty Roberts in *The Man Who Listens to Horses*.

www.horsetravelbooks.com

three individuals share power – but to my knowledge there is no expression to define the power exercised equally by two people, or by all people (because this is obviously impossible, although anarchy, communism and many other ideas have been tried and failed).

So, the first condition for the rider to achieve sporting success is to assume control of the partnership – whether his or her partner is a stallion, a mare or a gelded horse. Under a firm and loyal hand any horse will accept the rider's leadership, because this is the law that governs a horse community. But that is also when trouble might raise its ugly head. The practice of leadership stimulates the best and the worst in human character, as you have probably noticed. Neuroscientists are presently studying how human neurons react to the exercise of power. And the scholars are beginning to understand what determines a leader's success or failure. Let's have a look into this recess of hidden and weird surprises; we might find a clue to the Centaur.

The basic ingredients of leadership are equally valid to govern a nation, to run a company and to ride a horse. If a horse is subjected to tyrannical handling it may be driven to despair and rebelliousness, and will try to topple the government. Contrariwise, if an animal is ridden without a firm feeling of leadership, it will surely take matters into its own teeth – because two individuals cannot exist without a political division of their roles. To take over leadership or to submit itself to a subordinate position is natural and necessary for the horse – that is the way Equus Caballus has survived successfully for millions of years.

Except for the ancient Central Asian nomads' equestrian culture that was developed in an environment that can never be repeated again, horses have rarely been ridden with a total understanding of their nature. In our historical past horses were exploited as slaves. In last century's England, it was believed that manual workers were unable to become good riders because their callused hands were thought to have lost the sensitivity for equitation! Which is just another gross equestrian misunderstanding. Some people are not capable of becoming good riders – not because of their callused hands – but because of their callused minds, which was probably the reason that landed them in a lower position in the human hierarchy, anyway. (Marx wouldn't agree with me here, but as I don't agree with him in some other accounts, we're quits!)

For a better understanding of the concept of leadership in horsemanship, we must proceed to a brief analysis of what this word means in the practical world: to exercise leadership is basically to make people obey you. The most elementary form of making others obey is by means of tyranny (if you can get away with it). This form of leadership has been adopted in military organizations for millennia. The repressive form of leadership was consolidated because it is more economic – it dispenses palavering, subtlety and diplomacy, and thereby facilitating the administration of a great body of soldiers by a small number of officers.

But we also have examples of charismatic leadership from the high military echelons. The speech Henry V made to his men before the Battle of Agincourt according to Shakespeare, is one of the best examples of charisma ever professed by a leader:

"*If we are mark'd to die, we are enow*
To do our country loss; and if to live,
The fewer men, the greater share of honour.
God's will! I pray thee, wish not one man more....
He that outlives this day, and sees old age,
Will yearly on the vigil feast his friends,
And say, tomorrow is Saint Crispin:
Then will he strip his sleeve, and show his scars,
And say, these wounds I had on Crispin's day.
From this day to the ending of the world,
But we in it shall be remembered, --
We few, we happy few, we band of brothers;
For he to-day that shed his blood with me,
Shall be my brother; be he ne'er so vile,
This day shall gentle his condition.'

Almost six centuries after that chilly morning, these powerful words are still moving.

The repressive military system became so deeply consolidated in the West that until the middle of last century it served as an administrative model for great corporations. So, it is quite understandable that for hundreds of years, Western relationship with the horse was also copied from the army. And we all know the results of that.

The sporting horse has basic wants – physiologic and psychological – that need to be satisfied so that it can reach a high level of performance. The best way to deal with the animal's nature is by charismatic behavior – which is the ability to inspire others to give maximum efforts and constitute the essence of success in war and peace. That tenth of a second in a flat race, that extra centimeter in a show jumping trial, the great precision in Dressage figures, the extra effort to out-maneuver an opponent in Polo, are impossible to attain by means of coercion, as Xenophon made clear more than 2000 years ago. That 'extra commitment' comes from the absolute complicity between horse and rider, when these two individuals cast their human and equine qualities into one overpowering force to achieve their common goal.

The success of horsemanship involves, more than anything else, an intelligent form of leadership: to motivate the horse, to develop its athletic vocation, to

www.horsetravelbooks.com

recognize its psychological and physical limits and to find big and small solutions to favor its performance. This is the road map that leads to the podium.

It is not by mere chance that leadership and horsemanship are associated with humanity's individual and social development since the first nomadic warrior societies learned that equitation was the key to conquering the world.

The sensitivity of developing intelligent leadership, of assuming responsibilities, of solving problems, of considerate behavior towards others, of recognizing mistakes, and trying to succeed again and again, lies at the basis of all great achievements. Horsemanship is intimately related to a person's qualification for leadership and his or her wisdom and capacity to understand, motivate, inspire, and find solutions to enhance the good performance of subordinates. There is more behind the word 'chivalry' and 'nobility' than meet the unsuspecting eye.

16. On Horsemanship and Draftsmanship

Ancient Western "horsemen" were primarily chariot drivers and European riding methods have been an adaptation from the use of the horse for draft. Therefore many classical authors present us with riding techniques that undoubtedly survived from ancient driving practices. But modern riders should understand that there is a big difference between driving and riding and that mixed techniques may have negative consequences upon a horse. Through a neurophysiological evaluation of riding we'll see that the reflexive response used for driving should be different from the one triggered for riding.

To gain a better insight into the sensorial world of equitation we'll have to start to explore the very source from where the horse's movements spring – the *unconditioned* responses with which Caballus reacts to external stimulation. The origin of movement, neuroscientists explain us, is the unconditional reflexes with which horses (and humans) automatically respond to environmental stimulus and challenges. So to understand the integrated movements effected by Homo-Caballus in equitation we must first take into consideration two of the horse's unconditioned reflexes that men have used for driving and riding purposes since the time of the Hittite war chariots and the Mongol cavalry.

Therefore let's focus our attention on animals' nervous system and movement: when moving around in their territory, animals have developed a sensory-motor system, which triggers two primary reflexes: one of them may be called the 'withdrawal response' and the other the 'opposition response.' The 'withdrawal response' can be sparked by the sight, sound, smell or anticipation of some dangerous or unpleasant circumstance, and the 'opposition response' may be triggered for fighting or to break through any opposing barrier that may impede the animal's free movement. Some authors call these responses the fight or flight instincts but, whichever name we choose to use, the fact is that in the horse these automatic responses can be molded through training into draft work *and* equitation.

In the natural habitat obnoxious smells, threatening sounds, and dangerous situations, which instinct or past experience associate with intolerable, or potentially lethal situations, may prompt the horse's 'withdrawal response'. Two opposing stallions will ostensively display menacing attitudes, wild rears and challenging neighing, and this behavior is intended to trigger the opponent's 'withdrawal response'... or else...

In the wild horse, the 'withdrawal response' is instinctively activated the moment that the animal becomes aware of an oncoming predator and its motor-system automatically triggers a gallop. The 'withdrawal response' is very well developed in the smaller oriental hot-blooded horses, and the 'opposition

www.horsetravelbooks.com

response' is a key feature of the cold-blooded European horses, as a result of their greater weight and strength, which also made these animals ideal for draft work.

Because he lived in forests, the 'great horse' had to break through foliage barriers and other natural impediments to escape a pursuer or else rely on its size to confront the adversary. Therefore his defensive strategy relies on force rather than speed. In such cases powerful bunches of muscle are positive qualities that helped the European wild horse to survive and after domestication to pull a wagon or a plow more effectively. Through the 'opposition response' the animal tries to annul or to overcome an opposite force by exercising a still greater force. The 'opposition response' provides a stronger, slower and more forceful surge of muscle power aimed at breaking outside resistance. In a wild state the 'opposition response' leads the animal to try to overcome any impediment which hampers its free movement as, for example, to pull the lasso from a cowboy's hands.

All types of horses are equipped with both reflexes—opposition and withdrawal – that humans have learned to orchestrate into horsemanship or draftsmanship.

The 'opposition response' became the basis of Europe's ancient draft technology that flourished for thousands of years. When a horse is harnessed to a plow or coach, and feels the vehicle's weight impeding its forward movement it will instinctively try to produce a superior force against the collar to break the impasse and move. With training, the horse learns to pull the coach and to do lateral maneuvers pushing 'against' the vehicle's shafts, always producing an 'opposition force' by applying a greater force 'against' the factor that impedes its free movement – the collar and the shafts.

In draft techniques, the coachman only triggers the horses' 'withdrawal response' when he uses whip and voice – at which the horse will produce a 'withdrawal response' to move away from the commanding sound or the pain of the whip. In drafting, the reins serve to connect the coachman's hands with the horse's mouth for emitting signs of direction changes and speed reduction. The whip, as we saw, accelerates the horse and the bit when pulled backwards, produces the counter-force that indicates the coachman's desire to reduces or interrupt the vehicle's progression. In draft technology man and horse have no direct physical contact and therefore the technique doesn't involve the complexities of the neurophysiological interaction of equitation. Draftsmanship is essentially a mechanical technique and works with the biological principle that force must produce a counter force.

Hot-blood horses, though smaller than draft horses, also have the 'opposition response.' This is the reflex used when an animal rears violently against the ring

www.horsetravelbooks.com

or another object it is tied to, or runs away with an inexperienced horse person pulling frantically at the reins – and the more the rider pulls the faster the horse runs. By pushing against the bit the horse will be using its 'opposition response' to counter the rider's pulling – and not the 'withdrawal response' as it might look like at first sight. Though once the horse has learnt to break through the force of the rider's hands the 'opposition response' will turn into a 'withdrawal response' – and the mismatched combination will be heading full steam for the barn.

The 'withdrawal response' is the unconditioned reflex mostly used to organize the chain of human and equine riding reflexes in equitation. The 'withdrawal response' is not an act of force but an act of speed that may be triggered instantly, with the slightest provocation. This response is of course more used in equitation because it is faster, and this is a 'plus' for most equestrian disciplines. For example, the 'withdrawal response' induces the forward movement of the horse when the rider's spurs touch his flanks. Acting as thorns, the spurs induce the horse to move away from the prickling sensation.

Studying the old horsemanship manuals you will find that some of them approve of cues that stimulate the horse's 'withdrawal responses' and others recommend the 'opposition response'. Some texts recommend that for a lateral movement the horse should oppose the rider's leg pressure moving *against* instead of withdrawing *from* the horseman's leg. This is a classical 'opposition response.'

L'Hotte, in his book *The Quest for Lightness* is aware of this problem: "Where disagreement exists is in the use of the heels. Some urge the use of the outside heels, also known as opposing heels (opposing in the view of the rider); others the use of the inside heels, known as the direct heels. If these two methods are correctly used, both can give the sought result".

Of course both methods work, but should two conflicting responses be used in riding the same horse? It is not my intention to differ, in case some readers use the direct heel, but I believe that through a deeper neurological study aimed to standardize a natural and universal code of biological riding cues, it will be essential to reconsider the use of two different cues in equitation. A horse should never oppose a rider's cue, but always move *away* from leg and heel pressure.

As we saw, the nervous system and animal responses to stimuli were only discovered in the 20th century, and therefore these issues have never been mentioned in academic texts. But riding schools should analyze carefully the use of any 'opposition responses' in equitation. These reflexes are probably still used as an inheritance of Europe's ancient draft practices and should be discarded in the light of modern neurophysiology. The stimulating of the horse's 'opposition responses' is undoubtedly at the basis of a mechanistic driving philosophy, which transformed the horse into the motor of a cart, plow, chariot and carriage.

www.horsetravelbooks.com

It is possible that some of the troubles of Europe's old conflicting schooling methods have been due to the use of two different parameters in organizing the horse's chain of riding responses. The movements derived from the 'withdrawal response' are always faster than the ones generated by the 'opposition response' – therefore the 'withdrawal response' seems more indicated for modern equitation.

If the horse is taught to oppose the rider's cues, no wonder so many horses learn to run away with their riders frantically pulling at the reins. The horse may have learned the trick in the riding school.

The 'opposition response' is a slow muscle force that the horse applies against opposition and is very useful for draft work. The 'withdrawal response' is a fast response that automatically makes the horse cede to pressure. As agility and speed are the elements that we look for in advanced equitation, the 'withdrawal response' is certainly the best reflex to be used for the schooling of a high performing horse.

17. The Power of Pleasure

The history of the man-horse relationship has mainly been of work and war, two unpleasant businesses for the unlucky individuals involved (except for 'workaholics,' sadists, and incurable utopians of course). Under these dire circumstances it is understandable that the handling of horses and the riding techniques employed under work and war conditions were mostly of bad emotional quality. Two stressed beings are apt to quarrel. But the pleasure horse and the sporting horse should be taught to take pleasure in equitation, for there is no limit to the performance of a horse that enjoys what he's doing.

A hundred years ago, English officers alleged that they could foretell the arrival of the French cavalry by the 'smell of the festering wounds' of their war-worn horses. Though in John Florio's opinion, England was "women's paradise, men's purgatory and horses' hell." The truth of the matter is that work and war was nobody's cup of tea – especially for the work-weary war-horse. Let us see how in *biological sound equitation* the concept of pleasure can be the driving force of a winning performance.

More than fear, which provokes a 'withdrawal response,' and rage, that may provoke an 'opposition response,' humans and horses share a reason for cooperative behavior in equitation – the feeling of pleasure. In the animal world the feeling of pleasure is responsible for gastronomic and sexual appetite – the pillars of life. When the feeling of pleasure overcomes man and horse a chain of biological modifications originates in the central nervous system, which inhibits the formation of negative feelings, increases the energy rate and decreases the feeling of worry and concern. Knowing how to stimulate pleasure in the horse can be the basis of a successful training program. And though it may start with a lump of sugar, it doesn't stop with an affectionate pat.

As you may well remember, our forebear Federico Grisone mainly used the emotion of *fear* to school his horses. He started the young horse with a lunging session in which the animal was whipped around in a circle until the 'devil of disobedience' was exorcised from its body – remember? His training procedure had emphasis on breaking the horse's resistance and rewarding its 'submission' with the ceasing of punishments. The horse, to avoid more chastisement after great emotional stress, would 'learn' to do what was demanded of it. (Very awkwardly and with a great waste of horse and man power, because some manhandled horses did, once in a while, kill a horse abuser.)

When Antoine de Pluvinel adopted Xenophon's methods of gentling and training, he tried to convey pleasure to the animal during schooling sessions. *"The horse should feel pleasure in equitation, if not the horseman can do nothing right. It is important that the bit gives pleasure to the horse's tongue. We have to seek what the horse prefers for its comfort. We should be careful so that the bit fits well on the animal's bars. The curb chain should be inserted correctly in its groove. Take care so that the bit doesn't pinch the horse's mouth. Be prodigal in reward and poor in chastisement,"* recommends Pluvinel.

With his thoughtful training system he moved Europe's equestrian center from Naples to Paris (which would be like moving Silicon Valley from California to Osaka). The power of pleasure has, for centuries, been widely acknowledged by most great horsemen, so it's surprising that it hasn't been widely adopted, as humans will generally embrace anything that works well.

Pleasure and comfort are recommended as the best working conditions for all trades, say contemporary psychologists. High performance equitation has also increased its success by using the feeling of pleasure produced by the horse and horseman's emotional minds. And it works like this: in the first days of their partnership an equestrian bond is formed between man and horse which springs from a feeling called empathy — which is the ability of two partners to feel each other's emotions and makes it a pleasure to be together.

Later on, this sentiment can be turned into the pleasure of working together. If a horse doesn't like the rider, whether for his or her temper or nature, or his or her way of conducting the exercises – then they can't blend their nervous systems into a winning performance. The reverse is also true. Don't ever ride a horse you don't feel comfortable with – your disquieting sentiment is probably also shared by the horse. Even if it is not specifically you that the horse is wary of, don't ride it. Go and find another one you feel you can trust.

The horse's and horseman's daily training sessions are aimed at organizing their athletic movements into a chain of interactive conditioned reflexes and should occur in a harmonious mood, which produces the pleasurable feeling of working together. That is what highly sensitive, or high performance, equitation is really about. The same pleasure that the rider feels by doing fast maneuvers with speed and dexterity – movements which are beyond his physical power – is transferred to the horse who, stimulated by the horseman's creativity, will also be doing sequences of movements that he would not accomplish in his natural life. This physical exhilaration can stimulate a flow of chemical substances, such as endorphin and dopamine, which produces a strong feeling of pleasure in both partners.

Pleasure is a physiological sense of warmth and satisfaction that conveys the feeling that this is how things should be done. Pleasure has been the power behind humanity's greatest triumphs in art and technology – it should therefore also be part of man's greatest biological conquest – which is undoubtedly the techniques of equitation. Horses, like humans, enjoys their body movements and speed (their physical constitution was developed for speed, remember?). The

www.horsetravelbooks.com

horse may be led to do many complex movements in dressage, show jumping, steeplechase, eventing and Polo, driven mainly by the pleasure of his physical action. But pay attention here: only the experienced rider will be able to distinguish the fine line between the pleasure of equitation and the stress of work. Long and tiresome training sessions, corporal punishments (which sparks rebelliousness), sharp muscular day-after pains and a repressive working environment stimulate the horse's emotional memory to build up an instinctive *rejection* for equitation. Barn sour horses will procure every sort of escape solution, which are only healthy signs from the horse's defense system sending out messages aimed at preserving the animal's physical integrity.

"My objective is to work the horse calmly, for little time, but always," explained the equestrian genius Antoine de Pluvinel, who understood almost 400 years ago the power of pleasure in the horse's learning process. Why so few people have understood and used this basic concept, which leads to good equitation, is a total mystery.

In the new sporting cycle, pleasure for the horse in its work can elevate horsemanship to a high degree of excellence. But there is still another element in equitation that should be analyzed by the modern horseperson: the psychology of games and play that, besides empathy and pleasure, conveys a common feeling of joy to people and horses. Is it possible to lead a horse to play a game as we play ourselves? Let's follow the trail of the Centaur.

www.horsetravelbooks.com

18. Equus Ludens
With the inspiration of Johan Huizinga

In a more optimistic age than the present, our species received the designation (or rather, we pompously entitled ourselves) Homo sapiens! Later we understood that after all is said and done we were not as rational as the naiveté of the time of Goethe and La Guérinière, the 'era of enlightenment and reason,' made us believe. So we began to designate our species Homo Faber. But there is a third important motivating factor present in human and animal life and that is the lust for games. Here is probably another piece of the biological puzzle that can help explain high performance equitation.

In our quest to discover the horse's nature – its life motivations and priorities – so as to use all its neuropsychological potential for the advanced practice of biologically sound equitation, we have already analyzed the interaction between the horse's and the rider's cooperative reflexes, and how this synergy is the result of training. We have also examined the feeling of pleasure that leads to good equitation. So, now we will seek inside the horse's psychological constitution for other elements that may help us to complete the picture of Homo-Caballus psychological and physiological merging. Let us analyze games, in a wider meaning and in the sense of 'fun,' evidencing how this ludic[41] sentiment could be shared in high performance equitation, according to Johan Huizinga's philosophical studies in his famous treatise *Homo Ludens*.

"The game is a fact older than culture because, even in its less rigorous definitions, it always presupposes the human society; but animals just as man also play," wrote Huizinga. And this fact is absolutely true. If you see a colt at play with other companions, you may see that in his happy pranks (where we can already detect all the movements which will be his future contribution to equitation), all the essential elements of the human games are present.

Look at the colts frolicking in the meadow: they are inviting each other to play by means of a certain ritual of attitudes and gestures. As they gambol around they show respect for the rules that forbid them to bite or kick their companions, at least not violently. They pretend to be angry with one another, lay back their ears and threaten to bite and to strike – and what is more important, they obviously feel immense pleasure and fun in all this merriment. The free playing of colts constitutes a simpler form of game between the horses. But there are true competitions in speed and agility, sometimes in group behavior, with lovely presentations of highly articulated gaits and collected movements performed to

---

[41] A Latin word adopted by the philosopher Flournoy to serve as an adjective for the word 'game.' A 'ludic' activity is when a game is played.

www.horsetravelbooks.com

be seen by the other horses. Does this ring the Pavlovian bell in your mind? Are you starting to drool like me?

Even in its simpler forms, the game is more than a physiologic phenomena or a psychological reflex. 'It transcends the limits of a merely physical or biological activity. It is an activity that has a definite sense,' thinks Huizinga. My attentive traveling companion has probably already understood what I'm driving at, and has already come to the brilliant conclusion.

Yes, I am suggesting through the perspective of human and equine psychological connection that the two partners can interact by means of another important link – the instinct we know that both humans and horses harbor in their psychological make-up: the joy of the game and the pleasure of playing.

Sporting equitation, which seeks not military violence or enslaving working tasks, may be practiced purely to the satisfaction of the partners. The necessity to practice sport is a common desire for most healthy people and horses (as one can see in Kipling's enthralling story *The Maltese Cat*).

Psychologists are trying to determine the nature and the meaning of games, attributing them a place in the system of life. "As a phenomenon, the game transcends the sphere of common life and it is impossible that it has its foundation in any rational element because, in that case, it would be limited to humanity," wrote Huizinga.

And as all horse people know, horses are also able to play, and thereby prove to be much more than mechanical beings, as Descartes or Loeb thought in their time. As they play, with obvious feelings of joy, they are more than simple irrational beings, "because as a game is irrational, it can only be practiced by rational beings," concludes Huizinga. The game involves us in a sort of magic – it is fascinating and captivating. It is full of rhythm and harmony. It produces tension, balance, compensation, contrast, variation, solution, union and disunion – involving elements that have as much appeal for man's intelligence as for the horse's. And is this not the description of a high performance equestrian presentation?

Yet if we are to associate games with equitation it is necessary, first, to remember that the game is a voluntary activity. The children and animals play because they like to play, and it is in this aspect that we will find the freedom of it. So, the first and fundamental characteristic of the game is the fact of it being free and at the same time representing the meaning of freedom in itself. (So if equitation is basically a game of freedom – no wonder the Central Asiatic nomads were so good at it.)

It is clear that, to make possible the merging of playful intentions between humans and horses, the pleasure instinct of the animal has to be understood and captivated by man. In all the definitions of the word 'game,' the starting point of its meaning seems to be the idea of fast movement. The game is a voluntary occupation, practiced within certain limits of time and space, according to rules freely accepted, but absolutely obligatory, endowed with an aim in itself with a feeling of tension and happiness and a characteristic of being different from the daily routine. As we define this, it comprehends every sort of action that we call 'a game' between humans, animals, children or adults: it is an exhibition of force, speed and dexterity. "It seems," writes Johan Huizinga, "that games can be considered one of the basic spiritual elements of life".

If Johan Huizinga is correct in his analysis, and there is no reason believe the contrary, (if you have seen colts gamboling in the field, you'll know what I mean, and if you haven't, you must take me at my word) it is possible to evaluate the phenomenon and to look for its relation with the equestrian games practiced by Homo and Caballus

How's this? If equitation is to be understood as a game enacted for fun by the horse (who enjoys speed and fast movements as much as the next guy – because that is the way he plays with his fellows) the animal has to feel freedom of movements. The good rider manages to move with the horse, control its steps, direction, speed and movements, and obtain complete dexterity, with rhythm, cadence and freedom of movements, which are the basic principles in all riding disciplines. The idea of *harnessing* the power of the horse for riding purposes is as old-fashioned as an Amish horse and buggy rattling along a four-lane highway. (See more of this in *Riding in the Comfort Zone*, Book Three.)

As we have already seen, the animals invite each other to play, using a certain ritual of attitudes and gestures. The good rider will know how to give his work the feeling of being a 'game,' by means of a ritual of attitudes, gestures and words. To be like a game, the duration of the training should be exact, for the horse should only work within a time compatible with his age and physical condition – so that joy doesn't turn into toil. The game is practiced with rules freely accepted, but absolutely obligatory, with an aim in itself. If the trainer works the horse within a definite time period, with obligatory rules and creativity, the 'game element' can be perfectly understood by the animal's biological intelligence. If training has a biological foundation and is accomplished with the feeling of happiness and a perception of being different from the 'daily routine' it will be successful.

This feeling of happiness is perfectly understandable by the horse who may be led, by a skilled partner, to play the game of equitation with pleasure and detachment. In fact, every good trainer and rider knows this, even if he or she has not formulated their thoughts exactly this way.

The rider who can capture the horse's natural inclination for games can also elevate his equitation to a superior grade of excellence. I'm sure that most of

www.horsetravelbooks.com

today's best riders will agree with me. (And if some don't, who cares? I live in Brazil, where the coco nuts come from).

Working with the feeling of pleasure and looking for the 'fun' nature of equestrian games (which we know is also an important element in the horse's emotional mind) – the good rider may transform his partner into an unique companion of adventures and, to boot, get unrivalled results in equestrian performances. This powerful interaction is absolutely impossible in sports that depend on inanimate objects such as bats, rackets, vehicles and other mechanical devices. 'There is no mutual feelings of joy between a car and a driver,' commented Gabby Hays once, as he unsaddled Partner, after helping his team win a game of Polo in San Izidro, Argentina.

19. The Bit, a Connection to the Mind

No mouthpiece has ever had the power to accomplish what its inventor proclaimed. Bit efficiency has always been enormously exaggerated. "No major innovations and no advances of any significance have been made in the systems of bitting and these are, if anything, as little understood as they were two thousand years ago.[42]" For lack of a sound bitting theory the incompetent use of mouthpieces is responsible for most of the miserable and useless horses that have inhabited this planet. But nowadays bits are becoming simpler, softer and more intelligent – and with the help of neuroscience their positive and negative effects can now be better understood.

The most polemic subject in equitation's long history has always been the use of bits. Which mouthpieces are the most appropriate for which type of horse? Do different types of work require different bits? Do different ages demand different mouthpieces? Should the bit be an instrument of gentle restraint or a tool for rough subjugating? Does the horse have to enjoy the mouthpiece? Does the horse, in order to be ridden, have to wear a bit at all? In which case should a snaffle be used and when to use a curb bit? When should a hackamore be considered? Will people, a thousand years from now, still be using a snaffle in the horse's mouth or is an equitation chip, to be grafted under Homo and Caballus's skin, on the way from Intel? Horsemen have formulated such questions for thousands of years, and literally hundreds of types of bits have been invented to correct the 'problem horse'. But the most important question of all has yet to be asked – What is really the mouthpiece's role in the human and equine chain of riding reflexes? How does the horse relate to the bit? Or put in another way, how does the well-schooled horse use the bit to his advantage?

The simplistic idea that a person's equitation can be improved by "improving" the horse's mouthpiece is particularly stupid, even for Homo Faber who has a long record of hare-brained ideas. This practice goes back to the beginning of Western equitation, which, as we saw, was mostly adapted from cart driving. As we also saw in the chapter *On Horsemanship and Draftsmanship*, the physical distance between horse and driver made for the development of a one-way communication system, which doesn't work well in equitation. The driver shakes the reins, hollers his orders, and whacks his whip in no subtle manner, while the rider connects his nervous system with the horses' and communicates by touch and the feeling of intentions. If modern equestrian thought is correct in defining equitation as a sophisticated inter-communication system, which calls for the interplay of all the rider's and horse's senses, there can be no doubt about one

---

[42] Elwin Hartley Edwards is the author of many books, including "Bitting."

www.horsetravelbooks.com

fact: few times in the history of technology has Homo Faber's one-tracked mind galloped so far in the wrong direction, as with the old bitting theories that offer mechanical solutions to solve neurological problems. (When Homo's whiz-bang mind hijacks his excitable brain there's no telling in what intellectual soup it's going to land him.) In sheer unbridled irrationality, no other idea, bar the invention of cigarettes, alcohol and snake oil, has been supported by its makers with such twisted logic as the philosophy of bitting.

Jointed snaffles, serrated mouthpieces, cheek rings with hedgehog spikes, curb bits, ring bits, nose bridles, flute bits, anti-rear bits, straight bar, French bradoon, Dick Christians, racing snaffles, full cheek snaffles and Fulmer snaffles – you name them – some made more powerful with rollers, spikes, levers, martingales and German reins which are sure recipes to ruin the pleasure of horse and rider. This, and a thousand other permutations of the basic bitting theme, *"was a situation that revealed all too clearly the continuing obsession with mechanical exactitude and the control and positioning of the head by those same means that had so occupied the minds of horsemen in antiquity,"* writes Elwyn Hartley Edwards, in his book *Bitting in Theory and Practice*.

Now, you won't believe this of course: during the Renaissance the bit started to be defined as the 'key' to good horsemanship. When the first academies were started, the mouthpieces were of the curb-bit type with rigid bars, long levers or enormous internal rings – and you won't believe this either – these 'horse-keys' were equipped with wheels, rollers and even bells, inside the horse's mouth, and people thought they helped to produce willingness and lightness of the horse! The right side of the mouth-bar was often built differently from the left side to act with greater leverage for the horse to become 'lighter' on his right turns! Descartes must have been delighted. Long cheek pieces were devised to increase leverage and produce maximum pain.

As we have seen, in the Neapolitan Riding School directed by Federico Grisone, the rule was to counter Equus Caballus' strength with Homo sapiens' violence. In most sedentary horse cultures past and present, when the horseman hasn't savvy enough to manage the horse, he will promptly purchase a more powerful mouthpiece. Which can be compared to a bad soccer player who, unable to score a goal, asks the coach to change the ball; or a second-rate painter who, recognizing the mess on his canvass, asks for a better brush. The bit, like any other tool – saw, chisel or lancet – has no competence in itself. It is only a way of transmitting the competence of a skilled craftsman.

The mechanical view of equitation, which spread unchecked in Europe from the Middle Ages to modern times, produced an infinite variety of bits, each with detailed 'recommendations' for use. A mouthpiece was supposed to accomplish a certain mechanical operation to solve certain behavioral problems in horses (for these people the 'horse' was always the problem – don't laugh, its true!). In the 19th century, the book *Origines de L'école de Cavalarie et Ses Traditions Équestres*, written by L. Picard of Saumur, has illustrations of more than 150 bits, each with a specific 'indication' for its use. There were bits for pregnant mares, Turkish horses and English hackneys; there were bits to correct shying, balking, rearing, jibbing, bucking horses; there were bits for horses that had the annoying habit of running away! (No wonder we have produced so few good riders.) To modern ears, all this sounds like the crazy Don Martin yarns published in Mad magazine.

But the new understanding of the horses' nervous system can radically change the conception of the use of bits. People are now mentally prepared to understand that the bit is placed in a spot of the horse's anatomy, its mouth, which, having an important function in the selection of food stuff, presents a great number of sensor nerves linked to the brain. The horseman's hands, like the horse's mouth, has also a great amount of nervous terminals because Homo developed his hand movements for the same purpose as Equus – for food selection.

So, it must be clear that the bit's role in equitation should deal with the fine movements in equitation, communicated by sensitive hands and decoded by the horse's sensitive mouth. The human legs stimulate the horse's wide movements and the human hand deals with the fine movements. When a cowboy performs a spin, his legs will produce the wide movements and his hands will determine when to stop – the fine movement. When a dressage rider does a piaffe, his legs and pelvis will induce the horses' leg action and his hands will keep the horse on the spot, which is the fine movement of the act.

The bit has also the practical advantage of giving command over the horse's bone structure. With the use of the mouthpiece it is possible to induce the flexion of the horse's neck and backbone thus making him slip his legs into the initial position to start the chain of reflex responses that the rider requires. Or in other words, the bit can induce the horse to take the position that his natural movements require, which is a natural cue for the horse to perform the required movements.

The horse should not be controlled through the rude leverage of a bit, because this destroys his nervous terminals and when he loses his feel he'll need a stronger bit, which starts the vicious escalation towards ever harsher bits. The mouthpiece should be used, during early training, to give a light 'mechanical advantage' to the horseman. This 'mechanical advantage' will be less and less necessary as the horse and rider progresses in their *neurophysiological identification* and their minds connect to each other's sensory-motor system. The reins that connect the rider's sensitive hands to the horse's sensitive mouth may be described as a duct that 'plugs' the human mind to monitor the equine mind and vice versa. The rein's function, in biologically sound equitation, is not 'to pull' the horse's head mechanically from one side to another, to make the changes of direction, or to pull the horse's head backwards for a stop (this is the way to drive a cart). The reins transmit the horseman's subtle hand cues to the bit, which conveys them to the horse's nervous system, which decodes them and automatically starts the requested chain reflex action, which has been automated during the combinations schooling sessions.

Now how does the horse relate to the bit? The bit is actually a practical way for the horse to monitor the limits of the equestrian movements. By the position of the bit the horse can anticipate the length of each muscle cycle, and this is why the well-trained horse will willingly connect with the competent rider's hands. The bit draws the line of the equestrian act. The bit must also be worked with one thought in mind: a horse will automatically be drawn to its 'comfort zone,' where comfort can be found, which means that when the horse is going at the right speed and performing the correct movements it must gain the sensation of be performing with absolute freedom. When the bit is activated to help produce a change of speed or direction the pressure must cease the moment the horse has responded. By giving the horse's mouth comfort, the rider can ensure the animal takes the precise direction and keeps the right speed by seeking its 'comfort zone'. Which means that the bit is exacting no pressure and following the horse's head movements smoothly. (We'll go further into this in the third part of the book.)

When General L'Hotte made his famous Dressage performance with his reins substituted by a string, this was a clear demonstration of the fine neurological Homo-Caballus connection we are talking about here – though the master had no inkling about the neurological facts that caused the horse's lightness and obedience.

In the gentling stage of the horse, during the organization of his first conditioned responses, the snaffle is worked with a mechanical function, and during basic training the bit acts like a 'teacher' that helps the reinforcement of the body and legs cues that will, when learned, substitute the mouthpiece's mechanical action.

In advanced schooling, the snaffle functions as a subtle 'transmitter' of the horseman's code of cues and, when lightly worked, indicates the head position, the collection and the curvature of the spine to facilitate the action of the horse's legs, necessary to start and to maintain the required chain of riding reflexes. ("The bit should not bother a working horse any more than a tie should trouble a man at work" – commented Gabby Hays to Partner, after the combination won the Volvo Cup Final in Geneva, back in the old Century.)

So it can be concluded that the construction of a bit should only have one real

www.horsetravelbooks.com

aim: to fit as comfortably as possible in the horse's mouth – which the plain old snaffle used by Xenophon seem to have done very well. In biologically sound equitation the stirrups are the stabilizers of the mouthpiece and though they are attached to the saddle they really belong to the chapter of bitting – so I think we must talk about them now.

The stirrups have been underrated in equitation in the exact proportion that the bit has been overrated. They have mostly been dismissed as a device that the rider steps on to hoist himself into the saddle. The stirrup, though, can be turned into an instrument of great precision. And though the bit was never the 'key' to the horse the stirrup was the key to cavalry success in world history. But what makes the big difference between riding with or without stirrups? As we know, in antiquity all good horsemen could acquire almost the same balance riding without saddle and stirrups, as Xenophon and his cavalry did.

To the human nervous system the stirrup act as a 'reference to the ground'. When the rider gets the feel of having the ground under his feet, his nervous system and sense of equilibrium perform better – as if the rider really has got his feet on the ground. And this makes a great difference for posture and balance. (For more details see chapter *Cracking the Centaur Enigma* coming up soon.) In the modern horse world the stirrup should be thought of as an instrument of scalpel precision that works in combination with the bit. The precise action of the mouthpiece, which advanced equitation requires, gets its stabilizing affect from the stirrup. In cavalry battles where warriors fought with saber or lance the stabilizing effect of the stirrup would be the 'edge' which could lead to victory. In modern sports, the smooth working of the bit-cues can only be accomplished with the precise coordination of the stirrups, from where the rider draws the exact equilibrium, weight distribution, and body tension required for effectively commanding every cycle of the chain of his riding reflexes. "Give me a point of support and I'll move the world," challenged Archimedes – and that is exactly what the stirrups gave the horseman – and with which he actually did move the world!

The bit has been the "solution" that created most of the problems in the history of horsemanship. Homo Faber, with his 'habilis' origin, inherited a compulsive tendency to rely solely on his visor-hand-motor coordination to 'steer' the horse. But the horseman that 'drives' the horse manually ends up by destroying the nervous terminals of the animal's mouth, rendering it 'hard mouthed', insensitive and unwilling to play the game of equitation. Such riders will never be able to interact with the horse in a biologically comprehensible way. In horsemanship manual driving is low-tech, as typewriting compared to word processing.

www.horsetravelbooks.com

20. The Saddle, a Double-Lane of the Senses

The history of saddles has been less polemic than the history of bits. But maybe this is just another mistake caused by our biological shortsightedness. The low profile of saddles is probably related to the fact that their function in equitation is very, very, subtle. But if we carefully scan the evolution of saddles with a neurophysiological view of equitation, a certain functional pattern starts to emerge between ancient, medieval and modern types of saddles. The building of rigging capable of uniting two different creatures for combined action may perhaps hide more secrets than its exterior reveals.

Bareback riding is notoriously a sweaty and sore business, so cloths and leather coverings began to be placed on the horse's back many thousands of years ago. But it seems that these ancient coverings served mainly to soften horseback riding for sedentary people's daily comings and goings. The Assyrians used cloths to soften the ride nine hundred years before Christ, and the Greeks did the same three hundred years after the Assyrians. At a time when curb bits and snaffles were already in use, riders still mounted without saddles and Xenophon, with the erudite's inclination for sarcasm, commented that only the 'soft-assed' Persians used blankets to soften their riding. "They cover their horses more than they cover their beds, and they prefer comfort to safety," criticized the famous philosopher-general.

The second stage of the evolution of the saddle was probably a contraption resembling a sawbuck packsaddle equipped with a leather loop designed to help the rider getting onto the horse's back.[43] But the introduction of wooden frames started the sore-back problem for Equus Caballus. A raw back is sorely limiting for long distance riding and this was also a drawback for a wider military use of the horse. So riders in horse breeding cultures strived for many centuries to devise a saddle that could give them and their horses a more comfortable and safer ride.

The saddle gained its final, almost perfect biological shape very early in time; probably sometime in the first millennium BC, and after that very few structural changes were made, beside functional adaptations for different kinds of work and warfare. Saddles can be divided into two types: light saddles for traveling and 'light' cavalry duty – reconnaissance, skirmishes and communication; and heavy saddles for cavalry charges, and cattle work. The heavy saddle was built with the concept of a 'chair' on which the horseman gained a firmer seat for wielding

---

[43] Charles Chenevix Trench explains the English etymology of stirrup: 'stir,' the archaic denomination for rope + 'up'=stirrup.

arms, shock tactics and ranch work. In the Middle Ages, the armored cavalryman was fitted 'inside' his heavy saddle, which was built with high, tight-fitting pommels and cantles, to help the knight resist the impact of a cavalry charge. The work saddle, of which the American western saddle is a good example, is an adaptation of the Iberian 'heavy saddle,' that was adapted to help the cattleman in his daily labor. This type of saddle should be as comfortable as possible, for the rider must spend many hours sitting in and getting out of it to accomplish his daily duties.

Recent historical data reveals that the great breakthrough in saddle making occurred in Central Asia and spread to Europe with the incursions of Hunnish, Magyar, and Saracen conquerors. The eastern saddle frame was very simple and ingenious like so many other intelligent technological solutions. With no leather covering, the eastern saddle was carved out of four pieces of wood – the pommel, the cantle and two side panels – that were so well shaped that when put together the saddle would spread the rider's weight on the two lateral saddle panels instead of pressuring the horses' spine. The side panels were slightly curved outward at the fore thus giving the horse's shoulders space to move. The empty space between the side-panels called the 'saddle room', avoided the pressure of the rider's weight on the horse's spine, which helped extend the autonomy of cavalry.

"This type of saddle expresses the connection and esteem of man and his horse, how much they depended on each other, how they tried to harmonize their relationship."[44]

The Hungarian saddle is of the eastern type and was probably introduced by Árpádian Magyars, a nomadic horse breeding people who by the end of the eighth century AD conquered the Hungarian plains. This eastern type of saddle is low in height, bow shaped, with pommels tied together by leather thongs. The front pommel leans forward and is higher, while the rear pommel juts back and is lobular, the seat is formed by a suspended ten-centimeter wide rawhide strip attached between pommel and cantle with the sides attached to the wooden side panels with leather thongs.

"This forms a comfortable, ventilated and mobile seat," says the catalog from the Ethnographic Museum of Budapest. But what do the Hungarian curators mean by 'mobile' seat? After spending the best part of a day at the saddle exhibition that traces the cultural history of this outstanding piece of Hungarian cultural heritage, I came to a very exciting conclusion: the rawhide leather strap was very possibly meant to enhance the rider's movements so that the horse could have a better feel of his movements and cues for changes of speed and

---

[44] Phrase from the catalog of the exhibition of saddles of the Museum of Ethnography in Budapest.

www.horsetravelbooks.com

direction. This would make sense for the ancient inventors of this type of saddle who were horseback archers and had to fire their arrows at the gallop, guiding the horse through a language of body movements (See *The Natural Language of Movements* in the third part of the book.) This 'mobile seat' theory is of course a conjecture, but I decided to tell you about it because it matches to perfection the nomad's natural blending with their horses, where a slightly movable seat would give the rider an 'edge' in horse control in critical moments. Therefore this particular type of saddle seems to be the perfect 'seat of the Centaur' where horse and human can monitor each other's muscle cycles and help merge into one galloping creature with matched movements and intentions.

The stirrup was perhaps the rider's most important invention since the bit. As we saw, the stirrup give the human nervous system a ground reference, which permits firmer movements, especially for the wielding of arms and the practice of sports. The use of a leather stirrup seems to have begun with the Scythians 2600 years ago and the metal stirrup arrived in Prussia and Lithuania from the steppes 1200 years ago. But it took centuries to become popular in other European countries because the Western carting mentality has always made it very difficult for people to understand pure equestrian principles.

All types of saddles have been built around the original eastern model because it is plain to see that all saddle frames are composed of four pieces – pommel, cantle, and two side bars – forming the saddle room, which was a major breakthrough in Central Asian saddle making. And the principal vector of the spread of the eastern type of saddle in the Western World was probably Hungary, a country situated in the last pocket of the steppe that stretches from Russia to China and where Scythians, Avars, Huns and Magyars had their headquarters before, during, and after Roman times.[45] The Hungarian plains have been one of the principal melting pots where Central Asian nomadic horse cultures blended with European sedentary civilizations.

Frederick the Great, the Prussian King and one of the foremost players of 18th century European power politics, equipped his cavalry according to the Hungarian style, and went as far as inviting Hungarian officers to help train horses and men. He also imported a great number of Tiszafüred saddlers, the best in Hungary, to make the Hungarian type of saddles for the Prussian army.

The Hungarian folk saddle and the military hussar saddle were basically the same until the turn of the 18th to the 19th centuries. In that period the hussar saddle was altered. The pommel head was eliminated after 1832 because "it caused accidents when the riders fell off the horse." At least, this is what the

---

[45] In Italy there is a modern saddle built with ancient nomadic know-how: the Maremman saddle formerly introduced by Hannibal and his Numidian cavalry in the third century BC.

www.horsetravelbooks.com

Hungarian catalog of the Ethnographic Museum says, though there must be a mistake here. The pommel head could evidently not hurt a man that *falls off the horse*, but would rather hurt him if the horse was shot and *rolled over him*. And this type of accident became frequent in Europe's nationalistic wars of the 19th century when a radical change in military strategy was introduced because of improved firearms that took an increasingly heavy toll on men and horses. In these wars, fought between the traditional and emerging kingdoms, Hungarian equitation and saddles had great impact on European cavalry tactics.

Now I believe that we should analyze the origin of the modern English saddle because in my mind its contemporary excellence is intimately connected to the Hungarian type of saddle. Let's take a ride in history and see how this may have come about. Let's turn our horses and head for the Hungarian plains.

In the 19th century Hungary was an unwilling partner of the Austro-Hungary Empire. In 1848 Hungarian nationalists fought the Rákóczi war of independence against a federation of Austrian and Russian armies. After a year of bloody battles the Hungarians were decisively routed and a Diaspora of Hungarian hussars landed men and horses in no less than thirty-four European kingdoms, including England. The modern English saddle, by its shape, structure and neurophysiological function, seems to owe a great deal of its excellence to eastern saddle making: it is light, with a low pommel and its seat helps connect the rider's center of gravity with the horse's. In the wake of the British Empire light cavalry, short stirrups, and English saddles, would be adopted worldwide, and nowadays remains a receipt to good horsemanship all over the world. And there is a reason for this.

The greatest technical innovations in the modern history of the saddle are happening right now, with new models projected with ergo-metric technology to assist current sporting demands. With new designs, new materials, and new computer techniques, the modern English spring-tree saddle places the horseman in a favorable position to unify the combination's gravity centers in all speeds.

With the intense traffic of the senses that surges at a very fast rate during the critical moments of an equestrian performance, this type of saddle serves many purposes: it provides the horseman with a firmer grip of knees and thighs; it stabilizes the rider's body, unifies the shifting centers of gravity and facilitates the free flow of the senses, which allows a clearer feeling of the horse's muscular vibrations and leg action. The spring-tree saddle allows the partners to perform with a greater synergy of movement and to monitor and adjust, in a hundredth of a second, their muscle cycles. It is a type of saddle that the Centaurs of Central Asia would certainly have recognized and approved.

The ancient nomadic saddle seems to have been built to assist the flux of muscle vibrations between human and horse, which would be favorable for horseback archery. The medieval saddles lost this quality in favor of the rider's adjustment to cavalry shock action. The modern English type of saddle is once again moving towards the close contact principle, and this is of course an asset for the biological values in equitation.

21. Other Thoughts on Whips and Spurs

The spurs have served since time immemorial to make the lymphatic cold-blooded horse move. Stiff pointed spiked spurs were in use for a thousand years and the medieval horsemen used them until the 13th century, when spurs with rowels, a little less subject to ill use, gradually substituted the dangerous device. Spurs and whips have always been the means to kick or whip life into a slow moving or unwilling horse, but nowadays, with better breeding and schooling techniques, these instruments have to be thought of as important communication tools, indispensable to good horsemanship.

The spurs were of course the products of low-tech equitation, when horsemanship and horse training techniques were based on provoking the fear of God and the Devil's pain in horses. After the discoveries in neuroscience, initiated by Ivan Pavlov and recently by James Rooney's research, riders can finally rest assured that to provoke pain in a horse is a self-defeating approach to equitation – simply because if the rider is able to give his horse a chain of soft cues the animal won't be aware that the decision-taking is not by its own volition. Good equitation is a natural marvel.

In biologically sound equitation spurs have lost their fear-inducing mission and are used with a more enlightened philosophy, which in recent years has greatly modified their design. Current spurs are mostly used as a reinforcement of the leg-cues, an expedient used when the rider need to emphasize a certain intention of action – and by no means as a way to speed up a lazy or unwilling horse. The 'atac d'epuron' – the attack of spurs – recommended by Baucher must be understood as a very last resort applied to a very intractable horse. The method is not justified in advanced schooling where the well-bred horse and the thinking rider have reached a high level of neurophysiological cooperation, and the partners are communicating through a code of extremely subtle cues. On our journey to the land of the Centaurs let's stop our horses a bit and analyze the historically swampy landscape of the use of spurs and crops.

The skin is the largest organ of the horse's constitution. It is the border between the 'self' and the environment, the limit between the 'house of the soul' and the natural world. The horse's skin is a very sensitive and agile organ. It is a mined landscape, full of receptor nerves that can 'feel' the land as the horse moves over it. In coordination with other sensor organs, the receptor nerves of the skin are vital to scan the environment for signs of danger. The distribution of receptor nerves over the skin surface which are connected to the motor coordination and creates a hyper-sensibility of the surface allows the horse to detect a fly as it alights on its skin, or a gentle cue from the rider for a series of flying-changes. (In the animal kingdom horses and deer are among the only animals capable of vibrating their skin to drive away insects.)

It is on this extremely sensitive organ that we perform with spurs and crops. The horse responds to the touch of the spurs through a *withdrawal reflex* – when the metal contacts the skin the animal automatically responds by moving forward. This natural reflex can be changed into a conditioned response for the purpose of moving at the rider's request. There is no need – or better still – it is not commendable to use the spurs to provoke pain. In a well-schooled horse the withdrawal reflex acts instantly and this cue is immediately sent to the medulla and provokes an instantaneous reflexive withdrawal response of the locomotive system. General L'Hotte once said that a good horse obeys not the spur, but the cold of the metal!

The modern spur doesn't need sharp rowels at all. Normally only the buckhook, which sustains the rowel is needed as a cue to spark the chain of riding reflexes. The spur's modern function is to keep watch on the horse's flank and if speed decrease is detected, or when a change of direction is accomplished less effectively, the spur should come into subtle action to reinforce the leg cue. Contemporary spurs are not a tool of torture, but a sophisticated communication device useful to the performance of the horse. See more on this in the third part of our journey.

The whip has a long and unsophisticated story. Since times immemorial, Homo troglodyte would cut a limb from a tree to beat the horse – and presto! The whip was invented. These rods can be made from any material — lianas, bamboo, leather, fiber and even from oxen penis, which in Brazil is euphemistically called a 'navel.' The whip, as a symbol of authority, is highly valued by all coarse riders, who love to swagger around with a leather switch in the hand and tinkling saucer-size rowels on the heels. The use of the whip as recommended by Grisone, and his long line of successors, can now be absolutely discarded.

"In highly sensitive equitation, big rowels are as useful as a double-barreled shot-gun", said Gabby Hays once to a Mexican cowboy in a rodeo down in Sonora, and Partner snickered in hearty approval.

The whip, nowadays called a crop, is a tool that has more to do with a maestro's baton than with an instrument of torture. As the conductor commands the orchestra with the baton, the horse-master conducts the horse with a crop. History has registered very few cases of a maestro beating the musicians with their batons – bar Herbert Von Karajan's assault on his musicians during a recital in the Berlin Philharmonic Orchestra. Though it did spoil the music, I was told. The modern crop comes in various lengths because as an extension of the rider's fingertips, they are used to 'touch' several points of the horse's anatomy as a cue to particular movements.

www.horsetravelbooks.com

Gaius Marius, the Roman general, during a military campaign in Africa, reported having seen nomadic horsemen riding their horses 'without saddles and bits, just using a rod to help guide the animals.' I personally think that the nomads must have had some way of stopping the horses, which the notorious general didn't notice – but I agree that to accomplish the changes of direction with a touch on the neck is more efficient than pulling a bit in the horses' mouth.

The crop may be used with great effect to practice turns and pirouettes. In this case, the crop will be acting in the horse's visual field, with absolutely no contact with its skin. Therefore the crop is only efficient if it is *never used as a whip*. The crop should act on the horses' receptor nerves like a touch – even when requesting to increase the speed.

In the 21st century, horse breeding and horsemanship will undergo the greatest philosophical and technological changes since the Biological Revolution's 'big bang' united Homo and Caballus into one galloping unity.

Now, in our quest to crack the Centaur enigma, we have wandered through some lost frontiers of Centaur psychology and neurophysiology and have at last reached the misty lands where Chiron the Centaur dwells. Let's ride softly over this sacred soil – for this is Asia Minor where Homer sighted the Centaurs more than three thousand years ago sweeping by on their mission to conquer the Earth. Don't miss, for any reason in the world, the forthcoming chapter where the second part of our journey ends.

www.horsetravelbooks.com

22. Cracking the Centaur Enigma

In our search for the biological foundation of equitation we started with Dr. Rooney's research on the chain of riding reflexes with which the horse responds to human cues. This led to our discovery of one of the missing links in the process – the rider's riding reflex chain, which is developed to spark the horses' chain of conditioned responses. And probing around this area we discovered another behavioral link, which fine-tunes the partner's mutual understanding – the love of games. Though, theoretically, in Homo's neurophysiological merger with Caballus, there should also be another factor – a law such as Newton's 'law of motion', which should connect all these reflexes into one double-lane of riding reflexes. But if there is such a sense, what is its name and how does it work? Now at last, let's try to crack the Centaur enigma.

Horseback riding conveys a powerful sense of 'self' to the exhilarated rider. Throughout the centuries, literate horsemen have grappled with words to put their feelings onto paper. And, as every good rider knows, there is a mighty feeling of unity in play when the rider can jockey the horse with almost the same control and precision of its gaits that he has over his own strides. Nevertheless 'self centered' Homo sapiens has always had a one-way perspective when looking at any phenomenon – specially the touchy feeling of 'self'.

Now let's pose the obvious question that seems to have eluded so many riders in the past: can the 'unity', which is evident in all fine horsemanship, be a one-way feeling? Is it possible to tie this mighty sense of oneness with the one-way traffic of human emotions? Is there any scientific evidence that the Centaur is formed by a two-way lane of fast traveling emotions, as the old Greek images of the Centaur appears to imply? 'Read me,' provokes old Centaur Chiron to challenge posterity's horsemen.

As we look at a fine display of show jumping, it is fascinating to notice all the movements that horse and rider produce simultaneously in their performance. On the approach to each obstacle the partners calculate their strides for perfect timing. At the exact moment the horse raises its forepart, leaves the ground with a powerful push from the hindquarters, collects his legs under the body and sails over the fence, with a beautiful precise movement.

Let's run the video back so we can observe the human role in the action. Notice that at the approach of the obstacle the rider also 'crouches' forward in anticipation for the jump and accomplishes very similar body movements to the horse. As Caballus goes over the fence Homo is flexibly standing in the stirrups, his spine as horizontal and aerodynamic as the horse's. His arms will also re-enact the basic forward impulse of the horse (of which he is obviously a part). On impact, the horse lands on its forefeet as the rider's body swings back to the

www.horsetravelbooks.com

vertical position, and the moment that the horse touches the ground with its hind-feet the rider also lands on his feet – in the stirrups.

What we are seeing is a smooth chain of perfectly matched athletic movements, produced by two super-athletes-in-one – a phenomenon unheard of outside the world of equestrian sports. No wonder. High performance equitation is accomplished by the cooperative interaction of two great athletes – Homo sapiens and Equus Caballus – who have acquired the ability to merge their nervous systems into one galloping being.

But how can these two marvelous creatures join their athletic prowess and perform so many movements, so fast and so perfectly coordinated? How can two athletes detect and compare, in a split second, each other's sensorial information to produce the correct movements each situation calls for? How can they channel their physical resources, which flow from two distinct bodies, into one chain of joint action, which results in the accurate timing of a winning performance? Is there a 'law of motions' which controls a double feedback of sensation and perception so that the partners can coordinate their wide and fine movements to form perfectly synchronic actions? How can they rely on each other's perceptions, and why does it, most of the time, look as if the horse is orchestrating the performance? Does the law of physics, which undoubtedly must rule this enormously complex kinetic phenomenon, have a name? Lets search for the neurological facts.

The sequence of all equestrian movements must, like all high performance athletes, be trained beforehand to within a tenth of a second precision. And like all great performers, the sense that coordinates all the sensorial information flowing in from the senses of sight, hearing and touch, which coordinate the athlete's limbs towards a sporting goal, is called *'proprioception:'* a fantastically complex sense which synchronizes the body movements of all human and animal physical activities. With the sense of 'proprioception', which means *perception of the 'self,'* the athlete can 'feel' the position of his limbs, his body and head as he moves. To be aware of his posture, his equilibrium, the angle and the tension of his body parts while on the move, the athlete receives information from anatomic sensor receptors connected to all his joints.

But 'proprioception' is not a clear-cut sense like vision, touch, smell, taste and hearing, because of the complex web of nerve receptors sending messages simultaneously from all the joints, which feed this sense. Nobody is aware of his or her proprioceptive sense before being informed about it! Now let's see how this extraordinary physical sense fits into the physiology of exercise. Great human athletes are capable of receiving and processing a lot of fast information and transforming them into precise movements.

For example, a soccer player has to follow the trajectory of a ball, which varies constantly during the game. The player will receive a permanent influx of information from sight, hearing and touch coming from the progression of the match. His senses will keep him informed of the ball's whereabouts, of his teammates constant moving, on the adversary's approaches and the position of the goal. At the same time his sense of 'proprioception' will feed him a constant flow of information about the position of his body so that he can put himself in a favorable playing position to perform the right action at the right moment. Because very precise movements are called for when the player gets the chance to tackle the ball. During these vital seconds, his sensory system will indicate when a movement is right, or is incorrect and should be stopped or radically changed.

As the human brain has a time limit for informative processing, some very fast movements must be programmed beforehand – that is, they must be automated to fit into the athlete's motor-program. Thus, during training the coach breaks the soccer game into tactical parts so that the players can train recurrent movements separately, to have them previously 'wired' into their mental "soccer program." This motor program is developed to coordinate his body movements automatically during his performance. When in action, his feeling of proprioception will constantly inform him how his body and legs are performing and, through previous training, some complex chain of movements can be performed automatically, dispensing with rational control.

A tennis player faces a different problem – because this game, as you know, is played with an instrument called a racquet. To handle a racquet poses new kinetic problems for the athlete. A racquet, depending on its weight, flexibility, length of the handle and tightness of the strings, will have to be maneuvered in different ways. A stiffer racquet offers more control, but a flexible one is more comfortable to use (although the player may lose control of it when his light titanium racquet collides with a 'topspin' ball). But attention now: great tennis players will develop a strong proprioceptive feel for their racquets. All the physical proprieties of the instrument will be incorporated into the player's 'tennis motor program' as he trains with his racquet. With practice the instrument will also start to send him feedback info on its performance as though it was an extension of his arm – and he'll be able to hit an oncoming ball as if it was the palm of his hand! Humans, we've got to hand it to them, show great dexterity with the handling of objects and can develop a wealth of reflexive responses in infinity of games. But all human skills in handling objects and vehicles pale in the light of the complexity of equitation.

The incredible fact about 'proprioception' in equitation is that good riders develop a strong proprioceptive feel for the horses' movements – and learn to read its two, three and four-beat gaits and transitions as clearly as if they were

www.horsetravelbooks.com

produced by his own nervous system! Every great rider can feel the horse's foot beats as if they were his own, and know the position of the animal's body and limbs in any given moment, because his proprioceptive sense has learned to read the horse's movements! And now hold your breath – all first class horses are capable of extending their proprioceptive sense upward, and feel the rider's movements, his subtle cues and, with time and schooling, even his intentions – as if they were feedback information coming from its own 'self'! In the fast double-lane of the senses the well-schooled horse, through his 'proprioceptive' sense, will not know from where the riding cues are coming! And lo, fair traveler! Here at last we must be peeping at this distinguished millennium old creature – the Centaur!

The complex cross-wired sense of mutual 'proprioception' shared by humans and horses is undoubtedly the unifying 'law' which connects all the other senses in high performance equitation. If we look carefully into this matter some equestrian theories can be confirmed and others discarded. But let's tread softly on this unbroken soil to avoid being led astray in this exciting new world – the incredible merging of the 'proprioceptive' senses of two highly developed species – Homo and Caballus! As an example of this interaction of human and equine senses, let's review a piece of the action of the mother of difficult equestrian sports: Polo. It's a fast game, so hold your breath, calm your horse and keep your eyes peeled.

Look, a polo player and his polo-pony are closing in to intercept the ball a split second before his opponent. The horse stretches into a dead gallop and the rider feels the speed through the pressure of the wind on his face, the thunder of the galloping in his ears, the green sweeping by under him, so he is well aware that he is flying at a greater velocity than his own physical means would permit (though his brain has safely been wired for it). A millisecond before the mallet stroke, the horse automatically alters its course so as to be in a better right-hand striking position. (Future research on the equine physiology of exercise will probably show us that the wiring of the polo pony's motor-program has been carefully developed in the horse's brain, and the animal has acquired a reflexive automatic response to the movements of the ball and the main features of the game.)

Rushing at the ball, the mind of the horse is directed toward the lay of the ground and to the course of the little white ball, while the player's rational mind is set on out-maneuvering the approaching opponent, on the changing positions of his fellow players, of the whereabouts of the adversaries, of the position of the goal, and on the course of the racing ball – while his emotional intelligence is automatically controlling his balance, connected to the furiously galloping horse. The Centaur's united 'proprioceptive' sense is orchestrating the intense flux of neurological information, which travels at the speed of light between the partners. The horse's strides are smoothly emulated by the rider and a split second before they come into striking position the rider leg-cues the horse for a 'delta-x of extra speed' to put the ball in the precise reach of his mallet – and standing lightly in the stirrups, and stabilizing his body for a split second – (as did the horseback archers of the steppe), with a well-aimed backhand, he scores!

The Centaur's 'high goal' has been accomplished! The neurons of Homo are working at a high frequency rate and his cues to Caballus occur at tenth of a second in a very, very, fast moving chain of events. All the rider's senses are fine-tuned and his flux of rational and emotional senses is channeled for a complete interaction with the horse's sensory motor system. Human limbs are the driving forces behind the horse's legwork, for his motor-system is strongly connected to his horse's motor-program. Adrenaline flows as freely in the veins of the Centaur as bubbly at Mayfair Baglioni on New Year's Eve. In the battle for each chukka, which has a duration of seven and a half minutes, the senses from the rider's nervous system send feedback messages, at machine gun rate, to the nervous system of the horse, who answers with a cascade of physical information to the rider. It's the feedback of the feedback, and Homo and Caballus' united senses are multiplied in an endless chain, as two mirrors reflecting each other into the infinite.

During such a grand display of equitation, the body and the mind of the rider are probably put to the harshest test of brainwork and motor coordination ever attempted by man. When galloping on the green, the greater part of Homo's brain areas are inter-connected and his emotional and rational minds are furiously interacting with Caballus to keep control of the ever changing factors of speed, equilibrium, and muscle action, powered by the horse, and the external whirlpool of environmental factors much beyond his own physiological capacity and original brain wiring.

Now brace yourself for a laugh! This fine display of horsemanship was in old King Cole's day called the 'independent seat,' and the aging monarch was once heard grumbling to his 'fool' – "no-one can ride properly in that manner!" And the fool told other fools about the "impossible independent seat" and all fools have believed it right up to our time!

The first thing that meets the eye in this neurophysiological landscape is that the latest concept of leg-use in equitation is correct. In the natural flow of the proprioceptive senses, the rider's principal means of controlling the horse's gaits should naturally spring from his own leg coordination. Theories such as 'The bit, in concert with the driving influence of the legs and seat, is used to regulate the gait and effect the transitions, both upwards and downwards,' and 'To regulate

www.horsetravelbooks.com

the gait the legs drive the horse into the hand,'[46] should also be accurate, for in the neurophysiology of equitation Homo should primarily connect his leg actions with the horse's leg action, while his free hands control the fine movements, for perfect timing.

Why should human limbs connect with the horses' leg action? Because in Homo's equestrian motor pattern the nerve sensors of his limbs will probably have a stronger proprioceptive connection with Caballus' leg action. And why should the hands regulate the timing element of the game? As we saw in the bitting chapter, Homo's hands and Caballus mouth were built for the fine task of alimentary selection, which is connected to a very sophisticated motor program in the brain. When human hands and the horse's mouth join, these super-sensitive organs can interact and control all the fine movements of the action, like a duo of ballet dancers performing the Nut Cracker in NY Public Theater!

And one other clear cut fact stands out in this proprioceptic moonscape: the application of force in equitation, and the stimulation of fear with the use of pain, will instantly denounce the rider to the horse as an *unfamiliar body* (a fake) – for a horse, unlike man, would never dream of inflicting pain on himself. (So undoubtedly the package jerking frantically on the reins upstairs, sitting off-balance, and digging in the spurs, must be from another planet — so let's get rid of the pest before something awful happens!)

When humans and horses turn their combined physical power into one fine-tuned machine, they can cross-wire their brains for an infinite amount of work, or learn to play a diversity of games, performed in a velocity superior to human biological speed. When thoroughly studied, equitation will by any standard comprise the most extraordinary sport ever invented by man. And moreover, if the cracking of the Centaur enigma here described is proven scientifically correct (and my horse says it is), equitation stands revealed as the greatest biological technique ever devised by human knowledge.

And we, the riders of a brave new horse world, sincerely hope that scholars find the time to study the Enigma of the Centaur, although we know that they are probably up to their high-brows with the genetic engineering of an olive without the inconvenience of a stone, or of an egg without the intervention of a chicken, for the glory of humanity and the cash from the sponsors.

The complete transition of equitation from a scientific no-man's land into a sound biologic study to safeguard stable solutions for all kinds of equestrian problems will possibly take some time. It's a kinetic jigsaw puzzle of gigantic proportions. Though we'll probably see the scientific slack on equitation being taken up soon. And mind you – when it starts to rain it'll pour. Until then, let's

---

[46] From Elwyn Hartley Edward's *Bitting in Theory and Practice*.

continue to instigate our fellow riders and scholars with our rash reports from this brave new wonderland populated by full-fledged Centaurs. And now get your horse and gear ready for a journey into the future.

www.horsetravelbooks.com

III – ODYSSEY IN SCIENCE

1. Are the Echoes of the Past the Music of the Future?

With the help of the echoes of the 'big bang' cosmologists are beginning to understand the origin of the Universe. Through the same comparative reasoning what do the echoes of the origin of equitation suggest? They imply that equitation evolved in only one place – Central Asia – and throughout centuries of expansion became the principal tool for human ambitions, and West Europeans were the last civilization in Eurasia to adopt the powerful technology into their lifestyle. The echoes of the past also suggest that horses and equitation were more important for human physical and mental development than for warfare. And it is from this point of view that scholars should analyze the future importance of horsemanship for city-bred people with a craving for a healthier life in communion with the natural world.

With the evolution of life sciences and new research into history we can finally start to understand that Europeans were never the finest horsemen in the world and that the Central Asian nomad's 'natural horsemanship' probably represents the best-tuned sensory-motor interaction between horse and horseman in the history of equitation. But then, what was Western Europe's contribution to horsemanship? In the past, I fear, relatively little. Western contribution to equitation seems to be reserved for the 21st century, when the current scientific revolution will benefit horsemanship as in no other time in history. For a better understanding of the music of future let us listen to the echoes of the past.

When the ancient Central Asian pastoralists developed the techniques of advanced equitation, cavalry assaults became an effective way to gain advantage in the dispute for the material resources on the steppe. The principle of the nomad herder's riding techniques was to blend into the horse's movements and create a biological unit that resulted in a super-efficient predator.

After a thousand years or so, the neurophysiological bond between horse and rider became so deep that the Centaur-like combination was able to plunder cities, even whole Empires, with the sole use of horse speed. But bows and arrows, swords, lances, and maces were not the exclusive property of the warriors of the steppe, though the strategy and tactics based on speed to wield these weapons became a nomadic hallmark. All witnesses in history acknowledge that nomad cavalry were capable of cooperating in unison, and during attacks, hundreds of horsemen could coordinate like a single unit – as a flight of eagle warriors! In the history of warfare no Western cavalry commanders have ever accomplished such feats of tactical coordination. But why do European horsemen, less connected to their horses, deprecate nomad equitation by calling the riders 'primitive horsemen' or at most 'natural horsemen?' Let's ride into Middle Age Europe and examine the motivation that lies behind the development of Western horsemanship.

If Western horsemen didn't invent equitation they undoubtedly introduced modifications in their riding style so as to serve their aims. What were those aims? Sociobiology teaches us that human genes motivate man to attain 'social status' because this, like fame and fortune, attracts partners – the so-called 'aphrodisiac of power.' Therefore when the elite of the urban-agrarian sedentary societies adopted *'equestrian dynamics'* they expanded their power and wealth beyond imagination. By horse communication much larger areas of land could fall under the control of one leader, and in order to maintain the political cohesion and economic expansion of their ever-expanding economy, Western social structure was organized into a complex hierarchical work force.

In this growing social web, the men who occupied the upper echelons continually worked to create unequivocal symbols of their high position in society. And the populace would copy these tokens of nobility as best they could in order to be mistaken for the ones on top. But pointed shoes, big buckles, loud capes, laced gloves, fancy trousers, frilled shirts, feathered caps, embroidered doublets, Tudor collars, gleaming jewelry, and many other cool fads could readily be imitated by the upstarts. Therefore, in this competitive environment, beautiful horses and refined horsemanship – dear to buy and hard to learn – had an important function in society: to show, beyond a shadow of doubt WHO was really the cock of the coop.

And so, in Western societies the emphasis in the use of the horse changed from Eastern military mobility to Western social mobility. That is, social status was the main factor in consolidating the type of equitation developed in Europe, because the horse became the main instrument of hierarchical distinction.

In sedentary cultures the horseman's social ascension didn't lie exclusively in the field of warfare, but rather in the military parade. For example: Gaius Julius Caesar published his book, *The War in Gaul,* to convince the Roman Senate to vote him a 'Triumph.' Being a victorious general he requested the right to perform a procession in Rome to evoke his martial feats and promote his social ascension. The 'Triumph' was held in 46 BC, and it included the defeated enemy generals, the captured soldiers and standards, and the conquered booty (most of it, anyway). The victory train was headed by the Roman legions, led by the triumphant Roman generals, mounted on beautiful prancing stallions.

And the apogee of this mega-pageantry was the magnificent and noble *Gaius Julius Caesar,* turned out in golden breastplates and aboard a gilded war-chariot that presented the triumphant hero in his moment of glory. This quadruple parade

www.horsetravelbooks.com

elevated Caesar from general to Consul and Dictator of Rome. But were these Roman war leaders really great horsemen, with a full sensory-motor connection with their horse? What does that matter? If they were not great riders at least they looked like it on that glorious summer day in July. What else matters anyway?

Knowing human nature, we may rest assured that in sedentary civilizations military parades became more important than bloody wars. "To die for the homeland is a peasant's ideology – the nobility must survive to rule it," remarked Gabby Hays once as he and Partner were watching the opening of the British parliament in London.

Any historian worth his books knows that the aristocratic wars of the Middle Ages turned into carefully planned mock combats, which could afterwards be mended with a band-aid. And these jousting tournaments were later transformed into the fine art of Antoine de Pluvinel and François Robichon de La Guérinière. During the Renaissance, the purpose of Academic Riding Schools was to prepare the noble horsemen for pageant cavalry presentations, and not really for bloody warfare. In these parades there was no need for the nobleman to be absolutely indivisible with his horse – on the contrary – it might be opportune for the plebeians by the wayside to notice WHO was really in charge here!

Only brilliant horsemen like Pluvinel were aware that in equestrian presentations of the highest order 'the horse seems to command the action.' Anyway, after the Middle-Ages Western generals were not expected to be good horsemen, but rather to be good generals. Newcastle was a good horseman and a lousy general, and Napoleon was an indifferent rider but an excellent general. (And Cardigan of the British Light Brigade is still a mystery, but some said it wasn't his fault, because he wasn't even there!) All this also helps explains the excessive collection of the horses verified in Europe's *'ceremonial equitation'* – slow, elaborate, recherché and baroque.

But, knowing that horsemen do not invent new movements of the horse, and that equestrian art consists in coordinating the animal's natural reflexes into highly complex patterns, how did the promoters of Europe's *'ceremonial horsemanship'* discover the movements used in pageantry and in high school equitation – so different from the use of the horse for military purposes? In antiquity horsemen had observed the movements that a stallion uses to court a mare or to impress a rival stallion. To perch up for coupling, or to fight for the privilege, the stallion arches his neck and gathers the legs under his corporal mass to look *bigger, more virile and magnificent*. With this carriage he demonstrates great nobility and vigor to impress the courted female or a great fighting disposition to intimidate the adversary stallion. All these attitudes are also important to accelerate the adrenaline flow and to heat the muscles, besides

www.horsetravelbooks.com

being excellent to impress the equine spectators: the female might go hot and the rival might go away.

But, with the adoption of these spectacular reflexes by the rider a long-standing misunderstanding took hold in Western horsemanship. In all chapters of the history of horsemanship we have seen the horse-masters trying to justify the high-school movements by their use in warfare – a supposition that we can now definitely discard as a mere 'warrior ideology.' (Even Xenophon dreamt of producing a battle horse that could at the same time be used as a parade horse, remember?) A horse is *not a bow* that needs to be bent to shoot an arrow – a horse has also agility when it is not collected – just watch an American cutting-horse at work. Collection is used as foreplay to action, but not necessarily during the actual performance. Even Trench's good sense plays him false when he tries to associate the 'collection' recommended by Xenophon to the rough topography of Greece – "the Greek horses had to be collected so as to balance themselves in the uneven terrain," wrote he, "but according to modern physiology..." Caprilli was right again. Collection does not necessarily produce better balance.

Collection is a natural reflex that the horse uses to magnify his presence as a prelude to battle or sex — the behavior is for 'show' and so it should be considered. The *'ceremonial equitation'* developed in Europe, and now called Dressage, was efficient to present the horseman in an aura of dynamic glory. And as pageantry was psychologically important for the social cohesion of Western nations, there is no need to invent excuses for it. To mistake the beautiful high prancing horse in the military parade for the hardy horse that really fought the war is false, but comprehensible in a romantic pre-scientific society.

The shine of armor, the gleam of breastplates, the splendor of uniforms,
The high plumed helmets, the luster of medals; the brilliance of silver studs on saddles, reins, and cruppers; the jangling of sabers; the chiming of bits, the tinkling of spurs;
The creaking of saddles, the swaying banners, the fluttering standards, the flickering streamers; the military music, the ruffle of drums, the blare of horns, the dazzling pomp, and the deafening pounding of thousands of hooves on the pavement, obscure the vision, accelerate the heart, and create the illusion of superior horsemanship.

And this is as it should be.

To Western horsemen, the glamour of *'ceremonial equitation'* took the place of the speed of the steppe horseman who, as a true predator, didn't require any artificiality for the well-planned strike, the objective dash, and the precise wielding of arms to assure success in battle.

But in the present equestrian sporting cycle, which will be consolidated in the 21st century, the neurophysiological bond of the ancient Centaurs begins to make sense again, when the *tenth of a second* and a *mere centimeter* may stand between Olympic victory and tragic defeat. And the upgrading of the human mind to adjust to the speed and power of the horse was ultimately the true legacy inherited by sedentary civilizations from the Centaurs of antiquity. Will the echoes of the past become the music of the future?

The Central Asian horse people's 'natural horsemanship' and West European's 'ceremonial equitation' had specific military and sociological aims that brought great benefits for Eastern and Western societies. And today, when riders again need speed and precision to conquer victories in modern equestrian games, life sciences are supplying new data on how horse and human can form one equestrian athlete like the 'natural' horsemen of antiquity. And 'natural horsemanship,' as an equestrian subject, takes us back to the source of the revolution initiated by Caprilli.

2. A Revolution in the Making

One hundred years ago Federico Caprilli started a revolution which was never concluded. In those troubled years humanity did not have the scientific insight to understand and appreciate the Italian rider's advanced proposals on 'natural equitation' and therefore the 'old horse world' was left with all its biases, malpractices and vices for another century. But Caprilli's revolution did not die – like a stubborn seed it lay waiting for the appropriate time to germinate. And because the scientific understanding of equitation is primarily a revolution of the mind, in this new century life sciences will fertilize the soil for Caprilli's ideas to blossom.

Agriculture and equitation are the oldest biological technologies developed by man, and have been the principal means of his domination of the Planet. Agriculture has been practiced for at least ten thousand years and equitation for about six. To keep up with the demands of an ever-growing human population, agricultural techniques have been improved by countless mechanical, chemical and biological discoveries. A series of green revolutions have, since Lavoisier's time, disavowed all the prophets of hunger since Malthus' time.

In equitation however, the reverse has been the rule. Until the late 20th century our horsemanship was largely practiced as in the Middle Ages. If we analyze the history of equitation without biased beliefs, we shall come to the inevitable conclusion that Caballus has adapted more to Homo than Homo to Caballus. The capacity of the horse to accommodate the requirements of human needs had dispensed people from promoting 'real changes' in the philosophy and methodology of riding.

As we have seen, Homo Faber went to a great deal of trouble with the engineering of hundreds of different types of bits, but with a mistaken view of how these tools really work in the context of the horses' *psychology and neurophysiology*. Throughout the ages, equitation has been practiced with so many conflicting systems that each generation of horsemen was led to believe that somewhere in the past riding must have been much more efficient. Grounded in this belief horsemanship, unlike agriculture, has mostly been performed by people with their minds set in the past.

Therefore horses have adapted to technical errors in riding methods that, if they had been committed in engineering projects, all bridges, houses, and buildings would inevitably have collapsed! Horses have overcome errors in handling that, if such ghastly mistakes had been committed in agriculture, humanity would long ago have become extinct. Many horses have undergone such barbaric psychological and physiological torture that if applied to humans the victims

The Centaur Legacy

would undoubtedly have turned into maniac killers. (See chapter *Nomad Wisdom in an Urban Civilization.*)

If airplanes were flown with the ineptitude that most horses have been ridden, commercial airlines would be impracticable. No profession could ever have progressed with such conflicting principles as equitation. In sheer incompetence, only auto driving can compare to horseback riding. The United States suffers a death rate of almost one Vietnam a year in motor vehicle related accidents because a car performs exactly the dumb maneuvers that the driver makes it do.

In equitation, the horse can be relied on to avoid most of the steering problems caused by the rider. A horse hardly ever overturns, never has a frontal crash, rarely falls into holes, never ever crashes headlong into trees, at no time sinks in deep water, if given the choice will avoid stepping on a fallen person and is usually capable of averting most of the common rider's incompetence. Sometimes smart horses will even take the bit into their own teeth and scamper home and out of harm's way with the terrified package clinging onto its back.

The horse has, for some six thousand years, accomplished its duties so successfully that equestrian societies have from time to time been able to inaugurate a new era of prosperity! Viewed as an engine, *the horse has been the most perfect machine man has ever laid his hands upon.* But now, in this new century, when Faber is starting to understand how the brain works and is rehearsing his first paces in the technology of giving life to mechanical devices, we can finally come to understand the almost miraculous phenomenon of equitation.

Technicians are now aware of the enormous engineering problems that underlie the building of a robot equipped with a simple viso-motor system: the sense of vision combined with a mechanical capability of action. They are discovering that optics, as used in television engineering and computer graphics, is a rather simple technology if compared to any biomechanical structure in nature. And more: that optics as a guide to accomplish motor actions would depend on such complex engineering that most honest scientists agree that it would be practically impossible to reproduce a complete sensor motor system artificially.

A physicist who wishes to calculate how a body moves when muscles are contracted will have to solve hundreds of *kinetic problems* in association with hundreds of *dynamic questions.* An artificial intelligence devised to calculate *how to contract hundreds of muscles* for a body to move, would also have to solve *inverted kinetics* and *inverted dynamics* so as to calculate *how much force* should be applied to every move of the robot.

All this is giving scientists a good idea of the cognitive complexities that the brain of a horse is capable of solving in a millisecond, and the speed of action

www.horsetravelbooks.com

that the brain of an advanced rider must be wired to deal with. *The wonders of equitation are many light-years ahead of the simple feat of putting a manned vehicle on Mars to explore the Red Planet's environment!*

But now for the good news: in this new century man will accomplish the first reengineering of equestrian techniques in history. Finally, Homo Faber will be able to understand the biological principles that govern horsemanship. Although, to prove scientifically *how the rider's nervous system merges with the horse's muscle cycles* may still be some years away. Finding out the precise mechanism of neuronal coherences is a difficult task that the researchers must face in the future. As in the case of intelligence, it is easier to identify an intelligent person than to explain *how* his intelligence works.

There are probably three main causes for the revolution in equitation that will occur in the first decades of the new century.

The first one is the growing understanding of the individuality of the horse – its behavior pattern and learning mechanism – which will revolutionize equine handling and training.

The second is the growing understanding of the neurophysiology of equitation – the merging of the human and the equine motor systems into one harmonious biological combination.

And the third are new multimedia strategies for the teaching of horsemanship, which will use a wealth of electronic techniques and devices – from computer graphics to virtual reality – to explain the Centaur's neurophysiological merging and sort out humans' and horses' roles in advanced equitation. A century after Caprilli's totally misunderstood 'Italian seat,' the time has come for his revolution to become victorious. *"The equestrian wheel completeth its turn,"* would Shakespeare have said, had he known the horse's mind as he knew the human psyche. Let's ride into the storm of our first biological challenge: is the current horse-human relationship symbiotic or slavery?

The relative ease with which a horse can be mounted and ridden has dispensed riders from finding a breakthrough to the biological understanding of equitation. For this reason most riding systems were founded on conflicting mechanical theories whose biological errors powerful mouthpieces and abusive handling could annul. With the advance of modern science in the fields of biology, psychology, biodynamics, communication, cybernetics, neurophysiology, and physiology, the third millennium Centaurs will advance towards a fully understood biological philosophy in feeding, handling, training and riding horses for sport and leisure.

www.horsetravelbooks.com

3. Equitation: Symbiosis or Slavery?

Genetic mutations are the main strategy for animal species to survive changing circumstances in the biosphere. But millions of years of intercourse between different types of animals have taught many species to join their biological skills as a short cut for survival. This form of inter species cooperation is called a 'symbiosis' and equitation can be said to represent one of the most extraordinary forms of symbiosis ever to have joined two higher forms of animals on this Planet. But why did the original Homo-Caballus symbiosis eventually degenerate into the slavery of the horse that we grew up to consider "normal"?

Without social cooperation within a species and symbiotic associations between different species, life on Earth would be outright impossible. A symbiotic relationship may take many forms such as 'service in exchange for shelter,' 'service in exchange for protection,' 'service in exchange for food,' or cooperation between two species that have learned to 'join forces' to achieve what neither could do individually. From bacteria to mammals, cooperation between different types of animals has become the very pillars of life on Earth. "All organisms bigger than bacteria are recognized as symbiotic systems."[47] In a fiercely competitive environment a symbiosis is a short cut to survival where different species can often bring different 'skills' to work for mutual benefit.

But slavery is not unknown in the natural world, so let's ride into this land of 'mutual interests' to examine these issues at a closer range and see why high performance equitation can be classified as a symbiotic relationship and why other ways of riding and driving horses can be related to slavery. Lets start to visit microscopic life and work our way to symbiotic relations among fish, crustaceans, insects, reptiles, birds and mammals.

Humans, horses, and many other animals harbor in their intestines colonies of bacteria that help break up the molecules of foodstuff, which is a symbiotic operation that help digest our meals. This symbiosis is of the 'shelter for food' type and if perchance something should happen to these colonies of microscopic workers the host would be faced by serious digestive problems.

Our planet's oceans harbor hundreds of different symbioses, but the union of the pilot fish to the shark is one of the most evident partnerships of marine life. This symbiosis is of the 'services in exchange for protection' kind, because by swimming under the shark's belly the pilot fish avoids his predators and the shark tolerates his presence in return for the service of ridding his skin of parasites. (And the fact that the pilot fish has learned to move in almost perfect coordination with the shark has a cybernetic biological foundation similar to

---

[47] From Lynn Marguli's book *Minds for History Directory*.

equitation.) Keeping together makes sense for both animals.

'A lichen appears superficially to be an individual plant like any other. But it is really an intimate symbiotic union between a fungus and a green alga. Neither partner could live without the other. If the union had become just a bit more intimate we would no longer have been able to tell that a lichen was a double organism at all.'[48]

On the bottom of the sea live a type of fish and a kind of lobster that have formed a working partnership of shared skills for mutual protection: the lobster has powerful claws but poor eyesight and the fish has good eyes but no claws. To escape their predators the lobster digs a hole while the fish keeps an eye on the surroundings. By keeping in contact with the fish's swaying fins the lobster can feel the partner's emotions, and if a predator heads their way the fish becomes nervous and they both scurry into the hole dug by the lobster under the watchful eye of the fish.[49]

Among land animals the 'service in exchange for food' type of symbiosis is very common. Many kinds of birds offer 'cleaning services' to bigger animals and are therefore allowed intimate contact with the larger beasts. A crocodile on the banks of the Nile will sleep with its mouth open to have his teeth thoroughly picked by a little feathered friend. And the proximity to the croc will also keep the bird's natural predators at a respectful distance. But for thousands of years crocodiles have never changed their minds and swallowed their little partner for a snack, so the symbiosis persists unaltered to this day.

In the forest there is a kind of butterfly that, in the delicate larvae stage of its metamorphosis, has developed the capacity to intermittently exude a sweet substance that attracts a type of aggressive warrior ants that drink the nectar, and this service help keep the protectors close and the predators away. It is a symbiosis that has been perfected by thousands of years of natural selection and is still going strong.

There is, however, a type of ant that practices slavery. The strategy of this creature is to attack a colony of a slightly smaller type of ants and hijack their eggs, which are then carried home to the aggressor's anthill. When the hijacked eggs hatch the captive ants will be induced to work in their master's underground fungus plantation. This kind of relationship is not considered symbiotic because there is not an even balance in the mutual benefit that the two species gain from the association.

The Homo sapiens and Equus Caballus symbiosis that occurred thousands of

---

[48] Richard Dawkins, *The Selfish Gene.*

[49] This symbiotic relationship has a neurophysiological connection similar to equitation: the contact with the fish's fins permits the lobster to feel the fish's emotions and act in accordance with the cues.

years ago evolved into a very complex and perfected form of mutualism in which humans offered protection, grooming, and health care in exchange for milk, meat, and transportation. The human and horse intimacy marked by a common life on the steppe gradually flourished into advanced equitation. The capacity of one species to read the emotions of the other and act upon the evidence, thus forming a joint motor sensory operation, gave birth to a new type of predator: the mythical Centaur. It must be stressed that though the human protectors would periodically skim the horse herd of some individuals, mainly the old, the weak, and the superfluous males, the Homo-Caballus connection in a nomadic culture was symbiotic in nature because it did not evolve around fieldwork and forced labor. There was an even balance of service for service and the two species would benefit equally by keeping together in a competitive world. Let's ride further into this rolling steppe-land to see in what circumstances the Centaur was born.

For a symbiotic relationship to occur between two animals they must share the same habitat for millennia and intimately know each other's behavior. And for a symbiosis to flourish one of the partners must take the credit for having made the first 'move' towards the other, who for reasons of self-interest accepts the intrusion into its privacy.

Now how were horses and humans first attracted to each other on the vast prairie-steppe of Central Asia and what made the horses accept the human approach in a world that knew no fences, corrals, and other horse containing facilities? And why did the Homo-Caballus symbiosis later degenerate into oppression and the slave-master relationship that became the norm throughout most urban-agrarian societies where horses were kept?

As we have already seen in the Paleolithic Age, Central Asian nomads and the wild horses of the steppe shared the same ecological 'niche': the prairie that covers most of the lands between the 60th and 30th parallel of Eurasia's northern hemisphere.[50] In this natural habitat humans were predator minded and horses were prey animals and the two species were well acquainted because they had spent perhaps a hundred thousands years trying to outguess each other.

But to understand how and in what circumstances the Homo-Caballus connection was established I think we must discard outright the commonly accepted notion that human hunters one day 'decided' to capture some live horses with the intention of 'domesticating' them. Even if the first nomadic pastoralists got the idea of domesticating horses from the reindeer herders that were known to live

---

[50] The 60th parallel is the northern limit of the ancient wild horse habitat, and runs from Scandinavia to the Bering Sea in far eastern Russia; the 30th parallel, the southernmost limit, stretches from Spain through northern Africa, Iran, Afghanistan, Northern Pakistan and southern China.

further north in the Eurasian tundra, the human mind had probably not yet developed the systemic approach to technological development of Greek inspiration, and new discoveries would rather be accidental than intentional.

Therefore it is very hard to understand how and why one human group on the steppe suddenly changed its aggressive hunting behavior and chose to approach the horse herds and mingle with the animals instead of giving chase. As any psychologist knows it is extremely difficult to control such a powerful atavistic habit as the instinct for the chase, as anyone who owns a dog will agree. In fact, such a change of habit can only occur with a change of mentality. So what triggered a certain tribe of hunter-gatherer nomads to change their minds about horse hunting and decide to become horse herders?

The first biological clue to this mystery is of course that humans and horses share some alimentary habits that may have attracted equines toward humans. It is not hard to imagine that after a clan of hunter-gatherers had struck camp to follow the wild horses on their migration route towards greener pastures, some horses may have gained the habit of moving into the abandoned camp to scavenge for the leftovers of herbs, roots and grain. This habit would have accustomed the horses to human smells and this behavior would probably not be lost to keener human eyes.

But who in a hunter's world of professional killers could have accomplished the 'join-up' process,[51] the delicate task of approaching and mingling with the animals in a friendly way and showing the horses that not all humans are assassins? Here I must confess that I got a cue from Bartabas' film Zingaro Triptyk.[52] In this splendid telluric choreography of dancing horses and humans dancers we get a hint of who, in a tribe of hunter-gatherers, would have the wisdom to attract wild horses: women of course.[53] Bartabas' film show women approaching some horses and with beautiful choreographic movements feed them tidbits in an atmosphere of complete confidence and idyll. In the next scene we see men chasing the same horses in whichever way possible and causing the animals to stampede.

It is tempting to imagine that in an ancient nomadic clan, before horses were domesticated, a group of women out to forage for edibles could have attracted the horses' interest by shaking trees and by digging up roots and discarding the withered ones. To the wild horses the presence of a group of peacefully foraging

---

[51] Monty Robert's 'Join Up' technique is described in the book *The Man Who Listen to Horses*.

[52] *Zingaro Triptyk*, a film directed by Bartabas, is an allegory of horse people's powerful impact on agrarian communities.

[53] To men's chagrin Jean M. Auel was probably right: women probably did domesticate the horse, as she confidently wrote in *The Valley of Horses*.

www.horsetravelbooks.com

humans may have meant a chance to eat stuff that would normally be out of their reach. Moreover, women and small children, unlike men, would not necessarily harbor the aggressive instinct for the chase and therefore may have made the first decisive move towards the horses. Women could probably have attracted mares and their foals with tidbits and gentle handling. Tender hands, used to caring for human babies, could also cure a festering wound, extract a painful thorn, or feed an orphaned foal. And how long would it have taken for the mares to share their milk with these wonderful human animals, doted with their magic hands? Probably less time that it took the male hunters of the tribe to understand that herding is a much better idea than hunting.

In antiquity humans and horses kept together because the symbiosis became as vital for their survival as the union of fungus and green alga on the bottom of the sea. The horses profited because human hunters could keep the surroundings free of predators and the intimacy brought human hands into play for a series of health-care services. And once a footman became a horseman and learned to annul the human time-distance constraint at will, the idea of living without a horse would become absolutely unbearable.[54]

But under what circumstances did humans lose their ancient horse lore and became incapable of communicating with horses? What happened along humanity's road to culture and 'progress' that transformed the Homo-Caballus symbiosis into the abject slavery that we grew up with in 'civilized countries'? Why did urban-agrarian communities come to believe that aggressive behavior and painful methods were best to start a horse for riding? To induce a horse to become an equestrian partner by cooperative action obviously requires a different mentality than the method of breaking and handling usually favored by modern humans and that is best defined by the word 'rape.'

Rape was not invented by humans and does occur in the natural world, especially among primates, though this behavior cannot lead to a symbiotic relationship but rather to fear, submission and slavery. And though servility is good enough for travel and work, it has nothing to do with the high performance equitation needed for hunting, warfare and sports. A symbiosis is a pact of non-aggression between two different species designed to enhance the survival of both, where violence plays no part at all.

In reality a human marriage is also a symbiotic vow sealed to ensure people's genes to migrate into the next generation, but unfortunately some marriages also degenerate and become violent. So why can animal predators keep symbiotic partnerships going for thousands of years and humans are known to have broken most of their pledges, whether towards their own species or in interspecies relationships? Why are humans so fickle?

---

[54] In all horse societies the theft of a horse carried a death penalty.

www.horsetravelbooks.com

In the urban environment that commenced to take shape in the Neolithic Age, the human mind must keep changing so that people can conform to rapidly changing circumstances triggered by ever-expanding communities, which form new patterns of behavior and to counter all sorts of health and security problems that grow in a never-ending spiral. In antiquity, when humans settled and formed hard working agrarian communities which eventually invented the tools and utilities that would propel mankind from the Paleolithic to the Neolithic Age, all the links with the natural world were gradually severed in favor of the new artificial environment built to bring safety and to ease the drudgery of everyday life.

As these agricultural communities evolved people lost their biological outlook of life and a mass of herbal and animal lore disappeared forever in the vortex of the 'civilizing process.' When the agricultural communities of Eurasia, in a Neolithic stage of technological development, adopted horses to do the heavy duty of farming, the delicate symbiotic fabric that had kept horses naturally linked to humans for millennia was ruptured. As we saw in the chapter Horsemanship in Sedentary Civilizations, corrals, stalls, and pickets gave humans such immense power over the destiny of horses that the fragile balance of animal understanding and cooperation necessary to uphold the association in the wild was definitively shattered.

Nowadays it is interesting to see that a new generation of American cowboys, the kind of professional that in the past was a paid 'slave keeper,' is finally starting a trend toward creating a relationship based on trust and respect rather than force and violence. In an age that is slowly being enlightened by scientific information the human arrogance that stems from biological ignorance is starting to change people's minds.

THE RETURN TO A SYMBIOTIC RELATIONSHIP OF BALANCED BENEFITS BETWEEN HUMANS AND HORSES IS VITAL FOR THE FUTURE OF ADVANCED EQUITATION.

Nowadays animal handlers are learning that it makes biological sense to stimulate the horse's inborn cooperative instinct by wise leadership, gentle handling, and effective communication.[55] Therefore the most effective way to start an equestrian partnership, which is really a symbiosis built on humans' and horses' understanding of each other's behavior, is by gentle symbiotic persuasion.

The degeneration of equitation from the original symbiotic form to the abject slavery and abuse of the horse probably started when humanity made the

---

[55] A language that Monty Roberts calls EQUUS.

www.horsetravelbooks.com

transition from the Paleolithic to the Neolithic and confinement facilities marred the Homo-Caballus natural relationship. The delicate symbiotic connection that must be practiced by nomadic cultures did not survive the use of forceful methods later introduced by 'civilized' people to lighten their burden and better their lives in the urban-agrarian environment.

4. Dancing with Horses?

Biological or natural horsemanship can be described as the capacity of humans and horses to adapt their physical features, emotions, and behavior into one cooperative equestrian performance. By the mounted nomad's riding style and military achievements there can be no doubt that these horsemen were very close in body and mind to their horses. As equitation is a biological technique that employs the horse's natural movements for human aims, all mechanical thought should be cast to the wind and all restraining devices discarded, because freedom of body and mind is the ultimate goal for horse and rider. Federico Caprilli, the first rider to advocate this revolutionary philosophy, became of course the first 'natural horseman' in the annals of Western horsemanship.

Throughout time there have been two ways to learn how to ride: the 'ancient' and the 'old' way. On the prairie-steppe, in ancient times and later in the Arab world, horsemanship was an open book that every horse person knew by heart. If you had any doubt about a horse related matter you could ask your father, mother, uncle, older sister, or brother for advice. They'd all know what to do because horses and humans were two perfectly fitting pieces of steppe ecology honed by thousands of years of coexistence. As we have seen, ecologically adapted communities have a clearer grasp of animal psychology and behavior than urban societies.

The second way – the 'old' way – is how you and I learned to ride. This method consists of putting the student astride a horse and teach him or her to act like a coachman: drive the animal forwards with the 'aid' of legs, seat and hands, while striking a pose and pretending you're not doing so. With this type of teaching the odds are that you'll rattle around on the top of a horse for the time it will take your unsuspecting neurons to connect the necessary pathways and form the new nerve circuits essential to deal with the horse's specialized movements.

The third way – the biological way – is where ancient wisdom finally encounters modern science. In biologically sound equitation, or bioequitation,[56] you must learn to merge with Equus' nervous systems and follow the horse's muscle cycles as if they were your own. The changes of speed and direction must be

---

[56] Biological or natural equitation can be defined as the human use of the horse's locomotive system by stimulating chains of cooperative movements, in the same way as the animal would use them in its private doings. By the use of the word 'bioequitation' I'm not trying to coin a term, or establishing the dominion over a system, but rather trying to put equitation into a natural biological context. Lately I've read much about 'natural horsemanship,' which seems to embrace the same philosophy without a corresponding scientific background.

www.horsetravelbooks.com

indicated to the horse by clear cybernetic body cues.[57] As we saw in the second part of this book, the neurophysiological connection between horse and rider can produce a chain of cooperative movements and the combination's proprioceptive senses will tie a bond of biological oneness so tight that is has also been called the 'Centaur effect.'

The *neurophysiological merger* materializes when the rider can produce a smooth chain of body stances that reflect the horse's movements, which must indicate the changes of speed, direction, or the sustaining of the gaits, while the rider's hands connected with the horse's mouth must induce the limits of the action. This biological technique also requires the fine-tuning of the human and equine emotions, because mutual trust must underlie the combination's capacity to work together. Biological or natural equitation can only be accomplished by the rider who has learned to understand the horse's motivations and can follow the animal's movements, either by becoming part horse by cultural heritage, as the Central Asian archers in antiquity, or by scientific understanding of the phenomenon.

In 'bioequitation' the rider, *without losing his human nature*, becomes half horse, which is really an extremely sophisticated accomplishment only possible because of the wonderful plasticity of the human brain. In equestrian games, the Centaur is not governed by the rules of the old riding schools, but by the feedback of the horse's nervous systems that relays a flux of cybernetic information concerning speed and direction that will guide every muscle cycle of the two connected bodies. The correctness of the rider's body posture is important and should be worked out while the rider learns to blend into the horse's movements, because this will help maintain perfect equilibrium, correct breathing, and other physiological body functions.

Now if a novice rider is taught to focus exclusively on his or her outline, seat, hands, and legs, and doesn't learn to let the proprioceptive feel flow downwards and *feel the ground with her galloping feet* she or he cannot become much more than an indifferent rider. Novice riders should be taught that their physical feel should *not stop* at their seat, legs and hands because these parts of their body are where their receptor nerves are located and these are the rider's means to connect with the horse's receptor nerves, and through them the combination monitors each other's movements. But of course, the great masters have always ridden in this manner, though science in their time had not revealed HOW they connected with the horses' nervous system. In 'bioequitation' the horse is only vaguely aware of the presence of the rider, although the human presence passes a

---

[57] Cybernetics is the study of control and communication in the animal and the machine. Biological Cybernetics is the communication and control in the animal sensory motor system.

www.horsetravelbooks.com

comforting feeling of safety to the horse, and in certain moments the rider's leadership is vital to bolster the horse's confidence in the task ahead. A lone horse wouldn't dare to venture out so far and to face all those obstacles on his own, and an unhorsed person would be unable to do so. These are the ground stakes for a perfect biological amalgamation.

'Bioequitation' is made of perfectly coordinated movements, and though the action springs from the horse's natural movements it is a cooperative procedure which, like dancing, must be learned by both partners. So don't be allured by the mechanical devices invented for driving and nowadays much in use for riding. Can you imagine the comic situation of two polka dancers tied to each other with a 'Czech surcingle,' or the invention of special tack to Tango, or a 'standing martingale' to keep rockers' feet from cuffing each other's chins? – don't laugh – there's a parallel here, as all restraining devices were invented to *shape the horse's movements* and not to 'induce' them! Surcingles, martingales, muzzles, pulleys and special reins should only be applied *temporarily* to correct the horse that has had its natural movements distorted by poor riding. A sound well-ridden horse will never need them.

When today we can freely talk about the *neurophysiology of equitation* – the natural interaction of the human and the horse's nerve systems – it is because many horse people are discovering that 'riding' is different from 'driving.' Equitation can be said to be the accurate alignment of the horse and rider's movements, which must flow into one chain of joint action where the freedom of their movements is the ultimate goal. For this reason riding is not like 'driving' a horse, but rather like blending into the animal's muscle cycles. Like dancing!

A CENTAUR CAN BE DEFINED AS A HUMAN BRAIN CONTROLLING A HORSE'S LEGS

Charles Chenevix Trench, a true Centaur, put this almost bull's eye in his *A History of Horsemanship*: "We people can't be very bright, to take 4000 years to discover how a horse likes being ridden. And even now we are not agreed to it." Although, like most Western riders, Trench missed the fact that the Central Asian nomads could not have conquered the greatest empires in the world and altered the course of History, had they ridden as *neurophysiologically unconnected* to their horses as Western riders mostly do.

As we saw in the first part of this book, it would to be easier for Joan of Arc to conquer Orleans, for the Russians to vanquish the Chechens, for Americans to collar Osama Bin Laden and for the English to adopt the Euro, than for most Western riders to understand that a horse and a human are not physiologically different and that they must learn to blend into one biological unity! As you may

www.horsetravelbooks.com

remember, Xenophon compared the horse to a dancer, but he did not see himself as the horse's dancing partner. In ancient Greece the Centaur was only a myth and though Xenophon got the handling of horses right, the biological phenomenon that unite the two equestran bodies into *'one physical operation'* would only be understood more than two thousand four hundred years after the philosopher-general wrote his famous treatise.

Now let's have a look at what Gustav Steinbrecht[58] wrote in the 19th century: *"It is the rider's first obligation to keep soft and natural those parts of the body with which he feels the horse. If his seat meets this requirement, he will soon feel the movement of the horse's legs and will be able to distinguish each individual one; he will thus have the means at his disposal with which to control them as if they were his own."* Without possessing the scientific understanding that upholds this definition – the sense of proprioception – the German master knew how to blend the human and equine senses into one galloping unity.

And as science progressed in the last quarter of the twentieth century some riders did in fact start to envision the blending of Homo and Caballus' neurophysiology as the key to high performance equitation. Listen to this interesting description from *The Body Language of Horses,* written by Tom Ainslie and Bonnie Ledbetter and published in 1980: *'The familiar accolade that describes an expert equestrian as 'part horse' is not hopelessly fanciful. Every good rider functions as part of the horse, with hearing and touch helping communications in ways eyesight cannot.'* Although the authors didn't dive headlong into the neurophysiology of equitation they were already shedding some light on the Centaur's innermost secret!

Now see this excellent description by Peggy Cummings of *Connected® Riding*: *"Many riders are taught to ride as if they are perched on a sawhorse.* (hear, hear!) *Connected Riding is the cycle of a horse's movements going through the rider's body. Returning that movement back through the horse's body to form a synchronized, reciprocal, rhythmical system. It's an interaction, a form of expression, communication and action. It requires being conscious and aware, active not passive".* From her description you can see that Peggy Cummings' *Connected® Riding*, has a biological grounding.

And Linda Tellington-Jones, a Canadian horsewoman, has developed an entirely novel way of approaching and training horses through the human touch. This is of course a major breakthrough in horse relations and training. The *Tellington Touch*, which consists of circular touches made with the hands and fingers on the horse's body, strengthens relations, increases relaxation and disperses concentrated muscle stress. This may remind us of Baucher's method

---

[58] Gustav Steinbrecht is the 19th century author of *The Gymnasium of the Horse*, and the master who set the cavalry rules for the German Army of the Deutsches Reich.

www.horsetravelbooks.com

of suppling the horse before mounting, until you read his recommendation: *"Before commencing the exercise of flexing it is essential to give the horse a first lesson of subjection, and teach him to recognize the power of man."* From his words you can clearly detect the human hubris marring the fine horse master's mentality. The difference between the 'old' mechanical techniques and the new biological method is basically that the horse people who are really breaking new ground on equitation are science literate. Thanks to advanced science our historical incapacity of setting the natural chain of equestrian phenomena in the right biological order of cause and effect can now be overcome. Bioequitation is here to stay.

Biological or natural equitation is the result of two intelligent bodies that have learned to communicate and cooperate through a sophisticated intersensory relationship. It is a unique behavior caused by the symmetrical alignment of two different nervous systems that can read and respond to each other's movements. It is above all a case of exchanged identities: through the proprioceptive feel the rider believes that he's the great performer and the horse thinks that he is conducting the show. It is undoubtedly one of nature's perfect symbiotic mergers, and it starts with a profound emotional relationship.

5. Emotional Intelligence in Horsemanship
With the involuntary participation of Daniel Goleman

Humans and horses have lived collectively for thousands of years and the symbiotic merger has helped both partners to become common species, which is the ultimate biological drive of all animals.[59] But what was the key neurological feature that permitted fleet Equus to form a productive symbiosis with brainy Homo? One of the answers lies in the emotional intelligence that is highly developed in both horses and humans. And the leadership of man over horse is possible by a new form of intelligence developed only by humans – the rational mind. To understand how the human and equine emotional intelligence interact in equitation can help clarify some of the deeper aspects that underlie bioequitation. Let's try to ride further into this jungle of emotions and intentions.

The survival of all animal species on the planet is directly linked to their capacity to adapt their behavior to changing circumstances that may offer a sudden opportunity to eat or mate or avoid an unexpected encounter with death. And the ability to alter one's behavior to respond favorably to one situation or another is made possible by the emotions, which are highly developed in both humans and horses. Emotions are also the roadmap responsible for horse and rider to 'read' each other's intentions and build a relationship of trust and cooperation.

A new generation of neuroscientists is mapping out how the brain works and revealing many mysteries of the mind that past generations of scholars had thought impenetrable. Dramatic discoveries are now being made by new techniques in videotaping the brain at work. These images are showing how neurons work when humans think, plan, sleep, get upset and... ahem... lie, cheat, blaspheme and so on. Now researchers also know how the mind of other superior mammals (dogs, cats, rats, dolphins, equines, humans, chimps and the rest of the primate family) is similar and how these different creatures understand emotional circumstances and react in accordance to their biological interests.

Not counting the neocórtex, which is more developed in Homo Faber and allowed him to enrich uranium and build the atomic bomb (which lately isn't

---

[59] A nomadic horseman's genes traveled faster than a sedentary person's. A recent study has revealed that 8% of the population, and a total of 12 million people living between Japan and the Caspian Sea, carry the gene of Genghis Khan's family line. What Dr Chris Tyler-Smith of Oxford University and his team of researchers seem to have missed was the power of 'horsemanship' to spread the conquering horsemen's genes over such vast areas. No wonder the Chinese authorities built a 6000 km wall to surround their country in the fruitless attempt to keep their womenfolk away from Hun, Turk and Mongol conquerors.

www.horsetravelbooks.com

being considered a very good idea), the working of the mind of Homo and Caballus is structurally similar and this is the basis for their emotional connection and capability to build good relations and develop fine equitation. Let's follow the Centaurs footprints and take a look into the neurological wilderness where these creatures have lived for thousands of years.

In his book *Emotional Intelligence*, Daniel Goleman explains that the human brain is divided into two minds: the emotional and the rational. The emotional mind has existed for a longer time than the rational. Generally speaking the emotional mind feeds the rational mind with information, which sorts them out and turns them into rational attitudes. Even so, explains Goleman, the emotional and rational minds are semi-independent faculties, which may occasionally clash, with the emotional mind 'hijacking' the rational. When this happens, a person will be committing an impulsive or irrational act – like buying beyond the limit of his credit card, quarrelling with someone over a trifle, or abusing a horse while training. As Xenophon wrote, – Never ride a horse when in a bad humor. In one unfortunate moment all good work might be lost.

This is sound advice because training a horse is a type of work which demands the patient connection of nervous pathways in the animal's brain to form new nerve circuits capable of producing the automated action required in equitation. This delicate web of information can be ruptured by one outburst of anger, and the collateral damage will be the horse losing confidence in the human trainer. Humans, though, are born with an efficient organ that can be trained to control bad temper and avoid emotional fatigue: the neocortex, responsible for rational behavior.[60]

The rational mind is located in the neocortex and gives Homo Faber all his human characteristics: abstract and strategic thought, speech, high-handed megalomania and a strange compulsion to lie, gossip and 'la merde qu'est l'envie', as Napoleon Bonaparte would have put it, were he riding in our company. The neocortex elaborates the information collected and passed on by the senses of smell, taste, touch, hearing and sight, and with this information produces thought. The neocortex is also used for strategic planning, the triumphs of art, the creation of culture, the understanding of this text, and to help give humans the charismatic leadership required in good equitation.

In horses the emotions help a dam to educate her offspring who, through the mother's behavior, will learn what to eat, what not to eat, and what situations are nasty and should be avoided. After weaning the adolescent horse will learn where to feed and drink and how to behave in the herd, under the watchful eye of an

---

[60] Emotional fatigue that cause the rupture of relations in all species, must be avoided through the systematic training of patience. A rider that cannot master his or her own emotions cannot master high performance equitation.

www.horsetravelbooks.com

alpha female who establishes everybody's social limits. Emotions help animals organize their hierarchy into well-organized societies (something that humans don't seem capable of doing so well).

The emotional mind is responsible for a great part of the animal's learning process and especially to determine the mood and intentions of other animals. As we saw in a former chapter, horses generally isolate only one aspect of a situation, which functions as a direct sign that will provoke a direct response. This also means that a horse will clearly distinguish microemotions of human behavior and swiftly classify people in two categories: *enemy*, or *friend*. The horse's emotional intelligence will not distinguish other signs that could lead to mixed feelings, the intermediary situations between good and bad intentions. Through natural selection naïve horses do not survive and this type of behavior, if it has ever existed, must have become extinct. This is the main reason why a trainer, when schooling a horse, must keep a cool head and emit clear signs of friendly leadership.

Humans have also developed a dichotomous tendency to distinguish between the evil and the good guys and Hollywood often plays on this emotion in thrillers. In a highly charged emotional situation the audience may suddenly identify a supposedly friendly person in the cast as the real villain! By certain clues in the context, planted by the scriptwriter, the viewer suddenly becomes suspicious of subtle behavioral changes that may transform the charming person into the ruthless killer. The emotional change from the good guy to the bad guy did not flicker across the suspect person's features, but was flashed exclusively into the viewer's emotional mind by subtle details planted in the plot.

Now let's see how emotions, which are the radar of danger, can provoke instant responses according to Goleman's description. Stimulated by rage, blood flows to the hands of humans, which permits a man to grab a weapon and attack his enemy. The heart will accelerate and a flux of neural-transmitting substances and adrenaline generates great energy for vigorous action. If the adversary prevails, the blood flows into the big muscles attached to the skeleton and legs of rational men to facilitate flight (irrational individuals can be trained to die for any brainless cause).

To a horse in danger electric circuits in the emotional center of the brain also liberate a flux of substances, which puts the body in the state of instant alert and all attention will concentrate on the object of alarm and in 1/10 of a second the horse will be off to make good his escape. The emotional appraisal of the need to act must be automatic, so rapid that it never enters the animal's conscious mind.

The equine and human emotional repertoire, gathered through millions of years of trial by error, is very large and is also responsible for the 'riding reflex chain' developed in man, and the 'riding reflex responses' programmed by the

www.horsetravelbooks.com

human training of a horses. When all these reflexes, stemming from the partners' 'emotional mind,' are organized into one chain of interactive riding reflexes the partners will have attained the excellence that marks bioequitation. (This sentence was written to sound matter-of-fact, but of course it takes time and practice to connect the human and equine emotional responses into one web of equestrian learning, as we'll see in forthcoming chapters).

To survive, both humans and horses harbor the emotions of contentment, fear, anger, curiosity, interest, indifference, boredom, stress, pleasure, eagerness, friendship and so on. And some of these emotions—interest, pleasure, friendship – are traits that cause the miracle of equitation; when a cooperative feel allows humans and horses to overcome negative reactions towards each other, which is the benchmark of good equestrian performances. Instead of 'raping' the horse of its individuality and liberty by applying harsh, conflicting, and cruel methods, a horseperson can school a horse from groundwork to high school by indicating his riding intentions through a 'natural language of movements' that animals have understood since the beginning of time. The great horse masters of the past did not possess this scientific knowledge, although the neurophysiological process described here was also at the bottom of their first-class horsemanship. But scientific information will influence the great masters of the future, who will obtain a level of equitation never dreamt of by La Guérinière, Baucher or L'Hotte. Trust me.

Let's keep in mind what we have seen in this part of the Land of the Centaurs and move into other territories of the complex Homo-Caballus symbiosis.

The interaction of the emotional mind of horse and rider is at the root of bioequitation. When every movement is triggered by the rider and automatically carried out by the horse the partners are connected by an unconscious flow of emotions that forms a substantial part of the 'riding reflex chain.' This subtle connection of the emotions could obviously never be understood solely by mechanical analysis, as horsemanship cannot be taught with a purely mechanical and emotionless glossary.

6. The Natural Language of Movements

Why does a horse permit a human to mount and guide him? How can man control a horse from a position on its back? How can horse and rider learn to perform a variety of chores as one biological unity? These questions can start to be explained by the fact that in the natural world most creatures share a common language of movements. Throughout millions of years this communication system has conveyed clear messages of 'intentions' that can be read by any animal in the wild. Through the 'natural language of movements' animals can interpret the intentions of one creature towards another, both within a species and also in the relations between different species. The ancient nomads probably used the 'natural language of movements' to gentle and train their horses for equitation and modern riders can learn to use the language by understanding how it works.

In the natural world the way you move reveals your innermost intentions. Stealth betrays the intention to ambush and murder, high stepping muscle-swelling displays are the prelude to fight or courtship, and relaxed movements are a sign of indifference or, perhaps, of friendly intentions. All animals are expert readers of other creatures' intentions towards them, which are revealed by the outline, movements, muscle tone, rate of breathing, and eye focus of the approaching creature.

To a skilled reader of intentions, a body packed for hostile action looks very different from a body relaxed for peaceful doings. As most animals have better eyesight, keener olfactory sense, and sharper hearing than humans they are also better equipped to receive, process, and act upon emotional information emitted by other animals. And though humans developed a 'future memory' – the capacity for strategic planning – animals will generally have a better grasp of the emotional circumstances of any given situation. If a browsing rabbit suddenly comes to the attention of a prowling coyote the two will instantly know where they stand and what to do.

Many vets, researchers, trainers and other animal specialists are developing an acute understanding of animal behavior, which helps them with their daily chores of husbandry, handling and care. Currently some American cowboys are using their corral savvy to tame their horses instead of 'breaking them,' which makes biological sense, though I am led to believe that these techniques include only the initial stage of the 'natural language of movements' that helps a man to establish leadership over a horse. The 'licking of lips and the lowering of the head as a token of 'submission' by the horse' described in this method gives one the impression that the old human hubris is at play, but undoubtedly the technique works to initiate a horse for ranch duties.

www.horsetravelbooks.com

But the training of performance horses requires one unbroken chain of body postures and attitudes starting from groundwork, to mounted training, to high level schooling for show and sports, which the 'round pen' seems unable to provide.

To initiate a horse a trainer must have a clear strategy in mind that must unfold progressively from the first eye contact with the horse to the last stage of the animal's schooling, whether for polo, show jumping or dressage. The instructor will be using psychological techniques that must deal with the new circumstances of a horse that must learn to share his movements with a rider. The trainer must know that his or her task is to promote fast, profound and lasting changes in the horse's behavior, and any error along the way will install a defective response in the 'riding reflex chain.'

And perfect movements can unfortunately not be achieved by the old method of sitting on a bucking 'bronco' for ten seconds, or by persuading the horse to stay calm in the round pen and let you mount him in thirty minutes.[61] A biologically sound training method is much more like coaching a human athlete to develop his or her sporting ability by changing old habits, learning new chains of movements, understanding how to handle the sporting equipment, and becoming proficient and confident in the practice of the sport. Therefore the first requirement of a horse trainer is to be capable of transferring his requests through a language that the animal can understand. And this, of course, has been the main handicap of modern humans who have lost their capacity to communicate with animals. But then, what kind of communication can animals understand?

The 'natural language of movement' that has organized the social life of the higher ranking creatures for millennia is by itself a distinct language, which conveys the emotions and intentions of animals in the natural world: are you intent on aggression, friendly relations, or should we rather go about our business and ignore each other? Is your aggressive attitude designed to kill me or is it only to establish leadership between the two of us? Do you have any feeding habits or other skills that may be useful to me?

The 'natural language of movements' has been perfected by million of years of animal interaction and most species understand it to perfection, perhaps with the exception of city-bred folks. This language is based on body movements, some which are very subtle, and is used for mothers to teach the facts of life to

---

[61] The obsession with 'reducing time' to mount the horse for the first time must be overcome by intelligent riders because, although bioequitation does in fact accelerate the learning process of horses and humans, you cannot diminish certain chains of movements that must have a biological time to become automatic. Anyone that rushes the proceedings will leave holes in the 'learning process' as conspicuous as holes in the seat of his breeches.

www.horsetravelbooks.com

their offspring, and later for adult animals to establish the right to feed, drink, and mate.

Between strangers the language is dichotomous, which means that it conveys one of two pieces of information: an opposition or withdrawal response, also known as a fight or flight attitude. But within the 'natural language of movements' there is also the cooperative action needed for wolves to hunt, the frolicking between young fox pups at play, or for friendship grooming between horse pals. Animal vocal sounds convey supplementary messages that must be understood with time, but the 'natural language of movements' is most animals' first language, because it helps the young to survive from a very early age. (See the following chapter.)

As we have seen, a symbiosis is initiated by a friendly, and seemingly uninterested, approach, and this may lead to cooperative behavior that can eventually form a bond of lasting friendship. And this is precisely the part of animal behavior that should most interest horse people. As we have seen, when cooperative behavior jumps the species barrier, and two different types of animals can learn to perform a vital task that neither of them could perform singly, this is called a 'symbiosis.' To form a symbiosis animals must form a partnership so that their basic set of survival skills can come into play to benefit one another and the learning phase of the symbiosis is achieved by the 'natural language of movements.'

BIOEQUITATION OR NATURAL HORSEMANSHIP CAN BE DEFINED AS THE HUMAN CAPACITY TO STIMULATE COOPERATIVE BEHAVIOR IN HORSES.

Here we should again remember that equitation – the use of the horse's gaits for human aims – is formed by three fundamental actions: changes of speed, changes of direction, and the sustaining of the horse's natural gaits – walk, trot, gallop – and to stop. When training a horse this is what the 'natural language of movements' must address, in a biological and progressive way. But the first act of the Homo-Caballus connection is for the human partner to convey to the horse a climate of relaxed cooperation, which is shown by firm though friendly behavior, and above all by avoiding the stupid domineering whip cracking displays commonly used by low-tech trainers.

A wise horse trainer will also refrain from displaying all vestiges of human behavior – like hopping, arms waving, shouting, and whistling – and especially looking fixedly into the horse's eyes. All such hullabaloo is typical 'primate' behavior and only serves to confound the horse in establishing your identity and intentions. Horses are not as visually oriented as humans and therefore they also rely on smell, sound and touch to help identify the intentions of other creatures. To a horse, if you act like a horse and sound like a horse, well, perhaps you really are a horse, in spite of your funny shape and gangly walk. One part of animal behavior is instinctive and comes with its genetic program, and has been perfected by natural selection over vast periods of time. The other part of animal behavior is achieved by experience and imitating others in its everyday life.

The 'natural language of movements' is a language of body postures and attitudes that must convey the principal tempos of animal motor behavior – walk, trot and stop; walk, trot, turn, gallop, trot, stop, etc. Through the 'natural language of movements' a trainer can convey his lessons by means of a natural code of biological communication, which simulates walk, trot, stop, turn, speed-ups and slow-downs with clear-cut body postures. It is a subtle language of intentions that all creatures have understood to perfection since before Adam. Don't miss the next chapter, where we're really going to ride into some rough Centaur country.

7. Communicating with Horses

Is there any continuity between human and animal communication, or are modern humans and horses condemned to a life of misunderstandings caused by an unbridgeable gap in their social evolution? Can horses emit clear information about their state of mind and intentions or are they merely automats guided by instinct? Can humans learn to understand horse behavior or has civilization irretrievably cut the lifeline to man's ecological roots and animal understanding? The answers to these questions depend mostly on the human capacity to grasp the biological aspects of horse motivations, and how certain environmental circumstances can effectively change the animal's behavior.

Social animals have an active, intelligent, elastic means of communication that most people are completely unaware of, a fact aggravated by the domesticated horse's tendency to restrain his natural behavior in the presence of humans. When approached, a horse confined in a stall or tied to a ring will often 'play possum,' stopping all movement, sometimes even tail and ear twitching, in the hope that the intruder might go away. This defensive behavior has led many people to believe that horses are generally dull-witted, stupid and unfeeling creatures.

Human misunderstanding of animal intelligence has a long and illustrious history. In the past, many attempts have been made to submit animals to 'intelligence tests' with the intention of measuring their capacity for 'rationality,' to see if they are capable of inventing 'new' movements, or capable of learning to use tools to 'solve' their problems, or yet, to identify themselves in the mirror! This only goes to show that most people haven't got a clue to what 'intelligence' is really about, and what an animal's brain was designed to perform in the creature's lifetime. 'By the mid-1970, it appeared to many scholars as though language was to be defined as the part of human communication that animals were 'incapable' of achieving'.[62]

And there is of course an ocean of difference between human language and horse communication, though all oceans are connected somewhere and so is all animal communication. To discover the points of agreement in human and equine motivations is a step towards understanding and communicating with horses. But the big difference between human and horse interaction is that humans can communicate about almost any subject under the sun, while horse relations will be reduced to immediate moods, intentions, states of the mind and to a limited scale of vocalization. Though this may seem rather restrictive, horses seem altogether to be doing better at equine relations than most people do with human relations.

---

[62] By entomologist E.O Wilson, in *Sociobiology*.

But what we must be looking for in this journey into the misty land of the Centaurs is where humans and horses can find common ground to understand each other's motivations and thus organize their relations and equitation to the satisfaction of both. By comprehending the similarity and differences that exist between human and equine communication we may regain some of our ancestral capacity to understand and communicate with the animal world and establish the ground for the cooperative behavior that underlines all good equitation.[63]

Let's then first examine the general meaning of equine vocal expressions. In horse communication mixed vocalization combined with body postures can encode information on individual identity and intentions such as aggression, defense, sexuality, or alarm towards predators. Snorts, knickers, whinnies, bellows, squeals and screams gain their full meaning in combination with a variety of postural attitudes. During friendly exchanges two equines emit harmonic sounds in the lower frequency domain while the hairs around their muzzles touch as they assess each other's smells and attitude. But when Humans meet they are prone to do a lot of arms waving, hand shaking, body stances, and blabbering, which is typical primate behavior.

Therefore, when approaching a horse, one should behave with the discretion of a horse and not with the rowdiness of a baboon: approach face to face, stretch the neck respectively forward, keep the arms down and the tone low. A soft breath into the horse's nostrils is good form and will show the animal that you are aware of equine etiquette. And never approach an unknown horse looking it directly in the eye. Two strange human eyeballs piercing fixedly into the horse's eyes will give the animal an uncomfortable impression of 'great interest' with unknown intentions.

Treat a strange horse confined in stable or tied to a ring with the same cordial respect that you would treat a stranger in an elevator: if you stare too much you may provoke discomfort and a negative reaction. Horses, like all prey animals, are sharp readers of intentions, and therefore our first duty in communicating with them must be to convey clear attitudes of friendship and relaxation devoid of any 'special' interest.

A horse, when deciding on an antagonistic encounter, utters loud bellows in combination with a high head carriage and strutting movements. Therefore humans should avoid this type of cock-sure, domineering, loud voiced, arm waving

---

[63] Humans, until the Neolithic age, were completely integrated with the 'community of life' and were a natural link of their environment. In those times man could communicate with the animals living in the environment through the 'natural language of movements' and simple vocal exchanges. The Old Testaments refers to 'a time when animals could speak' and North and South American natives have a rich oral tradition of human and animal relations which indicate a great understanding of animal motivations.

www.horsetravelbooks.com

behavior when approaching a horse, because this may be taken for aggression. And a smart horse will know that you don't have the size and power to challenge him and this may lead to an escalation of violent behavior. The absence of a good human-equine relationship is the chief reason for a horse's behavioral problems to begin, persist and worsen.[64]

Be clever; approach a horse with a friendly demeanor and don't ever reveal to him that in reality you belong to a predator species. This could start the relation on the wrong footing. If you learn to behave like a friendly nag the horse will take you at face value. Remember that.

In horse communication loud sonorous neighing is meant to localize a family member or a friend. At a distance you may also hail your horse in the pasture, though keeping the tone in the lower frequency domain, which travels well and carries a note of sociable intentions. Never shout like a human; it excites the horses' nervous system and may trigger a fleeing response. Akin to human relations there's no way to mistake pleasant exchanges with antagonistic behavior. Wrong behavior enacted by a human is sure to be taken seriously by the horse, and before you know it you've put the horse on the defensive.

Roman Jacobson demonstrated in a series of studies that the thousands of languages spoken by human groups have a common structure, built in a composite way, starting with simple linguistic units. In contrast, horse communication does not display such structure, and equines communicate with a variety of rather discrete body postures that reveals contentment, interest, eagerness, acuity, fright, boredom, distress, anger, pain, infirmity, hunger, thirst, tiredness and submission. Note that all these states of the mind have a correspondence with human feelings and behavior. For example, horizontal head waving also has a negative meaning in horse behavior and if a vertical shake of the head doesn't mean outright agreement, at least it indicates the intention to parley. A high head carriage is a sign of interest, whether for antagonistic or friendly contact. A drooped head with hanging ears and an opaque stare means tiredness, ill health or submission. And though Equine communication may seem rather rigid and stereotyped if compared to human language, you must try to understand the whole picture of horse interaction.

Exchanges between two horses are a fixed set of signs that the receiving animal interprets as rigidly as the transmitter. In fact, horses generally isolate one aspect of a situation, which functions as a direct sign that will provoke a direct response that may frequently become an overreaction. If a stallion notices the presence of a two-year-old male in his harem he will launch all his fury on the hapless adolescent. The stallion will only see the 'rival' and remain blind to the physical details that reveal that the overgrown youngster is really incapable of

---

[64] *The Body Language of Horses*, by Tom Aislie and Bonnier Ledbetter.

www.horsetravelbooks.com

threatening his position in the hierarchy. And to deflate the full onslaught of the furious stallion the adolescent stretches his neck, lowers his head, and wags his jaw to convince daddy that he is really only a baby incapable of doing harm. And the stallion generally buys it and lets him escape with a snort as a warning. It is not how you look but how you act that will determine the horse's reaction.

In contrast, Bronowski say that the structure of the human language permits us to compose and recognize an unlimited number of phrases arranged with a limited number of words. This is what linguists calls 'productivity of the human language'; the fact that allows people to voice an unlimited number of phrases with an infinite number of meanings, from a limited number of words. This reflects the plasticity of human verbal communication, starting with a limited neurological stimulus. (But this of course also permits Faber to interpret the sacred Bible, the holy Talmud and the revered Koran any old way he wants to, with the direst consequences, as Salmon Rushdie can attest to.) Therefore it may be said that the signals that horses produce are 'direct' and 'total' and with an immediate meaning. A fact that must be taken into account when handling and riding horses.

There is no doubt that human language is largely symbolic, and many gestures have lost their primeval animal meanings and gained new social connotations, which does not occur with horse communication. Equus body signs mean exactly the same today as they did in Attila's time, or three million years back in the African savanna of Laetoli.

But human language is not composed entirely of arbitrary symbols and animal communication is not entirely devoid of symbols. We should not exaggerate the inflexibility of equine responses, regarding them as absolutely fixed. Each response occurs within a context that is wider than the direct stimulus and certain circumstance may totally alter the horses' response. A horse in a round pen may opt to assume a submissive behavior, but once free of the pen's constraint may completely alter his manners because he 'knows' he is free.

If a show jumper refuses an obstacle that he considers too high, the context of the obstacle has also changed the horse's response to his rider's cue to jump. A horse is by no means an automat and an individual horse has individual traits. If a horse under saddle is considered nothing more than a Cartesian automat, a group of automats must be considered to be one big automat.[65] And this of course does not happen within a herd of horses where slight humor fluctuations accumulate and reinforce each other creating a complex society of tensions, uncertainties, conflicts, submissions and triumphs; which is rather similar to human social relations. Therefore we should not consider human and horse communication as dif-

---

[65] *Das Sogennante Böse: Zur Naturgeschichte der Aggression* by Conrad Lorenz.

ferent in principle but only different in grade, subject to human and equine priorities.

Selective pressure has conditioned an equine alpha male's grunts, squeals, body action, and head gestures as means to convey to the band its immediate mood and intentions. To understand this behavior we must realize what specific signal indicates a 'definitive situation,' like a stallion lowering the head with the ears pinned back and the intent to shoo the band away from a predator or a rival stallion. Other signals may signify a 'specific situation,' like a twitching tail showing irritation and discomfort at the approach of a strange animal or person. Or 'symbolic signs' like pawing the ground that can mean a number of things, from a sign of impatience for the chow bucket, or the intention to unearth something to eat, or yet to symbolically clear the ground before a roll.

Because of some significant coincidences many people compare equine behavior directly with human manners, which is not always the case. For though there are many points of agreement, horses and humans have many different priorities to attend to, and therefore they see the world with different eyes. This individual cognitive behavior also exist in human relations: a certain face on a photograph may have no meaning whatsoever to one person, but if it is the picture of another person's mother a world of memories will be triggered by the features. The world and all the things that it contains will have different meanings depending on a creature's species, diet, age, sex, kinship and other priorities. To understand this cognitive phenomenon is part of good horsemanship.

It is also important to know that signals emitted from one horse to another are meant more as a definitive instruction than a piece of information subject to 'interpretation.' As we saw, equines transmit general and specific instructions with no intermediary variations. And the reason why a sign emitted by a horse is a singular unity of information is related to equine evolution. A signal may be triggered as an automatic response to the sight of a predator that favors the survival of the individual that responds to it, thus saving its life.

Therefore a horse's signal is a unity of information that must not be subject to wrong interpretations. It is a 'complete' piece of information that must trigger a total response, because one second in the natural world can become a life or death matter. For this same reason the cue of the rider for a change of lead at the gallop must likewise be absolutely fixed to produce a total response. Prey animals, contrary to humans, must trigger instant responses to external stimuli and this is exactly one of the features that permits the neurophysiological connection of the Centaur. The well-schooled horse's responses to human cues are practically infallible, and these reflexes were installed in the animal's motor system by millions of years of natural selection to act instantly on provocation.

www.horsetravelbooks.com

On the other hand the human mind, capable of reflection and analysis, seems to have developed a tendency towards freezing in sight of danger. Incapable of great speed, humans must stop to formulate an alternative course of action. And it is the *difference and similarity* of response to stimulus that make the Homo-Caballus symbiosis possible. For example, in competitive dressage, the emotional part of the human mind can induce the horse to a piaffe, while the rational mind can remember the sequence of the figures, an impossible feat for the horse. Humans can remember the sequence of dressage figures because they have developed a 'future memory,' the capacity to understand a time concept which is worthless to the horse's biological priorities.

Human memory can be said to be the accumulation of signals in symbolic form, so that these can be stored and used for future responses, which is only possible if the initial response is not 'total,' and can be sufficiently delayed, and thus be connected to an abstract symbol that can be fixed in the brain. The interval between the stimulus and the message in the human brain makes it possible for the stimulus to be processed in more than one nervous cerebral center. It is the process of embodiment of language that establishes the principal difference between human language and horse communication. When training a horse, if the animal responds inadequately to a correct cue, the trainer will have less than two seconds to amend the failure. If the horse is corrected within this interval it may not link the correction with the mistake.

The internal language of equitation, which combines the instant response of the horse with the rider's capacity for strategic thought, was also at the roots of the mounted nomads' cavalry achievements. Ancient horseback archers thought of their horses as highly rational and would treat them with the deference of a best friend. Though most city-bred humans would think this ridiculous, the warriors of the steppe learned to organize a chain of postural body stances that reflected the horse's gaits, walk trot, gallop, changes of directions, and stop, that the horse could feel and imitate and thus the nomad horsemen achieved great control over their horses. Therefore there seems to be no aim in advanced horsemanship other than to understand the horse's motivations and communication system and organize equitation into one chain of cooperative movements, cued by the rider and imitated by the horse.

Human language evolved originally from primitive animal communication and our equestrian language must therefore stem from the ancient human capacity to synthesize biological body cues and vocal sounds into one chain of primitive movements and communication. And to reach the ultimate goal—high performance equitation—much depends on understanding the similarity of human end equine emotions. And, as we will presently see, science can show

www.horsetravelbooks.com

us other pathways of senses and emotions that are at the core of the neurophysiological flux that we call advanced equitation.

8. Life Cycles and Strategies in the Training of Horses

Although they may look similar, an untrained horse is essentially different from a trained one. A well-schooled horse, like a human athlete, is an animal whose whole relation to his physical performance has been altered. To become an equine athlete, a horse must learn new ways to handle the psychological and physical effort of moving in collaboration with a partner who is in charge of some very important parts of the action – specifically the decisions concerning the speeds and the directions of his gaits. Therefore the training of horses demands a critical understanding of the time cycles that govern the animal's life, and a biologically sound strategy to coach the horse to develop a favorable symbiotic behavior towards equestrian sports.

As we saw, for horse and rider to blend into one biological unity the partners must form a psycho-neurological cooperation chain capable of aligning their movements and intentions into joint action. To understand this procedure neuroscientists are adding much new evidence for whoever bothers to look for it. Therefore, in the 21st century horse people will be able to form a much clearer picture of equitation than was ever possible before, and perhaps the horse world can now come to a scientific consensus about riding techniques, instead of the wrangling and squabbling of the old school systems. And as long as we're traveling through this remote part of the Centaur's home range let's analyze the progressive biological technique of wiring a horse's brain to instill symbiotic behavior and favor equestrian performance.

The intention of this and the following chapters is not to teach you HOW to train your horse, because you'll find better books written and illustrated specifically for this purpose. The aim here is to help modern riders to form a strategic idea of bioequitation and help fit the horse's training program to the horse's life cycles. A biological strategy will help connect the right sequences of 'riding reflex chains' and assure the animal's goodwill towards training, by avoiding the human errors that frequently end in the animal's desperation, hostility and violence.

THIS IS NOT A HOW-TO MANUAL, BUT RATHER A WHY-TO GUIDE

For a horse to tackle equestrian games with the high degree of efficiency verified in a winning performance, great changes must be performed in the horse's behavior and attitudes. In this strategy what you get out of a performance is what you've put in. More often than not the incompetent rider will blame the under-trained horse for an equestrian mishap and affirm that he himself did apply the 'aids' by the manual and the d----d horse didn't 'obey' his orders. As Gabby

www.horsetravelbooks.com

Hays used to say "bull-shit in, horse-shit out," and Partner would snicker with laughter.

The way the horse behaves in his 'private life' is of course very different from the way he acts in his 'equestrian life.' To automate the split-second reading of the rider's intentions when approaching a moment of high emotional intensity, when the combination's joint motor-program must tackle a jump, perform a piaffe, hit a polo ball, or the bull fighter must set the banderrilas on a charging bull's withers, is not like anything the horse would himself conceive when bantering about in the field with his equine fellows. Not essentially different, mind you, but different enough to require a careful step by step approach to introduce him correctly to his equestrian role. And one must always keep in mind that under training conditions the horse will not really be learning anything new, but only adapting his body and mind to the new cooperative circumstance that we call equitation.

When starting a horse for riding, the first thing that must kept in mind is that even though equitation is basically the human use of the horse's locomotive-system in a symbiotic exchange for good care, decent chow and jolly friendship, the horse was not created by God for riding purposes. Undoubtedly, God's favorite 'running machine' was created to run his own errands. But the miracle of equitation, like many other good things in life, can be far more rewarding than any of the mind-boggling products that the entertainment industry regularly spews out for human consumption.

The next thing to remember is that the horse trainer will be working with a many million years pre-tested equine brain developed to 'read' the environment and transform the collected data into the right attitude and complex footwork that helped Equus Caballus to survive successfully in a hostile environment. And footwork is exactly what the horse trainer must address in a natural and systematic way. But because the horse's biological intelligence evolved to see the world in a completely different light than primates in general, and Homo sapiens in particular, horses have a horse's way of learning, and humans have a human way of learning. And this calls for some very unconventional knowledge that you don't learn in a conventional riding school or in 'round pen' workouts.

When a professional horse trainer, who through years of experience has developed a keen eye for equine motivations and behavior, starts a young horse in equitation she or he must know that this complex biological technique involves weaving the young animal's mind into a solid net of automatic response to the rider's chain of riding cues, where *every little movement has a meaning of its own*. On the psychological level the trainer will be working to change the horse's behavior in relation to his original mental motivation and induce him to follow the rider's cues of intentions in a flux of fast synaptic exchanges.

www.horsetravelbooks.com

Here are some basic checkpoints that a trainer should keep in mind about some of the horse's life cycles that rules his health, happiness and inclination to cooperate.

1. The horse's body and mind is part of the same system and to become a good performer the psychological aspects of equitation must progress at the same pace as the physical action. What his mind cannot understand his body cannot perform.

2. The horse was born with all the resources that he'll need in his new equestrian life and the trainer's job is not to teach him anything 'new,' but to make him perform his natural movements in the multiple sequences required by sport and leisure riding.

3. The horse's equestrian learning must follow his biological cycle of evolution (ontogenesis) from the time of birth throughout childhood, adolescence, and adulthood (see more in the next chapter).

4. A 'complete training cycle,' the time spent from brushing, saddling, and mounting to the time when the horse is unsaddled and brushed after a workout, should repeat the horse's equestrian evolutionary cycle: the session should start with the 'join up,' then the mounting of the horse, a ten minutes walk including flexions, a trot, a gallop, and only then should the horse tackle the exercise that he is currently working on.

5. During one 'complete training cycle,' 'short exercise cycles' should be introduced in the ring. The smaller cycles – from immobility to exercise to immobility – may take one, two, or three minutes, depending on the type of work, the horse's age and his physical conditioning. When the animal has completed a 'short exercise cycle' he should be halted and only started again after *sighing*, which shows that he has reorganized his respiratory system, and may start another 'short exercise cycle.'[66]

6. After a complete workout his biological clock will have completed *one training cycle* and he should be congratulated and made much of. By working within the horse's natural life cycles, the animal will develop good will to the whole idea of equitation, an absolute prerequisite to advanced horsemanship.

7. During workouts the horse believes that he is performing the transitions and changes of direction by his own will, and it is the trainer's duty to re-enforce this belief and humor him to put maximum faith in his effort. The domineering

---

[66] The horse, like all prey animals, evolved to perform one burst of speed to escape his predators. Predators evolved around the capacity to outrun, in a successful chase, his chosen prey. Success and failure lie in these short one or two minutes bursts of speed. A biological training strategy must divide this burst of speed into shorter work cycles that can keep the horse training for longer periods. After stopping, the horse's *sigh* will indicate when he's ready for another 'short work cycle.'

www.horsetravelbooks.com

attitude "you must do what I'm commanding" should change to "I'm here to help you do the right thing."

As the training strategy unfolds, the horse trainer will be working on the two principal levels of Caballus' powerful brain: the conscious and the unconscious mind.[67]

The horse's conscious and unconscious equestrian learning must be stored in a natural order in the animal's memory,[68] so that the experience can be easily available for quick responses to the rider's cues which travel along the joint human and equine motor nerve fibers at the speed of the synapses. The horse's brain-wiring must be done by the trainer with the purpose of linking millions of neurons into new pathways that will permit the animal to undertake any aspect of equitation, from the correct reading of the environment – the jumping courses, polo fields, bull rings – to the task of performing complex figures of Dressage, or performing a jumping circuit in full neurological feedback connection with the human partner.

The fact to be remembered here is that a young horse has to learn literally every step of handling and equitation. He must learn to walk beside the handler; to be tied to a ring; to have his hooves picked; to be groomed; to be clipped; to be saddled; to step into a puddle or cross a river; to respond to the rider's cues. He has to re-learn to walk, trot, and canter in a straight line with a rider astride his back; he has to learn to rely on the rider's cybernetic indications; to monitor the rider's movements; to produce a chain of transitions in response to a chain of cues; to jump fences; to tackle polo balls; to ignore loudspeakers; to keep calm in the face of a host of human machines; he has to learn to be patient, and await the major equestrian cues to start a race, to finish a dressage test, and so on.

These experiences must be added one by one to the horse's neuron web, which must be connected from the simplest barn and pasture handling to the performance of the most difficult gaits, and to tackle the most arduous equestrian sports. As the horse's bipolar brain does not have the two hemispheres connected like the human brain,[69] he must learn everything, from the picking of hooves to mounting, on both sides of his body.

The horse's confidence and willingness to cooperate should slowly spread from barn handling to envelope his performance in ever-greater circuits of 'equestrian knowledge,' until his brain wiring is a complete web prepared to cope

---

[67] This, of course, is a necessary simplification of how the horse's mind works.
[68] By 'natural order' I mean that leg cues, that must trigger the ample movements, must precede snaffle cues that indicate the limit of the movements.
[69] The unconnected bipolar division of the horses' brain permits a bi-polar vision in which the horse can monitor his right and left side of his angle of vision independently, which is a great biological asset for a prey animal.

with the situations of one or more equestrian disciplines. As in any information-chain, no link must be overlooked or taught out of order for the neuron web must be thoroughly knitted to insure the proper path of synaptic responses under any equestrian circumstances. Any error in connecting the 'riding reflex chains' may later provoke a disorder in the animal's responses.

Therefore simple chains of movements must be learned before difficult ones. The direct transition from walk to trot must be learned before the indirect transition from walk to canter, and canter before backing. The principal transitions must be learned before lateral work, and jumping before dressage. And the same cues must not be used for two different purposes. Experience by experience, the trainer's strategy must build the horse's confidence, performance, and physical preparedness to tackle any incident that may arise in the riding ring or in the field. The trainer knows that the horse's brain is built much like his own gray-matter, and that the animal will act positively to one simple principle: anything that seems like an enjoyable proposition will be willingly acted upon! Don't laugh – us primates do exactly the same.

As no one had knowledge of these biological facts in the past it is a wonder that some horses were able to perform with the high degree of excellence seen over the ages. Gabby Hays used to say that this fact should be credited exclusively to the horse's skill, as the vast majority of riders worked with a mixture of intuition and hearsay, and that unfortunately the hearsay seldom came from the horse and the intuition almost always stemmed from the rider's anthropocentric mind.

A training system must conform to the horses' psychological and biological cycles. This fact must permeate high performance equitation, because low-tech riding is correctly perceived by a horse as a threat to its very existence. The horse will acquire a positive attitude towards anything that is understood as a 'clean deal', that respects his mental and physical integrity and also has something 'in it' for him. When working with well-bred and capable horses, and applying biologically sound techniques, no forceful methods or restraining devices are necessary to attain high performance equitation.

9. Building a Centaur from a Horse

Approaching a horse with the intention of one day riding him involves a subtle code of behavior: smoothness of action combined with firmness of attitude will indicate friendly intentions for a certain purpose. Groundwork training has the task of teaching the horse to interact with a human leader and to understand the purpose of the relationship, which is to walk, trot, gallop, change direction and stop by human command. The teaching process must unfold as one uninterrupted chain of cooperative behavior that the horse must learn by seeing, imitating, and responding to the trainer's cybernetic cues. In the initial stage of the groundwork the horse must learn how to learn by firm but gentle persuasion.

For a young horse to be initiated in the schooling process the most practical way is the time proven system of lungeing the animal in a circle and teaching him to respond to the instructors' intentions and movements to walk, trot, stop, and walk again. On the lunge the animal should go through all the phases of his *ontogenesis*, which is the evolutionary stages of the horse's life since birth: the 1st childhood, the 2nd childhood, puberty, and adulthood.

The first session of lungeing represents the neonatal stage where the "newborn foal" takes his first wobbly steps on the road to adulthood.

In the second phase—the 1st childhood—the horse must learn how to walk, and trot, stimulated by human cues.

In the third phase—the 2nd childhood—the horse will have become more surefooted and capable of responding automatically to cues to walk, trot, stop and sustain these gaits for short periods. In his equestrian 'puberty' the horse will find himself mounted and able to perform his gaits with a rider cueing him by muscle vibrations to walk, trot, gallop, and stop. After this phase of training the animal will have become ready to work on the ranch or serve as a pleasure horse. It is in the fifth stage, when horse has completed his physiological connection with the rider, and can automatically read his partner's body postures and cues, that the animal will blossom into the equine part of a Centaur, in perfect command of his equestrian movements.

Personally I start a horse on the lunge in an open 12m ring, but the work can be done in any dirt area of soft level ground with a wooden pillar in the center. The lungeing rein is tied to a rotating tool fixed to the pillar, so that in the first sessions a more excitable horse cannot pull the lead from the trainer's hands. This is the first rule that the young horse must learn for life: it is impossible to snatch the rope out of the trainer's hand. As Archimedes wisely stated: give me a point of support and I'll move the world. The wooden pillar, in the center of the ring, represents the human strength around which the horses' learning will gravitate. Given that in this manner he can never run away, not because he is barred by the physical presence of an enclosure, but by the apparent force of the trainer's hands, he will settle down and concentrate on the trainer, who will become the center of his attention.

And now a surprise to Grisone and his latter-day followers: during the groundwork a friendly atmosphere must be established for the horse to build confidence in his work. The trainer's calm and expert handling of any situation that may provoke a 'negative response' will overcome all difficulties. During every lungeing session the horse should be stopped for a couple of times for gentle finger rubbing and hand touches over the body, under the belly and along the ears.[70]

This is the natural 'language of friendship' and shows that the trainer appreciates the horse's effort and knows his pleasure spots and tender places. In the horse's mind the trainer must become the friendly all-knowing leader, the source from where the helping cues to his equestrian movements springs. Therefore the horse trainer's manners must jump the species line, which can sometimes be difficult for humans to understand, though the technique is as simple as breathing and almost anyone in her or his right mind can learn it.

During every session, the trainer must convey to the horse his wish to increase speed, and perform the transitions from walk, to trot, and to stop, not with a whip but by physical signs of these movements and by expressing the emotional 'urgency' to increase the speed. A whip-like tool may be used as a prolongation of his arm, with the purpose to point or touch the part of the horse that must increase the action: forelegs, hind legs, belly, neck or croup. To decrease the speed the trainer must convey clear physical signs of muscular relaxation and a soft tug of the lungeing rein to indicate the slowing down of the action. The horse must perceive in the trainer's body movements the signs of the action that must induce his own performance: walk, trot, halt.

The reflex to stop can successfully be reinforced by the hissing sound shhhhhhhhh... emitted by the trainer as he himself stops. Throughout the whole session the trainer's body postures and attitudes must clearly denote his intentions to accelerate or to slow down. If the horse flags in his action the trainer must move closer with his hand running along the lungeing rain, and as soon as the horse bucks up he will slowly move back to the center. When the horse has understood the cues for changing gaits - walk, trot, and stop – performed in both directions, six stages of tack additions will prepare the horse to receive the rider on his back.

The first piece of tack is a saddle with shortened stirrups. One or two lungeing sessions later, when the horse is comfortable with this, he should start circling

---

[70] Here I very much recommend Linda Tellington-Jones books on *TTouch* and *TTeam Training*.

www.horsetravelbooks.com

with lowered stirrups, and a day or two later, when the animal is comfortable with the dangling stirrups, add the snaffle, which must have been put on an hour or so before training and worn during a meal. In this way the horse will have become accustomed to the hard metal tool in his mouth while chewing a meal and will respond better to the ensuing lungeing session.

Next, connect the snaffle rings to the pommel rings under the saddle skirt with elastic cordons, a 'virtual' rein for the horse to become accustomed to a flexible contact with its mouth. Two or three days will suffice for every new tack addition to become comfortable, and between fourteen and twenty-one days the horse should be confident in his work and ready for the breathtaking moment: to willingly receive the rider on his back. Step by step the horse is having his natural movements organized in a chain of conditioned riding responses affected by clear visual and auditory cues that translate the act of walking, trotting, and sustaining the horse's natural gates for short periods in both directions.

There is no need to invent new movements or to exaggerate the performance. Once the horse gets the hang of the game all that must be done is to suggest the walk and the trot in different sequences. When the groundwork is completed and the horse knows when to walk, trot, and stop on cue, the mounted work may begin, and the lungeing rein gets a new mission in the Homo-Caballus communication system: Lo! Hey presto! The lunging rein becomes the rein fixed to the bit and connected to the human hands that the horse has learned that he can never pull away from! When mounting the 'virtual rein' of elastic must be removed, but may be attached again after the horse has become comfortable with the rider on his back.[71]

The critical moment of mounting the horse should start with a helper setting foot in the stirrup and gently heaving the body over the saddle. If a 'negative reaction' occurs the act should be stopped and tried in the next session. Don't try to force the issue. A 'negative response' only means that the horse has not built enough confidence to accept the new situation, so more time must be given on the lunge for him to build up his self-confidence to receive a rider on his back. As the horse has never been rebuked, whipped or manhandled in any way during the training sessions, receiving the rider on his back will become a casual consequence of the training process.

After the rider takes his place on the horse's back one fundamental change must be clearly effected: instead of the horse imitating the cues to walk, trot, stop, and to sustain his gaits by visual contact with the earthbound partner, the

---

[71] Some trainers like to be the first man up, which I don't do myself. In this critical moment I think the leader will be more useful by standing at the horse's head, holding the halter, and soothing him with a low tone of appraisal and his touch with his 'magical' hands.

www.horsetravelbooks.com

cues to spark the horse's sensory motor system will now be switched, step by step, to his feeling of touch, through the body contact with the rider. After he is mounted the horse must learn to perceive the rider's muscle vibrations: the cues for walking, trotting, stopping, and to sustain his gaits and changes of directions. In the first mounted sessions both the trainer and the auxiliary will perform the cybernetic cues in combination.

In this way, from groundwork to mounting nothing will really have changed but the source of the cues, from visual to tactile. And usually after only one session the horse will have switched his responses from visual to tactile. There must be no hurry, for every animal has its own learning time. Some are fast to learn (and also fast to unlearn) and others may be slower to understand what is expected of them, though retaining the experience forever. But what are fifteen or twenty days of ground work for an animal that may give you twenty years of service?

Starting with groundwork, and progressing towards mounted training and high school maneuvers, each phase must have a natural prolongation into the next stage of the training program. By letting the stirrups dangle after the horse is confident with the saddle, you will simulate the contact of the human feet; by connecting the snaffle rings with the rings under the saddle skirt with an elastic cordon, the horse will slightly flex his head; by transforming the lungeing line into the rein, the horse has understood the principle of rein work without the added encumbrance of having a rider sitting on his back.

And once the helper raises himself up on the horse's back the horse will know how to start, change directions and stop, which are the bases of all types of equestrian sports. And to boot you have become the center of the horse's attention, and by showing gentle care to anything that may occur, you have gained his affection and friendship (that with animals becomes a life-long bond). Tidbits are allowed in the beginning and end of each daily work cycle. Never give the horse anything to eat during the work sessions because this may create expectations in moments when he should concentrate on the training. (This rule should only be broken in the first mounting session of an excitable horse.) Young horses especially are prone to lose their concentration, so don't worsen this habit by untimely indulgence. As we saw in *Equus Ludens*, the game must be seen as a voluntary occupation, according to rules freely accepted, but absolutely obligatory. If you can pass this idea to the horse he may become almost unbeatable in your chosen equestrian game.

During groundwork the horse will be learning to imitate his friend and leader by the 'natural language of movements.' Each lungeing session should take fifteen minutes and one extra minute can be added every week. As we've seen, any show of impatience, threatening movements and haughty attitudes will spoil

www.horsetravelbooks.com

the relationship and wreck the delicate confidence build-up of the animal, so these self-defeating human quirks must be avoided at all cost. Patience, determination, and clear-cut, though subtle movements to convey your intentions, are the recipe for establishing a working symbiosis in the natural world.

And don't ever be persuaded by methods that promise to prepare a horse for mounting in thirty minutes, an hour, or a day. This can be done, of course, but the multiple problems of an under-educated horse, who has not had it's natural movements organized into a chain of progressive riding responses, will be awaiting you just around the corner.[72]

Biological time – the time to be born, the time to grow-up and the time to mature – cannot be successfully accelerated, as any biologist or responsible horseperson can tell you. It takes two or three weeks for a horse to learn his basic role in equitation and any attempt to shorten it may cause 'flaws' in the chain of riding responses. Starting a horse should not be made into a contest like barrel racing, pole bending, or calf roping. Any mistake along the line will mar the horse's future performance. A bad start is the principal reasons why so many horses are undereducated, and so many horse people unhappy.

Groundwork has the vital importance of establishing human leadership and teaching the horse to perform his gaits at human command by monitoring the rider's cues. They are the first steps to the neurophysiological connection of equitation, which is the ability of Homo and Caballus to monitor each other's movements through sophisticated cerebral circuits, wired to respond to each other's motor-pattern.

---

[72] The 'round pen' system is, I believe, the first chapter in the 'universal language of movements' and will correctly establish the horseperson as the leader of the homo-Caballus combination. The method seems efficient to start a ranch horse for work duties, but falls short of initiating a high performance horse in the complex disciplines of modern sports, where the horse's movements must be organized into chains of automatic responses induced by a highly ritualistic technique of visual, tactile and acoustic messages.

10. A Rider Named Homo-Caballus

Many riders are ingrained with a conservative mentality and look suspiciously upon science to solve their equestrian troubles. Most people believe that 'new techniques' are all they need to solve their old equestrian problems. But sooner rather than later life sciences will be the logical tool for riders to understand the meaning of ecology, to appreciate the biological codes of life communities, their own place in the natural world, their biological link to their horses, and that they are more 'like' than 'unlike' their horse. And this 'back to nature movement' will trigger the spiritual leap from the old mechanical view of horses to a new biological view of equestrian methods and techniques.

In our journey to understand the origin of equitation we must not rely on anything except *facts*, and the data collected must only spring from the horse's body and mind, which cannot lead us astray. By this I mean that all new equestrian findings must be submitted to the physical responses of the horse, and we must completely clear our mind of all the vices, biases and fallacies of the 'old horse world.' This must be the number-one law for the intersensory relationship of humans and horses that leads to understanding, communication and highly sensitive, or high performance, equitation.

The first thing to be noted here is that it generally takes longer to hard-wire the human brain for equitation than the horse's. A horse may take a year or two to reach the adolescence of his behavioral transformation, where he has learned to perform the basic movements of equitation. But to become a 'horse leader' capable of guiding a horse through high adventure from a position on its back, the human partner must learn to see, hear, and smell the environment like a horse. The rider must become conscious of odd shapes, strange objects, dark shadows, hissing noises, rustling sounds, and other 'dangerous' manifestations to avoid his better part taking fright under him. The rider must be trained to rotate his senses like a gyroscope and sometimes be led by sound rather than sight, by touch rather than sound, or by smell rather than by sound – like his horse. This is a difficult achievement for humans who evolved as a highly visual species and rely mostly on what they can see with the eyes rather than what they perceive with their other senses.

When the human nerve system is well connected to the horse's and the animal is suddenly frightened, the shock wave travels through the combination's body as if through one animal. (In the Middle Ages, for writing such blasphemous ideas, I'd probably be denounced to the Holy Inquisition for a pact with the devil and thoroughly roasted in the town square to the joy of the merry burghers!) This means that when your horse jumps with fright you jump with fright, because you have become neurologically attached to his emotions.

www.horsetravelbooks.com

One must learn to control the horse's fear by looking at the world through the horse's eyes, and apply a soothing and rational handling of the frightening moment. But to see the world like a horse does and merge your locomotion system to the horse's gaits is no mean feat and it takes a great deal of time to hard-wire the human brain to the horse's mind, thus forming one workable equestrian operation. It must have taken a couple of thousand years for the Central Asian horse-herders to develop biologically sound equestrian techniques to control their horses at all speeds, a feat only possible under the severe conditions of hunting and warfare induced by their atavistic capacity of communicating with their horses.

So what can we learn from all this? That to turn into a full-fledged Centaur a person must have her or his brain upgraded to perform athletic feats at speeds and power superior to the original human biological capacity. Or in other words: the human mind must learn to rely on the speed and power of the horse's legs as if these physical features radiate from the human body, and to be able to control the animal's emotions. The initial stage of connecting the human brain to the horse's motor system will remind one of the rite of passage in a Paleolithic or Amerindian community: the person must create a spiritual connection with the horse through the alteration of the human conscience.

But as modern minds are burdened by obsolete traditions and by the tensions of modern life, a person must ardently desire the change, 'because knowledge is best gained if the spirit is in harmony with the spirit of the knowledge to be received or passed on. A horse person must not belong to the class of people who choose to dominate nature as their guiding principle.'[73] The rider that receives his or her horse groomed, saddled and booted from the hands of a groom cannot expect to come anywhere near the performance of a rider that cares personally for the training and welfare of the horse. (If this warning was aired in a former chapter please disregard this notice.)

Bioequitation is the building of a completely new attitude towards nature in general and horses in particular. To develop the 'Centaur feel' the novice rider has primarily to learn to connect his legwork to the horse's locomotion system, fine-tune his hands to monitor the limits of the animal's muscle cycles and connect his mind to the horse's view of the world. To develop further sensitivity to the horse's movements the student must have his brain hard-wired to feel the four-beat gait of the horse's walk, the two-beat gait of its trot, and three-beat gait of the canter – rhythms which the horse drums on the ground as it sustains and alters its velocity. When this feeling has been connected, and the rider can read these movements and act upon them automatically, his proprioceptive feel will actually have reached down and touched the ground through the horse's legs!

---

[73] From Cassai Lajo's book *Horseback Archery*.

Like the horse, the student should also start her or his equestrian life on the lunge and undergo all the phases of his ontogenesis, which is the evolutionary unfolding of his own life: the stages of 1st childhood, 2nd childhood, puberty, and adulthood. The first days of lunging represent the stage where the "new-born Centaur" takes her or his first wobbly steps on the road to adulthood. In this phase the human body must feel the workings of the equine muscles in all their gaits. In the second phase – the 1st childhood – the rider must learn how to walk, and trot with the help of the instructor's cues. In the third phase, the 2nd childhood, the rider will have become more equilibrated and able to perform the cues to walk, trot, stop and sustain these gaits for the time required.

In the next stage, equestrian 'puberty,' the rider will have become capable of cuing the horse's gaits with muscle vibrations to walk, trot, gallop, and stop. In this phase of training she or he will have become ready to work on the ranch or ride for pleasure. It is in the fifth stage, when the rider has completed his physiological connection with the horse, and can automatically read the animal's body movements, that she or he will have blossom into the human part of a Centaur, in perfect command of all equestrian movements. By connecting the body and mind with the horse's, equitation will have become second nature to the rider.

The pupil will also have learned to help absorb the vertical attrition of the horse's gait with his joints, and at the same time keep his hands completely disconnected from this attrition and fully connected to the horizontal expansion and contraction of the horse's outline, as the animal executes its natural gaits. Gabby Hays used to say that a good rider must have the supple body of a dancer and the skilled hands of a pianist, to which Partner would laugh and say that he'd better, or he'd end with his seat in the daisies!

The student must also learn the art of leadership by tying an emotional knot to the relationship, through the combination's love of being together, by creative thinking during training, and careful handling after workouts. And slowly the rider will develop the powerful feel that she or he is the extension of the horse, and the horse will feel his rider as the continuation of himself. A double-lane of riding reflexes will have been established by the emotional and tactile feedback of Homo and Caballus' joint action, feeding each other's motor systems with precise cybernetic data,[74] which their equestrian brains have been hard-wired to understand and act upon!

The human bi-pedal motor pattern will have been re-wired to administer the horse's complex two, three, and four-beat motor system, and the rider's legs are now commanding the impulsion and changes of direction which, by the way, is basically what they were meant for in his own gaits. The human hands, con-

---

[74] Cybernetic data are the cues that indicate changes of speed and changes of direction, which are natural biological movements indicating the changes.

www.horsetravelbooks.com

nected to the horses mouth, deal with the fine action, as the partner's brain wiring was meant to deal with the fine work of food selection. The sensitizing of a human to a horse's movements is a flight towards greater physical and spiritual powers, and no man or woman can ever aspire to fully control the body and mind of a horse if he or she has not full control of their own body and mind. The learning of highly sensitive equitation is a rite of passage in which the rider must reach far back into human evolution and ransom the once lost power to deal with the biological nature of the animal world, a deep and wondrous experience to the sensitive person with a biological outlook on life.

Equitation is not similar to any other type of learning but we can find grains of the biological reasoning of horsemanship in other human practices like sports, dancing and yoga, for example. The higher achievements in these practices also depend on great changes in body and mind to reach the excellence of performance or an altered state of the conscience. Almost like a 'rite of passage' through which ancient civilizations attained the understanding of life. And perhaps they were right.

www.horsetravelbooks.com

11. Bioequitation—Turning "I Wish" into "I Can"[75]

A horse is not steered in the conventional sense of the word and this fact is bewildering to people who have been brought up in the mainstream of a highly successful industrial society where all vehicles are driven by the hands guided by the eyes. Therefore the mental leap from mechanical to bioequitation can probably be made more easily by the new generations brought up in a post industrial world where science and technology have taught people to transcend beyond their natural social and physical limits. A supple body and mind is of course the first condition for a person to transmute into a full-fledged Centaur.

As we have seen, to blossom into a Centaur a person has to have his or her brain upgraded to perform athletic feats in speed and power superior to the original human genetic ability. In the first part of this book we analyzed the historical outcome of this unique neurological upgrading, when God's favorite 'learning machine' struck a deal with God's favorite 'running machine' and together the Homo-Caballus combination overran Eurasia and became the master of most of its riches.

In the third part I hope to have set Equus Caballus' learning process into a clearer perspective and in the forthcoming chapters we'll try to ride further into the recesses of Centaur country and speculate on how the human and equine brain should be upgraded to match each other's motor system. But first let's have a look at how humans developed their visual-motor system to solve their daily problems on the African savanna and why this impressive ability became the foundation of Europe's industrial revolution and why the visual-motor system is inadequate for guiding a horse in highly sensitive equitation.

A horse is not 'steered' in the conventional sense of the word and this fact is bewildering to many people who have been bred in the mainstream of a highly successful industrial society where a multitude of vehicles and electronic gizmos are guided by handle bar, steering wheel, helm, flywheels rudder, computer mouse, and joystick. (See also *The Cybernetic Zone of Horsemanship* coming up next.)

And if we consider Valen's defeat at Hadrianopolis to be the starting point of European cavalry history, it would take over one thousand five hundred years for the Western world to master some of those techniques. But why did it take longer for Europeans to master the full extent of bioequitation compared to the Central Asians nomads?

Well, we can start by analyzing your surname or mine. As I have the facts of my family name here at hand let's start with these. The German surname 'Rink'

---

[75] By Pam Brown, b. 1928

is of occupational origin, belonging to that category of names based on the type of work a man's folks once did. In my case the surname 'Rink' is traceable to the Middle High German term 'rinke' which denoted a buckle maker (and so what? Shakespeare's folks were glove makers!).[76] And as we know, from ancient times people developed their *visual-motor skill* for food selection and starting in the Neolithic – the 'New Stone Age' – Faber initiated the skill of manufacturing tools, clothes, shoes, hats, buckles, gloves, jewels and all kinds of domestic, professional and warlike artifacts, besides fine art itself. All this work depended foremost on the capacity of artisans to work with their hands guided by their eyes. This *eye-orientated* mechanical technology led humanity from the Old Stone Age to the New Stone Age with all its handwork that would slowly turn into Western Europe's industrial societies.

Now, the first use of horses in European history was for draft work. This type of work depended on harnessing the horse's power to plow the earth and pull a wagon. A long list of contraptions was invented to improve these techniques. Some scholars maintain that the horse-collar was one of humanity's most useful inventions. And for sedentary societies it probably was.

It stands to reason that when our artisan forefathers, coming from an agricultural environment, started to work with horses for riding purposes their brains were wired for mechanical thought and thus were prone to invent a 'mechanical solution' to their everyday horse problems. So when my great-great-great-great grandfather, hailing from a traditional buckle-making family in Jenas Einwohner in Germany, decided to go from buckles into the horse bitting business, he started to manufacture bits with the idea that it would produce subtle 'kinetic operations' favorable for controlling the saddle horse (don't laugh, Mr. Smith, your ironworking ancestors probably did the same). And as scores of mechanical devices had been built to 'improve' driving technology, hundreds of mechanical artifacts were also manufactured to improve horsemanship. Remember: in old Europe the bit was the 'key' to the horse. But through modern eyes...

"THE KEY TO THE HORSE IS EQUINE PSYCHOLOGY"

In this manner Western equitation became an extension of Western draft culture and a host of tools and devises were invented to help 'harness' the horse's

---

[76] The escutcheon that William Shakespeare earned as an actor and playwright had, beside books, flowers and theatre masks, a falcon with the dexter leg raised holding a quill, signed with the axiom 'Non sans Droict.' Well, the blazon of arms of the old Rink swashbucklers had a falcon sable with wings raised, the dexter leg raised, holding in its beak a ring, over the motto 'A noble spirit in pursuit of enterprises of honor.' (It must have cost the old firebrand Rink from Jena Einwohner a bundle.)

power and transform its movements into good equitation. As we saw, mechanistic techniques in horse training were the approved practices taught by Federico Grisone in Naples, a contemporary of the Rink buckle maker family in Germany, and are still largely in favor all over the world in spite of Caprilli's innovative teachings.

Western societies, who had gained all their remarkable technological advances by mechanical thought, could also be expected to build a 'mechanical device' to solve any daily horse problem. From the Middle Ages onwards, the nobles and the rich burghers, who formed the cream of Europe's Cavalry schools, possessed a 'visual-motor brain wiring' which was then standard for all successful people. For this reason, all tools are invented with a grasping handle and all vehicles have a *handle bar* or a *steering wheel* to be manipulated by the hands guided by the eyes. This mechanistic technology formed Europe's old riding philosophy and all sorts of bitting theories became the focus of Western riding techniques.

And while our successful forebears were building their artificial urban environment they would move further and further away from a biological understanding of the natural world, which is essentially the capability of feeling yourself as an interactive part of nature. As urban populations in Eurasia developed a growing capacity for mechanical thought they completely lost their intellectual faculty to interact with nature and animals, and here we must include the handling and riding of horses. But the Central Asian horsemen, still in a Neolithic state of technological development, retained their natural ties to steppe ecology and this gave them their excellent horsemanship. As modern humans slowly built their 'perfect' urban environment, they gradually lost the ability to comprehend the natural world, and this degraded their horsemanship.

From the Middle Ages to the so called 'Atomic Age' no one could understand why you could drive sleds, coaches, bicycles, automobiles, and airplanes by hand – but you could not ride a 'simple horse' in all speeds and directions by the same method.[77] As the reason for this phenomenon was never discovered, most Western riders reduced the horse's speed to their own brain capacity and everything equestrian was built for 'slow motion' – from armor, to horse types, to war strategy (as we saw in *The Rise of Horsemanship in Europe*). Outfitted with a 'mechanistic mind' people were unable to grasp the fact that they could not

---

[77] In *The Canterbury Tales* Geoffrey Chaucer describes the Knight's son: *'He was a good rider and sat his horse well.'* As you can see, in the Middle Ages, riding was described as merely 'sitting' on a horse. From this point of view sprang all the subsequent attention to the rider's 'seat' and the misleading notions of the different styles of 'seats' and so on. But of course, in those pre scientific times, people could only describe what they saw.

'drive' a saddle horse effectively with the hands – and that to achieve absolute control you had to adapt to the horse's nature.

Does this sound reasonable to you? Well until the 21st century, most horsemen couldn't fathom it. The mystery and mystification of equitation would grow in exact proportion to the Western world's mechanical success that took off vertically in the 18th century and would land Faber simultaneously on the moon and back in the Cartesian Age.[78] But, after all the ecological tragedies of the 'Black Century' all this will probably change in the new century.[79]

Nowadays neuroscientists say that the human mind has at least eight recognizable abilities – linguistic, corporal, logic-mathematical, musical, interpersonal, intrapersonal, spatial and 'naturalistic.' At long last it has been recognized that a 'naturalistic ability' is necessary to understand nature's systems and cycles, and that some people, like Charles Darwin, Gregor Mendel and Francis Crick are born with a genius for it. And in the first decade of the 21st century, scholars will probably link high performance equitation with at least six of humanity's eight basic abilities: corporal, musical, interpersonal, intrapersonal, spatial and naturalistic ability – and I believe that few other human activities calls for so many capabilities.

The corporal ability is used in equitation to form the riding reflex chain. The musical sense is put to use when Homo merges into Caballus' shifting rhythm and cadence. Interpersonal capability comes into play for humans to deal with the horse's complex personality. The intrapersonal capacity is essential to understand your own emotional attitude to the complexities of equitation. The spatial feel is the sense used to react in one tenth of a second during equestrian maneuvers in the field or in the riding ring. (See also *The Cybernetic Zone of the Centau*r, coming up soon.)

As we have seen, to learn to interact with the horse's nervous system the rider's brain must be hard-wired into much more complex sequences of neuronal connections than for driving motorized conveyances – boats, cars, motorcycles and airplanes – vehicles which were built to demand a simple *visual-motor*

---

[78] By Cartesian Age I mean the split between body and mind, like the act of operating a computer sitting on a chair, and letting the mind fly worldwide while the body stays home.

[79] Gerald Edelman, an American neuroscientist, affirmed in the closing years of the 20th century that in a certain sense children were not their parent's offspring anymore, but the product of the new info-technology, because the new *body of knowledge* had changed the way children *learned to think* and this would help them to build a better environment in the future. The learning of natural, or biological equitation also depends on people building a new attitude towards horses and learning to think of equitation as an extension of their natural senses. And this demands a radical change of mentality.

www.horsetravelbooks.com

system to guide them. In equitation the reins do not represent the 'handle' or the 'steering wheel' of the horse, so here is where a more complex brain upgrading is necessary to connect human and equine senses into one Cybernetic operation. (Don't miss the next chapter.)

Biological equitation not only conveys the comforting feeling of 'control.' That is a feeling the rider must attain in the beginning of his classes. As Homo learns to blend with Caballus' nervous system and the horse's nervous system also merges with the rider's – when a tight proprioceptive knot is attached to unite the partners, a new feeling arises – the exhilarating feeling of freedom. And this must have been what Caprilli meant in the first place.

12. Caprilli and Beyond.

All scientific studies on equitation must start with a simple question: How best to control a horse from a position on its back? From groundwork to mounting the source of the rider's cues change from visual to tactile and the human brain must become the 'decision center' of the intersensory relationship between two different nervous systems. Affecting perfect biological control of a horse is a task far beyond the complexities of handling the weight and flexibility of a tennis racket, controlling a bouncing soccer ball, or managing the cybernetic challenges of a racecar. Shall we take a ride into this world of motor learning and high performance equitation and take a look around the rocky landscape?

Bruce MacFadden informs us in his excellent *Fossil Horses* that more than forty thousand books have been written on various aspects of horses. But of this overwhelming quantity of literature no more than twenty authors are responsible for the way Westerners think about equitation today.[80] As we saw in the first part of this book Xenophon, Grisone, Pluvinel, Newcastle, La Guérinière, Baucher, D'Aure, L'Hotte, and especially Caprilli, can be said to have laid the foundations of Western classical riding. And as we also saw, only Pluvinel and Baucher referred to equitation as a scientific matter, though they had no scientific basis to substantiate how humans and horses go about to do what they achieved in warfare and nowadays in sports.

As we have seen, horsemanship, especially of the military variety, was until Caprilli appeared on the scene based on the extreme collection, 'with the frontal line of the head perpendicular to the horizon' established by the Neapolitan riding school way back in the 16th century, while unfettered extension, with natural head carriage and neck, is Caprilli's sole doing. And the modern rider's forward poise, especially over the hurdles, is nothing more than its logical complement.[81]

The revolutionary Italian captain maintained that *a rider should leave his horse as nature fashioned him, with his balance and attitude of head unaltered, because, if there ever should be any necessity for modifying this same balance, the horse, in the course of the schooling, would be perfectly capable of doing so himself if allowed the necessary freedom.* [Therefore,] *the first rule of good horsemanship should be that of reducing, simplifying and even, when possible, eliminating the action on the rider's part. Without upsetting his equanimity, we*

---

[80] My personal choice for the 20 most read classical authors are Xenophon, Grisone, Pignatelli, Pluvinel, Newcastle, Sollissel, La Guérinière, Carlos de Andrade, Eisenberg, Brogelat, La Brove, De Previl, Baucher, Steinbrecht, L'Hotte, Fillis, Caprilli, Decarpentry, Podhajsky, Nuno Oliveira.
[81] *The Caprilli Papers*, by Piero Santini.

www.horsetravelbooks.com

should always avail ourselves of his [the horse's] *natural instincts and encourage his natural movements and paces. When the rider is capable, throughout the entire course of the jump, of smoothly conforming to the movement of the horse, he will have developed more than sufficient dexterity not to disturb him in anything else he may do,* insisted the Italian master. Caprilli was immovably opposed to anything even distantly savoring of artificiality. In the presence of this admirable simplicity we may well wonder what Caprilli, to whom *dropped nosebands were as alien as standing martingales*, would have said about the muzzles and pulleys that, from the show ring, have at present invaded even the hunting-field and the race-course.[82]

But how can modern science vindicate Caprilli's non-interventionist philosophy in equitation? How can the human partner maintain 'control' of the action without the aid of mechanical means like severe bits, martingales, and other forceful ways to restrain the horse? How can the equine and human body become functionally connected with bones, sinews, and muscles working in biological harmony striving towards the same goal? In the second part of this book I hope we came to a satisfactory understanding about conditioned responses and the exchanged feeling of proprioception that unite the Homo-Caballus combination into one galloping unity. So now let's try to speculate on how the human and equine nervous systems interact and how the partners sort out their functional roles during equestrian action. Bad equitation occurs invariably when the rider interferes with the horse's way of going or when the horse has a different notion of what to do. Therefore let's pose another difficult question and try to sort it out by neurophysiological information:

HOW CAN HOMO AND EQUUS FORM ONE BIOLOGICAL UNITY WHERE THE HUMAN PARTNER CONTRIBUTES WITH THE DECISIONS AND THE HORSE WITH THE LOCOMOTIVE SYSTEM?

"The first rule of good horsemanship should be that of reducing, simplifying and even, when possible, eliminating the action on the rider's part."

But how can a rider leave everything to the horse, interfere as little as possible, as Caprilli postulated, and maintain absolute control of the action? Caprilli knew how to do it, though he had no science to understand why it worked. Let's have a look into this jumble of sensory activity and try to see how the Centaur ticks.

First we must understand how a nervous system functions, so to sketch a handy simplification I'll use Humberto Maturana and Francisco Varela's defini-

---

[82] From *The Caprilli Papers*, translated and edited by Piero Santini.

tion.[83] *The internal relationship of the nervous system is relatively simple: it is the balance between sensory activity and muscle tone. As a rule, all behavior is an outside view of the dance of internal relations of the organism. The nervous system is wholly consistent with its forming part of an autonomous unity in which every state of activity leads to another state of activity in the same unity, because its operation is circular, or in an operational closure. The nervous system, therefore, by its very architecture does not violate but enriches the operational closure that defines the autonomous nature of the living being.*

Now let's picture a cat snoozing on a sack and the unwelcome apparition of a dog that interrupts puss's tranquility. The cat's sensory activity detects the coming of trouble. Instantly the cat's muscles spring from repose to action and catapult the cat out of harm's way. As you can see, the nervous system defines the autonomous state of the living being's interaction with the environment and each state of activity leads to another state of activity. After the fright, when the cat finds somewhere else to repose, the cycle of activity will have completed itself.

But how does the 'dance' of the internal relations of human and horse proceed during equitation, when the human nervous system enters into a chain of cooperative action with the horse's nervous system? I believe that the Centaur combination must imitate life and form a 'third' autonomous nervous system, within which the partners perform their distinct roles. This new 'virtual nerve system' is basically composed by the horse's locomotive system whose action is triggered by the human brain.

This means that the human brain, to avoid conflicting actions, must bypass the horse's decision center. And this can only be effected by the animal's total reliance on human leadership and by the fact that the human cues that spark the action are so subtle that they are picked up and acted upon by the horse's two enlargements of the spinal cord situated in the cervical and lumbar area without interference from the brain. Through correct progressive training the horse's responses to human cues will become automatic, and the horse's proprioceptive sense will read the cybernetic cues as coming from his own decision center.

Yet, how do human muscle cycles interact with the horse's muscle cycles? Why should the rider 'eliminate' the action on his part, as Caprilli suggests? This is relatively easy to explain: a rider who has reached the 'mature' stage of equitation, where his neurons can read the horses' movements as if they were a product of his own nervous system will, without losing his human nature, have become half horse. By this I mean that the rider has reached far back into his animal past and revived the genetic archive of his quadruped motility, long dormant through

---

[83] Humberto R. Maturana, Ph.D & Francisco J. Varela, Ph.D are the authors of *The Tree of Knowledge, the Biological Roots of Human Understanding.*

his hominid evolution.[84] The nerve system of his legs can be plugged with the nerve system of the horse's legs and they are the source of the combination's speed and changes of direction. Yes, in high performance equitation the rider's legs will become responsible for the triggering of all the ample movements of the horse's legs, and also for the sustaining of the gaits, and changes of direction.

Now faithful traveler, we are zeroing into the neurophysiological 'frontier' where human and equine senses merge and the Centaur comes to light in his entire splendor. The cybernetic zone,[85] the area that indicates the combination's direction and speed is in fact the human pelvis. In many horse books the author identifies the human "seat" as the center of the human action. No end of "seat" positions are related to horsemanship. But this is of course an *outside* view of the reality that does not tell the *inside* story. The complete story that Caprilli postulated, but had no way of proving, is that horses and humans change direction by switching the position of their pelvis, a movement that when performed by the rider the horse can be trained to monitor and imitate because it is the natural way that all superior animals change directions.

And the human hands connected to the horse's mouth by the reins will convey the 'limits' of the movements. As we saw, this can be effected because the rider's hands and the horse's mouth are packed with sensor nerves designed by nature to perform the delicate process of food selection. When a rider's hands and a horse's mouth are connected by the reins they are actually like two dancers holding hands: hands that can read and interpret innumerable combinations of the partner's body movements and can become the molder to the action: how long the strides, how fast the action, when to change direction, how much to flex the legs, where does one movement stop and another begin?

And as we saw the bit has also the function of helping the rider slip the horse's scapula into position to perform lateral work and flying changes and the reins form a corridor that the horse learns to follow through. In all strides the rider's muscles protract and retract in absolute unison with the horses' muscle cycles, the arms and fingers following the advance and retreat of the neck and the body, the legs cueing for increasing speed and the pelvis indicating changes of direction. What we see is a smooth chain of perfectly matched human and equine movements operating like one fine tuned machine.

To change gaits or direction the rider will, instead of imitating the horse's movements, take the lead for the change and perform the movement required,

---

[84] By reaching back to the arboreal stage of evolution Olympic gymnasts perform their ring, beam, parallel, bars, vault and floor exercises with such mastery that no 'normal' person could dream of doing the same.

[85] Cybernetics is the study of the control and communication in the animal and the machine.

www.horsetravelbooks.com

and as the horse complies will again fall in line with the horse's muscle cycles. L'Hotte put it like this: *"The more experienced the rider on a more experienced horse could use what Baucher originally formulated in his nouvelle méthode, the idea of "effects d'ensemble" (coordinated effects), which entails the simultaneous use of leg and hand aids. In other words, the more experienced a rider was and the more confidence the horse had in the rider, the closer could the aids come together."* The old masters had no neurophysiological information to envision the horse and rider performing exactly the same muscle cycles with the blending of the nervous systems into one winning performance. They knew how to do it, but they didn't know how it worked.

The full control over the horse requires the full connection of human and equine senses. Equitation is probably the most demanding of sports because all human senses will be linked to the correspondent equine sense, and the alignment of the 'Riding Reflex Chain' can take a long time to accomplish. But once the neurophysiological connection has been performed it will be a more reliable system than the old mechanical devices designed to restrain the horse's movements and way of going.

13. The 'Cybernetic Zone' of the Centaur
With the guiding hand of Norbert Wiener

The steering problems for control and communication in equitation cannot be compared to driving a mechanical vehicle in any way. In advanced equitation the equine effector organs must receive simultaneous clues of the speed and the direction to be taken from all the human effector organs. To orchestrate the interaction of the 'third nervous system' by the rider demands great knowledge of horse behavior and automatic control of the informative feedback that riding produces. The Homo-Caballus symbiosis is probably the most spectacular learning process ever to have adapted two species on this planet. And the image of the Centaur depicts to perfection the end product of this astonishing biological transformation.

Cybernetics is the study of control and communication in the animal and the machine. *Cybernetics* is also the name of a book written by Norbert Wiener, which was thought by many historians, economists, educators, and philosophers to be one of the works which most significantly altered the direction of our society in the twentieth century. In the first chapters of this work Norbert Wiener informs us that the steering engines of a ship are indeed the earliest and best-developed forms of feedback mechanisms. But although I enjoyed his book very much I fear that this affirmation is historically incorrect. The first vessels invented by humans were log rafts that came into use about six thousand years BC, and were probably propelled by poles; and pole steering does not have the feedback mechanism of rudders, which was probably what Norbert Wiener had in mind.

But equitation, which also evolved some six thousand years ago, is certainly the earliest and most complex and perfect form of feedback mechanism in the history of human technological development. To me, it is a total mystery that no scholar has ever concluded that the intersensory relation of humans and horses in equitation was probably the first and probably remains the most complex form of interlinked feedback ever tackled by the human brain. The traffic problem of the nervous systems in the Homo-Caballus symbiosis poses Cybernetic questions of huge proportions, which are much beyond the simplification that Marshal McLuhan used when he proposed bicycle wheels to exemplify the extension of human legs!

To see if we can find more evidence about how humans and horses interlink their nervous systems, coordinate their equestrian movements, and decide where to go and what to do, I suggest we take another ride into the scientific no-man's-land of equitation where humans and horses become one. Biological cybernetics, the control of and communication with the animal, may help us to put equestrian techniques in the proper order of cause and effect and establish a method in the feedback of the Homo-Caballus symbiosis. By screening equitation in the light of Cybernetics, the most influential technological subject of the twentieth century, and flash some psychological and neurophysiological tones on the picture we may be presented with a blueprint of equitation beyond Xenophon, Baucher and Caprilli's wildest dreams. C'mon, let's ride, we can do it!

The role of feedback both in engineering and in biology has come to be well established. The role of information and the techniques of measuring information constitute a whole discipline for the engineer, for the physiologist, the psychologist and the sociologist, says Norbert Wiener. If a new scientific subject has real vitality, the center of interest must and should shift in the course of the years, explains Wiener in the preface of his book. So let's start our trek towards the control and communication in horsemanship by following Norbert Wiener's explanation of a classical example of mechanical cybernetics:

"In machines, an example of the cybernetic phenomenon is the anti aircraft artillery where a soldier and a cannon are part of a system of firing control. An airplane has a velocity, which is a very appreciable part of the velocity of the missile to bring it down. Accordingly, it is exceedingly important to shoot the missile, not at the target, but in such a way that the missile and the target may come together in space at some time in the future. We must hence find some method of predicting the future position of the plane. Firstly it is necessary for the soldier to know the range and the speed and curvature of the missile to explode the plane. But we also know that aboard the plane there's a pilot who will know how to perform evasive maneuvers to avoid being hit. The feedback sequences necessary to calculate a hit is a classical question of Cybernetics."

In equitation we must start our speculations with an opposite view of the missile's antagonistic hit or miss tactics: in this biological phenomenon there are also two brains interacting, but in this case the two brains have been connected by training to handle the psychological and physiological aspects of moving in 'collaboration.' The rider is invested with the steering problem, the specific role of taking decisions concerning the speed and the direction of the action, and the horse has the explicit role of tackling the environmental obstacles, of keeping his balance despite all sorts of challenges, while keeping connected to the central steering decisions.

In envisioning the two partners forming a 'third nervous system' by the feedback of their cooperative muscle cycles we may have solved the question of how human and equine 'riding reflex chains' interact and proprioception is obviously the sense that keep the partners from straying from their roles. As the phenomenon of equitation can be summed up as a human brain controlling an equine locomotive system, Cybernetics seems like an adequate tool to investigate the sequences of biological feedback, where one of the secrets is obviously the intercommunication of tactical info used by horse and human to decide on speed and direction in the very fast world of protracting and retracting nerve fibers produced by the human and horse's aligned body movements.

At this point of our investigation it would be useful to remember that most animals on the planet have a similar reaction time to external stimulus. Throughout millions of years of natural selection most species in the animal feeding chain has stabilized the same reaction time to fight or flight. As an example to this fact Norman Wiener reminds us of Kipling's story "Rikki-Tikki-Tavi", the battle to death between a mongoose and a cobra.

Let's stop our horses and watch one of these dramatic confrontations. As Kipling tells it, the fight is a dance with death, a struggle of muscular skill and agility. The mongoose is not immune to the poison of the cobra, although it is to some extent protected by its coat of stiff hairs which makes it difficult for the snake to bite home. But there is no reason to suppose that the individual attacks and retreats of the mongoose are faster or more accurate than those of the cobra. Yet the mongoose invariably kills the cobra and comes out of the contest unscathed. How is he able to do this?

Look closely – the mongoose begins with a feint, which provokes the snake to strike. The mongoose dodges and makes another such feint, so that we have a rhythmical pattern of offensive and defensive activity on the part of the two animals. However, this dance is not static but develops progressively. As it goes on, the feints of the mongoose come earlier and earlier in phase with respect to the darts of the cobra, until finally the mongoose attacks when the cobra is fully extended and not in a position to move rapidly. This time the mongoose's attack is not a feint but a deadly accurate bite through the cobra's skull and brain.

In other words, the snake's action is confined to single darts, each one for itself, while the pattern of the mongoose's action involves an appreciable, if not very long, segment of the whole past of the fight. To this extent the mongoose acts like a 'learning machine,' and the real deadliness of its attack is dependent on a much more highly organized nervous system. By this amazing outcome it becomes clear that the mongoose and the cobra have the same reaction time to each other's attacks, but the mongoose's mind has developed a strategy beyond the simple reaction time of the cobra.

The parallel of Kipling's story to horsemanship is that the steppe nomads, to control and communicate with their horses, developed a strategy to interact with the horses' muscle cycles by connecting the human and equine nervous systems into a chain of transmission and return of information in what in Cybernetics is called a 'chain of feedback.' By contact with the horses' movements a rider is capable of conveying his intentions for speed and direction to the horse by direct cybernetic cues and *postural feedback*. This method of control, which we may call informative feedback, is not difficult to schematize into mechanical form.

We generally do not know which muscles are to be moved to accomplish a given task, and neither does the horse. Therefore horses and humans must be trained to respond to a feedback system of control. The well-trained horse will react almost instantly to the tactile cues of the rider with a 'withdrawal response.' When a tactile cue arrives, the muscular activity, which it stimulates does not occur at once but at about 1/10 second. It is as if the central nervous system could only pick up incoming impulses at every 1/10 second, and if the outgoing impulses to the muscles could arrive from the central nervous system only every 1/10 second. The human's and horse's brains cannot handle and react to information faster than this; therefore the combination's 'riding reflex chain' must be automated.

The learning of equitation must follow the self-propagation of the horse's muscle cycles in which the two central nervous systems must learn to adapt to the other's feedback info, despite the two species highly varied pattern of behavior. But the mature rider has learned to feel the horse's movements and these have become familiar to him. The horse has learned to feel the way the rider moves on his back, and will pick up the cues for changes of speed and direction as if they had originated from his own nervous system. Remember that the horse is a 'cursorial machine' created for a certain purpose: to move with celerity and precision. And the riders' cues affected in the same 'brain wave' as the horse induces it to move at the rider's cues, in a smooth chain of muscle cycles. Bits and spurs can produce negative pain and discomfort, which the well-ridden horse, by producing the desired movements, can turn into the *right* movements. The horse that has learned to 'read' the rider's postural feedback, and the rider that has learned to replicate the horses' movements are neurophysiologically connected. So to be successful, the rider like the mongoose must have total understanding of the horse's behavior plus a strategy to induce the action that must progress towards a successful conclusion.

The intersensory relationship of humans and horses in equitation produces a dense complexity of feedback messages that address exclusively questions of space and time. The messages that flow from one nervous system to the other are related exclusively to speed and direction, the classical Cybernetic question, and therefore the two nervous systems of the symbiotic partners must be organized to respond to each other's movements. This refinement of behavior is always attained at the cost of increased sensitivity.

'But if he [the rider] *handles scientifically and voluntarily, one must decrease all the aids so that the spectators can truly say that the horse is gentle and well schooled and that he moves on his own",* wrote Pluvinel, almost 400 years ago.

www.horsetravelbooks.com

The bits of information flowing between the two systems must thus be limited to 1/10 second, the speed that the two brains can handle and produce cooperative movements. Man, who has the best-developed nervous system, and whose behavior probably relies on the longest chain of effectively operated neuronal chains, must follow the precise cycle of the horse's movements. To gain speed, to reduce speed, to sustain speed, or alter the direction of the action must be given by Cybernetic cues within the scope of the 'natural language of movements.' We thus see that the plasticity of the human brain is capable of adjusting to and replicating the horse's movements, which permits the rider to assume the Cybernetic control of the powerful Homo-Caballus machine. It must be understood that the degree of neuronal organization required to fulfill the task must be very high, and perhaps not all people are able to handle the info overload. Though I believe that to understand the cybernetic rules of the game can better any rider's equitation.

The neurophysiology of equitation can also be explained as the ability of Homo and Caballus to monitor each other's movements through sophisticated cerebral circuits wired to match each other's motor-pattern. This biological technique has no similarity whatsoever to the driving of a mechanical vehicle, since the rider's control of the horse's movements is counterbalanced by the horse's control of the rider's movements, which requires a biological feedback exchange non-existent in the handling of vehicles. The feed-back and feed-forwards of bioequitation forms a double lane of the senses that leads towards the liberty of performance for horse and rider.

14. Riding in the 'Comfort Zone'

Depending on the cultural enlightenment of their time the classical masters described the use of the 'aids' as means to produce 'submission,' 'obedience' or 'lightness.' Submission was the word used in the time of slavery, 'obedience' was the word used in the age of rationalism, and 'lightness' the word used in the high industrial era. But now science can shed new light on why horses really respond positively to bits and spurs, and what modern riders should know about these tools when they are used exclusively for communication, and also the negative consequences of their faulty uses. But let's also pose the most obvious question of all: are these 'old fashioned tools' really necessary in a world of cybernetics and changing equestrian technologies?

Around forty years ago neuroscientists discovered a psychological rule that governs the behavior of all living creatures and has played a major role in the survival of most animal species, especially mammalians that developed a more complex brain. This behavioral trait was achieved by the natural selection of animals that could 'save energy' in a world of unpredictable events and frequent shortages of food resources. Scholars call this psychological predisposition the 'comfort zone' and the expression means that an animal, given the option, will choose the course of least resistance, of least expenditure of energy, and the least chance of discomfort, pain and injury. This type of behavior makes a lot of sense in the natural world where waste of energy and physical harm can lead to suffering, disablement, and death.

Though the horse masters were unaware of it, this psychological feature has always had a preponderant role in how horses react to domestication, schooling and training. After reading the classical manuals from Xenophon to Harry Boldt[86] it has become quite clear to me that humanity has wavered between the uses of force or wisdom to overcome all the horse's natural resistance to work and pain.

In this chapter I have transcribed the opinion of some of the most famous classical masters on the use of bits and spurs as the means to produce 'submission,' 'obedience' and 'lightness', to see how modern psychology and neurology agrees or differs with them. Let us start with Pluvinel, 'the best of all those who ever donned spurs.'

"Pluvinel always sits in the same posture, up straight, whether he is putting the horse into the airs or at a walk; and I have often heard him say that for a Horseman to be graceful, he must never, when making the horse perform, move, except to raise very gently the arm up and down, back and forth, to make the

---

[86] But lazy behavior is usually frowned upon in a utilitarian culture, and animals and people that show this feature of animal evolution will be called indolent, lethargic, sluggish, and slothful – you name it.

www.horsetravelbooks.com

switch whistle, as he will discuss later. <u>Neither must the horseman appear to be using the aids, so that those watching him will judge the horse to be so accommodating and so well schooled that he gives the impression that he is performing of his own accord and in harmony."</u>

In Pluvinel's time the necessity for the horseman to appear 'graceful' and almost 'unconcerned' to the public sitting in the galleries was almost as important as the riding technique themselves. The rules of court behavior were as rigorous as the rules of horsemanship. So sitting up straight and never moving throughout the horse's gaits was just as important for good court manners as for good horsemanship. But this impassionate rigor had its positive side because it permitted the horse to pick up the slightest cybernetic indication for changes in gaits and direction from a first-class rider. And Pluvinel is absolutely right to say that the horse must give the impression that he is performing of his own accord, because that is what really happens when a rider knows how to ride in the 'comfort zone'.

Baucher: "Unfortunately, we search in vain in ancient and modern authors, on horsemanship, I will not say for rational principles, but even for any data in connection with the forces of the horse. All speak very prettily about resistance, oppositions, lightness and equilibrium; but none of them have known how to tell us what causes these resistances, how we can combat them, destroy them, and obtain this lightness and equilibrium that they so earnestly recommend. It is this gap that, I think, I am able to fill up. And first, I lay down the principle that all the resistance of young horses springs, in the first place, from a physical cause, and that this cause only becomes a **MORAL** one by the awkwardness, ignorance and brutality of the rider. The rider will remember that <u>his hand ought to be an insurmountable barrier, whenever he would leave the position of "ramener."</u>

When Baucher points out that the 'resistance' of young horses may become a 'moral' issue by the awkwardness, ignorance and brutality of the rider he touches on a very important nerve of high performance equitation. The horse should never link the use of bits and spurs directly to the rider. The animal performs better when he believes that he is capable of avoiding discomfort and pain by making the correct movements. Making the horse aware that the rider is the cause of discomfort or pain may provoke a battle of wills. Another important point is when Baucher suggests that the hand should be an 'insurmountable barrier' whenever he would leave the position of 'ramener'. As we'll presently see, this can also be explained by 'riding in the comfort zone'.

Steinbrecht: "Correct dressage training is, therefore, a natural gymnastic exercise for the horse, which hardens its strength and supples its limbs. Such exercise causes the strong parts of the body to work harder in favor of the weaker ones. The latter are strengthened by gradual exercise, and hidden forces, held back because of the horses' <u>natural tendency towards laziness,</u> are thus awakened."

Steinbrecht has a wonderful holistic way of explaining every equestrian phenomenon. Here he gives good counsel on 'obedience' and mentions a very important aspect of a horse's nature – the tendency to laziness, which can now be explained by the psychological attitude of the 'comfort zone'.

L'Hotte: The more experienced rider on a more experienced horse could use what Baucher had originally formulated in his 'nouvelle méthode,' the idea of 'effets d'ensemble' (coordinated effects), which entailed the simultaneous use of leg and hand aids. In other words, the more experienced a rider, the closer the aids could come together. *Regardless of the discipline to which the horse will be put, the horse must be taught to obedience.* <u>It is not in his nature to obey because he wishes to be agreeable to us or for his love of work. He obeys out of self-preservation and avoidance of pain</u> *that cause him to react to those that can provoke it and, if necessary, produce it. This in the language of the aids that the horse must obey.*

General L'Hotte, a follower of Baucher, is a better interpreter of horse behavior than his former master. In very few words he correctly explains the 'coordinated effects' which we here call the 'human riding reflex chain,' and points to the natural inclination of the horse to obey solely as an impulse of self preservation and to the avoidance of pain, which can again be explained by riding in the 'comfort zone'. As we have seen, it is a scientific truth that a horse does not obey the rider because he wishes to be agreeable, a fact that Dr James Rooney confirmed in the following century.

These four passages, written over a two hundred and fifty year time span, show that the great classical masters were well aware of the natural rules of bioequitation though they were of course unaware of the psycho-neurophysiological facts behind a horse's behavior and willingness to perform.

Now let us try to see equitation from the horse's point of view and imagine how he uses bits and spurs to his own advantage in a dressage competition, which requires the greatest neurophysiological organization in Western equitation. Let's take a seat in the stadium of CHIO Aachen and see the performance of the amazing German horsewoman Nicole Capellmann Lüthemaier as I saw her in 2002.

> The horse is moving into the arena at a collected canter to initiate the dressage trial. He halts to salute the jury, and proceeds in a collected trot, calm, equal, and straight... at the end of the arena the horse feels the snaffle sliding slightly rightward, and the human body turning slightly in that direction, which is a foolproof cue that a turn right is called for, and without displacing his hindquarters the horse turns, and then feeling the

www.horsetravelbooks.com

rider accelerating her muscle cycles he also accelerates to an extended trot, that is followed by a collected trot… the horse can feel the totality of the human movements and the light pressure of the bit and a touch of the spurs is a sure indication for a change of speed or direction… the bit is now pressing slightly at the corners of the mouth and the human body is slowing the muscle cycles to a collected canter, and by conforming to these movements the horse immediately performs the collected canter, and then reduces the strides to a walk, and as the snaffle slides faintly to the right preceded by a micro-twist of the human pelvis, a perfect right turn is performed down the center of the arena where the horse performs a pirouette, with the rider's inside rein indicating the turn, and the inside leg on the girth preventing the inside leg of the horse from falling in, and supporting the outside leg so that the animal does not step back… the horse, by ceding to leg pressure, following the slight twisting of the human pelvis, the shifting leg contact, and following the direction of the sliding bit… believes that in reality he is performing on his own accord, because by cooperating and thus avoiding discomfort every figure turns out right… Now a half pirouette to the left, followed by a collected walk, and then a collected trot, a half pass to the right, collected trot straight ahead, change of rein in extended trot and suddenly the human body induces the horse into a passage, a shortened, measured and cadenced trot, very easy for the horse to imitate, and an exhilarating chain of movements to perform… now the pressure of the human legs in combination with a slight pressure of the bit on both corners of the mouth indicates a collected canter and a change of rein in medium canter is a sure sign for flying changes of leg… in fact the human body that was perfectly following the horses' muscle cycles in the medium canter suddenly changed the body posture and leg cues for the flying changes of leg… which the horse follows within a tenth of a second and then goes into a change of rein in extended walk, collected walk, with a cadenced touch of the spur proceed in passage… transition from collected walk to passage… to piaffe some twelve to fifteen steps… proceed in passage… transitions from passage to piaffe and from piaffe to passage, piaffe, twelve to fifteen steps, proceed in passage transitions from passage to piaffe and from piaffe to passage… and now the horse advances at a collected canter, down the center line, five counter changes of hand in half pass to either side of center line with flying changes of leg at each change of direction… this is great sport… the first half pass to the left and the last to the right of three strides and four others of six strides… guided by the human muscle cycles it is easy for the horse to forget the presence of the rider… collected canter, track to the right, change rein in extended canter without displacing his hindquarters…great fun… collected canter and flying changes of leg… down the center line… when the human body moves ever so slightly into one direction followed by the sliding bit, perhaps a touch of the spur, this is a sure indication of the way to go, and by conforming to the direction indicated by the bit and spur these tools stop bothering… pirouette to the left, flying change of leg… pirouette to the right, flying change of leg… track to the left… on a diagonal nine flying changes of leg every second stride, finishing on the left leg, incredible how the rider can follow the horse… on the diagonal fifteen changes of leg every stride, finishing on the left leg… change of rein in extended canter, collected canter and flying change of leg… down center line… halt, rein back six steps… proceed in passage…transitions from collected canter to halt and from rein back to passage… piaffe, twelve to fifteen steps, transition from passage to piaffe to passage… halt…immobility… salute… the combination leave the arena breathing hard though perfectly composed at a walk, and the horse knows he's done a great job. And if you asked the horse how he felt about the rider's performance, he'd probably say, "I don't know how dear Nicole was actually able to hang on through it all!"

In the same way as ancient wise men learned to follow the gyrating stars, smart horses learn to use the mobile bit and subtle spurs to help guide them through their gaits. The bit in the horse's mouth and the spurs on either side must of course be as infallible guides as the stars in the Milky Way to the wise men, or the horse will lose faith in their guiding powers. The bit should never be understood by the horse as being connected to the rider's will, or a struggle may ensue and perhaps turn into a 'moral issue' as described by Baucher.

The horse must feel the bit and the spurs as a dividing line between comfort and discomfort that *he can perfectly avoid by performing the correct Cybernetic chain of movements in the correct muscle cycles.* Did the spur make hard contact…? Ooops, I must have stepped beyond the line, thinks the horse. Therefore the rider can trigger the horse's riding responses and monitor the course of its movements or completely change them at will. Every single movement of the 'riding reflex chain' has the two athletes working on it – the rider activate the movements, the horse produce the action, and the rider works the muscle cycles into the right speed and direction. When the horse is executing the gaits, holding the course and maintaining the speed determined by the rider he'll be riding in the 'comfort zone', the feeling that he is completely at liberty and performing on his own accord and in harmony, as described by Monsieur Pluvinel.

www.horsetravelbooks.com

In high performance equitation the feeling of horse and rider is of absolute freedom, and in this moment the genie of bioequitation has been let out of the bottle to move the partners to adventure and the spectators to applause! And now let's pose the prime equestrian question: are bits and spurs really necessary in a world of changing equestrian technologies? You bet they are. Modern bits attained their 'biological perfection' thousands of years ago and like good books they will probably be on the scene forever.

14. Why Ride?

Many good manuals have been written on how to train horse and rider and to improve the horse's well being. Especially in the last decade new innovative techniques stressing 'body awareness,' 'soft eyes,' proper breathing, 'centered,' 'balanced', and 'connected' riding are meant to enable humans and horses to learn to work together naturally, without pain and to achieve harmony, understanding, communication and great equestrian performances. Perhaps the time has also come to introduce another grass root question: Why ride at all? What's in this symbiosis to benefit humans and horses?

Psychologists and neurologists explain that the brain is like a system of organs of computation designed by natural selection to solve the problems faced by our evolutionary ancestors in their foraging way of life. Scholars maintain that the engineering problems that humans solve as they walk and plan and make it through the day are far more challenging than landing on the moon or sequencing the human genome.[87] So, by moving about in their everyday chores people can let their brains collect experience, which their mind transforms into knowledge. But how does this relate to equitation and the benefits of riding for humans and horses? Put on your saddle and let's ride out and try to seek an answer in the biological, anthropological, and historical environment produced by horsemanship.

As most of the earth's land is accessible to feet, and some feet are better than others, and the better they are the more complex mental software the animal must have to control them, when Homo Sapiens decided to adopt the best legs in the world – the horse's – he had to wire his brain into millions of new connections to control the horse and to understand and act in the fast-changing environment that the new speed generated by riding horseback. This is probably the most complete hard-brain wiring that the human brain has ever gone through, and it is called equitation.

Now, humans have, between their ears, a constellation of neurons greater than there are stars in the Milky Way, and even in Hollywood. If some exacting somebody suddenly decided to count his own neurons, at two per second, he'd have to rise very early in the morning – for it would take him all of 16 million years to finish counting. And the startling thing about neurons is that it is theoretically possible to connect them all into a totally integrated web of knowledge, which should then expand one's brainpower into a boundless web of almost infinite knowledge and wisdom. The only 'catch' is that nobody has yet figured out how to do it. But one thing seems certain to scientists, who disagree about almost

---

[87] From Steven Pinker's book *How the Mind Works*.

www.horsetravelbooks.com

everything: to succeed in life, neuron connecting is the name of the game.

Back in old Mesopotamia, before man developed equitation, many young people would probably dream of galloping over the sands of the Syrian Desert mounted on a fleeting wild horse. As you know, daydreaming is an exclusive human faculty. But to imagine what he or she would find over the horizon, beyond the Tigris and Euphrates, was probably not much thought about. Most humans will find their interests decreasing in the exact proportion of the distance that a prospect is removed from them. And although reverie is part of Homo's genetic make-up, real brainwork is his hardest task, and that's probably why so many people talk their way out of it. And though the brain weighs a little more than two pounds, and represents only 2% of the body's weigh, it consumes 20% of human energy. Man's 10% inspiration consumes proportionally more energy than his 90% perspiration.

For this reason it is quite understandable that dreaming about horseback riding, as a means of getting rid of his or her awful pedestrian condition, could have been part of humanity's daily dawdling for the last thirty thousands years. And once the Cybernetic questions of equitation had been solved by the Central Asian herdsmen, an extraordinary phenomenon occurred to the horse people's perception of life: with the new mobility provided by 'equestrian dynamics' they started to notice that the distant horizon was coming within the human grasp, in a way that no red blooded pedestrian could ever have envisioned!

The fact is that the steppe horseman had discovered that by overcoming the human time and space constraint he had the world at his feet. From this extraordinary discovery, the horse people's culture, learning, self-organization and social arrangement would be centered on producing an ever-diminishing phenomenon of time and space by horseback riding. So, theoretically, the faster that you are able to move in the environment – by foot, by horse, by automobile, by airplane, by rocket – the more you will interact with the surroundings, collect experiences, super-wire your brains and become ever more brilliant, in a never ending spiral of successful learning and brain development. But this idea is physically wrong, as the wise man from Ulm has proven and even got a Nobel Prize for! Let's ride back in time and out on the Mongolian steppe to sort out fact from fiction on the impact of speed on human learning.

In 1237, when the Mongols with their highly wired equestrian brains unleashed their amazing cavalry forces on Europe – when this mobile people decided that the time was right for the Western world to receive the 'golden bit in its mouth' – the Khans put in motion the greatest flood of neuron power in the history of mankind. Now, you have to understand that a five-year ride for a horseman would be a fifteen-year odyssey for a two-beat pedestrian. Mind you, to Homo sapiens 'getting there' is *not* half the fun, as McCormick Lines would

www.horsetravelbooks.com

shrewdly advertise in a later century. Without a horse to ride, hobbling from Mongolia to Austria would be a fearful nightmare. (And Mark Twain would certainly have roared – "walk to Mongolia? Not bloody likely! I'm going in a taxi!")

But even though the Khan's army moved at a brisk velocity of 60 kilometers a day, scientists will agree that their speed was strictly within a biological time parameter. By this I mean that the speed of the horse, even though greater then man's, is within the cognitive power of an equestrian wired human brain. By neuron connecting, the rider can merge into the two, tree and four beats rhythm of the horse's gaits, and by hearing the sound and feeling the wind pressure the horseperson can learn to maneuver the horse at a gallop of up to 35-50 km an hour, while still being able to react to the world around – boulders springing up in front, a rider coming up from the side, the swift changes of equilibrium in sharp curves, jumping over creeks, fording rivers, the soft uphill lope, and the thundering breakneck downhill gallop. By achieving a perfect neurophysiological merger with the horse, the horseman will have control over every single hoof-beat and tactical maneuver of horsemanship. By merging with Caballus, Homo's physiological performance will be charged by high-powered energy, like a 16-volt battery plugged to a 50-megawatt dynamo. Connected with the horse all human senses are magnified and the rider's brain is wired to adapt to the horse's physical power, speed and land-roving capacity.

As we can see, the mighty Mongolian cavalry force advancing on Europe will consist of five years' intense interaction with the environment, with the rider's senses being constantly challenged by sights, sounds, smells, light, wind, weather, people, their horses and other people's horses. Every mile is intensely lived by the horseman, and the experiences added to his brainpower and biological reasoning.

An airplane is also built with the idea of reducing time and space. But its maneuverability is greatly limited in a time and space context. Although a plane has a much greater capacity of reducing time than a horse, it is not capable of fast maneuvers within a time and space limit. The pilot of a modern fighter plane will be dealing with a fast machine which doesn't change its gravity center very often; curves are made in great loops, inside the cockpit, the monotonous sound and speed of 500-600 miles per hour is beyond human comprehension. Human neurons cannot be wired to fathom this kind of speed. Friendly and enemy planes will be moving more or less at the same speed, and though a hostile aircraft may zero in from any side the pilot will have a very limited visibility range, though many seconds to work out an evasive strategy.

So, as incredible as it may seem, piloting an aircraft is less neuron stimulating and therefore makes for less brain wiring than riding a horse! And besides that, the pilot flies with the knowledge that he is in a precarious position inside this 'heavier than the air' contraption, he's also well aware of the unreliability of a combustion engine, the danger of flak being shot at him, and that there's nothing he can do but pray (which is good for the soul but useless for the body).

Now let's imagine a flashback, in which a commercial airplane is flying at 650 miles an hour on the route from Ulan Batar in Mongolia to Vienna in Austria, in the year of 1240. The aircraft is flying directly over us and the line of advance of Ogodei Khan's army, also on its way to Europe.

On the ground we can see that the horsemen are constantly being challenged by the changing features of the landscape, opposition forces sent out to check their advance, the horse's speed, and the moving columns of warriors as they advance at a brisk pace. Each horseman is coping with the problems posed by every yard of the terrain, while billions of brain connections are interacting with the ever-changing environment. Cut. Scene two.

Up in the commercial airliner, also heading for Austria, the stewardesses have just served lunch (full of saturated fat) and collected the debris, and the passengers are settling down to digest their meal while watching Mr. Bean's latest antics. In the cockpit at the fore very little is going on either, except for the pilot's and co-pilot's eventual button and lever pushing on the flight control panel, which has hundreds of switches from the floor to the ceiling, forming a completely predictable environment. The pilot knows that theoretically he is moving at almost the speed of sound but his brain cannot fathom this fact. This kind of speed is beyond human biological comprehension.

At takeoff, back in Mongolia, the pilot received his rout number and Jeppesen chart that should lead him to Vienna's Wien-Schwechat airport without much ado. To verify their position the co-pilot sometimes checks the plane's position and navigation conditions on computers wired specially for the task. The pilot is sitting with the control wheel in his hands and his galaxy of neurons is virtually gravitating in a timeless and eventless environment. But six miles underneath the plane's silvery body, in one of humanity's greatest neurological challenges, the Khan's boiling cavalry is advancing by the force of sheer brainpower toward a quailing Europe!

Almost seven hundred and fifty years after this event, the wise man from Ulm observed that if his tram to the patent office reached the speed of light, time would have to stand still – which also means that his neuron interaction with the environment (which he knew little about) would also have to slow down – because his body and mind would not be traveling in a biologically comprehensive time.

Now for the paradigm: when humans break out of their original biological speed the concept of time slows down proportionally, and if a body attains the speed of light, 300,000 km/s, the person's time concept would stand still – as time stood still on blueberry hill! Surpassing the human biological dynamic, which is probably set at around a maximum speed of twenty kilometers an hour, Homo's slow bipedal brain loses its capacity to understand the speed it is traveling in and loses the notion of time and space. As people move from bike, to car, to airplane, to rocket, their capacity of coping with time and space goes from the pan to the fire. But is this really true?

Yes. Because skin, hair, flesh, bones and all human physical fact-gathering equipment has to be protected so as not to disintegrate with acceleration beyond the speed they were created for. You see skin, hair, flesh and bone don't travel well at great speed. The skin goes white, the hair blows wildly, the flesh trembles, the heart thumps, the bones shakes, and the mind goes whinny. So, as we have seen in a former chapter, the body of cars, airplanes and rockets must be designed to protect human life and limb from the effects of speed.

And the more Faber has to be protected, the more he will be cut off from the feeling of speed and movement, and lastly from all the sensations that are the clues to understanding space and time. As his mighty rocket speeds toward outer space, poor Faber's galaxy of neurons, floating between his ears, goes practically blank for want of stimulus. Inside the spacecraft the crew becomes as 'life connected' as a bug under a rug. Though some sedentary people seem to love this dull feeling and folks are lining up to buy a ticket to Mars.

So, believe it or not – a horse-wired brain beats an airplane-wired brain any day. And that is probably the reason why horses survived the twentieth century and are here to stay. But what's in riding to benefit horses? Well, that's an easy question to answer. Horses are fed and cared for, and have become a common type of animal far from the verge of extinction, which is the vital objective of any species, especially in these dangerous times.

For people to understand the advantages of equitation for human body and mind improvement, equestrian sports must be scientifically understood to be scientifically taught. And as the frontier separating the social and natural sciences starts to disappear, as the biological basis for human behavior begins to be comprehended, as the pioneering work of psychologists and neuroscientists recognizing the mind as the product of natural selection that should exhibit biases and aptitudes that fostered survival in the ancestral environment, the benefit of riding will become self evident to the general public.

www.horsetravelbooks.com

16. Nomad Wisdom in an Urban Civilization

The big philosophical difference between the steppe nomad's horse husbandry and the urban-agrarian type of horse keeping is that the Central Asian horse people adapted their lives to suit their horses and city-bred people adapt their horses to suit their lives. In other words, Western horses became sedentary and inherited all the psychological and physiological miseries of confinement. But the 'new horse world' which will emerge in the 21st century will be entirely built on scientific standards, because as this text is being written the equestrian know-how in urban civilizations is for the first time starting to surpass the equestrian savvy of the Central Asian nomads.

Until the twenty-first century most stud farms, training centers, pony-clubs and other horse facilities were built with Homo's view of Caballus' nature, which had seldom much to do with the horse's view of himself. On the contrary, Homo Faber has a long curriculum proving that the world was made for Faber alone, and anyone that contested this status quo had the 'mark of the devil' and should be exemplarily tortured by the Spanish Inquisition.

But in this century people are becoming aware that the 'old horse establishment' had been on the wrong scent since before William the Conqueror took England by horseback and now will have to be totally re-engineered. Nowadays biologists have discovered that horse breeding and horse handling should follow the laws of Equus' particular genome because the horse, surprisingly, is guided by his own genetic code! This remarkable scientific discovery would become the starting point for a revolutionary way of handling horse and herd in the new millennium.

Today any horse loving nerd can tell you that the horse's physiology evolved around its ability to run. The horse's feeding habits, digestive system, sexual urge and defense strategies were developed to sustain perpetual movement. When the great nomadic horse cultures perfected their horse handling techniques, their success in equitation stemmed from the simple fact that they had *adapted their way on living to the horse's way of life* and not the other way round. They understood instinctively that their path to fame and fortune depended on following the horses on their year round feeding cycle, and learning every detail of horse behavior and herd handling. By adapting psychologically and physiologically to the horse, the warriors of the steppe brought the whole world into their grasp.

But urban-agrarian civilizations have done the exact opposite: they made the horse become sedentary and this biological aggression would only start to be perceived by urban dwellers in the Digital Era, when all information on horses became available to all horse people everywhere. So in the 21st century the Asian

www.horsetravelbooks.com

horse herder's ancient wisdom finally encountered modern science, and started forming the biologically correct horse management that will mark the third millennium Centaurs.

By understanding disease management, nutritional values, athletic development, physiological and psychological questions related to equitation, Western horse culture jumped from the Dark Ages into the light of the scientific world in less than thirty years. Never had Homo Faber amassed so much understanding about horses and equitation than in the Digital Era.

And it is a clear fact that in the last decade of the twentieth century land development and urban planning had already begun to change, in view of horse owners' quests for new ways of enjoying their horses, and their willingness to move to wherever these conditions could be found. In an ancient yellow Equus magazine dated November 1998 unearthed in my dusty library I read an interesting article about equestrian communities and their plans to *weave horses into the complex fabric of modern municipal life*.

Can you imagine in those wild times, the aftermath of the 'Atomic Age,' when people were brainwashed by daily TV programs to develop explosive strategies to solve their daily problems – when Osama bin Laden bombed the American embassy in Nairobi and Dar es Salaam back to Washington; when the American Navy bombed the Jumiat-ul-Mujahedin guerrilla camp back to the Abbasid Caliphate; when the Israelis where trying to bomb the Palestinians back to the Old Testament; when the Russians were bombing the Chechen separatists back to their Scythian way of life; when Richard Reid tried to down a commercial airliner with a bomb in his shabby shoe; when President Clinton bombed Slobodan Milosevic back to Philip of Macedon's times…, *in those wooly days a group of American 'horse lovers' were actually building a community where horses were not a novelty but a way of life!*

Such an equestrian utopia may sound too good to be true, but it already exists, revealed the old edition of Equus magazine. It's called Norco, California, located about 50 miles east of Los Angeles, and even 'Jack in the Box', (the name of the ancient fast-food establishment which archaeologists are now planning to unearth) had watering troughs and hitching posts to attend the horse people! In America this new type of horse complex, besides uniting people bound by a strong commitment to horses, also attracted professional services and equestrian activities that welded together the horse community and the wider society – the government, the business world and the general social attitude toward horses.

This type of community was aimed at creating the correct environment for 'horse enthusiasts', (as horse people were then called by hard-core urbanites) because riding on the beaches and in the parks had been fine, but now people were yearning for special riding and driving trails so they could enjoy their favorite horse activities in peace! To please the equestrian soul, the new horse communities were concentrated where open land was available and where mountains rivers and lakes would be part of the scenery – and a little solitude was also welcome, as the project manager told the reporter.

The old article also revealed that the desire to be in the 'thick' of equestrian activities was already strong enough to cause people to consider relocation. The urge of the horse-involved population to get away from 'city dudes' (motor dependent pedestrians) who know nothing about animals, people who don't like the smells, who abhor getting dirty, was a big motivation. And moving to these equestrian communities was also a means to get away from poor horsemanship and the 'horses as livestock' mentality, which were extremely common in those times.

Yes. Equus magazine had once more pointed its finger in the right direction. In the last years of the 20th century the horse world was busy building a place in the sun in post-industrial civilization. However this type of horse complex was still being constructed to accommodate man's *passion for horses* but not necessarily to serve a horse's real nature.

Nowadays the idea is to build equestrian facilities planned to satisfy the horse's nature, which is of course also the best way to produce happy horses for high-performance equitation. This means that horse facilities should be built considering two specific biological requirements: the horse's needs for 'perpetual movement' and the maintenance of his 'herd instinct' to keep him psychologically and physiological sound.

The first problem that the 'new wave equestrians' had to overcome was the old idea that equines, like humans, are fond of houses and every worthy horse should have a domicile with its name plaque on the door! In the new century, the old practice of stalling horses was discovered to have taken the highest toll on horse happiness, health and performance, only surpassed by the ancient feeble-minded 'bitting theories.' But, as this is not a book about biologically correct horse handling, of which there are many good works nowadays, let's keep riding, looking and talking as we go.

There are three grave syndromes that mar the domesticated horse's life, and that must be mitigated for the animals to keep healthy.

The "Prisoner of Zenda" syndrome, in which a horse is kept incommunicable in a dungeon for much of its lifetime, and which provokes the anguish of being all alone in the world, is depressing and dulling to a superior creature and leads to serious behavior alterations.[88]

---

[88] The 'Prisoner of Zenda' syndrome, provokes behavioral disorders such as 'weaving', the rhythmical swaying of the horse from side to side in which the horse shifts his weight from one foot to the other while nodding or swinging the head and neck back and forth.

www.horsetravelbooks.com

The "Spartacus" syndrome, the 'fight to death' situation in which a slave horse, when it is abusively ridden in the training ring, has a feeling that is has lost control of its body, and has no chance to clear its mind, get its wind back, and reorganize its emotions; this is at the root of 'stable sour' animals that hate to leave the barnyard (as we saw in *Strategies and Life Cycles in the Training of Horses*).

The " Gut Yearning" syndrome, in which the constraint of being unable to eat when the guts are yearning for it, is aggravated by the horses' physiologic structure that evolved around a virtually continuous feeding process. This syndrome leads to the horrible vice of dung eating, gnawing at anything within reach, and cribbing,[89] which are the horses' emergency strategies (B plans) to keep the system from breaking down. The basic elements of Equus Caballus' herd instinct are, naturally, to live among other horses, eat like other horses, in a horse-oriented society that is continually on the move.

HORSES ARE NOMADIC BY NATURE AND THIS FACT HAS GONE UNHEEDED IN SEDENTARY SOCIETIES.

But to sustain modern breeding and handling techniques the original herd system would be, if not impossible, at least highly unproductive. But even so, in high performance horse facilities the feeding, handling and breeding habits must be modified, though not entirely ruptured by human incomprehension of the horse's biological constitution.

A horse needs other horses as much as it needs to breathe. A horse needs to move, as much as it needs to drink. And a horse needs to chew for most of its waking hours as much as it needs to eat. This physiological chain reaction should not be broken in a modern horse facility. But how can we go about achieving it?

Horses can be kept quite happy if they can see, hear and smell other horses day and night. The herd instinct – the good feeling of being among fellow horses – can also be maintained when the horses can keep count of each other, by daily sighting their comrades inside their paddocks in well designed horse complexes.

This 'vice' is not provoked by boredom as some maintain, but by the necessity that the horse has of walking to keep his digestive system working, mainly his salivary glands (a theory proposed by Gustavo Braune from the Homo-Caballus Institute, Brazil).

[89] Cribbing is also known as 'wind sucking', the aspiration and swallowing of air by the horse through the mouth; the horse arches his neck and inhales air, and swallows it. The 'vice' may be controlled by the use of a crib collar say the 'old timers,' but in the new century the problem will be entirely solved by giving the horse freedom to live more like a horse.

A 'stallion' is etymologically a 'horse kept in a stall', and the word 'stable' represents a Latin twist to the German 'stall', a building for horses. But a 'stallion' kept in a stall will have his life expectancy reduced in the proportion to the time he spends in that stall. I have seen horses being turned out every day for two or three hours, with the handler proudly believing that this is 'good management.' The short-minded dupe didn't realize that three hours of freedom means 21 hours confinement! This kind of procedure obviously takes its toll on equine health, happiness, and performance.

Although costly stallions cannot be turned out with the herd they will be happy to have a view of the horse herd from their private safety picket. The physical contact with other horses that stallions and other high performance athletes need must be furnished by interaction with well-trained handlers who must be taught to behave like horses. And the dependence on human contact need not be negative for the horse. (If some lonely horses can be relieved of their solitude by the presence of a common goat, why not by the attention of a 'loving ape'?)

The layout of the new millennium horse facility will be totally re-engineered by the 'new wave equestrians'. Stables will NOT be planned exclusively for easy maintenance. The idea behind stables is to keep horses, especially mares and foals, out of intermittent bad weather. Stallions, however, will have to undergo a name change, as they will spend more hours outside than inside a stall. Paddocks will be bigger so that a horse can gallop whenever he feels the urge. Corridors separate paddocks from one another so the stallions cannot touch and quarrel, but are able to stimulate each other into galloping games (each animal running, prancing and showing off in his own paddock). A modern horse complex conveys to the individual horse a feeling of herd life – where he will see, smell and interact with other horses by eyesight, smell, and hearing all day and night. The biologically sound horse environment must arouse the pleasure of living and the feeling of self-confidence in the horse, and these are primary conditions for leisure riding and for winning performances in competitive riding.[90]

Humans act mainly upon what they can see, but in their new role as the guardians of Gaia[91] people must also learn to act upon what they can feel. In

---

[90] Any horse complex that does not conform to biologically acceptable conditions for lack of space should be relocated to a suitable location.

[91] The *Gaia* Hypothesis postulates that the physical and chemical condition of the surface of the Earth, of the atmosphere, and of the oceans, has been and is actively made fit and comfortable by the presence of life itself. This is in contrast to the conventional wisdom, which held that life adapted to planetary conditions as it and they evolved their separate ways. This we now know to be wrong. James Lovelock is the author of *Gaia, a New Look at Life on Earth*.

www.horsetravelbooks.com

the first decades of the new century, the pooling of humans' and horses' life-resources in equitation will reach a high rate of performance. This new standard in horsemanship will bring the scientific community's recognition of equestrian games as being the finest sports ever devised by the human mind. Science will help to raise the measure of excellence in equitation as never before, though there are still some problems lying ahead in building the horse world back to its ancient splendor with the knowledge of modern science. Don't miss the next chapter.

17. On Culture and Horsemanship

From the ancient world to the 19th century horses and equitation were part of everyday life. From work and war to social advancement, culture and horsemanship were two interrelated subjects. The equestrian renaissance of the 21st century is being marked by a growth of scientific understanding of equitation, which will completely change modern man's perception of the horse in history and its role in a modern civilization. As equestrian studies take off in the universities and equestrian sports come of age the 'new horse world' may again become the stage of cultural development, job opportunity, joy of living for many, and for the lucky ones the road to fame and fortune.

You may wonder why during our conversation I keep falling back in time and frequently try to make a point by referring to our Central Asian or Greek forerunners. I have a reason for this of course. Scientists have informed us that Homo sapiens was endowed with a mind that tends to compartmentalization. This means that humans will usually only grasp one angle of a matter – the social, the economical, the psychological, the ethical, or the philosophical – and people will rarely analyze these subjects through new angles such as biology, anthropology, sociobiology and other life sciences.

As horse handling and equitation reached a relatively high technological degree in ancient times, I have referred to these periods to help us build a systemic view of equestrian subjects, and tried to escape the Euro-centered notion of horsemanship that prevailed into the 20th century. It must be understood that today we are merely living a time of change between past and future equestrian practices, between a pre scientific and a biological way of handling and riding horses. In the twentieth century, science amassed such a wealth of knowledge that the equestrian culture in the 21st century will undergo a revolution as it adapts old practices to biologically sound procedures, much like the ancient Central Asian horse people who reached a high degree of horsemanship by sharing the horse's life.

Some day modern historians will acknowledge that the development of equitation was the 'motor' of all modern societies and that in the last four hundred years, horsemanship was the booster of Western dominance. And of course, Western equestrian culture, like all our other dominions of knowledge, started in classical Greece whose citizens adopted their horse lore from Central Asia, the cradle of the Centaur. Let's ride back to ancient Greece and witness Socrates' trial in Athens, and see how the master of contradiction refers to horses and trainers in defense of his philosophy and physical integrity (though the prosecutors got him in the end). Let's tip one of these Greek urchins to hold our horses while we enter the forensic building and watch the trial.

www.horsetravelbooks.com

The galleries are full of spectators and the Greek magistrates, wearing flowing embroidered tunics, are grilling Socrates who is coolly standing in the dock facing charges of impiety and corrupting Athens' youth. In his own defense Socrates refers to the Greek horse masters as an example of *good* teaching. Said the old philosopher to his accusers, with a vigorous voice: "Take the example of horses; do you believe that those who improve them make up the whole of mankind, and that there is one person who has a bad effect on them? Or is truth just the opposite, that the ability to improve them belongs to one person, or to very few persons, who are horse-trainers, whereas most people, if they have to do with horses and make use of them, do them harm?"

This argument bears the stamp of absolute logic, but even so the jury decides the verdict 'guilty' and when Socrates has a chance to pledge the penalty he says ironically: "What do I deserve for behaving in this way? Some reward gentlemen (...) nothing could be more appropriate for such a person than free maintenance at the State's expense. He deserves it much more than any victor in the races at Olympia, whether he wins with a single horse, or a pair, or a team."

Notice, fellow traveler, that when battling for his life, and carefully choosing metaphors from the daily Greek scene, Socrates talks about horses and trainers. The age of Socrates, the fifth century before Christ, was a period of extraordinary achievements in the Greek horse-world. Equitation was part of the noble's daily doings, and the 'equestrian class' was the pinnacle of Athens hierarchy. Professional trainers were in great demand, and good horsemanship was reserved for the very few. Therefore we see Socrates affirming bluntly "most people, if they have to do with horses and make use of them, do them harm." (Europe's sedentary populations were never capable of riding horses as well as the Central Asian archers, from whom they received the equestrian legacy.)

After Socrates' death and the fall of the Greco-Roman civilization, European riders didn't increase their equestrian qualifications much. But this will probably change in the present century when Western nations finally have the chance to bypass the Central Asian's ancient horse cultures in horse handling and in the understanding of the psychological and neurophysiological aspects of equitation.

But does this fact carry any cultural significance? Of course it does. A mature horse culture embraces members of all segments of society: males, females, young and old. And to understand the meaning of 'culture' related to equine subjects let's analyze the word as the Greek understood it, and link it to classical culture rather than to cattle wrangling and rural work practices, which became the norm in the decline of horsemanship in 20th century society.

Xenophon, a disciple of Socrates and the patron of Western academic equitation, besides being a horse master was a statesman, a general, a philosopher and a writer. When the mass of classical works of the Greek culture was discovered in the Renaissance, the intellectual movement that this ancient body of knowledge sparked was also followed by the resurgence of the long-forgotten equestrian art, and riding once more became a part of the cultural baggage of intellectually well-prepared citizens.

Monsieur De Pluvinel, one thousand nine hundred years later, was a counselor, diplomat, vice-governor, riding master and the director of an academy where fencing, dancing, philosophy, mathematics and astronomy were taught, but with an emphasis on equitation. The riding schools of the past also helped shape the ethics and moral virtues of the young nobles. Equestrian art was perpetuated down the centuries through academies such as Naples, Ferrara, Vienna, Versailles, Saumur, Pinnerollo, Sandhurst, Weedon, Saint-Cyr, Warendorf and West Point. The riding schools were important cultural centers and their principals were men of political or scientific prominence, the students the future leaders of their countries. Academic equitation besides being a sport was a byword for culture.

In the 21st century, as never before, sports will probably be understood as the means of perfecting a person's physical and mental abilities, be it by the free practice of exercises or through competitions. The governments who include athletics in the student's curriculum from grammar school to university reflect the importance of sports in modern societies. As we have seen in the last thirty years, the discoveries of the grave health problems related to sedentary behavior will probably change humanity's unhealthy alimentary and sedentary habits in the centuries to come. (As Felipe Fernández-Armesto recently wrote "The purpose of the next revolution will be to undo the excesses of the last [the biological revolution].") And history has taught us that equitation has a time proven property of disrupting sedentary habits. With the fast progression of a new equestrian philosophy, equitation will inevitably be associated with cultural development, because it will be understood that to attain high performance equitation, the rider will have to acquire a good formal education with a solid grasp on medicine, neurology, physiology, psychology and ecology, which are correlated subjects to advanced equestrian disciplines.

Stirred by the growing importance of equitation, horse-related subjects will become optional in many American, Canadian and European high schools, colleges and universities. Private equestrian academies require a good cultural degree of their students as a preparatory basis to bioequitation, and equestrian sports are being state-sponsored as many games were in American and Soviet universities back in the Black Century. As equitation can be rated as the most complete form of stimulating the human body and mind, equestrian studies will open new fields of research.[92]

Today many universities are offering horse-related courses. Currently there are many careers linked to the equine world and in the United States every one of these professions requires a school grade. For example, *Horse Appraiser* demands the 2nd grade; *Extension Horse Specialist* requires a Bachelor's, Master's or Ph.D.; Architect, a Bachelor's degree; Auctioneer, a high-school certificate; Bloodstock Agent, a Bachelor's degree; Broodmare Manager, a Bachelor's degree; Construction Contractor for barns and arenas, a Bachelor's degree; Event Announcer, a Bachelor's degree; Insurance Sales Agent, a Bachelor's; Journalist, a Bachelor's degree; Lawyer, a Bachelor's plus Doctor of Jurisprudence; Librarian, Museum or Curator, a Master's, and so forth.

Many schools in the U.S. offer equine studies designed to help equestrians to get this type of job. Students can choose careers as horse trainers, personal trainers to student riders, riding instructors or else join the 'ground staff' as administrators to horse enterprises and many other horse-related businesses. In the twenty first century, equitation and equestrian professions will involve culture and technology as in no other period in history. At the universities, equitation is linked to subjects such as biology, physiology, veterinary, zoology, zootechny, psychology, economy, sociology, history,[93] law and physical education which allow students to complete their studies with an university extension and postgraduation in equitation.

In the near future, doctorate holders in professional areas such as physiology will certainly include advanced studies on the physiology and neurophysiology of show jumping, dressage, polo and horse racing, endurance riding, as well as research on the mapping of brain activity of horse and rider under training conditions. (See chapter *Odyssey in Science*.)

Psychologists will have the chance to work on horse behavior under practical training conditions.

Physical Education careers can be built on the manifold studies of the *neurophysiology of equitation*. In architecture, biologically correct horse facilities – stud farms, training centers, horse clubs, horse communities and all-weather

---

[92] It is most probable that in the 21st century most of human history will have to be rewritten in the new light of biological, anthropological and neurological discoveries. I am convinced that great parts of history will also have to be rewritten by equestrian historians; by horse people who can understand the power of equitation, as past sedentary scholars have showed no insight either into the crucial importance of equitation in the development of nations or any understanding of the 'equestrian mind' in the forming of past and present cultures.
[93] *Food and History*, by Felipe Fernández-Armesto.

riding rings – will challenge human creativity to divide space for humans and horses to live and work together in perfected ecological conditions. In computer engineering lies the opportunity of developing software for training programs for horses and humans, horse breeding and management, as well as host of programs and equipment for the spectators of sports events and TV broadcasting, far beyond the ones described in *The 2012 Olympics,* coming up soon. In the 21st century, the sky will be the limit for high performance equitation and horse-related business careers for bright people with a love of horses, riding, and the outdoor life.

With the steady growth of the equestrian industry and sports in all advanced societies, public and private universities are including equestrian disciplines and correlated professions in the school's curricula. And besides that, the cultural growth of the 'new horse world' will have an added advantage: only a horseperson with an equestrian mind will be able to ransom the importance of equitation in world history. If this were not so historians would have done it a long time ago.

18. On Modern Riding Ethics

Ethics is the part of philosophy that studies what is morally good and bad, right and wrong in people's behavior. Aristotle, by studying the customs of his own society (ancient Greece in the 4th century BC), deduced a series of ethic virtues: firmness, generosity, moderation, frankness, prudence and so on. As people's behavior must change with the changing environment, ethics has undergone many twists and turns, and its basic virtues have sometimes been lost. To anticipate the new ethical tendencies introduced in the 20th century, let us debate the human–horse relationship, to avoid any ill understood opinions about 21st century's horsemanship as an extension of the 19th century slave mentality.

When a motor-dependent pedestrian sees a horse carrying a man you can assume the following premise: if the advanced equestrian societies, almost all of them pro-slavery until the 19th century, had few ethical misgivings with relation to some people enslaving other ethnic groups, their equals, they could have had no humanitarian feelings for horses, also considered as slaves. For this reason slavery is still a very present issue in people's minds.

In Europe, societies against cruelty to animals are questioning as never before the training methods of show jumping horses. How long will it take for some pedestrian freak to sue you or me for maintaining a slave horse for riding purposes? Society is obviously speeding on a fast lane where 'new' ethics are very high on the agenda. Attorneys, specialized in class causes and minority groups, are this very minute honing their tongues for the coming legal battles which the changing ethical values have been causing in these biologically incorrect but politically correct times. Class vengeances, like when the English Labor Party banned fox hunting, are also reasons for concern. The 'new wave equestrians' can rest assured that the age-old concept of the horse as man's slave will not be forgotten by folks specialized in minding other people's business. Horse people of the world – be prepared for the attack of people that have made it their business to mind other people's business.

The 'horses as slaves mentality' can be expected from the most surprising quarters. "If the dog is man's best friend, then we can certainly describe the horse as man's best slave", wrote Desmond Morris in his Book *Essential Guide to Horse Behavior*, written in the Black Century. The most worrisome aspect of the reasoning of the eminent zoologist (from who I pilfered the 'naked ape' expression) is that, as he is apparently not a connected rider, he still associates equitation with slavery, which was very true when the horse was bound to the economic and military machine of the world.

But today this concept is totally out-dated in all advanced societies, where the horse is a precious partner in sports and adventure. Now mind you, if even

Professor Desmond Morris thinks of the horse as a slave, what does the rest of the population think about the Homo-Caballus connection? By reading books, magazines and news from all over the world, one gets the feeling that public opinion has not yet realized that the *'slave horse'* faded out in the latter part of the 20th century and Equus Caballus was reborn under a new sign: the symbiotic leisure and sporting partner. But keep yours eyes peeled, fellow traveler, for trouble from activists may be lurking just around the corner.

At the present time we have two groups of animal activists who 'defend' the rights of horses, as they loudly proclaim. One is the *Humanitarian Society,* a radical association whose members are against the use of the horse in any way – neither for work, circus, rodeo, sports or leisure. These activists 'defend' the 'total liberation of the horse.' (These sedentary pedestrians probably haven't got around to figuring out who's going to support all the world's pensioned off horses. The welfare state?)

The other group is the *Society for the Protection of Animals,* whose motto is 'use but don't abuse.' Any red-blooded Centaur worth his ration is totally for the *'use but don't abuse'* spirit; but the naïve idea of the total liberation of the horse might at any moment seduce the sensationalist tabloids which live by strident headlines:

WOMAN IN STRANGE BREECHES CAUGHT RIDING ON THE BACK OF A HORSE

Not that cruelty to horses has ended with the new century, though. But it's a known fact that crime and cruelty is a dark side of humanity, which unfortunately seems to be present in all levels of society. Crimes against the public patrimony, crime against the individual, wife and child beating, pedophilia, corruption, terrorism, kidnapping, rape, druggism, hackerism; which country can say it is free from these plagues? All societies have psychotic individuals and it seems that we will have to live with these creeps until the day genetic engineering is capable of repairing the faulty genes and turning criminals into choir-singing Trappist monks.

However, let's be rational: motor related accidents are responsible for a very high mortality rate in all age brackets. Yet nobody has ever seriously proposed closing car factories to save human lives. In Western countries almost half of all marriages end in divorce – but nobody thinks of abolishing the marital knot because of this unfortunate situation.

I see a big love in the eyes of the German horsewoman Gabriella Grillo, when she speaks about her sentiments working with her beloved horse Grandison – *"In this moment, we are working together, shoulder to shoulder, trying to succeed,"*

www.horsetravelbooks.com

this is not the way you talk about a slave. Reiner Klimke, the Grand Master of Dressage, emphasizes the great pleasure that his horse Pascaly feels during training. Anne Grethe Jensen, the Danish Olympic champion, spends four hours a day training and caring for her precious Mansur. Anyone who has heard Chris and Jane Bartle, both renowned Dressage trainers, talking about their horses… *"The pleasure of being able to communicate with Nero, to see him understanding me for the first time and both of us doing a movement we have long worked on,"* can understand the emotional knot that ties Homo and Caballus in their work. Nobody talks like that about a slave.

The ethical question of riding can be put this way: is equitation a form of enslaving a living being or is it a symbiotic relationship that benefits both partners, like most symbioses in the natural world? This question will sooner or later come to the forefront of public debate, and the 'new horse world' should be prepared and not be taken off guard. The best thing to do is to take the initiative and discuss the matter publicly. As a matter of fact, 'equestrian ethics' arrived in the horse world long before catching up in some other rather obscure areas of human endeavor: may a woman use her womb to have another woman's child? Should it be legal to make a product, which has proved beyond doubt to provoke cancer? May a laboratory clone people for obtaining spare parts for organ transplants? Is euthanasia included in the right of the individual to *come and go*? Is it a murder of first or second degree to abort a three-week-old fetus? In which circumstances is a person allowed to declare love to another without being sued for sexual harassment? If a scientist clones himself, will a Xerox of his ID card suffice to put him in jail for counterfeiting himself?

To avoid misunderstandings, public opinion has only to comprehend the ethics of high performance equitation—when the human physiology merges with Equus' and a Centaur emerges to dazzle the world. So let's tell them about it.

The confrontation with the Humanitarian Society and other such assemblies are unavoidable in modern societies. Ethics in equitation is an all-important issue, which must be made clear as horsemanship is readying to compete in all its plenitude with other modern sports. It is material that public opinion understands and approves of the 'new horse world.' But as we shall see, there are still other questions that call for solutions in modern equestrian societies. As science is opening the inner secrets of the DNA a question must be asked: what is Equus Caballus' contribution to the mental development of Homo sapiens? For the love of science, don't miss the next chapter.

19. Odyssey in Science

The understanding of equitation as one living system will transform the 'new horse world' into an expressive economical force in the world. And scientists, who in the 20th century seemed more interested in resurrecting the mammoth than understanding the anthropological, sociological, and historical role of Equus Caballus in human history, will in this century also prove why horsemanship was and can still be an important factor for human physical and mental development. With the equestrian boom, new research in the physiology of equitation will bring many interesting answers on how humans and horses react to the intersensory pressure of full equestrian activity.

In the 20th century, cosmological science made colossal strides in the exploration of the Universe. Telescopic observation and mathematical calculation brought fantastic returns, such as the observation of gas and dust in the solar system, the structure of the stars, the building of galaxies, the explosion of supernovas, the gravity force of the black holes, the radio waves of neutron stars, the detection of the first planet outside the solar system, the discovery that the universe is composed of three billion galaxies, and many other data collected from the vast recess of the cosmos.

Nevertheless, in the 21st century computer science and cosmology will probably not be at the fore of scientific progress. In the new century, science is pushing its way into a universe as complex as the cosmos and certainly more important to mankind – the depths of the human mind, with its trillions of nerve connections and many unexplored areas. Let's gallop a few years' forwards in time and see what's up in science around the world.

Already in the year 2010, neurophysiologists are the heroes of the day. They work to try to answer questions even more pertinent to humanity than the cosmological matters so much in vogue in the closing years of the last century. Scholars are slowly finding scientific answers to the following questions: how can one single fertilized cell be the origin of a whole person? If the brain is dozens of times more complex than DNA – the molecule that transmits the hereditary characters – how can it produce the brain? Where does the brain end and where does the mind begin? And how, exactly, can immaterial thoughts be stored physically in the brain by the way of biological and chemical interactions in the process we call memory? Or yet, how do these biochemical connections function when body and mind are working in high gear?

The research of the human mind is, undoubtedly, one of the most spectacular scientific endeavors of the new century (to heck with the rock festival on Mars and down with Barnacle Bill, Yogi, Casper, Scooby Doo, the space toys of *fin-de siècle* scientists. Nothing in nature is really as important and as complex as the workings of Homo sapiens' mind, say modern scholars.) Research on how the mind works which started timidly with the monitoring of the human mind in repose is now being directed at the study of the human mind in full activity. Through new techniques in computerized neuron tracking it is now possible, with a new generation of wireless electrodes developed by microelectronic scientists, to map the workings of the brain during equitation!

In this kind of research, the one hundred billion nerve cells wired with 100 trillion connections in the human brain are bombarded with various types of highly emotionally charged situations in equestrian sports. Scientists agree that the human mind can reach maximum working rate when directly connected to Equus' brain, because the electrophysiological interaction of horse and rider in equestrian sports is probably the biggest functional test for the full capacity of the human brain!

Neuroscientists are studying the complexities of the inter-species communication in competitive equitation, which is now also being considered a moment of maximum efficiency of the human psychophysical system. Under such circumstances all human senses are fully alert, totally connected to recognize the unexpected, to take lightning-fast decisions and to find instant solutions to problems that appear at speeds superior to Homo sapiens' original speed. The monitoring of the interaction of Homo and Caballus' brains offers a fantastic spectacle of the two species' neurons working interactively at maximum capacity to keep rational and emotional control during very fast action. (Anthropologists have also discovered that this powerful brainwork has to do with the Central Asian nomad's military domination of great parts of Asia, and Western horsemen's leadership over many horseless people up to the 19th century.) Let's follow one of the latest tests in a microelectronic hot-shop.

As we look onto computer screen 0 we see that a horse and rider are entering the ring and are about to start a show jumping test. The bell rings and the Centaur start to canter. On two other screens connected to the combination's brains the mental areas flare up like one fine-tuned equestrian machine as the horse's and the rider's cognitive processes are engaged by the sound of the starting bell and the portent of the action to come. On screen 1 we can see the human brain activity and on screen 2 the horse's brainwork, while screen 0 is giving us the visual picture of the combination working in the riding ring. On screen one and two the inside of the two brains are looking like a nocturnal aerial view of two great cities. Billions of synapses are glimmering in colored splotches that represent the different mental areas at work.

On approaching the first obstacle the related areas of the two 'cognitive cities' suddenly flare up in bright lights and deep colors, as neurotransmitters stimulate the brain and body of the athletes at the approach of the highly emotionally charged situation. The two monitors glimmer in different areas of the brains as Homo and Caballus have their mind directed at *different parts* of the action, though at the crucial moment – the jump – when the proprioceptive feeling reaches its *highest pitch,* the two brains flash up in the motor, sensorial and associative regions.

At the second obstacle both the human and equine brains flare up as they sail over it, and glimmers down as the barrier is left behind and they focus on the next challenge. On approaching the next jump the human and equine brains glow up in different areas as Homo anticipate the next jump and Caballus' brain glows in the areas responsible for his sensorial attention on the ground and the associative feel of the rider's cues. For the partners, it is an exercise that fully occupies the body and the mind, accomplished under high emotional pressure, involving an infinite combination of rational and emotional activity, as the rider's conditioned stimuli interact with the conditioned responses of the physically powerful horse. Throughout the course it becomes clear that no area of the human brain is left out of the sporting challenge.

In the twenty-first century researchers will probably rate equitation as the sport which demands the greatest effort of the human brain, in perfect equilibrium with the working of the body. And this type of research is being considered even more fantastic than the first human landing on Mars which occurred in 2009, when a Russian from Sverdlovsk, with an impossible first and last name, was overheard by the NASA staff grumbling as he made the first imprint of a human's foot on the Red Planet – "Nyet. I knew there'd be nobody home!"

With new computer technology scanning the human genome, professional and amateur athletes are also getting to understand their real sporting vocation, and are capable of understanding the genetically strong and weak points in their chosen sports. Super athletes are now able to precisely select two or more sports as an ideal cross-training technique to benefit the action of their primary sport. And equitation is often chosen for cross training, as it generally involves more brainwork.

Let's ride a bit further into this new frontier of the senses and have a look: all sports played with balls – when the brain has to anticipate the probable course of reception and emission of balls have been ranked by scientists for their capacity to stimulate the brain and by their capability to benefit Homo's motor coordinating system, as well as their general advantages or disadvantages in comparative sporting physiology.

Games involving vehicles, with or without wheels, are also being researched and ranked by their capacity to develop the athlete's mental and physical agility. A very popular outdoor game, very much practiced by the top echelon of the sedentary population in the 20th century, proved, with the new research, to be practically useless to human health – a mere sporting placebo, with which the urban sedentary 'athlete' fancied he was getting adequate exercise! (Women didn't take much to that game, although a feminist group tried to gatecrash a certain club in America.)

As most equestrian games mobilize *the majority of the human mental areas,* they are now considered to be the most complex sports ever devised by man. Equitation probably comprises the most efficient games for an athlete to exercise the maximum power of his mind in perfect coordination with the body.

Equitation is probably the most efficient way to unite the human body and mind, which have been separated by 'modern' inventions designed to make life easy and 'spare' the sedentary consumer from the slightest physical and mental effort. Through sports in general and horsemanship in particular each individual will be able to attain maximum psychological and physical equilibrium with the lowest emotional wear, thus helping to preserve a person's health and happiness throughout life.

20. Sport is War by Other Means

Homo Faber is not a killer species that throughout the ages has developed a murder instinct, as old-fashioned poets, historians, philosophers, screenwriters and the producers of computer games seem to have believed up to the 20th century. Warfare is probably the unchecked progression of the hunting instinct, as the ground elements of the chase are clearly present in war. In the 21st century sociobiologists stoutly affirm that the social and economic factors of war are present in the phenomena of sports, and it has been said that 'sport is war by other means'– *with more brain development and a happier ending.*

If Homo sapiens were a killer species, the hominid bands that once foraged in Africa would doubtless have wiped each other out, long before the start of the Biological Revolution. Sapiens is not naturally friendly or naturally hostile, but only *naturally interested* in anything that might advance his personal interests. This fact is neither good nor bad but only a fact that should be kept in mind if you're in the service of God, of science, of industry, of government or in any other service for the matter.

Homo sapiens has an excitable brain, say anthropologists, and the individuals of this species will stampede in any direction that their shrewd leaders tell them that there's a nut and a treasure trove for the taking. After the war for the treasure trove is over the leaders will keep the treasure trove for themselves and hand their stalwart followers the nut with a pat on the head and a moving speech on the 'hero's noble deeds in defense of the mother country' – a story that the happy monkey will retell over and over until his unfortunate relations threatens to boot him out of the family tree.

But on the supposition that his or her excitable brain is not disturbed by the opportunity to 'win' something 'free' and the monotony of his or her dreary city routine is unbroken by other exciting incidents, Homo sapiens is not specially bred for killing, even though it might look that way if you consider the Schwarzenegger junk and Doom and Quake garbage most young apes gobble up raw without chewing.

The fable that the 'naked ape' has developed a murder instinct comes from the peculiar way that the human specie have of twisting the truth of their 'noble war experiences' and have written them down in history as 'heroic adventures', though war had in reality represented the most miserable time that these guys and dolls ever had in their lives. But if a poor Homo sapiens, living in an urban cage, is suddenly let out on an official violence spree, after armistice has been signed and he or she is back in the coop the recollection of the 'excitement' might linger forever in his or hers otherwise monotonous memories – that is *'if'* they outlive the 'exhilarating' battle experience.

www.horsetravelbooks.com

As we know, all war efforts are the means of pillaging a neighbor's accumulated wealth, and started when the first Bugs bunny surreptitiously pilfered the first Elmer Fudd's carrot patch. Afterwards when the horse was domesticated and equitation developed to a point where arms could be wielded from horseback, 'equestrian dynamics' gave a dizzying boost to the war effort, and sped people along to the two awful World Wars of painful memory.

All through history, naïve humans have been led to believe that war was the express *order* of God. The Old Testament declares, 'If God, by special prescription, commands you to kill, homicide becomes a *virtue*!' According to the Koran, the propagation of Islam by arms is a religious *duty*. War was transformed into an ideal, a command of God! Saint Bernard became the reasoned defender of the Christian Holy War, and Mohammed was the instigator of the Muslim Jihad.

Raymond d'Agiles, Canon of the Cathedral of Le Puy, writes on the occasion of the capture of Jerusalem by the Crusades: "Admirable sights were seen... Heaps of heads, hands, and feet were seen in the streets and squares of the city... In the Temple and the Portico the horsemen rode through blood up to the knees of the horsemen and the bridles of the horses."

But let's skip the gruesome war reports and concentrate on the phenomenon of war. For political reasons, war has always been blown-up beyond its true significance by popular myth and naïve historians. Just listen to the theories that Gaston Bouthoul, professor at the School for Advanced Social Studies, wrote in the 20th century: 'War is unquestionably the most spectacular of social phenomena. If, as Durkheim[94] says, sociology is history interpreted in a certain way, war can be said to have given birth to history: history began by being exclusively concerned with armed conflicts, and it is unlikely that it will ever entirely cease to be 'the history of battles.' What the eminent professor failed to see was that it was the people that 'wrote' history that had become fascinated with war and not warfare *per se*.

When cavalry came of age wars escalated dramatically and throughout time poets, theologians, philosophers, historians, sociologists and economists would whip these social tragedies into treatises such as *Theological Doctrines* and *Philosophical Doctrines on War*. And in antiquity Heraclitus would humor the Greek troops with the aphorism: "War is the mother of all things. It makes gods of some and slaves of others." As economies grew and the booty of war increased, economists started to write theses such as *The Need for Prior Accumulation* and *Economic Consequences of Wars*. To these propositions Machiavelli, always on the prowl, added: "Every war that is necessary is just".

---

[94] Emile Durkheim: French sociologist (1858-1917) generally regarded as the founder of sociology.

These assumptions were so well accepted and sold books galore that Sociologists began to write theories such as *The Demographic Effect of Wars* and *The Primordial Functions of War*. In the midst of this war-worshipping hysteria Hegel would shamelessly encourage Napoleon Bonaparte, his "universal ideal on horseback," with the moronic concept of the "civilizing character of violence." All these theories were so successful that sociologists would enthusiastically add another chapter to war studies: *War Festivities and War Rites*. To which poor Nietzsche, the icon of warmongers, (but deep down a good fellow)[95] would add, "You must love peace as a means to new wars, and the shortest peace rather than the longer!!!" (The three exclamation marks are all mine!!!)

When psychologists saw the enormous successes that sociologists were having with their *war theories* they pitched in with *Warlike Impulses and Aggressiveness* and *The Psychological Consequences of Wars*. When other scholars saw the wild success of all these war theories they enthusiastically added other chapters harping on *The Historical Importance of Civil Wars* and *Plans for The Balance of Power Between States*.[96]

In the poor twentieth century, the *ideology of war* finally escalated into a worldwide frenzy and the efforts to 'explain' the war phenomenon had turned into a profession, as everything 'exciting' does in a consumer society. And professor Gaston Borthoul also wrote, "For wars are not only the clearest chronological landmarks we possess, but also, whether we like it or not, mark the big turning points in history..."

In the 21st century war will probably not represent either the 'clearest chronological landmarks' or the 'most remarkable change' in developed countries (whoever can remember what he was doing the day that the northern Alliance entered Kabul, or when the Iraqi population helped topple Saddam Hussein's statue in Baghdad?) Nowadays the world's clearest chronological landmarks have been taken over by sports.

But whatever happened to the good old war effort? Sociologists registered the turning point in human history, when sports would substitute war as humanity's clearest chronological landmark and become the biggest promoter of social change, in 1998, during the World War... sorry, the World Cup in France. People's involvement in this event would surpass anything that man had ever thought of before. During the 1998 World Cup the cumulative figures of television viewers hit the 37 billion mark! Twenty four thousand journalists, photographers, reporters, radio and television technicians invaded Paris and the other host cities to cover what would become the greatest media event of that

---

[95] Deep inside Nietzsche may actually have been one of ours: he was first seized by madness when witnessing a cabbie severely whipping a horse.

[96] All the theme titles were borrowed from Gaston Bouthoul's book *War*.

www.horsetravelbooks.com

century! Throughout the event France probably received more media attention than any allied military campaign in the Second World War. How can this be explained?

Because among the sporting nations football IS WAR! Or, as George Orwell aptly put it: "Serious sport is war minus the shooting." After Zinedine Zidane scored two goals, and Emmanuel Petit provided the 'coup de grâce' against mighty Brazil, waves of national euphoria spread across France. The joy could not have been greater in August 1944 when the swastika was dragged down from the Eiffel Tower and the Tricolor reinstated, after Charles de Gaulle had entered the French capital!

In 1998 sports definitely became a state affair of great national prestige. In France's cabinet, after the victory over Brazil, an awed opposition leader commented: "When you see all these French, seemingly so different but in fact so similar, sharing the same enthusiasm, you wonder whether there isn't a cement, a principle, a solution to all our problems." And of course a great victory and historical landmark had been achieved.

FRANCE IS THE WORLD POWER OF SOCCER!

In the last World Cup of that century, the games themselves had become generally more dramatic and better structured than ever before. When a team scored a nation roared! England's prince Harry jumped high on the sofa when his country scored against Romania, and the pope, having been a goalie in his youth, followed some of the games. And to boot, the Three Tenors happily sang a World Cup concert!

Today it can be said that the most astonishing happening of the 20th century was not the globalization of the World's economy as economists then made us believe. The single fact that caused the greatest social changes was probably the end of the myth that wars are solutions to international disputes, and the shift of sports as humanity's greatest interest focus. In the 21st century the leisure industry may finally overshadow the arms industry.

In 1997, the ball that Mark McGuire hit to make his 70th home run in the American Baseball League was auctioned at 2.7 million dollars. Ronaldo made 34 million dollars in that year, and Beckham is not telling what he's worth. In the last decade of the century Michael Jordan increased the American GNP by ten billion dollars a year and when he announced his retirement in 1999, Nike's shares in Wall Street fell six per cent on the stock market! Manchester United, the most valuable sports team in the U.K., besides having 20 million fans in China, had a turnover of US$141 million in 1996-97. All major football teams turned into corporations with shares in the World's Stock Exchange. With a million here and a million there, sports had turned into real money! The much vilified television system had forever changed the human view on war and helped instate humanity's natural love for sports.

Warfare represents a predatory competition where human life is squandered to sustain the so-called war effort. Sport, on the other hand, is the valorization of the individual, and the athletes who stream into the stadiums come from most countries and all social standings. Around the globe – from Germany to Cameroon – tens of thousands of towns and villages have a leveled rectangle of dirt marked with goal posts at each end. On these football fields youth prepares for the greatest show on Earth: soccer – a game where David can actually vanquish Goliath! Sport is an important step toward international cooperation, which has become the most important issue on the global agenda. At the dawn of the Third Millennium, humanity had the chance for a fresh start to build a happier life in a warless world. (Though as we saw, even in the more advanced countries the old truculent war mentality would occasionally erupt over trifling matters; old habits die hard).

However, this is where equestrian sports get aboard our bandwagon. In the sedentary environment humans have worked themselves into a dualistic separation of body and mind. In the urban environment people are overworking their brains and under-working their bodies, and therefore sports and gym are the only solutions capable of bridging the chasm that is creating costly health problems to sedentary folks around the globe.

In this new century more brains will probably be put into the task of developing sports than have ever been directed to war efforts in previous ages. And modern neurophysiological tests will at last prove that the neurons in an horse person's brain are better connected to cope with speed and fast decisions, which is increasingly useful in the ever changing environment of the Digital Era. And as the biological importance of the balanced use of body and mind has finally dawned on most societies, equestrian Sports will be considered the most complete form of integrating Homo's mind and body into one harmonious working machine. It hasn't been accidental that equitation was the 'big bang' of the Biological Revolution and that 'equestrian dynamics' was the power that fueled all technological revolutions until the twentieth century.

A victory on the battlefield or a medal on the sports field – to Homo sapiens it is probably irrelevant. Anthropologists maintain that the point of the matter is to overcome the challenge of life and exhibit your winning genes. And scientists can now say that to win in the riding ring has an added advantage: it shows a brain knit beyond the human genetic programming. "If sport is war by other means," as Clausewitz[97] famously stated, "equestrian sport is war by *all means,"* as Gabby Hays commented as he and Partner were leaving the 2002 equestrian games at CHIO Aachen in Germany.

Equitation is probably the greatest biological technique ever devised by man, and equestrian sports among humanity's most difficult achievements. And in the 21st century Homo and Caballus started the second chapter in their joint history – the Sporting Cycle – that will probably carry the partners to even greater adventures than in the past War Cycle. But you and I must continue our journey, for much is yet to be done for horses and people in this fast new world of ever changing fortunes.

---

[97] Carl von Clausewitz (1780-1831) a Prussian soldier and writer, who served with distinction in the Prussian and Russian army, advocated a policy of total war and revolutionized military theory with one book "On War."

www.horsetravelbooks.com

21. A Modern Structure for Equestrian Sports

A sport may be considered to be modern when it enchants the public and the media. But classical equestrian sports are very, very, traditional! Horses undoubtedly have a way of captivating people but their riders do not always have the bent of charming public opinion. Maybe the horse people's aversion to massification and the public's misunderstood concept of 'elite' are at the root of the relatively low popularity of equestrian games in the eyes of the general public and the media. To fit into the Digital Era, equestrian sports will have to become faster and with clearly understood rules, which is important for TV coverage. In show jumping and dressage, for example, the rules still obey the 'old army discipline,' which has definitely lost touch with reality.

The more developed a country, the more advanced its sporting spectacles. Sports have such a powerful capacity of mobilizing people that their effects on the human mind can only be compared to the *drive of faith* and the *urge of hunger,* as sociologists correctly point out.

The first commandment for modern sports is to offer a game of art and quality. To this recipe the boldness of spirit which leads to victory must be added. A game must be a show of beauty with sporting actions of great technical quality, style, and pluck. Psychologists say that to the public, the sporting spectacle helps escape from the individual's reality – a sedentary, monotonous, stressful and frequently unjust existence. The sporting spectacle creates the perfect world where the struggle to prevail is rewarded with victory. With humans' and horses' joint performance, equestrian games have all these qualities in double – but somehow classical equestrian sports do not quite capture the public imagination. How come?

When a fan, for personal reasons, chooses an idol or a team to root for, the squad's success or defeat will be felt as a personal matter. The fan will develop a deep identification with his hero, who will become his personal 'guru.' The success of soccer reflects these facts to the dot, so let us horse people look and learn from the 'beautiful sport.'

Modern football appeared among students, workers and clerks during the Industrial Revolution. Football is a very democratic sport. All that is needed to start a game is a vacant lot, a group of loafers, and a ball. And all that is required of a soccer player are his own physical resources, to run and kick a ball into a net, or between two sticks stuck in the ground. This material scarcity made football the first game to be adopted globally – almost any person and any country can afford to play soccer. FIFA, founded in 1904 by five member nations, swelled into 150 by the year 2000.

www.horsetravelbooks.com

Soccer is an agent for world enthusiasm that has no rival in modern sports. It has been played globally for a hundred years. But even with this early success it would take FIFA's officials many years to understand and adapt their old soccer rules to favor television transmission and mass media. Only in the last years of the Black Century did football finally take the plunge that took it from the mechanical age to the Digital Era.

However, the sporting story of equitation has been even more attached to tradition than football, and it has taken longer for horse people to see the world through the eyes of info-technology. Classical equestrian sports are by their nature strongly attached to the luster of nobility and the idea that cavalry tradition can only develop in affluent societies becomes clear when 22 riders require at least 22 horses (though in a game of Polo the number of horses will jump to 48). In equestrian sports the intellectual, physical and financial resources involved are of a much higher order. In equitation the human athlete will have to develop the physical and mental capacity to deal, not with a bouncing ball, or an impersonal vehicle, but with a live partner many times stronger than himself, and together the combination must face obstacles and opponents at speeds frequently beyond human means.

In soccer the player will have to handle the ball, possess the ability to pass it with perfection to a better positioned team mate, develop strategic thinking of the game's possibilities, and train chains of movements to kick, dribble and score a goal with his feet or head. The soccer fan identifies with the individual player and in the purely psychological aspect, football may represent an individual's heroic battle to succeed in life by his own physical resources – which is all that most people have going for them anyway.

But in equestrian sports the fan can admire the whole context of the game: the intellectual, physical, aesthetic and social environment of equitation. Equitation may represent the battle of a leader who has powerful resources of speed and power at his disposal. For this reason some people will identify with the equestrian champion's sweeping victories, but others may find it more natural to identify with a pedestrian hero's personal struggle. The equestrian fan is frequently a junior ranking rider out to see his hero perform and the football fan is mostly a vicarious player rooting from a sofa. For this reason it can safely be said that there is a social line that has to be crossed from football to equitation, and the more developed a country becomes the more equestrian sports will grow.

Equitation faces serious problems, however: the immutable character of the games. In any equestrian sport there are some 'tribal leaders' who will defend to a standstill what they call 'the authentic rules of the game.' Normally these people will have a nostalgic feeling for their youth and want the sport practiced exactly as it was in 'the good old times'.

www.horsetravelbooks.com

In show jumping, one of the rules is to give the contender a second and sometimes a third chance after a refusal, or in Three-Day Eventing the elimination only comes after the second fall. There is an excuse for this, they say. The custom comes down from military practice when the biological equitation was not understood and competitions were a means of 'comparing' the various training systems adopted in different cavalry schools, so each competitor was given a chance of staying in the game until the victor was known. (But as the neurophysiology of equitation becomes an established scientific subject matter there will be no great differences between one training system and another, so this problem can eventually be overcome and the rules changed.) To maintain a spirit of equilibrium, FEI, the Fédération Equestre Internationale, created rules so that a competitor would not be suddenly eliminated from the competition, as in skiing, or suffer a great loss of points, as in gymnastics. 'In the era of mass communications, this has turned into an inadequate system when all sports must vie for the public's and the media's attention', alerted *L'Anneé Hippique*, the publication that maps the international equestrian year.

We live in an era of ever-fast communications and equestrian sports must fight for the sponsors' money against other sports of which the majority are based on the element of a quick win or lose situation. For media effect, even soccer, the number one sport worldwide, has the penalty shoot-out – an element of unfairness because it is based on chance. All modern sports are organized basically as media events, and equestrian sports must be structured with rules that enhance the spectacular power and sophistication of the games on television, where 99.99% of the audience is to be found.

To succeed, both the public and the media must cherish a sport, and therefore a sport must become popular. Looking back at 1905, when Albert Einstein, in an unprecedented spurt of genius. published the revolutionary thesis of *Quantum Light, The Brownian Movement and the Theory of Relativity*, the newspapers stamped on the front pages:

'BLOODY SUNDAY: CZAR'S TROOPS KILL 500 AND POTEMKIN MUTINEERS KILL THEIR OFFICERS'.

Nobody knew Einstein, so only a little note on a back-page of the newspaper announced in tiny letters:
'Time and Speed relative, says scientist. Nothing can travel faster than light and curious things happen as it is approached: masses increase, distances contract!'

And although, 'Bloody Sunday' and the Potemkin mutiny would lead to one of humanity's greatest tragedies, it was Einstein, the anonymous revolutionary scientist, who would have the greatest impact on the 20th century. But today, the

www.horsetravelbooks.com

name 'Einstein' is the perfect definition of celebrity: a person who is famous because he or she is known. Which gives us the bottom line of the celebrity concept: the media likes what the public likes, and the public likes what or whom they can best remember.

Modern equestrian sporting rules must be modified to attract television viewers. Journalists and commentators must be trained to offer interesting insights into the equestrian heroes – both horses and riders. The speaker should follow the equestrian event with a vibrating voice, charged with enthusiasm and not as if he or she was describing Lady Di's funeral cortege. And though it might sound offside to 'noble equestrian ears,' a bit of healthy antagonism – playing one combination against the other – works wonders with the public (it doesn't have to be done as crudely as in boxing – it can be done with charm and subtlety).

Equestrian games have more speed, beauty and power than any other sport. The problem is that classical equitation was created during the European Renaissance for a very small circle of noble riders and even in the current Digital Era the 'horse world' is taking a long time to understand the geography of Cyberspace.

Equestrian sports did not take off properly in the 20th century because riders seem to be very slow to pick up good ideas. Our horsemen sat on the wrong place on the horse for a thousand years, and the stirrup took eight hundred years to spread from Poland to the northwestern part of Europe. But in the Digital Era horses and riders may finally move from the Dark Ages into the Third Millennium's world of advanced technologies and universal sporting success.

www.horsetravelbooks.com

23. The Centaur Legacy

Why didn't horsemanship die out with the technological boom of the 20th Century? Probably because the Centaur symbiosis is made of two pieces of the gigantic ecological jigsaw puzzle that are capable of pooling their physical resources and overcome nature's obstacles in a space and time context; a powerful combination that left a profound social imprint on the human journey in time. As the new city-bred generations will have to perfect their physical and mental preparedness to deal with ever-faster events in the Digital Era, equestrian sports and outdoor riding are probably still the best human strategies to adapt people to the speed of cyberspace and to alleviate the stress of modern life.

After the Biological Revolution, when sedentary minded people started forming urban societies to protect themselves from the forces of nature and their human enemies, nomadic-minded horse people were the first to raise themselves against the rule of urban man.

Humanity's equestrian saga started some six thousand years ago when the nomadic cultures of Central Asian acquired complete biological control over their herds and developed a full symbiotic partnership with their horses, which enabled cavalry warfare at a tempo never seen before or after their time. The speed of the horse made possible the confederations of myriads of clans and tribes over vast areas of the steppe who formed looter armies to plunder the amassed produce of sedentary societies living in the fertile lands east, south and west of the steppe borders.

The new style of warfare completely unsettled the agrarian societies and cavalry warfare spread a spiral of greater and greater chaos over the Eurasian landmass. The "Cortez effect," when Spanish mounted troops overwhelmed the indigenous inhabitants of Mexico, had actually despoiled Eurasia's sedentary societies since the 3rd millennium BC, and these cyclical equestrian hurricanes only abated around 950 BC, leaving in their wake the myth of the Centaur. The 'migration of the peoples,' as historians euphemistically call the pre historic conflicts of pastoralists versus sedentary societies, was in reality big-scale cavalry onslaughts on agrarian settlements that caused a domino effect of refugee societies which, in their escape by land and sea, killed, looted and displaced other agrarian settlements in their path of flight, producing a holocaust that greatly changed the geopolitics of the Old World.

What historians seem to have missed in the nomadic versus sedentary power struggle is that each side went through alternate cycles of 'bright ages' and 'dark ages' as the fortunes of war favored one or the other side of the contenders. When Herodotus in ca. 440 BC inaugurated the annals of Western history this period corresponds to the sedentary civilizations' first rise to power after millennia of oppression, which corresponds to the horse people's first cycle of 'dark ages,' following Greek and Persian technological advancement that effectively quelled the fury of the steppe horsemen.

But eight hundred years after Herodotus traveled through the Middle East and Sicily "in the hope of preserving from decay the remembrance of what men have done, and of preventing the great and wonderful actions of Greeks and the Barbarians from losing their due meet of glory,"[98] the warriors of the steppes once again found their horses' legs and the classical civilizations were ravaged and thrown into another spell of 'dark ages' that had marked the dance of nomadic and sedentary fortunes over the last three thousand years of warfare.

In the Middle Ages Genghis Khan, in one more burst of nomadic energy, led the horse people to form the greatest empire on earth, but two centuries later the speed-factor of nomadic cavalry at last exhausted its military resources in a fast changing world, and Tamerlane, his spiritual successor, would become the last great nomadic conqueror on Earth.

The Middle Ages were also formative to the Western World's ascent to power and the nomadic nature of horsemanship deeply imprinted Western horsemen's ideals. All cavalry legends like King Arthur and the Knights of the Round Table, and Don Quixote have the ingredients of nomadic ethics with horsemen being equal under arms and roaming over the countryside in search of the 'holy grail.' Though the Christian faith had transformed the roving horseman into a paladin of holy justice rather than a seeker of bloody loot, the means to success were the same: the time/space effect of horses and equitation on Eurasian civilizations.

In the 8th century AD, the Age of Charlemagne and the Carolingian rule, Europeans started in earnest to build their materialistic world system with the aid of the Western version of the Centaur – cavaliers, knights, hussars and cavalrymen – who were the cutting edge of Western might. After the Italian Renaissance Western Europe extended equestrian power for another five hundred years by successfully adapting horsemanship and cavalry strategy to their type of civilization, a cultural formula that lasted until Queen Victoria's day, and the closing stages of equestrian power.

World history has been shaped by a chain of nomadic and sedentary horsemen (and also some horsewomen) who built or upheld the power of clans, tribes, nations, city-states, khanates, emirates, and empires around the world. Mo-tun, Cyrus, Darius, Xerxes, Alexander, Caesar, Attila, Charlemagne, El Cid, Count Belisarius, William the Conqueror, Genghis Khan, Subetei, Ogoday, Richard the Lion-Heart, Saladin, Joan of Arc, Tamerlane, Gustavus Adolphus, Frederic the

---

[98] From *The History of Herodotus*, by Herodotus.

Great, Charles XII, Wellington and Napoleon,[99] just to name a few war leaders who led their armies on horseback and achieved victories on a scale that no footmen could ever have dreamed of.

But though the kings in the Middle Ages were the last monarchs to engage in battle mounted on fiery chargers, the Centaur Legacy held such strong human values that cavalry lore and costumes were observed well into the 20th century and the Second World War. In that conflagration, when tanks had mostly taken the place of horses, the opposing forces, especially American generals and German high officials, wore riding outfits complete with riding breeches, high-legged boots and spurs. General George Patton[100] became one of the most daring and flamboyant US combat commanders in the style of his valiant cavalry forebears and Hitler, the creep, who had been a mere footman in the First War, strutted around the premises in full cavalry rig complete with cape, boots and golden spurs!

As we saw, the American West was to become the last chapter in human history where a sedentary culture set out to subdue a free horse society in the old Eurasian style: the Indians played the role of the nomadic Huns, Turks, or Mongols, the US cavalry was the agent of the sedentary government, and the settlers, cowboys and soldiers were caught in the struggle, like Kevin Kostner's lieutenant John Dunbar in *Dances with Wolves*.

With the invention of automobiles, sedentary civilizations, especially communist Russia and China, after thousands of years of nomadic oppression, were quick to swipe their backyards free of nomads, horses, and equitation, the ancient emblems of aggression and defeat.[101] But the icons of horse-lore are still all around us as both men and women wear pants, which were the universal garment of horsemen. Sedentary Etruscans, Egyptians, Greeks, and Romans wore tunics and sandals, the ideal dress for chariot driving. Pants became more than a symbol of being a man, it was the universal sign of being a horseman.

The modern necktie is also related to horsemanship as Prince Rupert of the Rhine, who fought for Charles I in the English civil war, is said to have invented it when he was unexpectedly summed to the presence of the king after a cavalry battle against Parliamentary forces. As the Price had lost his white embroidered

---

[99] Napoleon was not a real horseman but rather an artillery officer who stuck to the image of a cavalryman, complete with white horses and flowing manes, because soldiers were not prone to follow artillery officers into combat like they did cavalry leaders.

[100] Among General Patton's great exploits was to lead Custer's 7th army to the successful assault on Sicily in 1943. Unfortunately the intrepid cavalryman was later fatally injured in a car accident.

[101] In modern China equestrian sports are frowned upon and horses are only allowed for work.

THE CENTAUR LEGACY

collar in the fighting he rolled a broad silk kerchief around his neck so that in the royal presence the two ends could cover the buttons of his doublet. The fashion stuck, and is still going strong. And modern languages are full of equestrian figures of speech that enliven and give meaning to ideas. We live in a world that was built by horse people and we are still very 'equestrian' in our ceaseless fight for all kinds of freedom.

As people today are developing a more realistic attitude towards technology, realizing that cyberspace[102] and outer space are not really the 'magic wand' to adventure, many are turning to the thrilling vision of the medieval age, horses and cavalry (like Harry Potter).

Let's stop our horses under this sycamore and spy the two horse people down on the trail yonder negotiating a steep downward slope. The riders seem content, and the horses are agile and intelligent beings that offer the liberty to fly at a speed beyond human biological time and the opportunity to cross the sanctuaries of life on Earth – the world's multiple wildlife parks – where life is permitted to produce life, and no motors beyond wristwatches are allowed!

In the third millennium all the world's natural parks will probably be opened to horse people and at any given moment long and short distance riders around the globe will be fulfilling their equestrian vocation and developing their natural intelligence favored by multiple horse communities, pony clubs, training centers and eco-villages. In the centuries to come, the 'new wave equestrians' will be riding as never before in the history of humankind, because the born rider understands that equitation is not about transportation – it is about roaming in a faster biological time, over greater spaces, in timeless nature and accomplishing physical feats beyond humanity's original means.

In fact, Homo sapiens' mental, psychological and perhaps even physical exposure to the denaturalization of modern life can be effectively counterbalanced by the inspiring equestrian experience.

And this is perhaps the most precious jewel of the Centaur Legacy.

Through the symbiosis with the horse, the last three thousand four hundred years saw a dramatic upswing of human fortunes and in the third millennium horsemanship will probably assert itself as humanity's greatest cultural heritage. The chance to practice a sport that mobilizes all human senses in perfect harmony with the human body, the opportunity to develop a greater understanding of biological systems, cycles and animal communication, and the revelation of equitation as the catalyst of human genius, will keep the equestrian flame burning. This is the heritage that our equestrian forebears left us,

---

[102] People overexposed by television and Internet may develop a mental disorder called 'sensory addiction', so beware!

www.horsetravelbooks.com

and with the help of life sciences we may finally move from the Dark Ages into the third millennium's world of advanced equestrian technologies.

Acknowledgments

CENTAURS ARE FOREVER

As we gallop through the last pages of The Centaur Legacy we would do well to salute some of the Centaurs who bravely fought to uphold the fading equestrian flame in the 'dark ages' of the 20th century, and some horse people that helped me with my assignment of writing this book. Not all of them are professional riders and some of them I admire but don't personally know. Some are heads of state, others are journalists, writers, editors, medics, soldiers and vets with a special dedication to horses and equitation, and some have decanted from this neck of the woods and are riding with their horses in some other heaven.

Though I haven't yet been invited to Windsor Castle for tea on the lawn, I think that in England we must honor HRH Queen Elisabeth, who rode out the anti-equestrian tornado of the last century, wisely upholding the values of equestrian tradition. I'd also like to salute Jeremy James, equestrian philosopher, writer, and Long Rider, who, after following the Centaur's trail, kindly wrote me: "I believe you to be right" and honored me by writing the preface of the book.

In Italy we must remember Federico Caprilli and Federico Tesio, great riders in their own right, who are now gone, though we still have our beloved maestro Pavarotti, an utopian in all things horse.[103]

France, oh France, had and has so many heroic riders, but we must never forget yesterday's General Decarpentry of Saumur, and today's Bartabas and his theater in Versailles, who is setting the ancient art of horsemanship into a modern perspective.

In Germany I salute Hans Heinrich Isenbart, rider, author and commentator, "the voice of equestrian sports" who popularized and strengthened equestrian sports, and Harry Boldt, the dressage rider and coach who helped the Germans to no less than three Olympic wins and whom I had the pleasure to interview for this book.

In Spain I must greet the brave bullfighter Alvaro Domecq, who with Prince Dom Juan Carlos, founded the Royal Andalusian Equestrian Art School in 1973, in a decade when equitation was at its lowest ebb. It was at Domecq's 'oficina,' in Jerez de la Frontera, which lies in the shadow of an old Arab fortification called 'Torre de La Estrella', that Gabby Hays, in 1998, watching Dom Domeq battling a bull on his horse Sagitário, heard a warm Moroccan breeze whispering

---

[103] Luciano Pavarotti, at the games in CHIO Aachen in Germany, confessed to a friend of mine that he only sings to pay for his love of horses and riding. Bravo maestro!

www.horsetravelbooks.com

"it's proprioception", and the scales had fallen from Gabby's eyes and the old Centaur enigma had stood revealed.

In Austria our admiration must go back to Alois Podhajsky and the Spanish Riding School who in the Second World War braved out one more army to threaten the Imperial Horses (and were saved in the nick of time by Gen. Patton and his armored cavalry).

In Portugal we must salute Nuno Oliveira, the departed master of horsemanship, and Felipe Figueredo Graciosa the present-day director of Queluz Riding School in Lisbon, who gave me great insight into the glorious past of Portuguese Men of Arms.

In Hungary I salute my friend Kassai Lajos, who has revived horseback archery in the Hunnish style, shot his way into the Guinness Book of World Records, and now teaches archery in a valley where Huns once roamed.

In Brazil I hail André Luz, and his HORSE magazine, who believed enough in my work to publish my essays when I started trying to undo the Centaur knot back in the nineties; and Jorge Ferreira da Rocha, Olympic Dressage rider and a genuine 'new horse world' utopian who asked me the crucial question that triggered the first part of this book: "What would the world have become without horses?"

In Jordan we must honor Princess Haya who, leading the Women's Union, rode roughshod over patriarchal tradition to show the Arab world what a women can do on a horse.

And the US is perhaps the country were more people have given their hearts and lives to keep the equestrian spirit burning. But if I must choose only one name of the past we must salute the memory of Peter Vischer, the riding journalist who founded Horse & Horseman and helped keep the spirit of horsemanship alive in the first half of the 20th century. In the second half of the century we must salute Ami Shinitzky the founder of Equus, the Magazine which carried the torch into the new century and I, personally, must thank Matthew Mackay-Smith DVM, the riding medical editor who guided me to revise my first attempt on this book and for which I am grateful. And of course Dr. James Rooney who taught me about the 'Riding Reflex Chain' through his myth-busting article in Equus Magazine which started my search for the Holy Grail. And CuChullaine and Basha O'Reilly, founders of the Long Riders' Guild, who believed in my work and had it published in English. And Roberta Jo Lieberman writer, editor and horsewoman who patiently help organize the American editions of my work. And let us not forget all the riders of the Olympic equestrian teams that throughout the turmoil of the 20th century never lost faith in the horse world beginning with the Stockholm games in 1912.

www.horsetravelbooks.com

Our Current List of Equestrian Travel Titles

Abernathy, Miles, *Ride the Wind* – the amazing true story of the little Abernathy Boys, who made a series of astonishing journeys in the United States, starting in 1909 when they were aged five and nine!
Beard, John, *Saddles East* – John Beard determined as a child that he wanted to see the Wild West from the back of a horse after a visit to Cody's legendary Wild West show. Yet it was only in 1948 – more than sixty years after seeing the flamboyant American showman – that Beard and his wife Lulu finally set off to follow their dreams.
Beker, Ana, *The Courage to Ride* – Determined to out-do Tschiffely, Beker made a 17,000 mile mounted odyssey across the Americas in the late 1940s that would fix her place in the annals of equestrian travel history.
Bird, Isabella, *Among the Tibetans* – A rousing 1889 adventure, an enchanting travelogue, a forgotten peek at a mountain kingdom swept away by the waves of time.
Bird, Isabella, *On Horseback* in *Hawaii* – The Victorian explorer's first horseback journey, in which she learns to ride astride, in early 1873.
Bird, Isabella, *Journeys in Persia and Kurdistan, Volumes 1 and 2* – The intrepid Englishwoman undertakes another gruelling journey in 1890.
Bird, Isabella, *A Lady's Life in the Rocky Mountains* – The story of Isabella Bird's adventures during the winter of 1873 when she explored the magnificent unspoiled wilderness of Colorado. Truly a classic.
Bird, Isabella, *Unbeaten Tracks in Japan, Volumes One and Two* – A 600-mile solo ride through Japan undertaken by the intrepid British traveller in 1878.
Boniface, Lieutenant Jonathan, *The Cavalry Horse and his Pack* – Quite simply the most important book ever written in the English language by a military man on the subject of equestrian travel.
Bosanquet, Mary, *Saddlebags for Suitcases* – In 1939 Bosanquet set out to ride from Vancouver, Canada, to New York. Along the way she was wooed by love-struck cowboys, chased by a grizzly bear and even suspected of being a Nazi spy, scouting out Canada in preparation for a German invasion. A truly delightful book.
de Bourboulon, Catherine, *Shanghai à Moscou (French)* – the story of how a young Scottish woman and her aristocratic French husband travelled overland from Shanghai to Moscow in the late 19th Century.
Brown, Donald; **Journey from the Arctic** – *A truly remarkable account of how Brown, his Danish companion and their two trusty horses attempt the impossible, to cross the silent Arctic plateaus, thread their way through the giant Swedish forests, and finally discover a passage around the treacherous Norwegian marshes.*
Bruce, Clarence Dalrymple, *In the Hoofprints of Marco Polo* – The author made a dangerous journey from Srinagar to Peking in 1905, mounted on a trusty 13-hand Kashmiri pony, then wrote this wonderful book.
Burnaby, Frederick; *A Ride to Khiva* – Burnaby fills every page with a memorable cast of characters, including hard-riding Cossacks, nomadic Tartars, vodka-guzzling sleigh-drivers and a legion of peasant ruffians.

Burnaby, Frederick, *On Horseback through Asia Minor* – Armed with a rifle, a small stock of medicines, and a single faithful servant, the equestrian traveler rode through a hotbed of intrigue and high adventure in wild inhospitable country, encountering Kurds, Circassians, Armenians, and Persian pashas.

Carter, General William, *Horses, Saddles and Bridles* – This book covers a wide range of topics including basic training of the horse and care of its equipment. It also provides a fascinating look back into equestrian travel history.

Cayley, George, *Bridle Roads of Spain* – Truly one of the greatest equestrian travel accounts of the 19th Century.

Chase, J. Smeaton, *California Coast Trails* – This classic book describes the author's journey from Mexico to Oregon along the coast of California in the 1890s.

Chase, J. Smeaton, *California Desert Trails* – Famous British naturalist J. Smeaton Chase mounted up and rode into the Mojave Desert to undertake the longest equestrian study of its kind in modern history.

Clark, Leonard, *Marching Wind, The* - The panoramic story of a mounted exploration in the remote and savage heart of Asia, a place where adventure, danger, and intrigue were the daily backdrop to wild tribesman and equestrian exploits.

Cobbett, William, *Rural Rides, Volumes 1 and 2* – In the early 1820s Cobbett set out on horseback to make a series of personal tours through the English countryside. These books contain what many believe to be the best accounts of rural England ever written, and remain enduring classics.

Codman, John, *Winter Sketches from the Saddle* – This classic book was first published in 1888. It recommends riding for your health and describes the septuagenarian author's many equestrian journeys through New England during the winter of 1887 on his faithful mare, Fanny.

Cunninghame Graham, Jean, *Gaucho Laird* – A superbly readable biography of the author's famous great-uncle, Robert "Don Roberto" Cunninghame Graham.

Cunninghame Graham, Robert, *Horses of the Conquest* –The author uncovered manuscripts which had lain forgotten for centuries, and wrote this book, as he said, out of gratitude to the horses of Columbus and the Conquistadors who shaped history.

Cunninghame Graham, Robert, *Magreb-el-Acksa* – The thrilling tale of how "Don Roberto" was kidnapped in Morocco!

Cunninghame Graham, Robert, *Rodeo* – An omnibus of the finest work of the man they called "the uncrowned King of Scotland," edited by his friend Aimé Tschiffely.

Cunninghame Graham, Robert, *Tales of Horsemen* – Ten of the most beautifully-written equestrian stories ever set to paper.

Daly, H.W., *Manual of Pack Transportation* – This book is the author's masterpiece. It contains a wealth of information on various pack saddles, ropes and equipment, how to secure every type of load imaginable and instructions on how to organize a pack train.

Dixie, Lady Florence, *Riding Across Patagonia* – When asked in 1879 why she wanted to travel to such an outlandish place as Patagonia, the author replied without hesitation that she was taking to the saddle in order to flee from the strict confines of polite Victorian society. This is the story of how the aristocrat successfully traded the perils of a London parlor for the wind-borne freedom of a wild Patagonian bronco.

www.horsetravelbooks.com

Dodwell, Christina, *A Traveller on Horseback* – Christina Dodwell rides through Eastern Turkey and Iran in the late 1980s. The Sunday Telegraph wrote of the author's "courage and insatiable wanderlust," and in this book she demonstrates her gift for communicating her zest for adventure.

Ehlers, Otto, *Im Sattel durch die Fürstenhöfe Indiens* – In June 1890 the young German adventurer, Ehlers, lay very ill. His doctor gave him a choice: either go home to Germany or travel to Kashmir. So of course the Long Rider chose the latter. This is a thrilling yet humorous book about the author's adventures.

Farson, Negley, *Caucasian Journey* – A thrilling account of a dangerous equestrian journey made in 1929, this is an amply illustrated adventure classic.

Fox, Ernest, *Travels in Afghanistan* – The thrilling tale of a 1937 journey through the mountains, valleys, and deserts of this forbidden realm, including visits to such fabled places as the medieval city of Heart, the towering Hindu Kush mountains, and the legendary Khyber Pass.

Galton, Francis, *The Art of Travel* – Originally published in 1855, this book became an instant classic and was used by a host of now-famous explorers, including Sir Richard Francis Burton of Mecca fame. Readers can learn how to ride horses, handle elephants, avoid cobras, pull teeth, find water in a desert, and construct a sleeping bag out of fur.

Glazier, Willard, *Ocean to Ocean on Horseback* – This book about the author's journey from New York to the Pacific in 1875 contains every kind of mounted adventure imaginable. Amply illustrated with pen and ink drawings of the time, the book remains a timeless equestrian adventure classic.

Goodwin, Joseph, *Through Mexico on Horseback* – The author and his companion, Robert Horiguichi, the sophisticated, multi-lingual son of an imperial Japanese diplomat, set out in 1931 to cross Mexico. They were totally unprepared for the deserts, quicksand and brigands they were to encounter during their adventure.

Hanbury-Tenison, Robin, *Chinese Adventure* – The story of a unique journey in which the explorer Robin Hanbury-Tenison and his wife Louella rode on horseback alongside the Great Wall of China in 1986.

Hanbury-Tenison, Robin, *Fragile Eden* – The wonderful story of Robin and Louella Hanbury-Tenison's exploration of New Zealand on horseback in 1988. They rode alone together through what they describe as 'some of the most dramatic and exciting country we have ever seen.'

Hanbury-Tenison, Robin, *Mulu: The Rainforest* – This was the first popular book to bring to the world's attention the significance of the rain forests to our fragile ecosystem. It is a timely reminder of our need to preserve them for the future.

Hanbury-Tenison, Robin, *Spanish Pilgrimage* – Robin and Louella Hanbury-Tenison went to Santiago de Compostela in a traditional way – riding on white horses over long-forgotten tracks. In the process they discovered more about the people and the country than any conventional traveller would learn. Their adventures are vividly and entertainingly recounted in this delightful and highly readable book.

Hanbury-Tenison, Robin, *White Horses over France* – This enchanting book tells the story of a magical journey and how, in fulfilment of a personal dream, the first Camargue horses set foot on British soil in the late summer of 1984.

www.horsetravelbooks.com

Hanbury-Tenison, Robin, *Worlds Apart – an Explorer's Life* – The author's battle to preserve the quality of life under threat from developers and machines infuses this autobiography with a passion and conviction which makes it impossible to put down.

Hanbury-Tenison, Robin, *Worlds Within – Reflections in the Sand* – This book is full of the adventure you would expect from a man of action like Robin Hanbury-Tenison. However, it is also filled with the type of rare knowledge that was revealed to other desert travellers like Lawrence, Doughty and Thesiger.

Haslund, Henning, *Mongolian Adventure* – An epic tale inhabited by a cast of characters no longer present in this lackluster world, shamans who set themselves on fire, rebel leaders who sacked towns, and wild horsemen whose ancestors conquered the world.

Heath, Frank, *Forty Million Hoofbeats* – Heath set out in 1925 to follow his dream of riding to all 48 of the Continental United States. The journey lasted more than two years, during which time Heath and his mare, Gypsy Queen, became inseparable companions.

Holt, William, *Ride a White Horse* – After rescuing a cart horse, Trigger, from slaughter and nursing him back to health, the 67-year-old Holt and his horse set out in 1964 on an incredible 9,000 mile, non-stop journey through western Europe.

Hopkins, Frank T., *Hidalgo and Other Stories* – For the first time in history, here are the collected writings of Frank T. Hopkins, the counterfeit cowboy whose endurance racing claims and Old West fantasies have polarized the equestrian world.

James, Jeremy, *Saddletramp* – The classic story of Jeremy James' journey from Turkey to Wales, on an unplanned route with an inaccurate compass, unreadable map and the unfailing aid of villagers who seemed to have as little sense of direction as he had.

James, Jeremy, *Vagabond* – The wonderful tale of the author's journey from Bulgaria to Berlin offers a refreshing, witty and often surprising view of Eastern Europe and the collapse of communism.

Jebb, Louisa, *By Desert Ways to Baghdad and Damascus* – From the pen of a gifted writer and intrepid traveller, this is one of the greatest equestrian travel books of all time.

Kluckhohn, Clyde, *To the Foot of the Rainbow* – This is not just a exciting true tale of equestrian adventure. It is a moving account of a young man's search for physical perfection in a desert world still untouched by the recently-born twentieth century.

Lambie, Thomas, *Boots and Saddles in Africa* – Lambie's story of his equestrian journeys is told with the grit and realism that marks a true classic.

Landor, Henry Savage, *In the Forbidden Land* – Illustrated with hundreds of photographs and drawings, this blood-chilling account of equestrian adventure makes for page-turning excitement.

Langlet, Valdemar, *Till Häst Genom Ryssland (Swedish)* – Denna reseskildring rymmer många ögonblicksbilder av möten med människor, från morgonbad med Lev Tolstoi till samtal med Tartarer och fotografering av fagra skördeflickor. Rikt illustrerad med foto och teckningar.

Leigh, Margaret, *My Kingdom for a Horse* – In the autumn of 1939 the author rode from Cornwall to Scotland, resulting in one of the most delightful equestrian journeys of the early twentieth century. This book is full of keen observations of a rural England that no longer exists.

Lester, Mary, *A Lady's Ride across Spanish Honduras in 1881* – This is a gem of a book, with a very entertaining account of Mary's vivid, day-to-day life in the saddle.

www.horsetravelbooks.com

Maillart, Ella, *Turkestan Solo* – A vivid account of a 1930s journey through this wonderful, mysterious and dangerous portion of the world, complete with its Kirghiz eagle hunters, lurking Soviet secret police, and the timeless nomads that still inhabited the desolate steppes of Central Asia.

Marcy, Randolph, *The Prairie Traveler* – There were a lot of things you packed into your saddlebags or the wagon before setting off to cross the North American wilderness in the 1850s. A gun and an axe were obvious necessities. Yet many pioneers were just as adamant about placing a copy of Captain Randolph Marcy's classic book close at hand.

Marsden, Kate, *Riding through Siberia: A Mounted Medical Mission in 1891* - This immensely readable book is a mixture of adventure, extreme hardship and compassion as the author travels the Great Siberian Post Road.

Marsh, Hippisley Cunliffe, *A Ride Through Islam* – A British officer rides through Persia and Afghanistan to India in 1873. Full of adventures, and with observant remarks on the local Turkoman equestrian traditions.

MacCann, William, *Viaje a Caballo* – Spanish-language edition of the British author's equestrian journey around Argentina in 1848.

Meline, James, *Two Thousand Miles on Horseback: Kansas to Santa Fé in 1866* – A beautifully written, eye witness account of a United States that is no more.

Muir Watson, Sharon, *The Colour of Courage* – The remarkable true story of the epic horse trip made by the first people to travel Australia's then-unmarked Bicentennial National Trail. There are enough adventures here to satisfy even the most jaded reader.

Naysmith, Gordon, *The Will to Win* – This book recounts the only equestrian journey of its kind undertaken during the 20th century - a mounted trip stretching across 16 countries. Gordon Naysmith, a Scottish pentathlete and former military man, set out in 1970 to ride from the tip of the African continent to the 1972 Olympic Games in distant Germany.

O'Reilly, Basha, *Count Pompeii – Stallion of the Steppes* – the story of Basha's journey from Russia with her stallion, Count Pompeii, told for children. This is the first book in the *Little Long Rider* series.

O'Reilly, CuChullaine, (Editor) *The Horse Travel Handbook* – this accumulated knowledge of a million miles in the saddle tells you everything you need to know about travelling with your horse!

O'Reilly, CuChullaine, (Editor) *The Horse Travel Journal* – a unique book to take on your ride and record your experiences. Includes the world's first equestrian travel "pictionary" to help you in foreign countries.

O'Reilly, CuChullaine, *Khyber Knights* – Told with grit and realism by one of the world's foremost equestrian explorers, "Khyber Knights" has been penned the way lives are lived, not how books are written.

O'Reilly, CuChullaine, (Editor) *The Long Riders, Volume One* – The first of five unforgettable volumes of exhilarating travel tales.

Östrup, J, *(Swedish), Växlande Horisont* - The thrilling account of the author's journey to Central Asia from 1891 to 1893.

Patterson, George, *Journey with Loshay: A Tibetan Odyssey* – This is an amazing book written by a truly remarkable man! Relying both on his companionship with God and on his own strength, he undertook a life few can have known, and a journey of emergency across the wildest parts of Tibet.

Pocock, Roger, *Following the Frontier* – Pocock was one of the nineteenth century's most influential equestrian travelers. Within the covers of this book is the detailed account of Pocock's horse ride along the infamous Outlaw Trail, a 3,000 mile solo journey that took the adventurer from Canada to Mexico City.

Pocock, Roger, *Horses* – Pocock set out to document the wisdom of the late 19th and early 20th Centuries into a book unique for its time. His concerns for attempting to preserve equestrian knowledge were based on cruel reality. More than 300,000 horses had been destroyed during the recent Boer War. Though Pocock enjoyed a reputation for dangerous living, his observations on horses were praised by the leading thinkers of his day.

Post, Charles Johnson, *Horse Packing* – Originally published in 1914, this book was an instant success, incorporating as it did the very essence of the science of packing horses and mules. It makes fascinating reading for students of the horse or history.

Ray, G. W., *Through Five Republics on Horseback* – In 1889 a British explorer - part-time missionary and full-time adventure junky – set out to find a lost tribe of sun-worshipping natives in the unexplored forests of Paraguay. The journey was so brutal that it defies belief.

Rink, Bjarke, *The Centaur Legacy* - This immensely entertaining and historically important book provides the first ever in-depth study into how man's partnership with his equine companion changed the course of history and accelerated human development.

Ross, Julian, *Travels in an Unknown Country* – A delightful book about modern horseback travel in an enchanting country, which once marked the eastern borders of the Roman Empire – Romania.

Ross, Martin and Somerville, E, *Beggars on Horseback* – The hilarious adventures of two aristocratic Irish cousins on an 1894 riding tour of Wales.

Ruxton, George, *Adventures in Mexico* – The story of a young British army officer who rode from Vera Cruz to Santa Fe, Mexico in 1847. At times the author exhibits a fearlessness which borders on insanity. He ignores dire warnings, rides through deadly deserts, and dares murderers to attack him. It is a delightful and invigorating tale of a time and place now long gone.

von Salzman, Erich, *Im Sattel durch Zentralasien* – The astonishing tale of the author's journey through China, Turkistan and back to his home in Germany – 6000 kilometres in 176 days!

Schwarz, Hans (German), *Vier Pferde, Ein Hund und Drei Soldaten* – In the early 1930s the author and his two companions rode through Liechtenstein, Austria, Romania, Albania, Yugoslavia, to Turkey, then rode back again!

Schwarz, Otto (German), *Reisen mit dem Pferd* – the Swiss Long Rider with more miles in the saddle than anyone else tells his wonderful story, and a long appendix tells the reader how to follow in his footsteps.

Scott, Robert, *Scott's Last Expedition* – Many people are unaware that Scott recruited Yakut ponies from Siberia for his doomed expedition to the South Pole in 1909. Here is the remarkable story of men and horses who all paid the ultimate sacrifice.

Skrede, Wilfred, *Across the Roof of the World* – This epic equestrian travel tale of a wartime journey across Russia, China, Turkestan and India is laced with unforgettable excitement.

Steele, Nick, *Take a Horse to the Wilderness* – Part history book, part adventure story, part equestrian travel textbook and all round great read, this is a timeless classic written by the foremost equestrian expert of his time, famed mounted game ranger Nick Steele.

Stevens, Thomas, *Through Russia on a Mustang* – Mounted on his faithful horse, Texas, Stevens crossed the Steppes in search of adventure. Cantering across the pages of this classic tale is a cast of nineteenth century Russian misfits, peasants, aristocrats—and even famed Cossack Long Rider Dmitri Peshkov.

Stevenson, Robert L., *Travels with a Donkey* – In 1878, the author set out to explore the remote Cevennes mountains of France. He travelled alone, unless you count his stubborn and manipulative pack-donkey, Modestine. This book is a true classic.

Strong, Anna Louise, *Road to the Grey Pamir* – With Stalin's encouragement, Strong rode into the seldom-seen Pamir mountains of faraway Tadjikistan. The political renegade turned equestrian explorer soon discovered more adventure than she had anticipated.

Sykes, Ella, *Through Persia on a Sidesaddle* – Ella Sykes rode side-saddle 2,000 miles across Persia, a country few European woman had ever visited. Mind you, she traveled in style, accompanied by her Swiss maid and 50 camels loaded with china, crystal, linens and fine wine.

Trinkler, Emile, *Through the Heart of Afghanistan* – In the early 1920s the author made a legendary trip across a country now recalled only in legends.

Tschiffely, Aimé, *Bohemia Junction* – "Forty years of adventurous living condensed into one book."

Tschiffely, Aimé, *Bridle Paths* – a final poetic look at a now-vanished Britain.

Tschiffely, Aimé, *Mancha y Gato Cuentan sus Aventuras* – The Spanish-language version of *The Tale of Two Horses* – the story of the author's famous journey as told by the horses.

Tschiffely, Aimé, *The Tale of Two Horses* – The story of Tschiffely's famous journey from Buenos Aires to Washington, DC, narrated by his two equine heroes, Mancha and Gato. Their unique point of view is guaranteed to delight children and adults alike.

Tschiffely, Aimé, *This Way Southward* – the most famous equestrian explorer of the twentieth century decides to make a perilous journey across the U-boat infested Atlantic.

Tschiffely, Aimé, *Tschiffely's Ride* – The true story of the most famous equestrian journey of the twentieth century – 10,000 miles with two Criollo geldings from Argentina to Washington, DC. A new edition is coming soon with a Foreword by his literary heir!

Tschiffely, Aimé, *Tschiffely's Ritt* – The German-language translation of *Tschiffely's Ride* – the most famous equestrian journey of its day.

Warner, Charles Dudley, *On Horseback in Virginia* – A prolific author, and a great friend of Mark Twain, Warner made witty and perceptive contributions to the world of nineteenth century American literature. This book about the author's equestrian adventures is full of fascinating descriptions of nineteenth century America.

Weale, Magdalene, *Through the Highlands of Shropshire* – It was 1933 and Magdalene Weale was faced with a dilemma: how to best explore her beloved English countryside?

www.horsetravelbooks.com

By horse, of course! This enchanting book invokes a gentle, softer world inhabited by gracious country lairds, wise farmers, and jolly inn keepers.

Weeks, Edwin Lord, *Artist Explorer* – A young American artist and superb writer travels through Persia to India in 1892.

Wentworth Day, J., *Wartime Ride* – In 1939 the author decided the time was right for an extended horseback ride through England! While parts of his country were being ravaged by war, Wentworth Day discovered an inland oasis of mellow harvest fields, moated Tudor farmhouses, peaceful country halls, and fishing villages.

Wilkins, Messanie, *Last of the Saddle Tramps* – Told she had little time left to live, the author decided to ride from her native Maine to the Pacific. Accompanied by her faithful horse, Tarzan, Wilkins suffered through any number of obstacles, including blistering deserts and freezing snow storms – and defied the doctors by living for another 20 years!.

Wilson, Andrew, *The Abode of Snow* – One of the best accounts of overland equestrian travel ever written about the wild lands that lie between Tibet and Afghanistan.

de Windt, Harry, *A Ride to India* – Part science, all adventure, this book takes the reader for a thrilling canter across the Persian Empire of the 1890s.

Winthrop, Theodore, *Saddle and Canoe* – This book paints a vibrant picture of 1850s life in the Pacific Northwest and covers the author's travels along the Straits of Juan De Fuca, on Vancouver Island, across the Naches Pass, and on to The Dalles, in Oregon Territory. This is truly an historic travel account.

Younghusband, George, *Eighteen Hundred Miles on a Burmese Pony* – One of the funniest and most enchanting books about equestrian travel of the nineteenth century, featuring "Joe" the naughty Burmese pony!

We are constantly adding new titles to our collection, so please check our website: horsetravelbooks.com

www.horsetravelbooks.com

Printed in the United States
31008LVS00005B/87